CHASING GODS

Willard Berry

ISBN: 978-1-941066-36-2

Cover art by Scott Brooks
Maps by Tula Biderman
Book design by Jo-Anne Rosen

an imprint of
Wordrunner Press

"My actions are my only true belongings:

I cannot escape their consequences.

My actions are the ground on which I stand."

—Tich Nhat Hann

To my family,

Vanessa, Lucie, Nicholas and William

CONTENTS

MAPS

Buxton, Maine

BONNY EAGLE POND

SACO

THOMAS B. COOLBROTH CORNER
JONATHAN B.
EPHRAIM B.
ISSAC B.
JANE R
COFFIN
WARREN'S TAVERN
TORY HILL MEETING HOUSE
BAR MILLS
HOLLIS TOWNHOUSE
SALMON FALLS
KIMBALL BARN
CATHERINE'S GRAVE
RIVER
COCHRANE HOUSE

CATHERINE'S GRAVE - JOSEPH COCHRANE APPEARS IN BUXTON
HOLLIS TOWNHOUSE - COCHRANE MEETINGS EPHRAIM ENCOUNTERS GOD
KIMBALL BARN - ADAM+EVE NUDE DEPICTION ALL NIGHT LIGHTS OUT SERVICES EPHRAIM'S BROTHER ASSAULTED
COCHRANE HOUSE - RESURRECTION
TORY HILL MEETING HOUSE - COCHRANE DENOUNCES OTHER CHURCHES
JONATHAN BERRY HOUSE - COCHRANE ARRESTED+JAILED

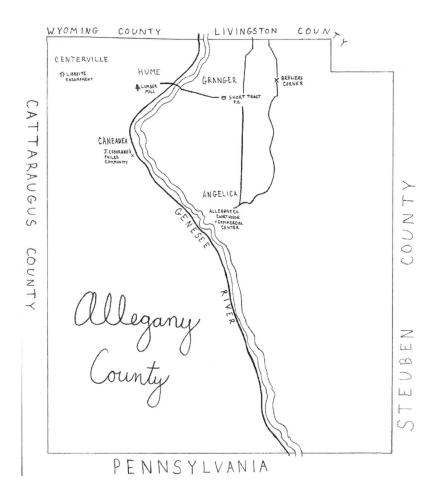

WYOMING COUNTY   LIVINGSTON COUNTY

CATTARAUGUS COUNTY

CENTERVILLE

⛺ LIBBYITE
ENCAMPMENT

HUME

🌲 LUMBER
MILL

GRANGER

✕ BREWERS
CORNER

✉ SHORT TRACT
P.O.

CANEADEA

J. COCHRANE'S
FAILED
COMMUNITY ✕

ANGELICA

ALLEGANY CO.
COURTHOUSE
+ COMMERCIAL
CENTER

GENESEE

RIVER

Allegany
County

STEUBEN COUNTY

PENNSYLVANIA

CHASING GODS

BOOK ONE

The Old Testament

ONE

"They say Ephraim went with the Mormons."
The only public explanation of his departure from his birthplace
in Maine is a note in the Buxton town record from 1840.

"Ephraim Berry is a no-account good-for-nothing and shameless. How did he ever come to this?" Jane shook her head from side to side.

"That's your brother," Mary snapped. "You tell me, you have been around him his whole life." Mary couldn't stay still; it had all been said before. Buzzing around the parlor dusting, straightening things as if guests were expected, the tight grip on her handkerchief never eased.

"To abandon you after twenty-three years and take your six children hundreds of miles away. Can't think of a more damnable act." Jane scowled.

"This cannot be my fault." Mary sat on the red stuffed chair, as if that would calm her anger. "There is nothing left for me to do." She patted her damp brow and looked at the prized china dish on the table beside her. How can he take my most treasured possessions? she thought. In the sun-streaked light Jane, swatter in hand, distracted herself in pursuit of a late-summer fly.

"The wagon is here, everybody," Isaiah yelled from the yard, but his words were heard and easily understood in the house.

"I guess I am as prepared as I can be." Mary grasped the arms of the chair, readying herself to face the painful farewell.

"Mary," Jane declared, "You have done everything you can."

"This is not as hard on me as it is for the children," Mary's voice faltered. "The breakup has been in the making for a long time. Ephraim and I are strangers, it is like we have been apart forever. But losing the children. They will be so far away I'll never see them. It will be hard to keep in touch. I'm not sure there is a post office where they are going." Mary tried to stifle her tears. "The children haven't grasped the fact that the marriage is over, and their parents already live separate lives. My absence will be a bigger adjustment."

"Father and Samuel have returned with the wagon," Isaiah said as he entered the front door. "They want us to load up right away. Father said that he will not spend much time here."

"We will take as much time as we need," Mary's voice did not waiver despite her fragile state. "Tell your brothers and sister to get the things they packed and carry them to the wagon. But I want all of you back here to give me proper goodbyes." For days she had been talking with each of the children about what they needed to take, the clothing and shoes, what had to be cleaned and repaired, and the personal items they could not do without. Mary was sure that everything was ready.

"I see Ephraim on the driver's seat and Samuel leading the horses," Jane said as she looked out the window. "I can't believe he brought that woman here. She is sitting next to him."

"The woman is not a problem for me," Mary said coldly. "I am not jealous." She looked out of the window and saw Ephraim sitting at the front of the long, wooden wagon with an arching canvas top. Storage chests fit snugly against the wagon box and barrels were lashed to the frame. Mary got up to look out at the team of large chestnut brown draft horses, strong specimens not usually seen in Maine. She didn't give the woman a glance, before she resettled in the chair.

"That wagon is large, but I don't see how everybody will fit inside," Jane remained at the window watching all the activity. The children lugged their things to the vehicle. Ephraim had raised the canvas top, and Samuel lifted the belongings to Ephraim who packed them in the wagon box.

"Most of them won't ride in the wagon, but walk alongside," Mary said. "The wagon has springs, but they say the ride will be rough. Mirinda won't be travelling with her father. She told me she is going with Ben and Mary Ann McKinney, who have more room."

"That is good. She won't have to watch her father with his new strumpet," Jane sniped.

"Please do not say that in front of the children. They have to get along as best they can," Mary said.

"Come outside, Mother. Everyone has gathered," Isaiah said as he entered the house. "Father's in a hurry and we have to go some ways before we meet the others."

Mary stood, fluffed up the folds of her gathered skirt and looked at herself in the mirror. She adjusted the combs in her hair which kept the long front tresses lifted above her forehead, pulled up the sides and swept back to her crown, where it was attractively knotted. Her attention then concentrated on the reflected face. She shifted her expressions several times in quick succession, seeking the proper image she wanted to leave with her children, the image they would take away in their memories. The powder did not remove the large bruise, the stamp of Ephraim's fist. She looked away, blinked her eyes and looked back in the mirror. It was hard to contain herself and not betray her troubled emotions.

She walked into the yard and made certain to stand so that the sun shadowed her face. The children lined up before her.

"Where is William?" Mary asked. "What has happened to William?"

The children looked about, but no one moved to find their brother.

"William? William! Get your ass out here," Ephraim yelled. He had been observing the farewell from the wagon. "William, mind me. Now."

The origin of the rustling was clear as William jumped out of a nearby tree, ran to stand next to his brother, Jonathan, and stared at the ground.

"You can't do anything right," Ephraim yelled at his youngest son. "You had better watch yourself with me."

Mary braced herself and walked to the head of the line. "Goodbye, Samuel. My first born," she said. "I will miss you, but I know you will be fine. You are a good man."

"Goodbye, Mother," Samuel said as he stepped forward and embraced her. "I will have my own farm before long. You will have a place there." He stepped back.

"Mirinda, my sweet daughter. How I will pine for you," Mary reached out to Mirinda, who seemed frozen in place. "I have taught you to be a strong woman, though I did not have to teach you to be pretty. You look beautiful today. Wherever you are, people will see you that way, and help you make a beautiful life." Mary looked deep into her daughter's eyes.

"I love you, Mother." The words eked out as tears streamed down Mirinda's cheeks.

Mary poised herself before Isaiah and he jumped forward, embracing his mother. "I don't want to leave you," he mumbled into Mary's ear. "Let me stay. He has all six of us and you have no one. How could he miss me with four boys to do the work? That should be enough for him."

Looking into Isaiah's eyes, she saw that her son's plea was unfeigned. She struggled to keep her eyes dry, aware that "tear" meant ripping apart.

"I had nothing to say in the matter," Mary said. So much involved, she could not explain.

"I don't want to lose you, Mother," Isaiah stammered. "I will write you. I won't forget you." The boy's trembling was involuntary.

"I will ever be with you, my dear Isaiah, even if only in my thoughts. My memories will never let you go." Mary eased out of her son's embrace. She had to appear in complete self-possession. "I will write you. I will keep in touch." She stroked his hair before she moved away.

"For God's sake," Ephraim yelled. "Why are you taking so long, Mary?"

The mother ignored Ephraim, taking her time before facing Josiah. When she looked at him, he smiled.

"You know how to make me happy, Josiah. I will miss that. How?" Mary faltered. "How, ah, I will miss watching you grow." *Ephraim is right*, she thought, her vitality diminishing. *I am taking too long. I won't hold up.*

"Father says that where we are going, I will have a new life. I like the one I have here," Josiah said. "But I have to go, don't I?"

Mary could not speak.

She nodded yes.

Mary was in a daze as she moved through her goodbyes to Jonathan and William. Had she taken the same care with her words, acted with the same sensitivity as with the other children? She remembered Jonathan's silence after receiving the news of his parents' separation and the move west with his father.

When William heard, his moods shifted dramatically. One minute he was caught up in the new adventure, using the knife just given by his father in imagined hunts with wild Indians. The next minute, he got angry, threw tantrums and disappeared for hours.

Mary would not remember how she expressed her sentiments and demonstrated her love to either of those sons. But she was certain that she had endured the departure gracefully. She had not collapsed in tears before Ephraim and his new woman. And she succeeded in controlling her anger, keeping the children's last glimpse of her from looking like a broken-down hag.

The wagon party started moving. When out of view, Mary's self-control vanished. Her shoulders tightened and she felt heavy in her chest.

"I tried to be strong, to be confident in my words," Mary said. "I didn't want to say that their lives would be fine and their futures secure; that despite their ages and my absence, they should not feel unprotected or that I don't want them. They should not imagine a future where their calls in the night go unanswered, or they reach out and find no one to embrace them."

It wasn't the worries of loneliness and penury that caused Mary's collapse. Her children were her life and without them life was over. Jane held Mary up and got her into the empty house.

"Why am I so weak?" Mary screamed, "So lacking in courage I cannot protect my children? That is a mother's job." Mary threw herself on the settee and sobbed.

"Mary you did everything you could," Jane said

"But they are gone," Mary cried. "Gone forever. I have no courage." In her frenzy she started to punish herself, slamming her head against the wooden arm of the settee. "No. No," she wailed. The hammering was unrelenting. The self-inflicted violence was manifest in the white froth oozing from her mouth and the sliding combs and falling hair.

Jane reached out to comfort her friend, who bolted at the gesture.

"Get away from me." Mary's anger shifted from herself to Jane. "You. You didn't help. A friend always offers help. You stood by, just watched. I counted on you being more than a bump on a log."

Mary's hair was no longer buoyant but drooping, damp, straight but for the few oleaginous curls. Her bald head, the shame of her childhood, was fully exposed. The rough scar that traversed her skull was unchanged, ruddy, a forever injury. She sobbed as she traced the indelible wound with her fingertips.

"I am coming apart. You let it happen," Mary howled. "I am falling to pieces." She shuddered, buried her face in the fabric of the settee, turning away from the world.

⌐

Ephraim stepped outside for the first time that afternoon to breathe the fresh air. *Will my father ever get off my back?* he thought. *Isaac criticizes everything I do, I'm never good enough!* The draft of cool air coming off the river and the pacing calmed him. *I'm twenty-eight years old, have my own farm and family. The old man still calls me toad.* His father came over this morning just to point out that he hadn't mended the fence by the creek. It was the third time he had stopped by to say the same thing.

From the Warren Tavern, Ephraim could see the Hollis Town House across the Saco standing alone on Brigadier Hill. Ephraim never left his farm during daylight to get a drink, but he was now downing several.

Turning east, toward the Lower Corner he saw a stand of great elms and heard the lowing of cows from the farm-yard beyond. The rumbling from Bars Mill did not muffle the sobs of the crowd coming down the road. Folks dressed well, better than what's seen on a Friday. He walked toward the train of people and found that the crowd was a funeral procession. He remembered hearing about a recent death of a child, a drowning accident by the river. Closer to the procession, folks became recognizable—Phineas Towle, Gideon Elden, and Timothy Ayer. Ephraim did not want to return home and filed into the line of grieving souls next to Abel Merrill.

The slow-moving mourners stopped when they reached a place Ephraim had never seen. But across the landscape of southern Maine small graves and family burying-grounds are scattered everywhere. It was said that this practice would cause the angels of the resurrection great difficulty in gathering the sleeping millions when they are called forth. Communities and the local churches must have had the angels in mind when they started planning public graveyards.

The secluded spot before Ephraim was the burial place for an earlier community, when mounds were formed and one's final resting place was higher than the surrounding ground. The mounds seemed arranged by families, but no identifying stones or markings could be seen. The ordered pattern, mounds in equidistant rows, formed a grid, although many of the raised graves had eroded over time. Small trees and sapling had taken hold here and there.

'I'll bet you don't know this place," said Abel, who was standing beside Ephraim.

"I have never seen anything like it," Ephraim responded, looking around the enclosure of sheltering pines atop a thick carpet of yellow needles.

"There is an old story," Abel began whispering. "An aging man, encamped down by the river, was shaving shingles, when he was seized by a fatal illness. He couldn't walk after the convulsions and with the searing pain. He could only crawl, on his unsteady hands and weakened knees, toward his house. He reached the closest dwelling and his neighbor, mystified by his disorder, did what he could to relieve the old man's distress. The stricken man's face was shrunken, his pulse weak and breathing intermittent. He could go no farther. Herbal concoctions and some strong spirits calmed the pain, but he was the first to die in this settlement. Happened the next morning. He was buried here, on his own land, and all his family followed."

"They were smart," Ephraim said, looking at the mounds, "never got plowed under, and a little closer to heaven."

"And further from the Devil's seeping corruption." Abel smiled.

Mourners gathered around the casket resting on a shelf of sod. The feet of the lifeless girl faced west, in the direction of the descending sun, and the family assembled on the south side of the coffin placed where the sun highlighted the child rather than their grief.

"The Andrews family must be Baptists," Ephraim said, since Pastor Abner Flanders of the First Baptist Church seemed in charge of the service.

"They are recent converts," Abel answered. Ephraim wanted to ask if that was why the girl was by the river. He thought better of it.

Pastor Flanders moved near the head of the casket, having a clear view of the little girl while offering her eulogy. Ephraim knew this preacher was his younger brother's namesake and came to Buxton to start the Baptist Society fifteen years before. Ephraim had never heard him speak.

"We gather here today to remember the precious life of Catherine Andrews. We come to say goodbye and celebrate the life she enjoyed here on earth." Benjamin Andrews and his wife looked forsaken. "We are here to thank the Lord for each precious moment and treasured memory. Catherine's life touched all of us," Pastor Flanders consoled.

"We are overwhelmed by emotions, the greatest being sadness. Sadness not for Catherine. She is in a far better place. We are sad for the loss of a dear child. But we feel great joy to know she is in the presence of the Lord Jesus Christ," the Pastor continued. "For the Christian there is no greater joy than to be in the presence of the King of Kings."

Ephraim wondered how he ended up among such forlorn faces. Were they crying because they were left behind? Unwelcomed in this life and no better place to be?

Flanders closed with a scripture from Corinthians: "We know that while we dwell in the body, we are apart from the Lord. We would rather leave our body and be at home with Him." The pastor closed his Bible and walked toward the grieving family to offer comfort.

At the close of the minister's remarks, a fashionably dressed man of impressive stature and commanding presence sprung from the assembled, moving decisively to the child's casket. Placing his hand on the forehead of the child, he began to talk.

"Catherine, we know that you are in Heaven in all your unblemished innocence. Your eyes are closed in this place, but they are open in the brightness of God's temple. The skin I touch is cool, but we know you are warm, wrapped in God's love. The ears I brush with my hand are closed to the sounds of this grove, but you are overwhelmed by song, angels singing all around you. Sweet Catherine, you know the glory of God and grasp the abundance of His grace." The speaker had a melodious voice.

Ephraim saw the mourners were captivated by this preacher talking of brilliant temples and angels singing, conjuring in his own mind a better place to be. Some ineffable spirit was aroused, which may have started with his drinks at Warren Tavern. But those around him stirred, provoked as well, adding to his euphoria.

"Through God's grace His kingdom is inside each of us. We can become more perfect in God's eyes, beginning right now, and in this life pleasure in God's gifts." The man spoke with intense earnestness, his dark penetrating eyes charmed the crowd.

God is inside of us? Ephraim thought. *Inside of me?*

"Paul tells us in Corinthians that we shall see God face to face and know the endless nature of His love." The speaker's voice seized Ephraim. "God does not say that He will love us if, and not until, we stop sinning. God's love has always been there. He loved us and sacrificed for us long before we were aware of His love, and how much we need it."

"Praise the Lord," a woman gasped, thrusting her bare arms above the circle of drooping heads.

"God dwells in the praises of His people," the preacher lifted his voice. "He is lodged in you," his roving eye teased the exuberant woman.

The congregants stirred, but Ephraim did not exult or move.

"Today, God and man are brought together again, the first time since Adam and Eve were expelled from the Garden of Eden," the man raved, "We are not sinners, but children of God."

Yes. Not a toad. Ephraim thought.

"Sweet Catherine leaves us with the message of life. We can make manifest the Kingdom of God inside ourselves. We can become one with God. Catherine tells us that we are at the entrance of a blessed life. We must go forward, our unpracticed voices joyfully praising the Lord. Thank you, sweet Catherine." The speaker touched the child's face.

The exceptional man took his leave from the burial ground. Rumors of his words at the child's grave rapidly spread throughout York County.

Ephraim had never experienced anything like this strange encounter. He never felt in need of comfort, but the words promised brightness he did not have in his life. He could imagine being swept up in God's love and overwhelmed by spirited music.

He looked at the mounds—the already raised bodies a promise. He needed to go over the strong fence that protected this place. The bank was treacherous, but a powerful force drew him to the river. He slid and fell, no glue to the soil. An unknown force pushed his face down into the dirt. Struggling, he stood and fell again, a jagged rock tearing his leg. He had to wash away the blood—the river drew him on. The trees were not friendly, one scarred and rotting fell across his shoulders, pinning him against the rough bank. Ephraim could not move. He caught his breath, prayed for strength. As he lifted the trunk with all his might, it splintered, freeing him. Impelled forward, his stunned body belonged to the river. He discarded his remaining garments.

Ephraim stood tall. His naked body, wounded and bleeding, faced the river. He plunged into the stream, relieved and weightless, until he tried to raise his head from the water. But he went deeper into the stream and was held down, the healing waters swirled and dragged him down. *God, stay with me. Keep this man, your child, safe and worthy of your love,* he pleaded.

The call worked. The pulling stopped, his flailing arms now loose by his side. *God heard me. I spoke to God and He listened.* A mysterious energy propelled him up, a substantial force hurried him toward the surface, the noisy water ushering his ascent. His head blew open as it encountered the air and his eyes saw a vast new sky. A rush of bliss embraced him, carrying him to more wondrous brightness. *I must hold on to this, never let it go. Thank you, God, for showing me your wonders. Thank you.*

TWO

In the summer of 1816 people could look directly at the sun through the murky atmosphere. It was red, larger than ever, dull and not brilliant enough to cast a clear shadow. Some folks could see spots traversing the sun's surface.

Nothing living in New England had experienced either the unusual sun, or a year without a summer. People were persistently cold, and every troublesome tooth was prompted to ache. The chill killed crops, serially, all summer and there was drought too. With failed crops, animals perished without feed and people experienced great privation.

New York City did not see snowfall, but in great numbers warm-weather birds fell in its streets, driven by cold and scarcity from distant forests. Wild animals starved. Packs of hungry wolves raided farmer's sheep and chickens. Four Maine townships offered forty-dollar bounties on the predators.

The last day of August observers watched with foreboding a mile-long iceberg float down the Maine coast. Icebergs always appeared in March.

No one could miss the white flag hanging from the front of the store at Coolbroth's Corner. It was large, five feet by three feet. No matter the direction of approach, customers could see the flag long before they reached the store.

Buxton was spread out over twenty-five square miles in 1816, but there was no town center. The township consisted of several distinct enclaves, with ten shops spread across the territory. Coolbroth's Corner served those living in the eastern part of the township. The store, run by brothers Ebenezer and Benjamin Coolbroth, stocked essentials people could not provide themselves, like salt, spices, sugar, raisins, and tea. Beer, whisky, and vinegar were dispensed through spigots from barrels, and some items were sold from bushel baskets on the floor. Farmers in the community usually found what they needed and got caught up on neighborhood gossip.

"The flag is a sign of surrender to the Almighty, Zeus and the whole pantheon of deities that governs the sky and weather," Eben shouted. "I'm telling all of them we've had enough."

Everybody laughed and appreciated the flag as an emblem of Eben's wild and prankish nature. Dancing around the porch with a lightning rod in hand, the instigator celebrated his daring feat.

"I assure you the act of raising the flag was dignified, I was appropriately haughty, insufferable. I want the gods to think that a sizeable resistance is hiding in the woods. We cannot surrender without a full display of Buxton bollocks," Eben hooted. "Hit me Big Boy."

"Do you think the flag is big enough that they can see it?" Nat Harmon asked. "The dry fog never goes away, despite the rain and wind. Of course, we can see the sun, so the gods may see us and accept your surrender."

Ephraim always felt relaxed at his uncles' store, for years a place of escape from his father's orders and harsh discipline. His mind focused on the same concerns as those around him. "Not a kernel of corn in Buxton—our lifeblood. Who would believe that the cobs have no milk in early autumn? They froze and there is nothing to harvest." He was in the company of his neighbors—Harmon, Matthias Redlon, Uriah Graffam, Paul Dresser, and Simon Plaisted, all farmers with nothing to do.

"We've been building fires all summer, except for those few days in July," Matthias said. "Here it is October and the foul weather hasn't let up. Hardly expected to see my wife knitting mittens in June."

Matthias and Uriah were huddled by the stove in the center of the store. The front door was tightly shut to keep in the meager warmth the old heater could generate. The furnace kept water hot for tea and cider ready for drinking. All but Eben, who claimed that too much clothing inhibited work, were dressed in heavy coats and sturdy boots.

"Everybody has suffered but going hungry is the hardest. Buxton has never been a land of plenty, but we haven't been given a chance," Paul said.

"Snow in June. That Canadian cold killed corn, beans, squash, cucumbers—everything gone." Uriah groaned.

"I imagine that you see a lot of people come through here, Eben, desperate for food," Paul said. "What can you do for them?"

"First of all, humility. I put up the flag," Eben smirked and saluted the white cloth hanging over the road. His face turned serious. "But food can't be given away and there's not much to sell. We get a little grain and produce. Portland's no better. Flour, meal, all breadstuffs are expensive."

Things not seen before were placed around the room. People traded some old mink pelts, elk antlers, a fine painted porcelain chamber pot, which must have been a prized wedding gift. A necklace made of bear claws was displayed, a long-ago reminder of personal courage. A used comb, hair brush, women's grooming items, were placed together on a shelf. The two chickens were still there. Rousted by the crowd from their usual resting places, they squawked and flapped around trying to find new spots to settle. Their number had not increased.

"There are some potatoes around and we've had some here in the store. We did get apples and pears—the cold being hard on insects and pests," Eben continued. "Summer was harsh on everyone."

Ephraim always wanted to get out of town, gain the respect of a soldier or find a new land and the excitement of an adventurer. Have stories to tell people had not heard before. But he was tied down by a wife and two-year old son, struggled more than ever, and watched his family grow skinny. The hope of change and of his betterment was gone. In the warm store he felt trapped.

"Let's not forget the boozers. Canada suspended import duties on grains and bans on distilling spirits. Not that anyone in this group has a taste for Canadian whisky," Paul got up and ladled himself more cider. He looked around to see Ephraim and Nat with their cups raised in request for more spirit. Matthias decided he wanted more too.

"As far as I know, no politician in this country has wiggled a finger to help people out," Uriah said.

"Cattle and hogs are a sad story. There's been no feed for livestock, or grass. Crop failure, shortage of hay, farmers forced to sell their cows and pigs for nothing. Beef prices down fifty percent, pork seventy-five. Nobody gets by," Eben said.

"If meat is so cheap, why are neighbors still killing and eating raccoons, squirrels, possums and even groundhogs?" Matthias asked.

"I guess they've developed a new craving. Been plenty of time to develop the taste, and it's not available in markets." Eben cracked. "We've never sold varmints at Coolbroth's Corners."

"Some farmers are left alone. Stephen Palmer and James Emery, down near Bars Mill, saved their corn, or the river did." Nat said. "The vapor from the Saco kept away the frost. Palmer and Emery will help neighbors with seed corn next year."

"Next spring Eben should find us some palm trees to plant down there. An expression of everybody's thanks," Uriah chuckled. "Folks are starting to call the land on that bank 'Little Egypt.'"

"Famine has become a frequent word for preachers," Ephraim was serious. "They are saying it is caused by sin. It is the beginning of calamities. The gospels talk earthquakes and famine. We've been spared the earthquakes, but the sky is always red."

"A reverend in Boston says it's Ben Franklin's fault and his experiments. The kite and the iron points he invented are butting into a heavenly realm—storms, wind and lightning bolts are God's response," Nat Harmon joked. "God is angry, and He has to take control."

"I'm sure old Ben passed off the reverend's remarks," Uriah said. "Franklin says people should pay as much attention to Christ's precepts as they do to Christmas."

"People are paying attention now. They fear the Last Judgment. They talk of Christ's Second Coming," Ephraim burst out.

"Meetings are everywhere, several times a week. People are scared. What does God mean by floating a mile-long ice coffin down the coast of Maine?"

"Well, no one's asking for caskets, and they come through all of the time. Preachers pass by, concerned with my salvation. I have been saved and back-slid so many times, I am unworthy of their attention and God's," Eben chortled. "That's what I say. I'm hopeless."

Nat stood by the closed front door, its back the space for messages and notices. Obadiah Jones's post was still there—an offer of fifty dollars to anyone with information concerning his wife, Nabby, who ran away. An announcement for a household auction up in Standish was tacked above notices of the sale of a fishing boat in Saco and cattle in Fryeburg. There was more than the usual number of "wanted posters" for outlaws.

"People clamor for these meetings, I am told," said Matthias. "Elder Buzzell and other Baptist ministers assembled north of here. People are so roiled, the ministers agreed to work together preparing for Christ's return."

"Have you ever heard of Jacob Cochrane?" Ephraim asked. "He's a part of this, although not a regular preacher. He draws flocks of souls to Scarborough and Reverend Clement Phinney's revivals there. Cochrane is assisting Phinney. He is becoming famous and earning the confidence of Baptists across York County."

"I have heard about him. He is fascinating. People go to the revivals because of Cochrane. He is in his early thirties and has a wife and two children. He gives great deference to Phinney, who always preaches, and stays in the background. Cochrane knows the scriptures well but just exhorts when Phinney is there," Paul said.

"Women are drawn to his meetings in large numbers," Nat cleared his throat. "I've heard he is fair to look upon. A woman told me he has a glance and expression that crave a second look. At the same time, he can assume the appearance and gestures of incredible sanctity."

"Do not forget his remarkable strength. In Portland, it is thought no two men are his equal. He can vault over the back of the tallest horse by simply putting one hand on the animal's rump. Ever heard of a physically intimidating preacher?" Paul joked.

"How does he draw people to these meetings if he doesn't preach?" Eben asked.

"Cochrane is in Scarborough all of the time but is not ordained. Phinney is from Gorham but preaches most in Scarborough. I went," Nat said. "It's not the traditional service where a minister is the only one to speak. The Baptist custom welcomes others to talk. Cochrane did not stand right away. He waited until the holy emotion brought on by the preaching calmed. Then he spoke: 'Today I have heard the gospel in its purity. God has sent this servant of his here for a great work of salvation,' he sobbed."

Ephraim's mind wandered, but his eyes fixed on the spider web, a shimmering orb in the rafters above his Uncle Benjamin's head. It was the sticky substance on the threads which caught the light, and they would hold the victim until the spider appeared to grab, stun and dismember its prey. He knew he was not a victim but could not escape his feeling of stuckness, the sense that he may never get away.

"Then Cochrane dramatically announced he would give up all his current work, everything, and commit his energies to Reverend Phinney and his mission of salvation. Cochrane follows Phinney, exhorting occasionally—'as the Holy Spirit might instruct.' Cochrane is deeply convinced that his help will lead to the most remarkable revival people in York County will ever see. Everyone in the meeting was enthusiastic with the proposal, but Phinney said nothing."

"All the goings-on among the Baptists, the expected appearance of Jesus, the Last Judgment—more bandits loose in the countryside," Eben yelped, then turned, "And it looks like Ephraim is getting serious on us. That could be real trouble down the road."

There was a slight smile on Ephraim's face as he shifted his weight on the wooden stool. He didn't exchange looks with anyone.

"I hear that Phinney's meetings have started, and Jacob Cochrane is always by his side," Nat said. "Phinney does the preaching, and Cochrane stays behind him. He's remarkable. When he exhorts sinners fall to their knees, he cannot stop weeping. His understanding of Christ's suffering is deeply felt, he is sorrowful as he listens and when he speaks. That's what folks say."

"He may be the man I heard speak at a child's funeral. He came out of nowhere, no one had ever seen him before. I was truly moved." Ephraim was sincere as he looked around at his friends. "He didn't know the child, but he spoke to the dead girl as if she could hear him, of God's presence in her, and her place in His kingdom. He talked of great hope," Ephraim said. "All of us can use more hope." During a long pause no one spoke. "I would be special if God were present in me. I am going to Scarborough to see if it is the same man and hear his words again. Excuse me." Ephraim stood and left the store.

Everyone was surprised and exchanged glances at the unexpected departure.

"Ephraim wants to escape, go where no one calls him Toad," Eben said without expression.

~

The meeting house was not what Ephraim had expected. It was big, a two and one-half story wooden structure with no spire— and old, maybe as old as he, built well before the Freewill Baptists established themselves. It was probably taken over from a less robust congregation. The entrance with its three steps may have been an addition. He sat in an original box pew, nothing that Baptists would build, and looked up at the balconies supported by hand-hewn pillars, extending along three sides. The pulpit was not Baptist either, with its six steps and a sounding board hung behind it.

Ephraim looked around the meeting house and observed people as they filed in. His eye was caught by a man sitting across the room. It was the man who spoke at the funeral. He was praying. His face shadowed in the faint light, but Ephraim was certain it was the same man.

Elder Clement Phinney entered and moved through the crowded room to the pulpit. He was a man of good stature, kind looking and strong. Mounting the steps with sure movements, he appeared self-possessed, not threatening or unapproachable. His ancestors had been war heroes, but his generous face gave no suggestion of a warrior behind it. He abounded with kindness and Christian charity. Ephraim could not imagine him in a fight.

"Freewill Baptists," Phinney began, "believe the decisive event of human history was the incarnation of Christ in the man Jesus." He said that Jesus did not come to collect the penalties for Adam and Eve's sins, but His appearance was motivated by love, "to restore the broken union of man and God."

Some new arrivals nodded at Ephraim, a request to join him in his pew. He welcomed them, and as they entered the box he looked again at the man from the funeral, who was avidly listening to the sermon. He nodded his head in approval and emoted sorrow when Jesus Christ was mentioned. *That must be Jacob Cochrane*, Ephraim thought.

"There is the need of self-examination, in all of us. We must be aware of sin and of our carnal natures, and turn our minds away from self-gratification," Elder Phinney continued. The preacher warned of backsliding, darkness and damnation and ended with a call for all to embrace hope.

The silence at the end of Phinney's sermon was followed by exhortation. Cochrane waited until several congregants spoke before he cried out, "My Brothers and Sisters, I realize I take up a very small place in this glorious meeting, as I do in the kingdom of God."

Phinney's humble assistant captured the attention of the worshipers, who turned to watch him speak.

"My quest for salvation has taken me to ten of the nineteen states in this country, and I have never heard such a man of God. Elder Phinney can help me open the doors to God's kingdom. I am humbled by his example, and how much I must learn before I am ready to meet the Lord."

Cochrane rose, embraced several worshippers and left the meeting house.

After that, Ephraim saw Cochrane under a big red maple tree across the church yard, talking to a few men. One was Ben Andrews, the father of the drowned child, and the others included John Dennett and Amos Kimball of Buxton. Ephraim didn't want to interrupt but had to listen. He waited behind the tree trunk for the right time to introduce himself.

"I must talk to Phinney and restore myself in his eyes," Cochrane's' voice was low.

"You tried that already, and got yourself into this situation," Ben Andrews was candid.

He must have become a good friend of Cochrane, Ephraim thought.

"I remember, and there were other elders present when you said it: 'Brother Phinney, you are very hard-hearted, you do not love me, and it is as cruel as the grave. For I never saw the man I love as much as I do you,'" Andrews was emphatic.

"Then, Mr. Phinney, pressing his cane against your chest said, 'Jacob, I love you at the end of this,' tapped you with his cane. 'I don't want you closer. I cannot ever take you into my heart,'" John Dennett finished the story. "Many in York County know that you were spurned."

"I have praised Brother Phinney ever since. In my preaching in Kennebunk, Hollis, Standish and Waterboro. Every place, I urge those gathered to go to Scarborough and listen to Elder Phinney and be truly uplifted." Cochrane's usually rich, smooth voice broke as he saw Phinney lead a handful of parishioners toward him.

"Brother Cochrane may I speak with you?" Phinney said as he and his group approached.

Cochrane and his friends moved as well, making the joint gathering visible in the moonlight. Ephraim moved out of the shadows to watch Jacob respectfully bow to Phinney.

"You are a remarkable man, Brother Cochrane, and you have successfully taken on the toils that the Lord has placed before you," Phinney began. "Your desire to work with all your heart to restore the church to the apostolic form preached by Paul is widely known. Your zeal, however, has taken you too far."

"I am completely committed to God and spreading His word." Cochrane was meek.

"Since I returned to Scarborough, I learned that you have grieved many, even your friends, by an attempt to perform a miracle," the Elder said.

Cochrane slowly sank to his knees, lowering his head as a supplicant. "I always place myself in the hands of God, trust His power and follow His guidance," Cochrane said with confidence.

"I have been told that you undertook to cast the Devil out of a man who was under deep conviction—possessed by the Devil. You placed your hands on the head of this man, prayed, expressing your deepest faith in the crucified Christ and invoking His divining power. I am told it was an impressive exhibition, ending with a demand that the devil depart. But there was no movement, disturbance or corporeal tumult in the prostate man. He appeared unchanged.

"According to the account given me, you tried to convince the man that he had been transformed, recovered. He insisted he felt no better after your ministrations than before. His story did not change despite all your persuasive efforts. The failure was more than an embarrassment for your friends, it was a cause of deep concern. They came and asked me to rebuke the evil spirit which they felt had taken over you," Elder Phinney finished.

The churchyard stayed quiet. Ephraim watched Cochrane, whose stillness and bowed head captured all attention. Like a sacrificial lamb, he made no effort to defend himself.

"Brother Cochrane," Elder Phinney broke the silence, "How can you account for your audacious and profane behavior? For Baptists, believers do not need miracles to know the truth of God's word."

"I am truly sorry, Elder Phinney," Cochrane raised his head. "I am sorry for my actions. But we know that Christ empowered the Apostles to cast out demons."

"In truth, Brother Cochrane," Phinney was curt, "you are no Apostle."

"We know from Mark and Luke that Christ promised believers generally the same powers," Cochrane sounded more like a teacher than a defendant. He elevated his head. "We know this delegated power was conditional, as we see from the fact that the Apostles were not always successful in their exorcisms. Certain spirits could only be cast out in certain ways, some only by prayer."

"Brother Cochrane, our church teaches reliance on prayer, not on miracles," Phinney preempted further discussion.

The scene Ephraim watched looked frozen, no one in this small congregation was able to move.

As he slowly raised himself up to look at Elder Phinney's face, the moonlight caught tears streaming from Cochrane's eyes. Cochrane struggled to speak. His low voice now rumbled in deep regret. "I bless God for such a faithful man, as you. I have sinned and am guilty of great wrong-doing. I have defamed Christ and abused His cause. God forgive me. Everybody forgive me. What shall I do?" Cochrane could not control his crying.

Cochrane was left alone, offered no comfort, but his penitence was not without effect. The confidence of his friends grew as the miserable body on the ground stirred, pulling up and restoring itself. Those watching saw a man of extraordinary gifts, superior in all his natural abilities. Without question, this meek man of God must surely be forgiven.

Reverend Phinney did not, as requested, rebuke the evil spirits which had possessed Cochrane and had shamed him and the Baptist church. He did not move and did not speak. He stood and watched as Cochrane straightened himself. One by one, Phinney's congregation moved to embrace him. Ephraim followed the congregation.

Few were present for Jacob Cochrane's comeuppance. But soon everybody in York County would hear of it. Ephraim was sure people would speak more of Cochrane's virtue than of his error.

⌢

Mary usually collected eggs earlier in the day, but with Ephraim leaving bed early, and the children's demands, she waited until Mirinda was down for her morning nap and Samuel was playing and could be left alone. The collection was routine. She entered the barn, watched the hens, and knowing their instincts for nests in places dark, quiet and clean, Mary knew exactly where to find the eggs.

The new planting season must be different from the past year. Hard work has to pay off, ease the mind and restore a bit of optimism. It would be good to have a life bright and full, Ephraim thought, working in the corner of the barn used as his workshop. He was sharpening the plow and had it on its side. The mouldboard rested on a small log so Ephraim could access the attached metal blade with his big file.

"I'm sorry about getting home so late," Ephraim turned to acknowledge Mary's presence, but avoided her gaze. "I was at Coolbroth's and we started drinking. We all drank too much and lost track of time. On my way back, I fell," Ephraim said. "As soon as I got up, I came home."

"You are not much of a drinker, Ephraim. What's come over you?" Mary asked.

"My bad mood is like the wretched weather. Months of dreariness and cold have spawned a sense of helplessness. It is discouraging," Ephraim said.

"It's been a bad year, for both of us," Mary said. While she collected eggs she always made sure the nests, which she made of pine shavings, were left clean. If an egg happened to break, the shavings helped absorb the remnants and the nest dried faster. Mary was on the far side of the barn, but she could hear Ephraim.

"I did not give up the idea that I could make a difference, my tenacity would defeat nature. There had to be a way to produce some crop income," Ephraim said. "I kept my hope for a long time through endless hard work. When that failed, I worried where the food would come from. Your pitching in helped us get by, but it did not ease my worry or stress. The family's welfare is my job."

"August was particularly hard with its frigid mornings. I was still suffering with morning sickness," Mary said.

"You were very strong, Mary," Ephraim continued, "And in the afternoon, you worked with me planting crops in the sheltered places we could find. You tucked rags and old shawls around the seeds. Our efforts were thwarted by ice and frost. I sought advice from the Portland papers on alternative plantings, fodder crops, on animal care—but nothing worked. I'm responsible for our family's welfare, but the constant anxiety and pressure eat at my confidence. I fight failure as my father's voice gets louder inside me, and it is hard to hush him up."

"Why haven't you talked to me about this before? You've kept it all inside. When you tell me your problems I feel closer. I am always here to support you." Mary sounded hurt, but stepped toward the workbench.

"My father's harping, reminders of my inferiority and weakness started long before I met you. They are an unending burden which you cannot lift from my shoulders," Ephraim was emphatic.

"Is that what takes you out at night? Someone to lift your burden?" Mary said harshly.

"Mary, I'm not seeing another woman," Ephraim countered.

"Ephraim. I don't know what to say. Should I ask if I can believe you?" Mary raised her voice. "You reveal so little, are so closed up. You say you are not lying to me, but isn't that like a lie too? Not wanting me to know the truth?"

Ephraim focused on the plough and his filing.

"Let's go into the house, I want to fix Samuel some eggs," Mary's words were short. She turned and left the barn.

Mary went about her business preparing food, readying the skillet, boiling water for the coffee and slicing bread. She looked on Mirinda, who was napping. Ephraim got down on the floor with Samuel. Ephraim lifted his son of two and one-half years and observed the precious face. He looked directly into his son's eyes with love—hoping that Samuel could see the deep affection that was never offered Ephraim by his own father, Isaac.

"You are my son, and you must know how much I love you. You are my gift and treasure. You entered the world so easily, causing little pain and so much happiness. Always think of yourself as a prince, a beautiful man and nothing less," Ephraim said. "And know I will never mock you with names like Toad."

Ephraim took Samuel firmly in his hands, raised him above his head and shook him playfully. Samuel giggled. A small shriek escaped Samuel's mouth when Ephraim released his hands and pitched him just above his fingertips. A second later he was in his father's full embrace. Samuel's giggles were hard to stop.

"Samuel, I want you to grow up strong, true to yourself, and assured. Nothing in your nature is shameful or deficient. Demand respect and never ignore your feelings, or let them be ignored," Ephraim said. "And as you find your place in the world, I will be behind you to help however I can. I will always be there for you, Samuel. I promise," Ephraim held his young son quietly and then put him down with his toys.

"The food is ready. Come," Mary persisted to get Ephraim's attention. "There is a plate of eggs and ham on the table, Ephraim. Get started. I'll join you when I finish feeding Samuel."

Ephraim took his place and started eating. It struck him that Samuel was the bright spot in his life. *Samuel, my son, gives me hope*, Ephraim thought. *He is human and true in a damaged world.*

"I am not lying to you. There isn't another woman, Mary," finally Ephraim spoke. Mary sat at the table and started to eat.

"How am I supposed to talk about it? I have been struggling to find my place in a confusing world and have depleted myself in the process. It isn't just me. All of Buxton, every family, has been injured. There is no help, and no one knows what to do, find a way out. Our souls are in anguish."

At Ephraim's words, Mary stopped eating. She stared at her plate, dabbling with her eggs. She let out a slow sigh, looking at Ephraim, her face urging him to continue.

"I went to a few meetings, mostly in Hollis." Ephraim's exhausted face exposed his journey into disillusionment. "They were not what I was after. The experience left me feeling worse and aimless, like asking for my father's help." Recounting his visits across the river wasn't easy for Ephraim. "I didn't go back right away, because my great hopes were crushed. The promises failed. I realized my place was at home, not worrying you with my absences."

Mary's eyes widened, showing both her concern and total confusion.

"Jacob Cochrane, the evangelist, began a big revival in Scarborough with Elder Clement Phinney, a Baptist, last fall. I heard about the meetings, Cochrane's message and miracles. I went to a meeting in Hollis. His preaching wasn't as moving as I expected, but what he said rang true. He says he talks to God and can help us find our place in heaven."

Mary considered what Ephraim said and tried to understand his story. "So last night you returned to the meetings, despite your doubt?" she asked.

"No. I went out and got drunk," Ephraim responded in a tone which showed he didn't want to talk anymore.

❧

The day was well underway when Ephraim entered the kitchen. The last of Samuel's breakfast, a crust of bread, was on the floor where he was playing with some wooden blocks. Mary, sitting at the table breastfeeding Mirinda, had her back toward the door he entered. As he walked to the place at the table, Ephraim heard Mary's sobs.

"I owe you an explanation for why I was out all night," Ephraim's voice was low and solemn. He pulled out his chair, sat and looked at Mary's face. It was red and puffy. Her look was blank despite all the tears.

"So, you are still up to no good. My nagging worked for a while, but it did not keep you from straying," Mary snarled.

"It doesn't have anything to do with the things I complain about. There's nothing wrong here in the house or my sleep," Ephraim said. "And, there is no woman involved."

"Can't you get your story straight?" Mary got up, put the small child in her cradle, went to the stove to get Ephraim some porridge and placed the bowl before him. Mary then picked up the baby, sat down and opened her dress to resume Mirinda's feeding. Mary did not say a word.

"There is more to the meetings than I told you. It started right after Mirinda's birth, in late February, I heard there was a special gathering in Hollis. You were mending, and still needed rest," Ephraim said.

Mary's sobbing subsided along with the tears. Her full attention was on her husband.

"I don't keep track of you. You always come and go as you please. I know you have business other than farming. I have things to do as well," Mary's look was hard. "I have always trusted you."

"I didn't go regularly to Hollis because of my responsibility here. I've said that. You and the children needed my attention— and still do," Ephraim's tone was even and then he paused. "I did go back though, and deep down was never sorry for it—even the times I left the meetings trembling, I thought that there was really nothing to hold me back. What was there to stop me?"

Mary started taking deep breaths, which had nothing to do with the baby's feeding. She looked fearful.

"I should have told you all of this before. Or let you know that through this whole experience, my heart had turned to stone. I felt all alone—in a dark forest I could not leave. I did not have the strength to leave." Ephraim stopped for a minute. "Then I gave myself up completely, knowing I should have done it before. That's why I was there until daylight."

"Where do I fit in to all of this, Ephraim? This double life? What about me, and your children?" Mary's voice was bitter.

"It's Cochrane, Jacob Cochrane. I have been drawn to him for a long time," Ephraim blurted. "He is a prophet."

"Ephraim. Ephraim," Mary yelled. "What are you talking about?"

"I am a committed Brother of Jacob Cochrane, a member of his society. My name is in the Lamb's book of life." The barrier crossed, Ephraim's words started tumbling out. "I first encountered Cochrane, who was not then a preacher, about a year ago. I stumbled upon the burial of a little girl where Cochrane gave a eulogy. When he spoke with his hands on the child's head, it seemed that God was speaking to the girl through him."

Mary's face changed. She appeared to be baffled as she moved Mirinda from her breast and buttoned her dress. She put the sleeping child in the cradle. After seeing that Samuel was still absorbed in his toys, Mary sat down again. A long sigh escaped her.

"Ephraim," Mary said, "I've known you for four years and it seems I don't know you at all."

"Sunday found me in Hollis again," Ephraim's trance-like state focused on his story. "Cochrane's sermon was not unlike what Elder Phinney said in Scarborough. Then he began to tell what was about to take place: 'There will be the greatest reformation that ever was known in this part of the world, and if there is not they might say God never sent me to preach.'" Ephraim stopped, his perspiration prompted by his agitation. "Nothing happened. Nothing followed. His prophesy failed, I felt dissolute. I don't know why I counted on it."

Mary stretched forward, her taut neck cracked when she turned. She was caught up in Ephraim's narrative.

"At the beginning of June, Jacob called a meeting in a Hollis barn which would last a week. I was seized to go, to tell Cochrane how much he had disappointed me. But my duties were here, and I had no time for the revival. But I could not stay away. I arrived at night and saw many of my friends rejoicing in the Lord. It was when I sat down that the power of the Lord came on me, causing me to tremble. The accursed pride of my heart kept me back, it would not let me cry to God for mercy. I left the barn and came home. The sins my father reminded me of all my life were still there and intact. Cochrane's meeting continued and when I went back to see if the Lord would not touch my heart, it was hard as stone. It separated me from everything."

"I am sorry, Ephraim, that I didn't soften your heart," Mary said with sympathy, reaching across the table toward him.

"Two weeks ago, a Sunday, I went back to Hollis and the Town House. People seemed different. There was singing. Some were standing, praising the Lord and some falling to the floor in great distress begging for mercy. I had seen something like this before—long before I met you—but I never really watched it. I could not see myself getting down on the floor like that and making all of that noise. It was not a way for me to connect with God. Everyone was friendly to me, some too friendly I thought—like they were selling things. A woman wanted me to come and praise the Lord with her, I knew she meant getting down on the dirty wooden planks and screaming. I moved away.

"My first encounter with God was not on the floor. On the other side of the room on a table, there the power of God sat me down. Hostile forces were present too, among those cramped around me. I was surrounded and afraid. My stone heart remained untouched as I moved to a chair, wanting to be unnoticed until the meeting ended, and I could get away. I would get somewhere apart and silent to beg for God's mercy. But God would not let me get away, there was no escape. More than my stone heart, I was so petrified I could not raise myself. I cried out for help—to lift me from my chair. I could not be heard because of all the noise, or my screams were hollow. I begged for God's mercy." Ephraim's breathing seemed to stop involuntarily. After a long pause he exhaled.

"My cries became groans as I plunged into darkness. I could hear my groans, they rumbled, as I opened my eyes to a landscape of destruction, an orange wasteland, smoke spewing from surface pores here and there, stanchions half-buried in the ground near bones of strange creatures and charred carcasses.

"There was a reason for my groans as I looked down at my naked and expanding belly and saw the green head of a serpent breaking through the tissue. I couldn't move with my hands tied behind me and my legs hobbled. It emerged, a grotesque creature with a large fanged mouth and black eyes and a long body which swelled as more of it surfaced. Its skin glistened with a slime so foul that it penetrated my crippled senses.

"The snake loomed over me, indifferent, its head pointed toward the discolored sky. That part of the serpent still inside me began to spasm and the slime gushed in its desperate effort to be completely free of my body. There was great hissing, venom spattered my face, when a huge shadow was cast over me. I watched the shiny ebony beak of a great bird pull up the serpent, tug it out of me, and carry it away. The bird had a furry yellow face, purple, browed eyes, great orange wings spangled with silver, and a long tail which was hard to distinguish from the snake's body as it flew away.

"Unable to move, my hollow figure wasted in the heat and foul air. Again, I called out for God's mercy when my mind and senses shut down.

"I was in a semi-arid place, the breeze, dry and warm. My frail, naked body rested on an old wooden bench. No one passed on the narrow dirt road in front of me, which was not untraveled. Dust rose above a rocky turn in the path and I realized someone was approaching. It was an old man, sandaled, with a staff and simple robe.

"He stopped, looked me over with his gentle eyes and finally spoke. 'You are not looking well. Is there something I can do for you?'

"'Thank you, no.' I found I had a voice, 'There is nothing you can do for me. I am dead.' I found I had tears too, as they started streaming down my face.

"'You are not dead, my son. But you are in need of nourishment,' the stranger said with kindness and assurance. 'Come with me,' he said, extending his hand. I was led up the path that had brought this stranger to me. We ascended to the base of a cliff, the stranger guiding him into a crevice which got wider as we walked. 'Keep up your strength,' the guide said, 'We are almost there.'

"When I saw the green pasture before me and the pool beyond, I was stricken—I was with my Redeemer. My mouth opened with astonishment and my eyes widened as I looked at him, His eyes bright and a halo lighting His face. He told me that He loved me, that He would care for me, always be there and that my life would overflow. 'You are free. Peace be unto you,' He said, wrapping His arms around me in a strong embrace. I was overcome by the most intense emotion." Ephraim looked at Mary, his face red and wet. He was trembling.

"How did you get home in this state?" Mary asked. She moved her chair next to Ephraim's and laid a comforting hand on his.

"I'm not sure. I roused to find myself in Jacob Cochrane's arms. He stoked my face and with the help of others, drew me to my feet. When I finally managed to stand, I was surprised how light I felt," Ephraim said.

"How did you keep from falling down?" Mary asked.

"We locked arms and danced and praised the Lord. I shouted along with the rest of the congregation. I rejoiced that my emptiness was gone, and my voice rang out, as foretold by Cochrane, that the Kingdom of God was now inside of me. There had never been room for it before. I exhorted, but all there were saved and converts. We all knew the meeting was done—most of us took the road across the river home."

"I don't know how you did it," Mary said, in bewilderment.

"I am worn out. As I came up Portland Road the sun started rising and freshness latched on me. All things looked new," Ephraim closed his eyes and smiled.

～

Ephraim and Mary headed to the Hollis Town House and were late. As they looked from Narragansett Road up to Brigadier Hill and the large, unpainted building on its crest, they could see a large gathering was underway. Teams were hitched to fences and trees down old Alfred Road and, from its junction, Union Falls Road appeared no different.

A large crowd led by Jacob Cochrane burst out of the Town House headed toward the Saco River Bridge and Buxton. The congregation was singing and hollering, women and girls waived handkerchiefs. The ecstatic, disordered band scrambled down the hill in excitement. Mary saw James Martin, the schoolmaster, stumble in the road and his wife drop to her knees beside him to pray. Soon his wife pulled him up, brushed him off, gave him his hat and trekked on with everyone to Captain Gideon Elden's pasture. In her rush, a young girl tried to jump a fence and got her foot caught on the top rail. Falling head first, her petticoats went in the same direction as her head, hiding here face. She laughed as two boys disentangled her from the fence and got her standing, her undergarments now in place and drawers out of public view.

Ephraim and Mary found a spot under a tree at the edge of the field, where they could hear Cochrane and stay cool in the afternoon heat. They could see a wagon that had been pulled up as a platform for Jacob Cochrane. There he would stand and view all his congregants. Singers stationed around the wagon, as well as musicians with drums, a horn and tambourines, would complete the scene for the prophet's service.

"Look, Ephraim, there's your cousin John and his wife Anna. Let's go over," Mary said. It was a short distance and still shaded.

"Mind if we join you John, Anna?" Ephraim asked. As greetings were exchanged, Mary could see that Anna was pregnant again. Anna lost her last child and always had difficult pregnancies.

"It's good to see you, Anna," Mary said. "Is the baby due this summer? You look well along."

"The baby should be here in August. We will see," Anna smiled. "I am glad to be here. Reverend Cochrane gives me strength and keeps me going. Have you heard him preach, Mary? He inspires and is a healer."

"No, I haven't heard the Reverend preach," Mary replied, "but no one can escape all the talk about him. He is on everybody's mind." She turned to face her close neighbor and friend, Joanna Harmon, with her husband Nat. "Oh, Joanna. Won't you and Nat join us?" Mary smiled. The neighbors settled, Nat by John and the women together. As if by some urgency, Ephraim got up and moved away. He turned and darted towards Cochrane's wagon. Ephraim was soon talking with two of Cochrane's assistants.

"Is Ephraim an enthusiast?" Anna turned and asked Mary. "He has that look."

"He is drawn to Cochrane's doctrine," Mary said.

"As well as to his miraculous powers and spiritual gifts," Anna nodded.

The music got louder, the singing and rhythms more robust, as Ephraim moved into the middle of the celebrants. Cochrane would be received by shouting and wild clapping. Ephraim needed to be part of it, and felt a euphoric rush as the handsome, fit man vaulted on to the wagon platform. Within seconds of the prophet's buoyant ascent, Cochrane's stance, feet apart, half crouch and arms stretched in a wide arc, made him appear ready to lift the heavy burdens brought before him by the down-trodden but expectant crowd. His powerful, mellifluous voice rang out:

> "Make a joyful noise unto the Lord
> All ye lands
> Serve the Lord with gladness
> Come before His presence singing."

The crowd jumped up and down, cheering. "Praise the Lord," "Glory Be," their shouts echoing around the field. With the measured pounding of the diviner's feet the marching began, people danced, alone or with others, whirling themselves into breathlessness. Along with the exertion of the dancers the music got more muscular and vigorous.

Cochrane raised his arms again to quiet his followers.

"We must serve the Lord with gladness. Be joyful unto the Lord. God is here. God is present and close to each of you," Cochrane began to speak over the joyful exultation.

"You are here because you know it is here where you can experience God in a new way. That is why you came to this place. The traditional churches, some call them standing churches, are standing. But they are standing in your way from truly knowing God and hearing His voice. You should not have to strain to hear God's voice. His promise is clear. Some of you cannot hear it, and others I know can hear Him now. I am here to help you hear His voice and, guided by the Almighty, to make God's word real to you," Cochrane stopped to catch his breath.

Ephraim tried to let himself free and join the dancers, but the movements of their feet were too quick and practiced. He did raise his hands high above his shoulders, allowing them to hang down limp from the wrist, and spin with the others, but he could not manage the quick steps. He easily merged with the less disciplined men and women clutched together, embracing each other and whirling. The laughing woman with saucy eyes who grabbed his hand tightly and tugged him from the clustered bodies he recognized as the one from the townhouse who invited him to worship on the floor. A large and more insistent man fueled by his flask pulled her hard in another direction, and she was gone.

"I saw Jesus, oh, I saw Jesus." Ephraim heard the cry but could not see the man in the tumultuous throng. "He showed me heaven— my grandmother was there. I saw my mother and father on the edge of hell. I was taken everywhere." An effortless energy lifted Ephraim to the side of the shaking man who continued to babble. "I saw my brother Ben enter the kingdom of heaven. My brother Esau was there, condemned forever. He was sobbing, waiting to be cast into hell. He never cried for mercy." The groaning and clapping did not keep Ephraim from being overcome by the weeping. He found himself in the dust, embracing the man who had just been with God.

Some chosen for a physical encounter with God were a surprise. Bobby McDonnell, the strongest man in the Saco Valley, was humbled through Jacob Cochrane's intercession. The mesmeric preacher's call to God caused Bobby to fall on the ground seized by convolutions, and froth at the mouth.

"He's experiencing his faith." Ephraim did not recognize the woman who called out. "Bobby's terrible power has been subdued. God has taken it away and made him his pure self. He'll never again make anyone afraid." Around the stricken form, men and women shrieked and laughed. Others trembled and shook. Some fell on the grass and were, or pretended to be, entirely overcome and irresponsible.

"The Holy Spirit is with us tonight," Cochrane shouted after returning to his stage. He is here, to purify and to empower us." The prophet walked deliberately from one end of the wagon bed to the other. "Quiet," Cochrane commanded and forcefully moved his extended arms up and down. "Listen. Listen to me. Be still. The Holy Spirit will not respond to the rowdy and inattentive." His stern gaze penetrated the darkness which now engulfed his believers. He waited until the crowd was silent.

"God," Cochrane said as he raised his arms to summon the Almighty. "Your humble servants await at your mercy. We are unworthy of your gifts but stand ready to receive your spirit."

"Come and get us, big boy," a drunken voice yelled from the darkness.

"Quiet," Cochrane shouted. "Shut him up. The Spirit will abandon you and seal your damnation."

Muffled admonitions and grunts of disapproval were followed by silence. Believers fell into a trance as Cochrane waited for the throng to quiet.

"You can feel the hot presence of the Holy Spirit. Some of you are already seized by it. Paul speaks of spiritual gifts. The Holy Spirit comes to your side with wondrous gifts of wisdom, healing, tongues and marvelous powers. Lord," Cochrane howled, "we ask that the marvelous powers of the Holy Spirit be made manifest," As his arms shot skyward, a flaming arrow came out of nowhere and struck the prophet's chest. He didn't fall back, but grabbed the burning arrow and pulled off the cloak in which it was lodged.

"Halleluiah," Cochrane yelled, "God has set my heart afire." He fitfully waved the flaming garment for all to see. "God's spiritual anointing. He has come by fire." Cochrane coughed, whirled and fell to the ground, disabled. "I am in communion with the Holy Father," Cochrane cried, raised the burning material before lifting his head toward heaven. "This Holy Fire is a gift of God for me to pass on, a gift for me to share and to sanctify each of you." Facing the awed believers, he rose and shouted. "Bring me the candles."

A handful of devotees appeared on the platform carrying baskets filled with candles.

"Let us ignite your heart. Come, receive the Spirit," Cochrane roared. "Each will have your own light. Each will be joined by burning hearts." As Cochrane set the burning arrow and cloak on a metal plate at his feet, a great flame burst upward. He grabbed a candle, and another, lit each to pass to acolytes who ignited more of the crude tapers. "Help me spread the light. All of you help me spread God's Holy Flame."

Powerful drums and blaring horns further excited the aroused crowd. The compelling desire for a flaming candle swept through the flock, the need for transcendence and belonging connecting the enthusiasts. All moved forward. Ephraim's fervent mood was heightened by the presence of other geared up disciples. As he rushed forward a shirtless man pressed against his perspiring body, offering a swig from his flask. Ephraim found a quick shot of whisky invigorating. The noise of those around him gave him pleasure. He was unbothered by the elbowing of a dazed man intent on beating others to the holy flame and ignored the spittle of chewed tobacco dribbled on his jacket by a passing pilgrim. A distressed man gripped his shoulder for support, although the meshed horde would check any fall.

Ephraim had flashes of memory and past deeds. No thoughts of Mary, her whereabouts, or the farm crossed his mind, but his father's rebukes were ever present. *I would feel no shame if my father saw me now. He couldn't tell his friends that I'm a black sheep, call me a ne'er-do-well, or toad. It doesn't matter what he says. Father will always be angry and never know this experience.*

The irresistible tide of bodies carried Ephraim toward the wagon where God's gifts were dispensed. He made no effort to get ahead of others, since his joy was enhanced by sharing the experience of deliverance. With all the excitement, no one noticed Ben Andrews crawl down from the tall tree fifty paces from Cochrane's pulpit, or think about the contents of the sack slung across his back. Andrews had carried wire up into the tree, which successfully guided the flaming arrow to it target. The other end of the metal strand had been attached to Cochrane's body just before he last stepped on the wagon platform.

Ephraim, head jerked up by a great roar, was stunned to see brilliant flames shooting up from Cochrane's pulpit. The crush of the relentless mob had overturned the makeshift stage, flinging torches recklessly about, and separating ignited candles from God's anointed. The grass caught fire and the old wagon was tinder for a small inferno. Ephraim stopped in his tracks and fell to the ground, his body exhausted, and determination diminished. Ephraim found contentment resting in the grass, knowing that he had found the right path and God's fire was within his grasp.

Mary wasn't present to see the flaming arrow and the fire. She was confused and bored by Cochrane's spectacle and jumped at Ned Harmon's offer to take her home. He and Anna were tired and their minds on the tasks that awaited them at home.

The evening offered Mary the chance to talk to Anna about her childbearing difficulties, the losses she suffered, her painful labors and the danger just months away. Anna said she bore the curse of Eve. Cochrane had told her that but promised to show her the way out of her suffering. As a prophet of God, Anna felt Cochrane knew her destiny and would safely get her through the birth of her next child. Mary marveled at her faith and hope.

The three traveled up Portland Road in a farm wagon, the women sitting on its straw-covered bed. Nat drove from an old kitchen chair he had placed at the front of the wagon.

"What did you think of Cochrane's meeting, Mary?" Joanna spoke first. "I have never seen anything like it."

Mary did not answer right away. "I have a problem—with God's presence," Mary began. "Many felt His presence tonight, but I didn't, not once during those hours. That must make me odd. I heard lots of people say God was with them, that He talked to them or they had a vision. I didn't know what to make of the seizures and possessions—I suppose they show God's presence. I felt no inkling of God. Did you feel in His company?"

"People sang with great ardor. Some of the music was inspirational and I was taken with its passion," Joanna said.

"How would I go about it?" Mary asked. "I want to feel the emotions that moved Ephraim so deeply tonight. Did you see him by that man who claimed to be with God? Ephraim looked so strange. I cannot imagine myself that way. I do not want to lose him."

"Spiritual transformation takes time," Joanna answered. "From what you have said, Ephraim went to meetings all summer before joining Cochrane's church."

"If God were present in me, Joanna, what would I feel or expect to see? Would I radiate love and kindness? Be visited by angels?" Mary was sincere.

"I have always seen kindness in you, Mary," Joanna said, "and love. You worry too much. But serenity and joy might take some time." Joanna smiled, trying to make a joke.

"I could rehearse the expected emotions. I could practice crying in the presence of the Lord, and then cry at meetings." Mary paused. "That might be hard to do. The emotions Ephraim expressed tonight I have never seen before."

"But Ephraim has experienced a powerful conversion and testifies to it, Mary," Joanna countered. "He told you all about it. That's so important."

"Yes. That is true." As Mary remembered Ephraim the morning he returned from Hollis, she started choking up. "You are right. In his heart Ephraim feels God loves him as he is. Isaac says he loves Ephraim, but that love falls short. We cannot feel loved unless the love includes all our faults. Ephraim's experience of God is full—he gets what he wanted from a father." Mary was silent. "Through Jacob Cochrane he found that love."

Mary was home. Goodbyes were exchanged as Nat helped her from the wagon. *Learning to know God will be a slow process for me*, Mary thought as she walked to the house. *But I can talk to God and act as if he listens. If I do it enough he may talk back. And I'll follow His instructions.*

God. How I resent Jacob Cochrane. The thought vanished as she entered the house.

THREE

Joshua Kimball's barn felt vast, though its dimensions were hard to determine in the darkness. Cochrane commanded attendance of his most ardent, so there were only fifty people sitting in a half circle in the middle of the barn. They faced an irregular construction higher than the loft, consisting of timbers and large tree limbs lashed together, covered and draped in discarded sailcloth to resemble the side of a mountain. Saplings and shrubbery poked through the canvas, appearing as trees adorned with brightly painted paper-mache fruit. A big green shoot in the center was strung with golden globes.

The large stuffed parrot-like bird was fastened to a branch on one side of the scene and another brightly feathered specimen was suspended from above. A brown bear skin with a glass-eyed head attached, was spread over a large log. The head of a small antlered deer stuck out of a gap in the heavy fabric.

A large hoop with yellow cloth stretched across it, fringed with orange yarn, dominated the foreground. Dark chalk was used to sketch the large triangular nose, broad horizontal mouth and slanted eyes of a lion. Just before it a live lamb, bleating softly, was tethered to a big rock. Some white rabbits snuggled in a wire cage. Stray chickens strutted in and out of the shadows.

Light from a dozen barn lanterns on benches and platforms outside the perimeter of followers cloaked the crude and artless design of the set. But all were entranced by the drama and mystery before them. A new kind of spectacle had come to York County. There was no talking, just silence broken by the squawking and clucking from the chickens.

The great ring of the gong changed everything. Nothing like it had been heard before, but Cochrane's acolytes were not frightened by the thunderous sound. They trusted that something important was about to happen.

Jacob Cochrane's commanding figure swept into the center of the gathering, his substantial frame cloaked in a great white robe. Cochrane's head was held high, his chin raised and his arms stretched wide, making it easy to see that his feet were bare.

"Praise Jesus," Cochrane's voice rang out. "Glory Hallelujah. Peace be with you, my Brethren and Sisters." The preacher's normally florid complexion was even-toned in the dim light, although with his arrival more barn lanterns had been lit. The followers could see the blond highlights in his hair, his high forehead and dark and penetrating eyes.

"Tonight, we are here for worship, but more for instruction," Cochrane's voice thundered.

"Not only will I talk about the Garden of Eden, I am here to show it to you." His back to the congregants, Cochrane stretched his body toward the canvas mountainside. "I will tell you about the Lord's wish that man live in a bounteous garden, and that man not be left lonely. All will behold His gift of the woman, in her full nature."

With graceful agility Cochrane spun around toward the assembled group into a half-crouch. His face contorted, he snarled, "And we will talk about temptation, sin, and evil. I will show you Adam and Eve's expulsion from the Garden." Cochrane straightened himself, standing tall—a smile slowly crossing his face. "The Holy Spirit will join us, my Brethren and Sisters, as we will learn God's plan of happiness for man and woman and for the ultimate restoration of the Garden."

The light in the barn dimmed as Cochrane again faced the cloth wall. "The Lord God planted a garden in Eden, in the east, and there He put the man He had formed. He made various trees that were a delight to look at and good for food," Cochrane paused, pointing to the colorful adornments on the shrubs and saplings, as a regular, muffled beating of the gong began. The congregants seemed enthralled by the harmony of the light, the drum and sonorous tone of Cochrane's voice. "There," Cochrane pointed to the large green shoot strung with gold globes, "we see the tree of knowledge of good and evil."

"As the Lord took the man and settled him in the Garden of Eden he gave a grim warning: 'You are free to eat from the trees in the garden, except for that one—the tree of knowledge of good and evil. The moment you eat from it you are doomed to die.' A loud strike on the gong fell ominously on the gathering.

"The Lord watched over the man and He realized that it was not good for the man to be alone." Cochrane walked easily within the gathered semi-circle. The muffled gong again sounded. "God formed out of the ground various wild animals." The preacher touched the glass-eyed bear and stroked its head. His hand reached toward the antlers of the deer, and he walked toward the lion. "The Lord created such a beautiful place where ferocious beasts," the sudden and sharp strike of the gong startled everyone and Cochrane's hand, extending toward the lion, was quickly pulled back, "where ferocious beasts lived peaceably with the gentle lamb." Cochrane knelt and petted the fluffy animal. "He also formed various birds of the air." Birds whistled as the preacher pointed up.

"Unfortunately, none of these creatures proved a suitable partner for the man." The narrator's voice sounded sinister as the rolling beat of a snare drum became louder. "The least suitable of all was the vile serpent." A fold in the canvas mountain parted and a green head, with great black eyes and dangling red tongue poked through. It could be seen by all because a lantern was held nearby to capture its malevolence. The drums intensified, and the snake disappeared with a prolonged hiss. Made uneasy by the snake, people took time to settle.

People were caught off guard when their religious guide jumped out from nowhere, his luminous robe streaming behind like a comet tail. Cochrane extended his arms as if embracing all the celebrants. His voice took a richer, deeper tone, imitating the voice of God. "It is not good for man to be alone. I will make a suitable partner for him."

The lights in the barn went out. The subdued rhythm of the gong was joined by faint echoes of "Hallelujah".

"The Lord cast a deep sleep on the man," the deep voice began.

Low moans started, and faint crying. Sobbing from the back of the barn lent an ethereal quality, before the wailing grew louder and constant.

"And while he slept, the Lord God cut out one of the man's ribs, then closed the slit in the flesh," the narrator interrupted the groans. "From the man's rib he fashioned a woman." Screams of excruciating pain mimicked those of childbirth. Silence followed. "God said he would bring the woman to the man."

Beautiful singing began. The light grew brighter. Cochrane's followers saw him beam, a sheen on his imposing flanks and the broad back, a strong chest lustrous. He was on his feet--stark naked. The humbled figure on the floor before God had recomposed and now stood triumphant. To all he appeared godly, an awesome form.

Cochrane's movements were measured, giving spectators sufficient time for adoration. Both the men and women were stricken by his glorious appearance. Cochrane rotated toward the mountain, placing his right knee forward so he could rest his weight on it, while stretching his other leg back its full length. He didn't say a word, arms spread upward, his body spoke for him: "Behold."

The gong sounded in its full volume and Cochrane began quoting from the Bible:

> "This one at last is bone of my bones
> And flesh of my flesh;
> This one we shall call 'woman,'
> For out of 'her man' this one has been taken."

Rustling coming from the thick shrubbery drew everyone's attention, and Cochrane's turned to his left. Eve took time in making her appearance. When congregants first saw a bare foot and the calf above it, there were gasps as well as some notable changes in breathing. Another leg appeared, and the young woman stepped out of the bushes with no hesitancy. After three strides she stopped, one forearm raised to partially shield her breasts and the other poised near her upper thigh, her sex was neither hidden nor completely unprotected.

Not more than twenty years of age, the young woman was lovely and self-assured despite her complete nakedness. She was radiant in the now-bright room, her auburn hair shining, skin fresh and lustrous. her body comfortably relaxed on feet set casually apart. Cochrane gave his followers time to assimilate the scene and admire every beautiful feature of this woman.

Cochrane walked slowly toward the woman, one arm reaching out to her. "Such beauty glorifies God," he proclaimed. Joining hands, they faced the congregants. "God has a true partner for each of us. They are ours for He has fashioned them from our own ribs. With our partners we are spiritually mated."

Cochrane's large white robe spread out on the floor. He settled on the robe with one knee, his gestures inviting the woman to join him. As the woman knelt to join Cochrane, the gong sounded, lights went out, leaving everyone in darkness.

A low voice gasped in disbelief, "How can this happen in church?" while another exclaimed, "It's a miracle. God has offered us a glorious vision." "I think that girl is Eliza Hill?" followed by "Shush." "The woman is a Jezebel, displaying her body for men to lust after," from one woman's voice, nearly drowned out by shouts of "Praise God."

Cochrane appeared fully robed when the light returned, his joyous countenance gone. "Praise the Lord," he started. "We must talk about sin, about the evil that surrounds us. You know God cast Adam and Eve out of the Garden. They disobeyed and ate the fruit from the Tree of Knowledge of Good and Evil." The preacher swung around, pointing at the green shoot strung with the golden globes. "Adam and Eve sinned against God, against their Almighty Father who created them," Cochrane thundered. "And loved them deeply," was said in a whisper.

"There was evil in the garden, as there is evil everywhere. Evil is here tonight. Look, look," Cochrane stomped toward the mountain waving his hands. The canvas backdrop shuddered and from under it, near the glass-eyed bear, a green head began to protrude. The black-eyed and red-tongued serpent slid forward, its head moved left and right to survey all present. It raised up defiantly. Ephraim's head was wrapped in tightly knitted fabric to portray the snake of his dream. Cochrane and he had agreed no one could better imagine the part. He moved forward slowly, powered by his elbows, which were wrapped against his body by a green shroud. He gave a loud slow hiss.

"You are evil incarnate, Serpent," Cochran howled, "leading everyone into sin, leading Adam and Eve into sin. We know from God," Cochrane began quoting from Genesis, "'Because thou hast done this, thou are cursed above all cattle, and every beast of the field; upon thy belly thou shalt go, and dust thou shalt eat all of the days of thy life.' You are evil, you are hate and infidelity. Go. Go from the garden."

Moving forward, the serpent again raised its head and hissed. From someplace in the congregation a hiss was returned. Moving toward the darkness Ephraim hissed back in anger, starting a volley of hisses. The barrage of hissing seemed unplanned, but the cabbage thrown at Ephraim could not have been spontaneous, nor the numerous vegetables to follow. The rising chorus of shouts, "Get out!" and "Go!," was more than Ephraim could take. In a panic he freed his arms from the green shroud. Gaining his feet, he ran out of the barn to the congregants' jeers, tumultuous shouting and applause.

Ephraim disappeared into a dark corner of the barn. When planning this reenactment, Cochrane mentioned Jesus's parable to the guests. "You have to be prepared to proceed shamefacedly to the lowest place. Then when your host approaches you and says 'My friend come up higher,' you will win the esteem of your fellow guests. The more you debase yourself before God, the more you will be exalted." Rather than exaltation, Ephraim felt that his crawling was something his father might have commanded. Ephraim preferred to be among the believers, not seen as a leper.

Reverend Cochrane asked his congregants to sit down and compose themselves. A follower cleaned up the refuse left by those who expelled the serpent from the Garden. "You must know my Brethren and Sisters," Cochrane returned to his story, "that the Almighty did not cast Adam and Eve out of the Garden because they were disobedient. Adam and Eve were driven out of Eden because they did not say they were sorry. They never asked for God's forgiveness or how to make up for the great displeasure they caused Him.

"We know from St. Paul the importance of God's forgiveness— that His forgiveness is there, it is there for everyone. It is everlasting. And," Cochrane was emphatic, "had Adam and Eve asked the Lord to forgive them, not only would they have been forgiven, but they would have been restored to the Garden." Cochrane walked around looking directly in the faces of his congregants, the light bright enough for them to be caught directly by his gaze. "You, my Brethren and Sisters, can ask—you just must ask for God's forgiveness. Ask and you will no longer spend your lives tending an ugly and fruitless land, not God's kingdom. You can leave Buxton for the kingdom of God. You can leave Buxton now." Cochrane roared.

"Why can't people…you," Cochrane pointed to a woman on the floor, "or you," pointing to the man beside her, "bear the burden of your own sin? And then ask God to lift it from your shoulders?"

"Are you like Adam?" Cochrane looked into the face of the man he had pulled up from the floor, "blaming his sin on the woman who gave him the fruit to eat?" Cochrane pushed the man back to the ground and walked to the other side of the gathering. Congregants were startled by the rebuke.

"You are a sinner," Cochrane took hold of a woman's hair,

forcing her to stand, "but, like Eve who told God it was the serpent who caused her to sin, you cannot accept your transgressions." The woman smarted.

"It's true for all of you. Your disobedience is someone else's fault. Isn't it? God have mercy on you who cannot recognize your sin and deny your foul deeds. God forgive you," Cries of "Have mercy on me" began, "Forgive me Lord," along with speechlessness and squirming. Cochrane stopped, letting his flock find communion in each other's discomfort and suffering.

"There is a way forward, a way to a new Garden. First, we must come together and stop lying to each other," Cochrane admonished. "Then, together, we must put aside our old selves and past deeds, allow ourselves to be new men, men who grow in goodness and knowledge and, like Adam, are formed anew in the image of the creator."

"Stand, everyone," Cochrane commanded, walking along the semicircle, raising his hands to get people up. "Come together, reach out, and hold hands." Cochrane grasped the hand of the woman at one end of the semicircle and gestured to the man at the other end to come closer and join hands. Cochrane joined in the circle. "All of us here in the circle are bonded by sins, each of us is a sinner. Despite our hard work to follow God's laws we have failed again and again. Almighty have mercy on us," Cochrane pleaded, prompting others to cry out for mercy. "Squeeze each other's hands and ask for God's mercy.

"Paul brought the news that Jesus Christ came to pay the price of our sins. By believing in Him, we are afforded forgiveness and a path to heaven. He tells us we are made right with God through faith. Let's keep our hands clasped and raise them up," Cochrane instructed. "We are going to tell the Lord that we are sorry for our sins and ask for His forgiveness." Congregants waited to be unburdened by Cochrane's pleas.

"O God, I am sorry that I offended you and am deeply sorry for my sins." Cochrane was interrupted by a woman from across the circle who collapsed. "Pull her up. God will help you."

Cochrane resumed. "Say, 'God, you are all good and deserving of my love. I promise with the help of your grace to amend my life. Forgive me for my sins. Amen.'"

Some in the circle sobbed, others mumbled, all called for forgiveness. The circle grew tighter as Reverend Cochrane began to sing in his beautiful voice:

> "Not to condemn your guilty race,
> Have I in judgment come.
> But to display unbounded grace,
> And bring lost sinners home."

The circle swayed side to side as Cochrane repeated the song. "Because of Jesus, we have become right with God. We are bound together by God's love, which will make us perfect." Cochrane called out. "Embrace each other." As Cochrane backed away from the circle he watched his adherents hug and clasp each other's hands. All of it satisfied him, especially the man and woman exchanging the "holy kiss."

Cochrane stepped on a small platform where he could see and be heard and would be elevated above his followers. "Tonight, you learned about the Garden of Eden and saw it. Now we start to restore the Garden of Eden, and improve your life, your community and unite spiritually. We will make a heaven on earth."

There was not a noise among the congregants, so drawn were they to Cochrane's words. As the preacher looked around he saw anxious and expectant faces. His glanced past Ephraim, normally dressed, rid of his green outfit, looking embarrassed and seated alongside a sister.

"All have an obligation to fulfill God's plan for a new paradise. We must cultivate and care for our new Garden and shake ourselves free of the laws and institutions which have compromised our freedom. They stifle God's vision for us. He wants our Eden vibrant, us exuberant and our social love and spiritual union entirely shared."

Cochrane's position caught the full light. He shook his hair loose and his torso assumed a statuesque pose. A soft, rhythmic beat of the gong started as Cochrane untied the sash around his robe.

"Paul tells us how we can ennoble ourselves while fully expressing God's love. It's from Corinthians: 'You must know that your body is a temple of the Holy Spirit, who is within—the Spirit you have received from God. You have been purchased, and at a price. So, glorify God in your body.' We must all learn to glorify God with our bodies." When the robe dropped on the platform, Cochrane took on the appearance of a Greek statue.

"And being true to our flesh and what God has wrought, our body can glorify his love and the union that springs from it." Cochrane's left arm stretched straight out to the congregants and the other stretched toward the canvass wall behind. The gong pealed loudly, as Eve walked to join Cochrane. With both their arms raised, Cochrane began to sing:

> "Faith is thy gift, almighty Lord,
> From faith in thy sure promis'd word,
> And from the hope of heavenly things,
> This social love and union springs."

⌒

Mary had been busy since early in the morning, feeding Samuel and Mirinda, settling the children and getting everything in the kitchen together before the arrival of her sister-in-law Jane. It had been three weeks since the apple season began in mid-September, and two of the barrels of freshly picked fruit Ephraim had brought into the house looked perfectly suited for Mary's project. She and Jane would be spending the day preparing dried apples for the coming winter.

The tubs for washing the fruit were set out and filled with water. Some apples were already soaking. A basket, bowl, knives and cutting boards were set out on the table along with the linen string. Drying apples was not complicated, but with Jane's help they could core, peal, string and hang the two barrels before day's end and enjoy themselves at the same time. The stringing and the hanging were easier with more than two hands.

After the knock on the door, Mary fussed with her hair, straightened her apron and went to greet her favorite sister-in-law. "Jane, how good to see you," Mary said as they embraced. "You are right on time. Come on in."

"It looks like you have everything ready," Jane said as she took off her shawl and surveyed the kitchen, then glanced into the parlor. "I see that Samuel and Mirinda are settled. My boys are happy next door with their grandmother. And they will get so much attention today from my three sisters."

"Here is an apron for you, Jane. And you might want to pull up your sleeves, so you don't get them wet." Mary said as she reached into the tub, put some apples in the basket and placed it on the table. The women got right to work, coring the apples, then peeling them, cutting them cross-wise in one-quarter inch slices and placing them in the large bowl. "When we get the bowl filled we will start stringing the slices." Jane was more experienced at this, being ten years older than Mary, but Mary was unconcerned about her assertiveness.

"How is everything at home, Jane—with James?" Mary asked.

"There is a lot of work for carpenters. Everybody's building something, so James is always busy," Jane smiled. "If he is not tired, I try to keep him busy too. I would like to have another child. After two sons, it would be nice to have a little girl."

The basket nearly empty, Jane pulled more apples out of the tub into the basket and put more apples into the tub to soak. "I want more children too, and there is no reason we shouldn't. I've had two babies with no problems. Ephraim also wants a bigger family, but he spends less time at home."

"I was hoping we would talk about Ephraim. My brother has changed so much in the past four years, he has become a new person. I see things in him I have never seen. I am grateful to you, Mary."

"Jane. The change doesn't stop. He does things I don't understand." Mary took the peels from the table and put them in a sack. "Jacob Cochrane. Ephraim is very involved in Cochrane's brotherhood. I believe he has taken a secret oath and is helping Cochrane gain followers," Mary said. "I can't explain Ephraim's behavior and don't understand Cochrane's charm."

"Cochrane is stirring people up all over the county," Jane said. "They are caught up in his preaching and his special powers. Some say he is an imposter."

"Cochrane's meetings haven't drawn me in. Ephraim is quite involved, becoming a disciple. He took me to a Cochrane meeting, but we didn't come home together. He stayed. There are special services for believers," Mary said. Mary got up to fetch more apples, paused and looked directly at Jane. "You know how much Ephraim and I shared, and intimacy bound us together. There is not much sharing now. It's confusing to me and undermines our closeness. I think it's my fault and my lack of a spiritual nature."

"There is a lot going on with Jacob Cochrane's deception, Mary. You cannot blame yourself for misunderstanding."

"We've got a lot of apple rings here; the bowl is overflowing. Let's start stringing." Mary had two spools of linen string and gave one to Jane. They were quiet until the bowl of apple slices was empty, and two strings of apples were set separately on the counter.

"I don't want Ephraim to get into any trouble," Mary blurted out. "His connection with Cochrane could have a sad ending." Jane slowed her pace in peeling the apples and waited to hear more. "There is not an adult in York County who has not heard about Cochrane being naked in church. A preacher exposing himself to his congregation is unthinkable, and a naked woman at his side. The depiction of Adam and Eve could not have been intended as a religious ceremony. It's decadent."

Mary heard a sound from the parlor and got up to give Samuel and Mirinda some crackers. "They are fine," she said as she sat down.

"I understand that authorities in Saco heard of the scandalous incident and summoned Cochrane to court. They say he was required to post bonds and promised a severe penalty if his depravity is repeated," Mary said. "I'm sure Ephraim was there, but I haven't had the courage to ask him. I don't think he would say a word."

"I know about the Adam and Eve incident," Jane did not look up from her work, and sounded contrite. "I was there. Ephraim snuck me into the barn."

"You were there?" Mary was astonished. "How could you expose yourself to such depravity?" Mary put down the apple in her hand, as well the paring knife, her hard stare demanding an explanation.

"Ephraim asked me to go," Jane said. The primary purpose of Jane's visit was to tell Mary about the notorious Cochrane meeting, but it was hard to start. "Cochrane's depiction of Adam and Eve was like a short play, and Ephraim was given a part in it. He had never done anything like it before and wanted me to see him play the serpent. He wrapped himself up in green cloth and crawled across the floor. Behind an awful mask he hissed. Cochrane stood by, the voice of God, waiting to drive Ephraim from the garden."

Mary was speechless, unable to conjure the scene in her mind.

"I knew about the service for a while. Ephraim was pleased Cochrane had asked him to be in it. It took courage for Ephraim to get in front of everybody. I helped him with some sewing on the snake head. He asked me to keep it a secret." Jane's narrative was sincere. "I went that night to see Ephraim play a nasty snake. The snake was hard to play. He didn't like it, although it pleased Cochrane. I never thought of seeing Cochrane naked, and a naked girl holding his hand."

"You saw Cochrane naked? And the girl?" Mary gasped in disbelief.

"I am here Mary, because I had to tell you about this. You are my good friend," Jane said. "And I care about my brother. You know I am puzzled by him, his spiritual experiences and his ties to Jacob Cochrane. You are the anchor in his life. You make a difference, as his wife and the mother of his children."

Mary resumed peeling and slicing apples. The two barrels of apples had to be strung that day, and the routine and rhythm of the work brought order to her mind.

"I was thinking about Ephraim and when we were so close. And I remembered talking about that time. It was during a quilting bee. Ephraim's sisters Anna, Elizabeth and Rebecca were there, and your niece Mercy and daughter, Ruth. We talked about the bliss and pitfalls of marriage." Mary was quiet, recollecting the quilting bee conversation.

"You seem very happy, Mary," Mercy observed. "But you and Ephraim had little time together before your marriage."

"Courtship was different for me, and special," Mary began. "Since I was in Scarborough, Ephraim and I had a long and extensive correspondence. That's how we got to know each other."

"That doesn't sound like much fun," Anna snickered.

"It was sweet," Rebecca challenged. "I was lucky to help Ephraim with his letters."

"We learned we could say things each had never expressed before," Mary continued. "I found myself opening up to Ephraim completely.

"I wasn't surprised when my mother insisted my wedding not be in Scarborough. But it was difficult to raise the subject with Ephraim. I would have to tell him why. The issue wasn't one of his worthiness. It was why was I was being publicly embarrassed, rejected by my mother. My incomplete explanation was in a letter to Ephraim. He had met my mother and had some understanding of her ways. My father and Uncle Joseph worked with my aunts here in Buxton and I had a wonderful ceremony. Ruth and Mercy know because they helped and made me feel at home."

"It was beautiful," Ruth said. "I think my mother put more into making sure you had a wonderful day than in arranging my wedding."

"All of the Moultons in Buxton worked to make sure you had a happy day," Mercy added.

"You know I do not like to talk about my hair," Mary confessed. "I'm bald. That's always hard to say. It's a horrible bit of information to divulge on your wedding night.

"While I started to undress that night, I mustered the courage to tell Ephraim about the accident. I was five years old with my cousins at Uncle Joseph's house. They had a big tree in their yard with a swing. I couldn't wait for my turn and begged for my mother's help. She was busy talking to my Aunt Catherine but relented. Mother got me settled on the wooden seat, then got me going. Immediately following a hard push, I fell from the seat. As I stood up the swing returned from the height of its arc. I was hit, a metal flange on the bottom of the seat scraped across the top of my head taking some of my hair with it."

Mary had to catch her breath to slow her churning emotions.

"A portion of my scalp was stripped away, the hair remaining of the top of my head was sopped with blood. But I was able to stand, and my vision was not blurred. I remember a noisy scene. There was my uncontrolled crying and my mother's angry screams. The shock did not diminish the pain which seemed to increase with some swelling of my raw head. Aunt Catherine wrapped her shawl around me, to protect my head and soak up the blood floating on its surface. My tipsy mother spent the next several weeks in some aimless fury, intent to let everyone know the accident was the result of my innate carelessness, not of her drinking."

Most in the room knew about Mary's hair, but none had heard her tell her story. She gave her friends time to picture the gruesome scene.

"Tears were pouring from Ephraim's eyes as I confessed my ugliness. Then his urgent embrace filled the great need my mother could never sense was there. I was surrounded by his overwhelming affection. We were one. I didn't want him to pull away, but he did. As he removed the rest of my clothing, he couldn't stop kissing me—kissing me all over."

"My gracious," Anna gasped.

"His body stretched beside me was reassuring. He touched my hair and gently spread my locks across the soft pillow. With tenderness he unfastened the combs that carefully held the hair piled on the top of my head, as he kissed my forehead. He exposed the ugly mark on my scalp, touching softly the long scar, telling me I was beautiful. And I felt beautiful and loved."

"That I should know such tenderness,' Mercy's voice was little more than a whisper.

"I never thought my brother could be like that," Anna added.

"He's never unkind, just never shows emotion," Elizabeth said.

"The intimacy wasn't one-sided," Mary explained. "It was deep—for both of us. We unlocked each other's heart. We were one."

"Ephraim has always been self-contained and private," Rebecca said, "That's what he seems to prefer. Parts of him are closed off from the family. He spent much of his time growing up alone and working."

"A lot of men are that way," Mercy said. "My Isaac can be a loner."

"Some time men don't talk. Most things they don't think are women's business," Ruth said.

Mary told Jane that the conversation with her younger sisters had been revealing. "Anna was a little protective of her older brother," she said, "but I think he was most open with me."

"Ephraim kept things to himself," Jane said. "Apart from all of us."

"He is like that now, Jane, always quiet and guarded. If he were more self-revelatory, he would be found unlikeable. That's what he thinks," Mary said.

Jane knew by her friend's tone of voice that any comment was unwelcome.

"It is a spiritual divide. He tells me of religious experiences where God was present. That's nothing I can imagine. I fear I am losing him," Mary started to cry, but tears did not slow the pace of work. She and Jane strung more apples.

"I can't imagine Ephraim portraying a snake," Mary said. "It's child-like, something I have never seen. I don't see his obsession with Cochrane ending if he stays away from home, not embraced, unable to toss Samuel in the air or to talk to me. Jane, what I can do?"

"You love Ephraim, Mary. Continue to show him your love is strong and enduring," Jane said. "He loves his children, so continue to be a good mother. Make sure Samuel and Mirinda feel loved and protected. Ephraim likes being a father. You should try to have more children. These are things you can do for Ephraim that Cochrane and his church cannot do. For Ephraim, Mary, you are indispensable."

"That is what everybody says, Jane. I have to be strong and be a good wife and mother," Mary tried to smile. "I think we should hang up some of the apples we have strung."

The two strings were long enough to span the kitchen rafters. Mary got up on a stool and reached a hook in the rafters. Jane handed her an end of a string of apples, which Mary attached to the hook. Mary moved the stool to the other side of the room, and Jane handed her the other end of the string to attach to another hook. They were pleased when two strings were hanging across the room.

"It is disheartening when I think of what I am working against," Mary chuckled. "I am in competition with a prophet of God, a prophet whose naked rituals are as important as the scriptures he recites. Can he be stopped?"

Mary was surprised by a knock. No one was expected. She went to the parlor, opened the front door and was glad to face her neighbor. "Please come in Joanna. Jane and I are busy, but always have time to talk when peeling apples."

"It's nice to see you, Jane," Joanna said as she entered the kitchen. "Give me a knife. My mother always said I was good at this."

"Thanks, but there is not room enough for another to work at the table. But join in our conversation," Mary said, as she moved a chair close to the table for Joanna. "We are talking about Adam and Eve."

"Dear me," Joanna exclaimed. "Are you talking about Jacob Cochrane and his meeting? Who isn't? Cochrane's Adam and Eve made him famous. Wouldn't you like to see it?"

"I did. I was there," Jane took some time before confessing.

"What was it like to see a preacher naked, especially one as handsome as Cochrane?" Joanna asked. "That's not a question I could ask my husband. You know Nat was there."

"I didn't see Nat, but it was dark in the barn," Jane said. "The nudity was a shock to me. I really didn't pay much attention to Cochrane's body. It was nothing like a religious service, except the quoting from the Bible. A strange meeting, and I cannot understand Cochrane's purpose."

"Many women admire Cochrane ardently," Joanna tried to explain her question. "Some embrace him in public meetings and unblushingly kiss him. He doesn't discourage that, calling it the 'holy kiss' of the Scriptures."

"I didn't realize that Nat was drawn to Cochrane and his teaching," Mary said. "He talks to you about services?"

"Nat is interested in Cochrane and goes to meetings," Joanne said. "He doesn't normally tell me anything. His attraction to Eliza Hill was strong, so he had to tell me all about the Adam and Eve depiction. He described Eliza as toothsome. When Cochrane does it again, I won't be able to keep Nat home."

"But he won't do Adam and Eve again. It means trouble with the law," Mary said.

"Cochrane thrives on attention. He likes crowds. Nat says that after Adam and Eve, Cochrane's following has grown bigger and bigger," Joanna said.

"You think Cochrane chose to stage the Adam and Eve story because of the opportunity to show a man and a woman naked? He knows people will flock to his meetings?" Jane asked. "Is that his purpose?"

"I only know what Nat told me," Joanna responded. "More

than that, Cochrane says the sacred bonds of matrimony are determined by God, like in Eden. Only God knows who should marry, according to Cochrane's vision. He says that God wants a new form of marriage."

Mary continued to peel and slice, unnerved by Joanne's disturbing words. In Jacob Cochrane's realm whatever she does makes no difference. The things she does best—being a good wife and mother, and the intimacy she has shared with Ephraim—may not be enough to keep him home. *A new kind of marriage?* Mary felt herself beginning to seethe with anger and disgust.

⌒

This is not about lust, Ephraim told himself. *This is about bringing people closer to God, strengthening their belief. That is why they come to church. It is why they are drawn here tonight.*

Everyone committed to Jacob Cochrane followed his plans without question, including how to get to meetings without attracting the attention of authorities. To ward off county officials, the gatherings for believers were held in different places. Tonight, devotees came to the dwelling-house just off the road from Saco Falls to Buxton Corner by various routes. Vigilant sentinels were posted around the property to detect interlopers or spies. The place was shuttered, and its doors barred.

I went to church looking for pleasure. That was long ago. I was only fourteen. Ephraim tried to dismiss the memory, but his mental habit of connecting sex and worship persisted. *The music, the swelling urgency, sense of belonging, everyone lifted from the world, the rapture of being raised up. Reverend Hutchinson urging us to share. God was there. I couldn't keep away.*

The large room had no chairs. Supplicants were standing and expectant, something remarkable would happen tonight. Timothy Ham, a prominent Cochranite with a strong voice, started the singing. Congregants joined in with dancing, whirling and jumping followed. Cochrane appeared. Congregants shouted "Amen," and "Praise Jesus."

Cochrane raised his hands to bring order to the room. "I can say in truth that God has a holy Church on earth, wherein He reigns. You are witnesses to His word and work. All of you are doing God's labor. Yet His chosen remain secluded people." The prophet liked to remind followers of their separateness.

Taking the lead in more singing and dancing, Cochrane motioned Ephraim to join in. The vigorous exercise left most out of breath. Rounds of dancing broke out, each with greater fervor, exuberant shouts, exhaustion. Ephraim, knowing Cochrane's plan to excite the crowd, worried that the raucous sound would be heard in the surrounding countryside and the meeting could be interrupted. Everyone else ignored the danger.

Cochrane stopped, invoking the angel in Revelations, "Thrust in thy sickle, and reap, for harvest is ripe." Dancing resumed. A sheaf of wheat in one hand and his other guiding a young admirer, Cochrane led half the group in a physical, and emotionally engaging movement called reaping. Another troupe lined up opposite, moved forward wildly, hands flapping, then throwing their arms in the air, closed in on those reaping and then moved back. These "winnowers" were separating the chaff from the wheat.

"Bow down your hearts and humble yourselves to the dust before me," Cochrane howled, "Thus sayeth the Lord. O ye worms of mortal clay. All flesh shall wither in my presence. The deceitful shall be consumed by the fire of my burning." Dancers fell to the floor breathless, some unable to move. Those still standing waited patiently for signs of vigor from the fallen, knowing some on the floor had entered a realm of celestial wonderment.

That night of the revival Reverend Hutchinson threatened damnation, while promising God's embrace. Celebrants could be with Jesus in paradise, drink with Him in endless pleasure. The doomed could be restored, strengthened by others who shared the gift of God's love. The words from long ago could not leave Ephraim's mind. *"There is no limit to how God wants to use us."*

"I just saw a large ball of light, a body of fire moving slowly to the south. It turned and passed by me to the north, divided into four parts, and moved swiftly each way, east, west, north and south. It vanished," a resuscitated man spoke as he raised himself to his knees. "I was blind but heard a loud and terrible voice thunder, 'I am the mighty prophesying Angel of the God of Heaven and Earth. I speak of that which has been, of that which now is and of that which is to come.'"

The unfolding vision of another zealot broke through an astounding hush, capturing the room with exultant cries. Believers were struck by the tone, authority and exceptional language in which the revelation was declared.

"The Angel said, 'If there is yet to be found in Zion, sinners or workers of iniquity, I will, without reserve, prophesy evil against them. They will be cast before the righteous like stubble. God's kingdom on earth shall be a righteous one. His own chosen people should be prepared and ready,'" the message ended. The speaker collapsed in exhaustion, a look of fear on his face.

A woman returned from a trance-like state with her arms stretched toward heaven recounting another vision. It ended with a loud groan and terrible shaking, which gave the woman physical and physic release.

The weeping girl beside him in the dark church cried for mercy. She clung to him as the pastor shouted, "Receive His love," and "Share your gifts." What excitement he felt as he was pulled down into the shadows of the bench. Ephraim's old memory didn't leave him.

Because these services generated much physical exhaustion, Ephraim had placed a bed in an adjoining room for those who needed time to recover from their terrestrial state. The bed was of special importance that night.

Sister Mercy was a regular feature in these meetings and regarded as a maiden of great personal beauty. Most extraordinary were her spiritual gifts and the ease with which she moved into the celestial realm. She had astonishing visions of heaven. It amazed Ephraim how she was able to discuss with extreme frankness various forms of forbidden behavior and at the same time project the guilt that would result from merely thinking about such sins.

"Her spirit wandered far away from her body," Cochrane announced. "Sister Mercy's spirit has left us." Cochrane rolled the young woman on her back to assess her physical condition.

"Oh my God," a voice in the gathering whispered, "You think she left her undergarments in heaven, too?" Despite the shadow cast by Cochrane's kneeling body, it was clear that the helpless girl was naked under her shear white gown.

"Sister Mercy is breathing, but her heartbeat is faint," Cochrane said after brief inspection. "There are no reflexes. She seems to be failing and I have no drugs to revive her. Ephraim, help me get her into the bed."

The two men picked up the limp body and carried Sister Mercy into the adjoining room. Cochrane left Ephraim with the girl and went back to the others.

"You should go home for the night. Rest and regain your strength. You despair and fear she may never regain consciousness, but I will watch over her and do what I can. Get some rest, Brothers and Sisters. This is in God's hands," the prophet was consoling as he guided his followers to the door.

My instincts took control that night, and the girl couldn't stop herself. Ephraim was mesmerized by his thoughts and gripped by the shadow of Sister Mercy's veiled pubis.

"You need some rest too, Ephraim," Cochrane said, reentering the room. "I will see to Sister Mercy's abandoned body."

Ephraim nodded and left the room. He had his hands in his pockets, so his prophet would not see that he was aroused.

Cochrane followers were not surprised when they returned the next day to find an open casket in the meeting room. Cochrane sat nearby in a chair, silent and meditative. Sister Mercy's family implored Brother Cochrane to bring the girl back and reconnect her fugitive spirit to the physical remains in the next room.

Cochrane was mute, appearing spellbound, but Ephraim knew Cochrane was thinking about his skillful legerdemain, that every step had gone as planned. Ephraim was impressed by the open casket when he returned, its placement and all the candles. *He is focused on the rest of the plan. All must go as well,* Ephraim thought.

Ephraim knew exactly what to do. He asked the group to stand and led the file into the adjoining room to view Sister Mercy, making it clear that nothing should be touched. Sister Mercy should in no way be disturbed, and no one should linger in the room. Cochrane wanted nothing to break the spell. Should the heavily powdered recumbent figure accidently sneeze, Cochrane had confided, the mood would be lost.

The beautiful young woman reclining on the soft white cover of her bed, her head elevated by a fluffy pillow, appeared almost floating. All looked white and black. She was dressed in a white robe, no contrast to the pale alabaster skin of her hands and face. Her cheek bones reflected the dim light in the somber room, as did her flawless forehead. The light was perfect. Her dark, shiny hair was spread across the pillow, lending radiance to this ethereal scene. Only Sister Mercy's long, silken eye lashes did not look subdued, curling up as they did. Her full lips were tinged the color of faded pink rose petals. Ephraim couldn't quell the sobbing and soft cries of the relatives and motioned all out of the sanctuary.

Jacob Cochrane was standing behind the open coffin when the mourners returned to the meeting room. His usually robust faced looked sallow, his sunken eyes lost all brightness. The affirmative tone belied his depleted appearance. "Sister Mercy has now been away so long that the powers of her spiritual attractions are overwhelming, so strong that she has become bound to them. She cannot be released without assistance, our assistance. Everyone, in your most earnest voice must reclaim her. Call out and ask the Almighty Lord to bring Sister Mercy back." He straightened up, inhaled deeply, posing to best display his powerful frame.

He entered Sister Mercy's room and went directly to her bedside. He stretched one arm toward heaven, and reached down with the other, passing his magic hand across her fair brow. "Mercy," Cochrane commanded, "Arise." Upon sweeping his hand upward with clear deliberation, Mercy sprang from her bed with a scream and rushed into the room where the bereaved waited. While fully conscious, she was completely unaware of the revealing nature of her sheer night garments. Her joyous, but prudent mother, alert to her almost natural state, grabbed a sheet from the other room, wrapped Mercy in it, and took her back to dress.

Those present, unrestrained in their rejoicing, clapped hands and started singing. The enthusiasm increased as they waited to hear Mercy tell of the wonders she had seen during her absence from her brethren and sisters.

Sister Mercy moved before them, the aura of light surrounding her head conferred the look of a sacred figure. The thousands of shining particles making up the aura appeared as tiny stars. Her voice, rich and soothing, was complemented by her descriptive powers.

"I have been led down different paths, shown many wondrous places," she began trembling and pale, "I saw a path of tribulation paved with the bitter grief, heavy sorrow, and the keenest of excruciation. On that path I walked day and night, headed to hell." The congregants were breathless, frightened, but made no sound. "But I was guided up a path of light, on each side were colored flames the size of human beings. It was like a beautiful rainbow."

With Mercy's recitation and visions, people started shaking. Murmurs of "Praise Jesus" and restrained shouts of "Hallelujah" did not intrude on Mercy's celestial tale.

"The path led to a great, luminous temple. Four thousand Angels trooped toward this place of worship, their steps quickening as they got closer. They entered the temple and I heard a band of heavenly music, many harpers, beautiful sounds coming from hundreds of strings. Angels raised their solemn trumpets and gave a sonorous blast. They heralded peace. Yea, peace, joy and tranquility shall crown your days," Sister Mercy paused. Never having been given such a vision of heaven, devotees were stunned. "I was shown the word of the Lord, it appeared on a great sheet that looked like fire, the words written in gold," Sister Mercy bowed her head as she finished, leaving everyone in awe.

The sharing of this sublime experience connected congregants with feelings of euphoria, purpose, belonging and superiority.

Cochrane looked exultant and Ephraim's old memories were forgotten.

The measures taken to protect the secrecy of Cochrane's meetings did not keep Sister Mercy and her resurrection from becoming a legend within days. Many living in the Saco River valley regarded the event as the greatest of Jacob Cochrane's miracles. Their adoration of him grew. Cochrane adherents gloried in repeating the story of the miracle and the details of Sister Mercy's visions. Cochranites were a growing force, not just a secluded people.

⌒

Harvest was over, cold on its way. Dairying was at its end, farmers slaughtered livestock to fill their meat barrels and prepared for a new winter diet of salt pork, beef and dried beans. Cider was made and stocked. At Coolbroth's Corners, the brothers sold the last of the cheese and replenished the store's shelves and barrels with foodstuffs—spices, sugar, tea, salt fish, coffee—items rarely found in the winter months.

One November afternoon Uriah Graffam, Nat Harmon, Paul Dresser and Ned Redlon gathered by the store's revived stove, trying to shake off the late fall chill with flasks of cider. Ben Coolbroth sorted new merchandise and Eben, outside, tended to building repairs. A big storm had just brought down a large tree limb, damaging the porch roof and busting its corner post.

Eben went into the store to check the cider and pass out dried fruit and cheese. "Well," the irrepressible voice blurted, "Do you think that Jacob Cochrane will get us all to Heaven? Seems he is converting everyone—maybe even some cows."

"Many think his reformation remarkable, hundreds baptized," Paul said in a serious voice. "He no longer works with the other churches, the Baptists and Methodists. Pastors Phinney, Stinchfield, all of them, once called Cochrane the revival's guiding spirit. They now speak against him and close church doors in his face. They are outraged by Cochrane's creed of spiritual wifery. Vigilante committees have organized."

"He's kept tongues wagging for so long they are wore out. People can't lick their own chops," Uriah chuckled. "First it was Adam and Eve, Cochrane promoting lust and nudity in church. Then the mystery of Sister Mercy's resurrection. Was fornication involved? That story is heard in Portland and New Hampshire. Anyone not horrified by spiritual wifery, don't know what it is."

"Some call it free love," Ned grinned.

"It's simple. Jacob Cochrane is preaching against marriage," Paul said. "He's issued a proclamation declaring that God wants all marriages annulled. Partnerships should be based on spiritual ties alone. Followers married according to Massachusetts law should renounce existing vows. In God's plan each member of his society has a spiritual wife, husband, mate or yoke fellow. God's intended are revealed to Cochrane through divine revelation. Members should yield themselves to Cochrane's holy directions."

"Lots in Buxton don't accept Cochrane's view of marriage," Eben said. "Most who come in the store don't like it."

"Cochrane benefits most," Uriah said. "I hear God continually reveals to him a different member of his brood of young lovelies to be his temporary, spiritual wife. Think that's for training?"

"Lustful men everywhere seize Cochrane's teaching to personally appraise his flock," Ned cracked, scratching his crotch. "Doesn't Cochrane have a wife? Is she frigid?"

"I have met his wife, Abigail," Nat said. "She looks alright, been married ten years and has a son born last year."

"I've been told that Cochrane's views do not please his wife. She laughs at his connection to the divine," Ned said.

"I heard that here in the store," Eben took an expansive breath before he continued. "There is the story that Cochrane met one evening with an enthusiastic disciple, Phineas Butler, who lives in north Saco. Cochrane told Brother Phineas that he had been in prayer that very morning and, among other revelations, God told him that for the time being they were given divine permission to exchange wives. Butler said he would obey God's wishes. Guided by the Holy Spirit, he went directly to the Cochrane house near

Saco Falls. Mrs. Cochrane greeted him at the door and asked him what he wanted. He told her of God's revelation and that he was prepared to accept her as his spiritual wife. Mrs. Cochrane turned red in anger, leaned until her face was five inches from his and yelled at Brother Phineas, 'You go back right now and tell Jake Cochrane that his God's a liar.'"

Everybody laughed—even those who had heard the widely circulated story. Eben went outside to check the progress on the repairs. Seeing that they would take another day and the sun sinking in the sky, he asked the carpenter to join the men in the store. Cochrane still dominated the conversation.

"His decrees are becoming less popular among the unbelievers, some calling them quackery," Paul said. "But his followers hold him up, almost as a deity,"

"Believers anger at the word quackery," Ned said. "They say spiritual wifery is not something concocted by Cochrane. It's based on Chapter Two of Genesis, justified by the story of Adam and Eve. Did anyone see Cochrane's show?"

"I have never forgotten it—seeing Eliza Hill," Nat Harmon blurted, before his face turned red.

"In Cochrane's portrayal of Adam, God creates Eve from his rib. She was 'bones of his bones and flesh of his flesh.' That's how people are spiritually mated," Ned explained. "I never saw his service. Heard he showed his bone." He grinned, looking at Nat.

"I wasn't paying attention to Cochrane or Genesis. The naked girl captured me," Nat said.

"Cochrane's foes explain the scripture differently," Paul followed the dispute. "Reverend Buzzell, the Baptist, says the origin of marriage was in Eden but God's plan is not Cochrane's. Marriage is not intended to encourage sexual union, but to propagate a virtuous race, protecting people from barbarism, heathenism and lust." Nobody disagreed. "Cochrane, he says, teaches and practices corrupting immoralities, living in ways common decency scorns."

Ben had kept busy, dressing some ducks a hunter had brought as trade for flour and dried beans.

"It seems that Cochrane has gotten many interested in the ribs, for better or worse," Eben did not interrupt the rhythm of Ben's work. "At Coolbroth's Corners we butcher but have never gotten involved in human ribs. That leads to trouble."

"Trouble is right. You could wake up and realize that the person next to you in bed is not your rib," Paul laughed. "I heard about Jack Coombs in Hollis, who realized that his spiritual wife was actually two years older. Someone confronted Jack and asked if he was fooled by Cochrane. He said that the birth sequence didn't make sense, but the outcome did. She was the best sex he ever had and took him right to paradise."

"It's like I said," Eben interjected, "In the rib business, you never see the trouble. Ducks are very predictable." Eben nodded toward Ben, not missing a chance to sell merchandise.

Uriah was the smoker, and the first to start coughing. Smoke was seeping out of the stove. "Eben, is this the first time you have used this stove? Not a good draft. Either the stove pipe or the flu is blocked." Noticing the smoke, the others moved away.

"Another thing to check with winter coming on. Just haven't done it," Eben groaned, as he looked up the length of the pipe. The cause could be fallen bricks, leaves, or a bird nest. It doesn't take much soot or creosote buildup to interfere with a proper draft. "Thanks, Uriah. I'm surprised you are the first to notice."

"Just as Cochrane erred in understanding God's plan for Jack Coombs, others have also confused the commands of the spirit," Ned chimed in. "How else explain the grown-up daughter who was given a spiritual brother?"

"Or the instance where a man took his step-daughter of sixteen for a wife, with the consent of her mother. When the law was to be enforced, they eloped," Eben laughed.

"If I were a purveyor of ribs, I would be losing business and gaining animosity from my female customers. When a husband brings that kind of provision home, who is going to cook it? The wife would be gone, taking all the kids to her father's house. Or she will be coming here to buy senna, manna, anise seed, and rhubarb.

She'll put it in his food. He would be defecating day and night, given no opportunity to enjoy the gift of a spiritual wife."

"The truth is that Cochrane is breaking up families that have lived happily under accepted ideas of love and matrimony," Paul said. "His doctrine is making converts of wives whose husbands are boring in bed, and of husbands with wives too priggish to embrace the new faith."

"What about you Nat, you go to Cochrane's meetings. What does your wife, Joanna, think of his preaching free love?" Paul was direct.

"She knows I was smitten by Eliza Hill. I never made it a secret," Nat responded. "She doesn't know anything about spiritual wifery, but she would never find my replacement satisfactory."

As Nat spoke the front door opened and Ephraim walked into the store. Ephraim's manner seemed odd. He was polite, but no more than expected when greeting strangers. He briefly embraced his uncles. His cheerless demeanor set him apart, but Eben was intent on Ephraim joining the lively conversation.

"Welcome back, Ephraim. We don't see enough of you," Eben playfully punched his nephew's shoulder and laughed. "You spend a lot of time with Jacob Cochrane. Maybe you can tell us about spiritual wifery?"

"Spiritual wifery?" Ephraim was defensive. "People talk as if personal relations are the business of politicians, government, or local officials, but they have no jurisdiction in matters of religious experience." Ephraim tone was flinty.

"Cochrane has caused such a clamor with his new doctrine, all of us are curious," Eben said calmly.

"A person's spiritual destiny is far more important than local rules and traditions. So many are stuck in Reverend Coffin's world, but those ways are gone," Ephraim sounded like both teacher and defender. "How could I obey Coffin's kind of religion, one corrupted by the State of Massachusetts? I would be putting my eternal salvation in the hands of functionaries and thieves."

"Church is seldom linked to free love. That's what we were

joking about. We don't know the connection," Eben said lightly.

"To be a member of the true church of God, you have to have experienced authentic New Birth, which is dictated exclusively by the Holy Spirit," Ephraim's earnestness separated him from his old friends. Ephraim's new evangelical posture had not been witnessed before. "Our religious and political institutions are corrupted. Corruption has undermined religious liberty, with the church subservient to the state. We must create and sustain our own, separate church. That's why I came by—I'm helping Jacob Cochrane create his great church." The usually modest friend seemed emboldened by his words.

"Our talk has been less serious, Ephraim," Eben was cheerful. "We were asking Nat about his attachment to Cochrane's society, and if it has anything to do with free love."

"I just haven't been chosen yet," Nat smiled. "As far as I know Jacob Cochrane and God have never discussed my marital condition."

'What about you, Ephraim? Has Cochrane eyed a spiritual consort for you? Has one of his swooning admirers planted the holy kiss on your innocent face?" Eben teased.

Ephraim seemed offended but did not argue with his friends. "Knowing me for a long time you may be surprised, but I am not here to talk about sex. And to your disappointment, I have no spiritual wife," Ephraim smirked, then became more serious. "I am raising money to build Cochrane's church and thought you might help out. It's clear that a soberer occasion will be required for that subject. Sorry, I must go."

Everyone was struck by Ephraim's mood, but they all tried to hide their surprise as he went around the room and shook everyone's hand. Then he turned to leave.

He stopped at the door and looked back. "I'll come again and spend more time with you. None of you is off the hook. You cannot deny the Kingdom of Heaven." Ephraim disappeared into the evening.

FOUR

The house sat comfortably on a pleasant stretch of land across the top of a ridge, catching every ray of sunshine during the short winter days. In summer, fresh breezes from the sea floated through it. The privacy lost by its placement on the corner of the property where the road bends around, was outweighed by the sweeping views and the advantage of seeing everything coming up the road. Most important about the location was the relatively large size of this level plot. Twenty-five yards from the west end of the house sat the large barn with an animal enclosure. Ephraim's workshop was attached at the end nearest the house. There was room for Mary's treasured garden not far from her kitchen at the east side of the house.

The children fed, Mary went out to look around the farm she loved so much. She walked through her garden, thinking there was another month before work would start. She faced a lot of weeding and some uprooting of plants that didn't survive winter. Going behind the house she checked the privy. She didn't want another skunk building a nest inside. Behind the house there was also a small grove of apple trees.

Mary did her spinning in the house, but her loom was in the barn—in a corner next to one of the hay cribs. She wanted to get ready for her afternoon's work—she would weave after the children were down for their naps. Passing the animal enclosure, she noticed two railings that Ephraim needed to mend before spring. She paused at the workshop door which wasn't completely closed. The jamb needed repair. *Ephraim would have fixed it if he spent more time in the workshop this winter*, Mary thought. *Ephraim spends less and less time on the farm.*

Mary was surprised to see Ben Andrews walking up the road toward the house. Not a neighbor, hardly an acquaintance. Mary had seen Ben at the Cochrane meeting she attended with Ephraim. She remembered that Ben Andrews had strong ties to Cochrane, and Ephraim talked extensively about Cochrane's eulogy for Catherine, Andrews's daughter. From the time of the eulogy, everybody noticed that Ben stayed close to Cochrane and helped as his Society grew.

Mary was chasing chickens toward the barn when Ben walked cautiously up to her. He had never been at the farm. "Good morning," Andrews said. "It's nice to see you."

"Good morning," Mary replied. "Ephraim is not here, and I don't know when he will be back. I'm busy. I will tell my husband that you came by." Mary turned to get the birds out of the winter air and back to their nests.

"I've just come from Jacob Cochrane's place," Ben's words stopped her. "Your husband Ephraim, Tim Ham and a few others were there. Jacob sent me here."

"I don't know why, what your business might be. My husband is a Cochrane enthusiast, but that has nothing to do with me. I have attended a few Cochrane meetings, but am not drawn to his teaching as my husband is. Never has his spirit overwhelmed me, and I don't feel deprived." After showing her irritation, Mary's civility returned. "I am unsure that we have ever spoken. What is it that you want?"

"There was a visitation with Jacob this morning. We do them almost every day," Ben continued. "Jacob revealed his recent communication with the Lord. Our lives must be aligned, he told us, with the Divine Plan. Jacob, transmitting the most recent expression of God's will, was told that Ephraim and I should exchange wives. You, Mary, are meant to be my true, spiritual wife."

Mary was mortified. The man standing before her was nothing like the loving man who once stretched beside her, unfastened her hair, spreading it across the pillow and gently kissing her scarred head. This man embarrassed her. "Spiritual!" Mary was incredulous. She showed neither anger nor fear. "Humph!" She turned quickly to the chickens who were headed toward the barn. Mary didn't hear the footsteps. When she was grabbed from the back by powerful arms, she had no idea what was happening. Her breath was squeezed out of her and her limbs lost strength. Her heels left tracks on the ground as Andrews dragged her into the barn.

Ben flung his spiritual wife onto a pile of straw. He sat on top of her using his powerful knees and thighs like a vice against her body, restraining the movement of her rigid, unyielding frame. "Let me go!" Mary screamed. Her natural defenses triggered, she instinctively fought back, freeing her lower body to knee him in his groin. Enraged, he struck Mary hard across her face. Her mind slowed, first thinking she was having a terrifying dream, but horrified to realize she was awake. This was not a dream. Mary had no shield. Overcoming her resistance, he yanked up her skirt and ripped her underwear. Exposed from the waist down, the shock of February cold barely registered in Mary's mind.

Her growing terror enflamed Ben's brutal assault, as he tore her blouse and ripped off most of her clothes. His weight made it hard for Mary to breathe. There was no relief from the grating of his rugged clothing, the digging of ragged nails into her flesh, and grunting in her ear. The rough straw covering the clay floor of the barn jabbed her back. "This is divine. It's God's will—we are living out His plan. My wife. You will love me," Ben grunted.

When he raised up, Mary thanked God for the chance to breathe, but it was only to remove his trousers. She did not struggle as Ben sat on her chest. His reach to her tangled tresses was not with affection. The gesture was to raise her head, as he spread his knees and arched his pelvis. Mary gagged, her eyes popped, as Ben roughly tugged her hair. *Oh my God! You did not intend for me to have this in my mouth*, Mary screamed to herself. *This dirty, stinking member is choking me. I want to bite it. No. Don't make things worse.*

Mary had no plan. She could only submit to the violence and Ben's pleasure. Her strength was nearly gone. She did not speak, too stunned to scream. Part of her was not there. Part was high up, floating among the rafters of the barn looking down on a paralyzed young woman, eyes screwed shut and wailing silently. *Maybe my fear and helplessness drive him on*, she wondered. From her station in the beams, she saw herself trying to catch her breath, relax and calm her body. *Give him what he wants and maybe he will leave me alone*, Mary thought as a way out.

Mary jerked her head back in horror when she opened her eyes and found young Samuel staring at her. His pale blue eyes were Ephraim's looking from behind the partition which divided the cribs of hay. Her mouth freed, she regained her voice to shriek. "Go back to the house," her inflection hoarse. "Go back to the house. I'll be there soon." Riveted by the violence and his struggling mother, Samuel did not leave. Ben looked around at the blank-faced boy with indifference, then resumed his bestial attack.

Mary had to get this over. "You know, I've been through this before, Ben—had men before," she lied and softened her voice. "It's nothing special, not part of God's plan. Just let me know what you want." Mary relaxed her strained neck and benumbed head as Ben released his hold on her hair. It took a moment, but his haunches were off her chest and his body crawled down the length of her vulnerable frame. The brutality was not gone.

Ben spread his victim's legs and the beastly and vicious incursion began. *How can he do this, feel free to stick this into me? The pain, the gouging. He wants to tear me apart. It is brutal, animal gratification. God is not involved. Where is God?* Her body jerked violently, even under his full weight. His painful stabs were brutal and unrelenting. She sobbed. *This is the closest thing to death. What but the end of my life could be worse? I am being taken over. I am nothing. There is no mercy.* Mary gasped for breath. *God, God have mercy.*

Then it stopped. Ben finished his business and got to his feet. He did not look at Mary's face. Maybe he could not stand to catch her eyes. It was better for Mary that he didn't see her hate. Ben turned away, mumbled something about his return to the

Garden of Eden with Mary by his side, and left without touching her again.

Mary couldn't move. Stiff and unable to open one eye, she wondered how a man should properly wish his spiritual wife goodbye. She squelched the thought. Mary doubted Ben knew what he did was wrong or that she would be forever haunted by his horrific assault. How would he react if his daughter, Catherine, had been plundered? Her rage subsided, but her sense of Ephraim's betrayal grew, crushing her mind.

How could Ephraim not have protected me? He must have known this would happen? It cannot have been Ephraim's idea, but he is complicit in this horror, this atrocity. How can I ever make sense of this? Of him?

Within her seething rage, Mary's sense of shame began to well up, along with thoughts of her own guilt. A succession of frightful thoughts marched through Mary's head. She knew the awful experience would have its own life, that it would never be over. She was scared that she would never heal, even though it would remain her secret. She could avoid Ben and knew she could muster the strength to subvert his crazy vision of God's plan. This would never happen again. She would kill him. Although her mind was hollowed out by the violence, she was certain that Ephraim would never acknowledge Ben's visit. He would not say a word or think the abominable event plausible. He would never boast that Mary was sacrificed to his new-found God.

It was that time of the month she was most fertile, so the next weeks and months would be fraught with the fear that Ben's corrupt seed would grow inside of her. She must pray to God that a child would not be a consequence of her near-death experience. How could she make sure that didn't happen? She must get the advice of a skilled midwife. She would take savin or snakeroot as a precaution.

If I carried a child everyone would assume it was Ephraim's fatherhood. No one would believe otherwise, Mary thought. *It's like Hannah Plaisted. No one wants to hear the unspeakable topics of wife-beating and rape. No one wants to know these things, even those who think Cochrane a lunatic and spiritual wifery an evil twisting of God's order.*

Mary's wandering mind returned to Ephraim's betrayal. The man she loved, her husband and father of her children, had violated her too. He destroyed her trust, severed marriage vows. It was treachery—the worst expression of faithlessness. It wasn't Ben Andrews alone. Ephraim was a party to this cruelty and her debasement.

There was no one to give Mary solace or offer consolation. She felt abandoned by God, deserted and alone.

It took a long time to pull herself together. *I must get back to the house, find Samuel and let him know I am all right. I must hold my children in my arms*, Mary thought. She rose to her feet and began dressing herself. *Thank God I have them and am alive to care for them.* She brushed the straw and smudges of dirt from her skirt and found her shoes. *I have courage and will regain my strength. I am not defeated. I will survive this and find a way forward.* She was certain she would make Ephraim sorry for what he did.

〜

Ephraim was tired and a little contrite as he trudged up the road toward the house. He'd been gone more than twenty-four hours, having spent all night at a Cochrane service. Looking down the length of the field, his eyes rested on the sheltered bottom, the woods where the snow collects in winter and becomes a wet and mushy bog in spring. He had always thought it a good place for cattle or pigs. But his ambitions for the farm had diminished as his commitments to Cochrane took more and more time. His preparation of the plow, checking the metal bolts and bars that held the wood frame together, had been put off several times, just as his interest in repairs to the barn and house had diminished.

He would get the farm in order. The welfare of his family depended on it. His home was in fact his only refuge, a place apart, a place of affection and serenity. Samuel and Mirinda needed to feel cared for and protected. Despite his absence, there would be some extra cash coming in. His efforts at raising money for Cochrane's church were showing greater success. Cochrane appreciated Ephraim's industry with small rewards, which was how Ephraim came to have a bag of special candy in his pocket for Mary. He knew he should do more for her.

As Ephraim approached the house, he saw Mary in the yard. It looked like she had gathered wood, built a fire and was ready to light it. Some of Ephraim's clothes were piled nearby. She lit the fire just as Ephraim was close enough to realize what was going on. "What in hell are you are you doing, Mary?" Ephraim yelled, as he realized that the fire was built to incinerate his belongings. 'What? What are you doing?" He dashed toward Mary and the growing flames. He kicked at the pile of wood, dispersing the small logs and branches and stomped on those that had been ignited. "Are you crazy?" Loose dirt helped him squelch the dying embers.

"I'm alive and standing, no thanks to you," Mary screamed back. "You monster. You treacherous pig. I gave you my love, everything. How could you betray me? Am I a sacrificial lamb? A tribute to your insane prophet?" Mary rushed at Ephraim, still screaming, her fists clenched and arms flailing. Ephraim blocked the swing she took at his face and parried another from her left arm. He grabbed her shoulders hard and pushed her away. Mary landed on the cold ground, her screams transformed to sobs.

Mary looked up at Ephraim, who was befuddled. "Why don't you beat me up? You know what it's like. You know how it's done. Be like your father when he thrashed you," Mary cried out. "Now I have had my own experience with violence. You are nothing special. Did Ben Andrews tell you about his pleasure with me? Was the fact that he stuck his filthy member in my mouth part of the story? I'll bet he described my rape as transporting and spiritual."

Ephraim did not know what to say or do and did not move. Ephraim knew nothing about Ben Andrews's visit or about any violence. He never forgot the beating by his father but could not connect that with his wife's screaming.

Nothing was burning, the flames gone. He was surprised by the smoke encircling the remnants of the fire, but it didn't hamper breathing. His clothes were intact. The smoke did impair his vision and he did not see tears in Mary's eyes. Ephraim, with the most casual look, could not miss the cuts and bruises on Mary's face.

"Did you bed Ben's wife? Cochrane ordered a swap. Was Ben there to watch you copulate, to protect his wife and make sure you didn't rip her? With him present, I guess you wouldn't tear her clothes off. Was she compliant? Did you stuff it in her mouth? Did she try to bite it?"

"For God's sake Mary, stop. You are making too much out of this. I didn't know Ben came here. I spent no time with his wife," Ephraim tried to calm her. "Cochrane did tell us there were spiritual affinities between the two of us and each other's wives. Affinities, he said, that are superior to relations formed by natural affection."

"He raped me! It doesn't matter to you. Look at my face covered with bruises, red marks and scratches. Were spiritual affinities at work? That's just what you can see. Worse, he brutalized my insides. My pain tells there is more injury to discover. Would I do this to myself? Make myself so disgusting you'd never come to my bed?" Mary raged. "Cochrane's ways are gruesome and the path to evil."

"Cochrane has led me to a new birth," Ephraim snapped. "He's changed my life. The first time I ever heard him speak he said that the Kingdom of God is inside each of us, and we can discover the divine in ourselves. He is showing me the way, and I will always be grateful to him. I'm proud of the changes in me."

Mary got up, walked to Ephraim and stood face to face. "You are a selfish bastard. Ben Andrew's cock was inside me, and Jacob Cochrane is an imposter and a fraud. He is sinister, a madman who has indentured you. You've lost your own good judgment and joined his world of deception and falsehood. What you see as improvement, Ephraim, only makes you harder to love. How can I love you at all?"

"Jacob is a prophet and a messenger of God," Ephraim ignored Mary and started walking toward the house. "I'm going in now to get myself some coffee. I'm tired.'"

Mary followed Ephraim into the house, where he started heating some coffee by the fire. She went to the cupboard and got a crust of bread, taking it to Mirinda's crib. Samuel barely looked at his mother while taking the cookie she offered him.

"Prophet and messenger, huh? Cochrane spreads lust and depravity," Mary couldn't stop. "You are a part of it. In the Garden of Eden where Cochrane showed everyone his privates and introduced a naked girl into his holy service. You bend to Cochrane's wishes more than your father's. He gets you to do anything. They say that you were involved in Sister Mercy's resurrection, not the fornication but the setup, the spectacle. Maybe some fondling on your own, depraved bastard? Being around him gives you the chance to satisfy your lusty urges?" Her anger simmered.

Ephraim sat down at the table with his coffee, and Mary took the chair across from him. He did not know how to respond to her challenging eyes. "I had never felt the Holy Spirit before Cochrane. I was lost and without purpose," Ephraim halted. "You saw me before my new birth and my experience of transcendence."

"What about the earth? What about the present?" Mary's voice got louder. "You have a farm to work and till, and a family to watch after. They can't take care of themselves. What must we pay for your transcendence? How are we supposed to live, to get along?"

"I have to get along too and make my way in the world. I faced hardships all of my life and tried to overcome them" Ephraim bolted from his chair and crossed the room, where he stood fidgeting. "I am still finding my own way, taking the right path and following it to the end. The walking is not the hard part. After all I entered this world feet first." After trying a joke of his breached birth. "I was raised to think I could do nothing on my own. I was not permitted to be sad or worried or angry. Feelings were strangers to me. You must not show feelings, experience emotions, unless you want others to see their truth and find them unreliable."

"Life is about survival and getting by. You provided for us and offered security. You have been good at those things. But farmers can't spend many nights away," Mary said. "Over the past four years I thought you were learning to trust your emotions and learning to love." She stopped and slumped on the table. The crying was not from anger. As it grew louder, it was clear Mary was weeping. She shook like she could come apart. She mumbled and gasped for breath at the same time. Mary could not suppress her agitation. She sprang from her chair and rushed to embrace Ephraim, as if her husband could pull her back together. Nothing changed.

"Ephraim, what is happening to you? Am I losing you?" Mary cried. "You have to tell me. What Cochrane and his church are doing to you is frightening. Where do we belong? We are left behind. Does my love make any difference?"

With unusual calm he slowly eased himself from her vice-like embrace. He backed away, his eyes not losing contact with Mary's. "You have to understand, Mary, Jacob Cochrane is my teacher," Ephraim said. "It is not only about my redemption. Jacob is my guide to a new world—a world of grace and goodness, abundance, justice and equality. I want to live the freedom I have found inside myself. I have to have the power to rise above my grim past."

Ephraim didn't answer Mary's questions. He mentioned the past, but not his wife or family.

"I need to be by myself. I'm going to the barn to rest." He picked up his coat, opened the door to leave, stepped out on the porch, and found himself facing his sister Jane. "Nice to see you, Jane," Ephraim said. "I'm going out now. Maybe I'll see you later."

"It's so good to see you, Ephraim," Jane said as she embraced her brother. "Stay out of trouble," she kidded and closed the door.

◦⌒◦

Mary was relieved to see her sister-in-law and friend. She went straight to Jane, clutched her and started to cry. "It's good that you are here. I need a friend." Mary took Jane's winter jacket and laid it near the fire to warm. "I'll make some tea."

"I went to see mother, she's fine, and thought I would stop by," Jane said. "It looks like I chose a good time to visit."

Mary put some water to boil, set spoons and cups on the table, and went to the cupboard for the tea.

"It's awful. I was raped. By Ben Andrews, who was told by Jacob Cochrane to follow a holy revelation he received from God. I am intended to be Ben Andrews's spiritual wife," Mary started to shudder again. "It was brutal, ugly. I hurt everywhere. I am degraded, and ashamed. There was nothing I could do to stop it."

Jane pulled up a chair next to Mary, who reached for a comforting hand. In the morning shadows, Jane could see all the signs of Mary's assault and beating. "Oh, Mary," Jane said. "How can I help?"

"I don't know. The worst part is Ephraim's collusion. He was there yesterday, with Cochrane and the others. Ephraim probably saw Andrews rush to come here," Mary held back more tears. "Ephraim did nothing to stop him—to protect me. Jane, what can I to do? I hate Ephraim for what he allowed to happen. I just told him that. But I don't want to lose him either."

Jane rose when Mary stood to get the tea. Jane put her arms around Mary, pulling her close and fighting her own tears. "Let's make the tea together," Jane said, leading Mary into the kitchen.

The tea poured, they sat down at the table and Jane was the first to speak. "You have done a lot for Ephraim, Mary. Everybody can see the changes in him," Jane began, "but he still doesn't know how to behave. Sometimes he doesn't understand his own feelings, he can't identify them or separate them." Mary reached to put her hand on Jane's arm. "He is quite like our father," Mary reached for her cup of tea, adding some sugar in it.

"Father tried to be good to Ephraim, and he offered himself as an example. He would quote the Bible and say, 'the Son can do nothing of himself, but what he seeth his Father do.' What did Ephraim see his father do? Father showed Ephraim how to farm and provide for a family. Father did a lot of things well, but he could not understand his emotions either. Father promised

Ephraim love, but Ephraim didn't feel loved. How could he when his father beat him mercilessly and left him on the ground?"

"What am I supposed to make of that?" Mary's anger did not subside. "It doesn't sound like there is anything I can do." Mary turned away, toward the light coming in the window, her breath palpable.

"Just continue to do what you are doing, but don't expect Ephraim to change right away," Jane said. "I don't think Ephraim ever wanted to be like Father. That's hard if you think your father never liked you. Jacob Cochrane has swept away Ephraim and Ephraim wants to be just like him. Like the Bible says, 'What things so ever He doeth, these also the Son doeth likewise.' Cochrane performs miracles. And he talks about a world where everyone has the same chance for redemption. Like Cochrane, believers can learn to talk to God. All are equal in God's eyes and free to pursue spiritual and physical perfection."

Mary moved out of her chair toward the window, hoping to catch a glimpse of Ephraim. He was nowhere to be seen. "But Cochrane is an impostor. Most people can see that. You can look back at the Adam and Eve spectacle and know that its purpose wasn't religious instruction. It was all about self-promotion, and Cochrane's self-indulgence. Who can believe that Sister Mercy was resurrected? Why can't Ephraim see behind Cochrane's tricks and fakery?" Mary asked.

"Lots of things get mixed up with everything going on—visions, trances, prophesies, naked bodies, singing and dancing. All is hard to balance, makes it hard to think," Jane stammered.

"Give me advice, Jane. What can I do? Where do I start?" Mary was desperate.

"I may not be of much help in saying this, Mary, but continue to be a good wife and mother. That's what you are and what everybody sees. You are constant and true. You have no tricks. There is no mask. Nothing false or deceptive. You know better than Ephraim how to get along in this world and your children count on that," Jane said. "Ephraim may not see you as his rock right now, but you are."

"Jane, I cannot be like Jacob Cochrane's wife. I don't know how she puts up with his depravity and acting like a goat," Mary said.

"From what's said about her, she knows the truth and draws the line," Jane responded. "She told a man, sent to her by her husband for sex, that she was not the man's spiritual wife and said, 'Jacob Cochrane is a liar.' She's said that spiritual wifery is hogwash."

"He treats her badly and she continues to have his children. I don't see how she can go to bed with him," Mary said.

"Mary, you are a strong woman and you can be tough. I've seen that. You've got to rely on those qualities. Everybody knows that you are Ephraim's wife. They don't know or recognize any other. You can't allow them to think otherwise. They know nothing of your rape. They don't want to know. As far as they are concerned, nothing in the past two days has changed your life, or your marriage. That's the way you must live," Jane said.

"Jane, that is going to be hard for me," Mary said. "How can I?"

"I will support you and help you. You can do this," Jane said as she embraced Mary. "We will stick together. You know, I am doing this for you, giving advice, because I care for you. I also care for my brother. It will take some time for him to see that he cannot live his life through Jacob Cochrane and see that Jacob Cochrane's selfishness will bring him down."

Jane was at the door and stopped. She turned and rushed to Mary, reaching out in a protective embrace. "Mary, my good friend," Jane started to cry. "I will never forget the terrible thing that happened to you yesterday. I can understand your horror. I must get home," she said closing the door behind her.

⌒

Before the meeting started, churchgoers enjoyed the bright June sunshine, some finishing food brought with them. Sunday was a day for giving out sweets and candy which made the frolicking youngsters happy. There were two girls sitting together on a bench, one braiding the others hair. A boy had removed his shoe, showing off his bare foot with three missing toes—the result of a farm accident. Two boys were teasing a dog by withholding scraps of food left from their lunch. Men enjoyed smokes and others had ready flasks. It was the kind of early summer afternoon that draws people to rivers or shade trees. Most didn't want to spend their day in church, but a throng from the Saco Valley gathered outside of Buxton's Congregational Church. The meeting was called "in the interest of all denominations."

The Coolbroth's Corners bunch was determined not to miss the event everybody talked about for days. Eben and his irreverent quips would be missed, but he didn't want to close his store on account of Jacob Cochrane.

"We will see how this turns out," Paul Dresser said, "All of the preachers in York County seem to be afraid of Jacob Cochrane. Clement Phinney from Gorham, George Pacher of Saco, and Ephraim Stinchfield of New Glouster are behind this. They want to bring Cochrane down."

"Remember Reverend Buzzell, who once asked Eben if he didn't think it was his duty to give the preacher a load of wood?" Uriah asked. "Eben said he'd pray about it and later told Buzzell that the Lord wanted Eben to mind his own business and Buzzell to take care of himself. He did. Buzzell was chosen to lead today's special meeting." Everyone chuckled at the memory.

"These preachers think of Cochrane as a predator. He's drawing too many away from their congregations," Paul said.

"Cochrane claims to have more than 2,000 followers," Nat Harmon added. "They don't just come from this standing church. They come from all levels of our community, men and women of all ages, and from the dissenting churches as well."

"I can understand how Cochrane, with his eloquent preaching, the raucous singing and dancing, glories in having a crowded field of worshiper before him. It excites him," Uriah said as he took another swig from his flask. "But performing five hundred full submersions in the water? That's a lot of time doing baptisms, but what happens to your body when you spend so much time soaked and shivering?"

"He has baptized more people than anybody, in Maine or anywhere else," Nat said. "For him, what could be more gratifying?"

"Well," Uriah smirked. "All that time in the water, his hands and feet must look like white prunes. I can't imagine a comely, young woman wants to have those wrinkled hands brushed across her forehead as Cochrane brings her back from celestial rapture into the real world."

"Five hundred submersions could be harmful," Nat said with a smile. "But the water doesn't make all of his appendages shrivel, not from what I have heard about his success in pleasing women." Nat cupped his crotch.

"Cochrane gets more popular every day. Moses McDaniel said that at one meeting more than five hundred people went forward to the Lord's Supper." Nat continued. "And the Lord's Supper is taken only by those who have been born again and baptized. Some converts are disreputable, but Benjamin Simpson, a Baptist preacher in North Saco, left his church to follow Cochrane."

"This church is not prospering, and many parishioners are leaving," Ned Redlon said, looking at the structure behind him. Ned's family were long standing Congregationalists. "Reverend Coffin is old, many say enfeebled and out of touch, and elders are talking about a replacement. I don't know how that will be worked out. Meanwhile, Coffin holds on."

"Watch out," Nat said to Uriah, yanking him sideways. Uriah was paying more attention to his flask than the two boys playing Graces nearby. One player had flung, with throwing rods, a ribboned hoop into the air. The other player, a rod in each hand, raced to catch the hoop and nearly crashed into Uriah.

"The kids ought to pay attention to what they are doing," Uriah said, whisky spewing from his mouth.

"I'm less concerned about Jacob Cochrane than the bad times I see coming," Paul sounded worried. "Banks make it too easy to get money. We've all watched the prices for our crops plunge. Europe has flooded our markets with farm products, and their cheap exports are squeezing us. Shops are closing. With more unemployed, people can't pay back the money they borrowed."

"You are too serious, Paul," Uriah said as he screwed the cap on to the stubby neck of his flask. "Let's go in and get a good seat. It's time for the fireworks."

The church was the biggest north of Saco and the coast, but the galleries on three sides were nearly full. Pastor Buzzell perched on the stilted pulpit, not looking the least bit humble. There was no question that he was in charge, despite the fact he had never been welcomed in this sanctuary. Pastor Coffin, a fierce critic of Baptists, was nowhere to be seen.

"Quiet please," Buzzell's voice was clear and commanding. People took their time to end their conversations and chatter. "Now all bow your heads for the opening prayer," Buzzell said and he stretched his arms toward heaven. "Praise be to God and to the Father of our Lord Jesus Christ, who has blessed us in the heavenly realms with every spiritual blessing. Bless us here today. Guide us and grant us your wisdom." Buzzell lowered his arms and raised his bowed head. "Pleased be seated."

The meeting had an ominous start. All the seats in the church were hinged and when everybody sat down at the same time there was a loud clamor, like a giant clap of thunder from heaven.

Those familiar with the church were unfazed as they settled themselves, but Buzzell's face registered alarm. He composed himself and began. "Our text for today is Mark 13:37, "And what I say unto you I say unto all, Watch.'" Buzzell raised his voice and repeated the scripture at a more deliberate but pompous cadence. After a pause allowing the scripture to be absorbed, Buzzell's face turned stark white.

"Behold, I stand at the door and preach," Cochrane's voice pealed from the back of the church. "If any man hears my voice and opens the door, I will come in and I will sup with him and he with me." Cochrane quoted Revelations. Cochrane knew of the well-publicized meeting. He knew the text from Mark and knew he was the target of the sermon.

Heads turned, and all eyes were on Cochrane. "Jesus is standing at your door," Cochrane thundered, "Jesus is knocking. He is seeking to enter your heart." Cochrane took time as he modulated his voice. "Jesus is speaking at your door, saying, oh, won't you please let me in. I will help you." Everyone could hear Cochrane's whisper.

Cochrane's stunning oratorical skills had everyone enrapt, seeming to be speaking to each congregant personally. Buzzell might as well have disappeared.

"It's your choice to let Him in or not," Cochrane's voice grew louder and his tone more challenging. "God gave men free will to choose, to let Him in or not. It's up to you to determine how much or how little each of you wants to let Him in." Cochrane offered up his hand. "He promises you rebirth. Will you let him in? To be born again?" Congregants were in Cochrane's thrall. "Matthew tells us the gospel of the kingdom shall be preached to all the world, to people here in Buxton. And the end shall come. God's word must be heard by everyone, by every group, by everyone here today."

There were murmurs of agreement and cries of "Praise the Lord." Many sat silent, mesmerized.

"I come, the everlasting gospel to knock, to reach everyone who heareth. All I want is my bigness on the floor," Cochrane's words stopped but his time was not over.

The pews creaked as people shifted to get a better look at the grand orator in his fine clothes, detailed, showy and eye-catching. There were murmurs and whispers, more than Buzzell could easily quiet. As Buzzell tried to regain the attention of the congregants, a feeble cry was heard from the back of the church.

"I found Jesus. Yes. I found Jesus standing at my door." The voice was from a haggard woman on the floor of the church. Locals recognized the coughing, wheezing, drooling woman with tangled hair as Anna Berry. She had been married in this sanctuary but was rarely seen in church because of illness. Her hand reached toward the top of a pew in her effort to stand and be seen. "I was weak, but have found the strength to stand," Anna, short of breath, wheezed after she was upright. "I stand to let Him in, into my humble heart." She turned, her look fixed on Cochrane. Anna's haggard appearance and drawn face made her appear older than her thirty-two years.

"Satan's presence, his efforts to overpower me, caused me illness and disease. He caused me the loss of babies," Anna's voice was still unsteady. "After I let Him in I was raised up. He is not a punishing God. He makes it easier for me to live. My new strength, my healing by God's grace and the forgiveness, comes from Jesus's death and resurrection." Anna was trembling, and tears were streaming down her face. With determination she boosted herself up as far as she could. "My healing is God's glorification of the human body. I am more robust and no longer wasting away. I will be strong enough to bear more children. I have answered the door, let Jesus in and I am healing. I am healing." Anna kept her tight grip on the top of the pew, then lowered herself to her knees. She bowed her head.

Silence followed whispers and hushed words exchanged. Anna's presence in the church, her apparent strength, and her uplifting story made for a small miracle. Anna's husband, John, and John's cousin, Ephraim, were standing in the back of the church near Cochrane, so there was no mystery about how she got to church. How she had pulled herself together, risen to this occasion, remained a mystery.

Pastor Buzzell took full advantage of the silence that gripped the room to finally speak. "We thank the Lord for the blessings He has bestowed on Anna. The Christian lives of Anna and her husband John give inspiration to all of us." Buzzell did not know John Berry. He knew John was a solid member of the Congregational church and one of the wealthier farmers in Buxton. "For Anna's healing we must credit her faith, her reverence of God and her obedience to His teachings." Buzzell gave Cochrane a dismissive look.

The two men faced each other in a showdown. Anyone with an imaginative turn could see the scene as a thrilling duel, but with no fight to the death. Buzzell mustered his strength and faith, pushing himself hard into the podium to resume his sermon.

"And what I say unto you, I say unto all, Watch," Buzzell repeated the day's text. "Mark says the Master wants us to be watchful—diligent and alert. Matthew repeats the Lord's warning that "many shall come in my name, saying I am Christ.'" Buzzell stared at Cochrane. "Be concerned that when our Lord returns he may not find us secure. He may find us indulging in ease and sloth. We must not give in to waywardness and perversity. We must be watchful lest darkness come upon us.

"We must be suspicious of pretended Messiahs. There are those, Luke warns us, who are deceivers, conjurers of false miracles. 'Go ye not after them,' Luke instructs. Beware of the false prophets, who come to you in sheep's clothing. They could be adorned by finery, but inwardly are ravenous wolves," Buzzell paused and faced Cochrane. "You will know them by their fruits. Grapes are not gathered from thorn bushes, nor figs from thistles. All of you know that." Congregants nodded in agreement.

Buzzell's booming voice had power and his words caught attention. No one missed his meaning.

"Peter warns us, 'There are false teachers among you.' He tells us they will introduce destructive heresies—heresies which deny the true teachings of our sovereign Lord. Adherents to these teachings are assured their own destruction. Many will follow the depraved conduct of these false teachers and bring the way of truth into disrepute. Yes, Peter warns us that 'In their greed these teachers will exploit you with their false stories.'

"Peter scorns the false prophets. Peter fights self-deception. It is better not to know the ways of righteousness, than to turn your backs on sacred commands. Peter has strong words. He reminds us of two proverbs: 'A dog returns to its vomit,' and 'A sow that is washed returns to her wallowing in the mud.' We must be watchful, alert, and be true to God and His word."

Cochran had the grace and courtesy to stand at the back of the church and take all Buzzell's lashings. At the end of

Buzzell's remarks and the closing prayer, Cochrane interjected a last word.

"I stand at the door and preach. If any man hears my voice, open the door. Open the door." Cochrane bowed, straightened up and surveyed the whole room with piercing eyes. With a flourish of his cape, he whisked himself from the church.

～

Centered in the well-settled parts of lower York County, the forces opposing Cochrane gained strength over the summer of 1818. But the prophet's efforts to expand his flock were unceasing. He extended his preaching north, beyond York County, and kept himself in the public eye with more mouth-gaping tales than anyone in the Saco Valley. His requirement for adoration was boundless and, combined with his infinite imagination, led him to deeds both outrageous and disgraceful.

Porter, a small town in Oxford County, was not unfamiliar to Cochrane since a deputation of his missionaries had operated in the area for several months. Townspeople were god-fearing, hardworking, sincere and pious, the kind of souls particularly attracted to Cochrane's teachings.

Determined to make an unforgettable first impression, Cochrane decided on a special introduction of himself to the community. He would imitate Christ's entry into Jerusalem, riding on an ass. It was set for Saturday when the market was in Porter, allowing a couple of days for Cochrane's closest associates to make arrangements. The prophet's team was adept at getting word out that a special event would highlight the weekly gathering.

Saturday's market crowd witnessed more than a simple entry; it was a procession. First came a band of drummers, followed by a small chorus singing a spirited song. There were no palm fronds for Cochrane's retinue to wave, but the bright green sapling branches gave the train a special flair. Bearers, like heralds of old, walked several yards ahead of Cochrane. Some members of the crowd dropped to their knees as the mounted figure approached.

Cochrane, straddling a white donkey, had the appearance of one from another world. He wore a linen tunic the color of an apricot, over which was wrapped a long pale blue toga. The combination, complemented by the red cloak draped over the animal's back, was stunning and regal. Cochrane's frame was erect, his tilted head with its benign look fixed on the path ahead. The prophet sat aloof, above the crowd, but could not have ignored the pause in the donkey's step, the sound of water splashing on the ground and the loud plunk.

Accompanying the party was the donkey's young foal, the same color as the mother, who kept close to its mother's rear flank. It occasionally nibbled at the red cloak upon which Cochrane sat. Thinking it would go unnoticed, Cochrane jabbed the foal with his sandal to keep it away from his garments. The catastrophe was sudden. The young donkey brayed loudly, its mother quickly spun toward her foal, bolting at the same time and throwing her rider into the air. A round-house kick followed, catching Cochrane hard in the torso and sending him into the pile of recently deposited donkey shit. Everyone was astonished. The prophet's imperious look was gone. No one could believe the supine man on the ground had been ordained by God to preach His everlasting gospel.

Cochrane's followers were disciplined and quick to act. All rushed to their master, formed a protective wall around him and kept him out of sight. The tight cluster of disciples moving together, slowly escorted their leader out of Porter.

A maxim in Cochrane's teaching was to never look back. When he and his believers regrouped in Limington, he was already conjuring another event to display his supernatural powers. The event would be carefully planned, with the utmost attention paid to the smallest detail. Only Cochrane's most trusted lieutenants would be involved.

The charismatic spiritualist gathered his close followers and solemnly announced his plan to go to Lake Sebago. There he would preach and walk on water.

Ephraim and Ben Andrews helped in the preparation. Traveling in a small boat along the shoreline of Lake Sebago, they found a place with long stretches of shallow water. Less than a foot of water covered an extensive area of swamp mire. Stepping from the boat into the mire, they found the bottom's composition just strong enough to support the weight of a man and not sink. As they trudged through the muck and carefully explored that part of the lake's perimeter, they found a regular bottom with occasional sinks and holes, some deep. But it was permeable enough to drive pine timbers deep into it and secure them.

The men worked hard and drove two parallel lines of pilings into the lake bottom. The underwater pier stretching more than thirty feet into the lake was locked together by wooden scaffolding, upon which wooden planks were laid down several inches below the surface of the lake. The planks were fastened with nails to keep them submerged and in place. Smeared with mire from the lake bottom, the underwater pier was almost invisible from the shoreline in daylight. In the evening twilight the structure would never be noticed at all. The way the mud was daubed on the planks, Cochrane would be able to see his way in the dark.

Working in the water and sludge, carrying and floating posts from the shore, and lifting and pounding with heavy hammers, the job took Ephraim and Ben several days to finish. It was a remote site, and the work was done in the early morning, so the project would not attract attention. Secrecy and vigilance were critical to the success of the plan.

When the construction was finished, Cochrane was taken to the site to inspect and test it in the morning hours. Cochrane, satisfied with the viability of the structure, soon announced that he had a special communication from God. Cochrane's numerous converts and disciples were summoned to assemble in the wilderness, a wild place on the shore of western Maine's largest lake, for a new revelation. The location for the miraculous event, though an unsettled area, was not difficult to reach. It was just two miles north of Standish and no more than twelve miles from Buxton's Lower Corner.

The long-awaited day finally arrived. It was arranged that horses and wagons would be left one hundred yards or so from the lake, and pilgrims, expected converts and Cochrane disciples would walk from there, then congregate where the slopes descended to the lakeshore and formed a rustic amphitheater. Judging by the impressive size of the crowd that assembled, word of Cochrane's special service must have spread through the entire valley.

The surface of the lake the was still and luminous in the twilight. Except for the fading sky no light was seen until the flames from the torches in the woods became visible. Flanked by two torchbearers, Cochrane wound his way down the slope in flowing white, like Jesus coming down from the mountain. Near the bottom of the trail, Cochrane stopped, adjusted the folds of his immaculate robe, and brushed off twigs and leaves that had attached themselves to it. Unaccompanied, he walked the final distance to the water's edge. The crowd was spellbound by the majesty of Cochrane's presence.

Ephraim and Ben Andrews were certain that their days of work had gone undetected. But the persistent county authorities who had been monitoring Cochrane's activities for months, had discovered something was going on at Lake Sebago. The spies watched from afar. The afternoon Ephraim and Ben finished work on the pier and left the lake, these agents took a closer look at what had been going on. From their raft, the county bloodhounds followed the submerged pier its entire length and understood Cochrane's scheme. Agreed that Cochrane's spectacle should not succeed, they removed some of the submerged planks, those over the deepest and most dangerous part of the lake. When their mischief was done, they left the site seemingly as they had found it.

Cochrane purposefully approached the lake and put a foot into the water, placing it firmly on the sunken pier. His upper body twisted away from the lake, and with the span of his long arms his white garment shimmered in the light of the torches. In a stentorian tone he called out, "Be not afraid" and stepped forward on the pier with his other foot. After another step he cried out to an imaginary boat in danger and buffeted by angry currents, "I go to the helpless." He paced further out on the invisible pier; his steps unearthly. All ears were wide open, and eyes were strained from their sockets in astonishment. "I will calm the frightened," he cried again. "Take courage."

As the God-like figure's smooth and regular pace confirmed the wonderment of the onlookers and bolstered their conviction of Cochrane's divine powers, the miracle-worker called a third time, "Be of faith. Banish all doubt. It is I." Just then his forward foot found no place to ground itself. He lurched side-ways, his widespread arms offering no help in regaining balance, and took an undignified plunge into the water, floundered, then sank into the watery mire. It was an unceremonious baptism.

The noise of the crowd was wild, the mingling of shrieks, shouts and screams. Spectators were frozen in place, while others, horrified, rushed to the water's edge where the torchbearers fully raised and waved their flames to illuminate the appalling scene.

A hand surfaced from the lake amid violent thrashing. Cochrane's head emerged, and he began to swim toward shore, his progress inhibited by the drag of his muddy and tangled robe. He found his footing and stood. He came out of the water with his clothes clinging to his near-naked body. Cochrane, eyes fixed straight forward, did not say a word. Ephraim was waiting for Cochrane on the shore but was not acknowledged as his master walked by.

Sometime the miracle works. Sometimes it doesn't, Ephraim thought as he moved himself away from the lake. He was reminded of the time months before when Elder Phinney admonished Cochrane for his attempt to cast the devil from a possessed man. Cochrane's reply was etched in Ephraim's mind: "We know God's delegated power is conditional, as we see from the fact that the Apostles were not always successful in their exorcisms." But Ephraim knew that Cochrane's perfectionism and self-pride did not permit failure. For the prophet there had to be an explanation for this debacle, and Ephraim would be found at fault.

FIVE

Six months had passed since Ephraim visited his father's house, the spring when he dropped off some bags of seed Eben Coolbroth had asked him to deliver. Isaac appreciated the gesture, but Ephraim didn't tarry. He embraced his mother and left after a brief conversation with his father about the planting ahead.

The visit was intentional, planned so his father would be home. Ephraim's primary purpose was to try to get money from Isaac to support Jacob Cochrane's ministry. That he might be turned down was not an obscure thought in Ephraim's mind. In fact, he considered a rejection likely. But the visit was an important way of redefining himself to his father. He was devoted to Cochrane's teachings, and his beliefs were compelling. He had experienced God, something his father would never understand, and it could not have happened without Cochrane's guidance.

Ephraim knocked at the door and was greeted by his father, who invited him in. "Good to see you, Ephraim. It's been quite a while," Isaac said. Ephraim's father looked slightly older, the eyes as dark as ever, but the receding hairline, the grey more prominent, and the brow more deeply furrowed. He went into the kitchen where his mother was baking, hugged her and greeted his sister, Elizabeth.

"We are making you a treat, Ephraim," his mother said. "Can I get you a cup of coffee? I'm getting one for your father."

"Yes, please. I'd like one," Ephraim said as he went to the parlor to join his father. Isaac was smoking a pipe. His sister Aphia was also in the room, still possessing a childish look despite her twenty-five years. Ephraim settled in a chair across from his father.

"What brings you by? Is this a special occasion?' Isaac asked.

"I realized that I hadn't seen you or mother in some time. I've been thinking that I need to spend more time with my family. I must get better at that," Ephraim responded. "Family is at the core of my life. Samuel is nearly four now and Mirinda is a year and a half. Mary's due with another in December, not far away." Looking around the room, it seemed livelier than he remembered. There were fewer chairs around the table, but it was covered with a bright cloth and a bowl of apples. "I should have brought Samuel with me."

"We do see your children now and then," Isaac said. "Mary brings them by. Elizabeth and Aphia enjoy having them around."

Anna brought in the coffee and set the cups on a table between the two men. "When I started thinking about family, Father, I think about you and what a good example you have given me, that of a good father."

"I've been thinking, too. I am lucky to have you. Time with your children is fleeting. So many things unforeseen," Isaac paused and suddenly looked sad. "You heard about your cousin, Thomas? When my brother, Jonathan, went off to the war, he left his wife, Sarah, and a baby, Thomas. I helped take care of them."

"What happened to Thomas?" Ephraim asked.

"A bad accident," Isaac said. "Thomas has a big cider mill. Last week he was making cider and was distracted by his young son, Stephen, who threw an apple at him, a prank. Something you never would have done. Thomas turned to see who threw the apple and his hand, caught in the apple crusher, was mangled. He got an infection and died yesterday." Isaac blinked and tears appeared.

"How awful. I'm sorry for the whole family. Who knows God's will? That after Thomas lost a son earlier this year. Your brother must be grief stricken," Ephraim took his time. "We have to be grateful for what we have. It's a strange coincidence. I'm here today to tell you how much I admire you and have for a long time. I remember, I was seven or eight when you and mother took the family to church to renew your baptismal covenants."

This shifted Isaac's attention from his nephew's death. "Why would you remember? I did that to fend off the Baptists who wanted me dunked in the Saco River." Isaac chuckled.

"It made me aware of your goodness and devotion. Your vows, to do God's will, to be obedient to him and keep his commandments, were inspiring," Ephraim said. "And that is how you have lived your life."

Isaac's silence showed that Ephraim's words were unexpected.

"I will never forget what you told me about fatherhood," Ephraim continued. "Fathers raise children who are really God's children, and fathers are God's stewards. You told me that. Fathers are charged by God to care for and love their children. I still think about what you said and follow that wisdom."

Still not sixty, Isaac's hand shook as he raised his coffee cup to his mouth. "Yes, I remember telling you that," Isaac sounded as if he were speaking to himself.

"Because of you, I thought deeply about being a good son. I understood that sons want to be like their fathers, and mirror their father's achievements," Ephraim said. "You drew me to God's word, where I learned from the story of Job that a son can become an inspiration to his father, through his expression of total love and devotion to Him."

"You are very thoughtful in sharing your memories," Isaac said. It was not clear to Ephraim if he had pleased his father. Before Isaac could say another word, the front door flew open, and after stomping the dirt from their boots, Ephraim's brothers came in the house. They looked happy to be home. "Alexander and Abner, you have come too late to dispute your older brother. He has just assured me that I am a good father." Isaac laughed.

"How can he say that after you left us in the field today to do all the work," Alexander joked as he affectionately embraced his father. The boys went into the kitchen to get some coffee and see what their mother was baking. The house smelled like cake.

"Father, there is something else," Ephraim said. His tone changed to that of a petitioner. "I wanted to tell you about my spiritual life. My faith has grown, and I spend more time pursuing God's work."

"I've heard that you have become a follower of Jacob Cochrane," Isaac said, "and you are spending a lot of time with him. Jane told me about this. She is pleased." Ephraim noticed that his father wasn't dismissive of his news and seemed anxious to hear more. Ephraim was surprised since his father didn't like to listen.

"Because of Cochrane, I have had a spiritual rebirth, a new beginning," Ephraim's words were emphatic and sincere.

Alexander and Abner entered the parlor with their coffee, moved some chairs close to their father and older brother, giving Isaac a larger audience.

"I don't really understand what is going on with these new preachers," Isaac said, straightening in his chair, assuming a more authoritative posture. "I think this country was blessed by the standing clergy, pastors like Reverend Coffin. They are enlightened, pious, faithful, and consistent. Clear in their teaching, they are worthy of our trust. We now have evangelists who act upon their own inner voices rather than the word of God. It's very confusing."

Ephraim had not come to talk about Coffin but followed his father's lead. "I thought you never really cared for Coffin, too pompous and distant. Rigid you called him. He's out of touch and his congregation has dwindled."

"The new preachers come from the lowest conditions of life, and that's where you find the most ignorant minds. These men don't know what they are saying, are uncontrollable in their actions and unbending in their views," Isaac said.

"If you ever heard Jacob you would find him highly intelligent and eloquent in his speech. People marvel at his command of scripture. He is not unbending in his views. He is sympathetic and listens to people," Ephraim replied, looking in turn at his brothers.

"I have never heard Cochrane preach, nor have I been interested. Most evangelicals appear out of nowhere, decrying and denouncing all that does not cave before them," Isaac cleared his throat and continued. "Their services always include an attack. The attack is essential and it's not just on those who disagree. They attack their own congregants. They denounce individuals as hopeless and evil. The new preachers get conversions through fear. Fear makes their revival meetings effective."

"Jacob has never denounced me," Ephraim said huskily. "He preaches love and forgiveness. Preaching fear would only separate him from his flock, which he ardently cares for. I know he cares for me."

"You know I study the Bible. I don't know where Christ, or his apostles, have publicly denounced a single soul," Isaac maintained his role as teacher.

"Jacob made me aware that the kingdom of God is inside me," Ephraim wanted his father to know his new understanding. "God does not denounce his own children and Jacob never diminishes me."

"I don't see in all of these revivals a healthy religion," Isaac continued his instruction while Ephraim counted the gaps between the floor joist supporting the loft above. "It is all excitement, and excessively frantic. I know people are prone to excitement, it is part of nature. Excitement is a great pleasure—like whiskey or a good smoke. They used to have revivals just one time during the year. Now they are ceaseless. People want the pleasure."

"I could use a little more excitement in my life," Alexander said with a twinkle, "and I'm old enough for liquor and tobacco. Maybe I ought to get revived." The boy seemed to enjoy needling his father.

"There is not one sentence in the Bible, or example to justify the attempt to excite the feelings of the churchgoer," Isaac stayed on course.

"I'll bet you could use a little excitement, too, Abner. I remember the restlessness that comes with being fourteen," Ephraim smiled at his youngest brother. Abner grinned.

"These preachers excite people to the point that they have no self-discipline, all order is forgotten, and in their bewilderment, no one knows what is and what is not the word of God," Isaac's voice had grown loud.

"You sound like you are an expert on these preachers, Father, but you say you have not gone to their services," Ephraim said. "How can we trust that your views are reliable?"

"I already mentioned that Jane told me you were becoming a follower of Jacob Cochrane. A lot of what is said about Cochrane could be gossip, but there are a lot of consistencies. He has come up with some startling and shocking events. His spectacles are dramatic, ingenious and shrewd. And he has an attachment to certain carnal novelties. Parents warn their children against him," Isaac cleared his throat. "To startle and shock is Cochrane's great secret—the source of his power."

"Jacob preaches the word of God—and His revealed truths," Ephraim countered. "He has extraordinary powers, a profound knowledge of the Bible and interprets scripture clearly. He does not invest his followers with fear. He emphasizes Christ's message of love—of encouragement and hope. We can be healed and become more perfect."

"Ephraim, you are a farmer not a clergyman. Leaving aside your salvation, what does Jacob Cochrane offer? It is a secret society. Is your involvement about women and sex? Are you making any money?" Isaac was candid despite the presence of his younger sons.

"Jacob Cochrane has been given a mission by God to spread his Word. He has been gifted in special ways to carry out the Lord's command to bring converts to His church," Ephraim said patiently. "Some of what you say is true, Father, but you don't have a comprehensive picture. Practical matters must be attended to in order to realize spiritual goals. People love Cochrane's magnificent preaching, but to experience it they have to actually come and hear him—and more are coming."

"More are coming? Why? What about the increasing accusations of 'humbug' and 'charlatan'? Doesn't that turn people away? People come when he is called a quack?" Isaac asked.

"More people are coming. Cochrane understands people—and his understanding of human nature is remarkable," Ephraim responded with unusual candor. "He knows that audiences are excited by deception, fascinated by potential fraud and stimulated by the fact that they may be tricked. He likes to stir controversy and is willing to take the risk of damaging his reputation. And to discover how the deception is carried out, may be even more exciting to those who come."

"Presenting yourself naked is shocking. There is nothing miraculous, just outrageous and depraved," Isaac said. "But the resurrection of Sister Mercy, I believe you were there, is a fabled occurrence, and obscene. It's said he has driven demons out of people, too. The final truth is yet to be determined in many of his legendary acts."

"Miracles do happen. There are spiritual mysteries—which is why Jacob's adherents grow in number. Your nephew John's wife, Anna, is certain she would not be alive today if it weren't for Jacob's healing. She said that in church."

"Said it in church? What does that mean? Cochrane shows off his manhood in church," Isaac was unrelenting. "Is that done in a sacred place?"

The idea of exposing oneself in church widened Abner's eyes. He exchanged looks with his older brother, their faces unable to suppress huge grins, though they didn't laugh.

"Trickery is usually driven by the desire for gain," Isaac continued. "Does Cochrane's preaching bring in any money?"

"Money becomes more important as the flock grows and everyone's needs increase. We want to take care of everybody in the flock," Ephraim's voice was confident. "Our last celebration of the Lord's Supper drew more than five hundred followers. That is a lot of mouths to feed and no one went hungry."

"There has to be a lot of money coming into Cochrane's church. And collecting a lot of money requires uncommon commitment. Your prophet cannot do that all by himself. Are you helping him and getting some for yourself?" Isaac asked.

Ephraim took his time answering Isaac's bold question. "Jacob's commitment to God's work is unbounded, and many people want to financially support it. Much is freely given, but many people must be asked. I do some of the asking, but I don't do it for financial reward. It is part of my commitment," Ephraim found nothing embarrassing in telling his father the facts. "Charity work benefits thy soul."

"It must be hard when you ask those who finds Cochrane's activities nefarious and shameful, or think of him as a swindler," Isaac said coldly.

"Actually, more think of him as a prophet and a victim of persecution. People's belief is strengthened by the bashing Jacob gets, and they want to give more. People make real sacrifices to ensure the work is carried on, that his ministry flourishes in the face of detractors," Ephraim felt unaffected by his father's critical attitude. "And they are inspired by his miracles."

Isaac said nothing right away, everyone hearing his even breath. "Did you come here to ask me for money?" Isaac asked.

"I came to see you," Ephraim halted. "But money is part of it."

"I know it's common now for folks to show open admiration for an outrageous charlatan and contempt for those they bilk. I will not be bilked," Isaac said. "I am giving you nothing."

The silence was profound. Shock registered on Alexander's face and disappeared when he stood to get more cider from the kitchen. Abner went with him. Unadorned and bare except for the cracked looking-glass, the stark parlor with its bare floor compressed the silence and gave the room a heaviness. The room was chilly. Seeing the faltering fire, Ephraim went to the hearth and put some more wood in the blackened fireplace. He returned to his chair and caught the fixed eyes of his father—they suited Isaac's rigid frame.

"Ephraim, I may never understand what you call your spiritual rebirth," Isaac broke the silence, "but I can see that you are sincere in your new beliefs. You belong on your farm, but I know you can always use more money. It was wrong to suggest that you were trying to bilk me. I raised you as an honest man and you haven't changed. I trust you won't. But men change in their desire for gain. In almost every popular story you hear these days ingenuity is praised and nothing is said of principle."

"Thank you, Father. I am honest and try to live by your truths," Ephraim sounded humble.

"I cannot give you money because I have no interest in promoting Cochrane and his controversial doctrines," Isaac's eyes were benign looking at his son. "I appreciate your success and it's clear you will not be changing the direction of what you are doing. You will do well raising money because everybody trusts you—they always have. I have a suggestion."

"What would that be, Father?" Ephraim said. He was surprised that his father would want to help him out.

"We will be going to my brother Jonathan's house in a couple of days for your cousin Thomas's funeral. You must come along. Your cousin John will be there as well as his wife, Anna. John is not a Cochranite, but Anna is a believer. John has holdings and there is money to give. You say Anna has benefitted from Cochrane's healing powers. Ask John for money—it would please his wife," Isaac sounded confident. "Maybe I'll say something to Jonathan as well about your commitment to the financial support of Cochrane's society."

Ephraim smiled. *Money, then converts, Cochrane had told him. Before I leave, I'll ask Alexander and Abner if I can take them to a meeting.*

༄

Alexander and Abner took fifteen minutes to reach the Narragansett Trail, where they met their older brother. The three traveled another mile and a quarter to Nathanial Kimball's barn but reached Jacob Cochrane's meeting before dark. Before sneaking into the building, Alexander and Abner were warned to never tell anyone about the meeting.

"Why do you have to sneak us in?" Abner asked.

"Jacob Cochrane's followers have secrets they don't want to share with outsiders," Ephraim answered. The awaiting mystery and growing darkness brought the brothers closer together.

"People say that Cochrane gained his holiness through sex. His initiations of virgins enhance his miraculous powers, especially his power to heal. Is that true Ephraim?" Abner asked.

"There are many popular notions," Ephraim answered casually, "but they are secrets."

"According to the stories," Abner continued, "he takes locks of hair from virgins he had sex with and puts them in special boxes which are hidden in a secret place. The special powers and spells the boxes confer are colossal."

"Power greater than a bag of rabbit's feet," Alexander exclaimed.

"Cochrane's powers come from God. But you will have a chance to see them tonight," Ephraim said, happy to have his brothers with him. Bringing his brothers into a meeting was a risk. He remembered Cochrane's scolding after seeing Jane in Kimball's barn, but Ephraim wanted to see his brothers' spiritual conversion. The place was packed, but Ephraim found the boys room on a narrow bench before he left to assist in the service.

The boys were barely settled when a trumpet sounded, and the barn quieted. The schoolmaster, Aaron Boynton, rose and started singing, congregants quickly joined:

> Come you sinners poor and needy,
> Try the cross as we have done.
> You will find the yoke is easy,
> If you'll only put it on.

Boynton delivered a brief sermon proclaiming that Jesus calls all men to Himself and everyone will be embraced. Following a short prayer, Boynton stepped from the pulpit into an area covered with straw, intended to protect those who might be overcome by the Lord's presence. The bed of straw was the only sparsely occupied space in the barn.

Past that refuge for seized zealots, two tall posts supported a loft. The posts were joined by a low beam against which several men knelt, as if in prayer, hands covering their faces. On one side of the barn about twenty females, mostly young, squatted on the straw. Opposite, on the other side of the barn, young men hunkered down, looking expectant.

The place was quiet until a loud, mellifluous voice was heard, and Jacob Cochrane entered as if it were Christ's Second Appearance. Finished with his song, he knelt in the center of the straw, shut his eyes and thrust his arms heavenward in prayer. He spoke like Lord of Hosts, as if angels were pouring the words into his mouth: "No prophet of the Lord can be hidden. I am here, no darkness thick enough to obscure my presence before you—and the gifts I offer. The gifts are for you."

It was a signal for exulting and ecstatic utterings. Confused and bewildering voices rang out, and the silver tones of a woman's supplications. The din increased with entreaties, petitions and pleas for forgiveness. Handkerchiefs were raised to bright eyes, and sobs intermingled with prayers and whooping.

The men and women crouched on the straw started crying out, each struggling to be heard. Shaking and thrashing increased. Boys, their heads buried in the straw, sobbed bitterly and choked from near suffocation. Some hands wrung to the point bones would crack, others pulled their hair.

One young man flailed on the floor, cried, "Satan ravages me and is trying to take me away. But I will hold fast. Help. He's dragging me down." A rough-looking burly man not seen before, grabbed the boy, sprawling on his body. A close observer saw the stranger with the rolled-up sleeves and powerful grip. The large tattoo on his forearm was that of a former convict.

Abner turned toward his brother, shocked and mouth agape. Alexander glanced back, protective and reassuring, but his face filled with excitement.

When the chaos and bedlam reached its peak, Jacob Cochrane appeared in the center of the room and called out, "Lord, Lord.

Receive into your fold those who have now repented, who eagerly seek your embrace and crave your compassion."

Cochrane's words did not immediately quiet his flock or dispel their fear and distress. He looked down and saw that the young men before him had not been raised up, still smothered by straw and choking. There were five and he went to each, pulled their heads from the straw. He embraced them before he rolled all on to their backs. Eyes clinched closed, bodies yet convulsed, groans intermittently escaped thorough fractured breath. He knelt, pressed his fabled hand on each forehead and raised his other hand heavenward, "Arise," he commanded—five times. When he finished his last heavenly call, a boy began to stir, the others followed, and all extended their arms to receive God's mercy. They cried out "Praise Jesus, Praise Jesus." Not far away, the burly man's body still covered the frame of the boy who had flailed and called for help. The boy was still and motionless, but the hulking man on top twitched, as if still overcome by the godly atmosphere.

Fever-pitch excitement and high emotion were unrelenting. The service that started with an individual's celebration of belief and commitment to live by God's rules transformed into an unconstrained, collective appetite for revelry and indulgence. Fervor, unbridled physicality, and expansive expression of natural affability collided in the barn.

The frenzied mood in the barn promoted an anonymity where no one had personal responsibility for their actions, and actions normally regarded as harmful were reframed as necessary for the greater good—serving everyone's pleasure. The scene got livelier and more licentious as the lights went down; music louder than the clapping, dust from the stomping on the straw clouding vision.

Morals and beliefs lost in the delirium were replaced by lust, infidelity, hysteria, hallucinations and brutality.

Though Alexander was caught up in the excitement, he didn't make a move. He remained next to Abner, watching what he could make out in the half darkness. The heel of a shoe mashed his toe, alerting him to the woman whose back eased into his lap. She touched his leg, lifted herself and started to run her hand up toward his crotch. Her head turned toward him, followed by her robust upper body. There was no other introduction, as she urgently pressed against him, then rubbing her breasts against his chest. When she looked at Alexander to speak, he did not recognize her. "Have the spunk to kiss me?" she breathed. Not waiting for an answer, she glued her mouth to Alexander's, grabbed his hand and led him away. Abner was alone.

A woman cried out from the darkness, "Jacob—Jacob Cochrane. Where are you? I need you now. My body craves your healing."

"No need to rush, dearie. He has enough for all," a voice cackled. "He will have time to honor you."

The expectation of sex and Cochrane's healing powers drove Abigail Clark on that night. She found the sex act was restorative, but Abigail knew that Jacob Cochrane's administrations endowed her with the power to heal. She fumbled through the darkness, driven by desire and her great urge to help others. Whether by chance or God's direction, she bumped into Jacob Martin and started to cry. Long ago, the man's head had been crushed been between a cart-wheel and a tree. The ugly, horribly disfigured face triggered Abigail's passion to attend to his suffering. She embraced him tightly and kissed him everywhere. The force of her hugs, like a bear's, pushed him back against a log on the floor. He stumbled backward, bringing Abigail with him.

"I know your needs," she murmured while pulling up her skirt and moving her sex toward his face. "Oh, my poor baby. I am giving you my warmth." In his jerks, she didn't recognize his struggle to breathe. She hunched wildly for some time, then raised herself to reverse her position, and reached into Martin's trousers so she could get him to squirt. She eased back and bleated, "I'm delicious. Don't you think I'm delicious? I'm sopping." While Abigail's haunches fastened around Martin's head, his body began to spasm and shake erratically. She convulsed, letting out a loud moan and collapsed.

"Great God." Martin's muffled exclamation transformed into a jagged smile.

Abner was surrounded by clamor, pushing and jostling, pungent smells. The sexual excitement was as inescapable as the pounding sounds and screams of fear that attend violence. His back pressed against the side of the barn. Yells, screams and cries for help were all around and shocking. Cochrane was known to have rough friends, even criminals. A pickpocket would find his job easy in this crowd, so many with their clothes off and no one paying attention.

Peter Rounds was soused. Having too much to drink, the intense craziness began. His natural disposition to hysteria and fantastic visions changed into an explosive fuse. He was lying on his back, his raised trunk supported by his elbows, his britches down, exposing a half-swollen member. Opposite, a young woman's face froze in shock. She appeared unconscious, except her eyes fixed in a wide-open stare. She sprawled on a plump gunnysack, arms askew, one clenched hand on her thigh and the other resting on her breast. Her bedraggled dress was pulled above her raised knees. The feet were more than two feet apart, remaining distant despite the fierce and constant trembling of her anguished limbs.

"She wanted me to drive out her sins," Peter hallucinated. "I did. Look. Look," he yelled, pointing at the dark space between the girl's knees. "See them. All the tiny rabbits running out of her hutch. God have mercy."

Naked Ben Andrews was in the center of the debauchery, beating a bare woman with a sheaf of reeds. She gripped his penis shouting, "I am your Eve, you are my Adam. We are meant for this."

Abner was in a dangerous place. Anguished and raucous cacophonies disguised the menace and approach of the man who had targeted Abner, moving from the wall toward the center of the barn.

Powerful arms coiled around Abner's chest from behind, making him choke and gasp for air. Not completely ensnared, the boy kicked back hard against the attacker's shin, momentarily slipping from his hold. Darkness disguised the assailant's face, but the white fist that shot out of the dark was clearly visible as it struck Abner's face, sending him backward. He was further battered when his body lashed against the low beam, where men had knelt in prayer. The attacker lunged, tossing the boy on his back. Abner screamed, but no one came to help.

Blood poured from the bashed face Abner could do nothing to protect, firmly pinioned to the ground and unable to move. After a time, the perpetrator, a massive man, stretched himself out on top of the helpless boy, to restrain him and to catch his own breath. With the victim inert, the attacker rolled off the boy and extended himself at his side.

The man pulled at Abner's limp arm, placed the hand next to his crotch and inched closer. Rather than fondle the attacker's genitals as desired, Abner fiercely jabbed the man in the balls. The man grunted, lashing back, striking Abner in his swollen face. A knife was pulled from the man's belt as he stood. The boy was yanked up and slung over the wooden beam.

"No. No, no, no," Abner screamed.

The enraged man pulled the struggling boy up by the top of his trousers, cut open the fabric of the seat, and pushed his victim hard against the timber bar. Abner's screams did not stop as the thug spread the boy's legs apart and pushed himself between them. The forced penetration provoked a hideous wail and involuntary buckling. Arms clutching the beam for support, the fiendish man brutalized the mute and comatose fourteen-year-old. He snorted as he pulled up his trousers, aware of a lantern nearby and people watching. His stance suggested the words beneath his dirty laugh—*I can do what I want and he can't stop me.*

Observers couldn't miss the distinct tattoo on the attacker's arm. It was a heart pierced by a dagger.

Abner finally moved in the pitch black and quiet. He pulled his arms up over the wooden bar, resting his battered chest. Deep breaths helped as he reached to his legs, bolstering them so he could stand. His legs were wet with blood oozing from his throbbing rectum. Abner strained to straighten himself and reform his body with a huge gulp of air. All his efforts to pull himself together could not stop the drool of flesh settling on the hard clay floor.

⤜⤏

Mid-morning light fell on the chair where Mary was settled, knitting. The midwife told her to stay off her feet as much as possible during the final weeks of pregnancy. Childbearing had not been easy before, but now she experienced pain in the lower back—pain in her hips, groin, lower abdomen and legs. Sometimes the discomfort was extreme, but she didn't complain. She didn't like the waddling gait that marked her movements around the house or the difficulty she faced climbing stairs. Not much longer before it was over.

It was quiet in the house, with Mirinda half asleep and Samuel on the floor building a house of blocks. When Ephraim stayed out all night he never returned early, so Mary showed no surprise when he casually walked in the door. He gave Samuel a hug, looked at Mirinda in her crib and then went to Mary. The glare on her face was not welcoming.

"Your father was here looking for you," Mary didn't get up and her words were cold. "I told him I didn't know where you were or when you'd be back. He was furious—in a way I have never seen. Your brother Abner was brutally beaten and raped last night at Cochrane's meeting and he holds you responsible. Abner was savaged and is almost senseless."

Ephraim turned white, stunned by Mary's revelation. He pulled up a chair near Mary and sat, silent. He remembered his father's burning eyes during the beating long ago. Ephraim's shaking body remembered as well, the savage blows and endless clubbing; the wild animal hulking over him and his total helplessness. Horrid flashes imagined himself in Abner's place, the torture and suffering.

"'It was Ephraim's evil doing,' Isaac yelled at me. 'He took Abner to a dangerous place, where criminals are protected, and boys preyed upon. Ephraim will answer for this. Tell him to come over, to answer to me and look at his brother. Do you think he has the courage to face Abner?'"

Ephraim covered his faced with his hands, hiding the tears. *Bad memories never go away,* Ephraim thought, *they are always there to haunt you—you're never rid of them.* He still winced at the word "toad." Over time, the word had less force with no accompanying urge to strike back. *Memories of violence never recede. The memory of my beating still haunts me, it's always there. It cannot be contained and seeps out. It jumps, transform itself, and turn on me. 'It is all your fault' it yells, 'your curse.'* Ephraim can't hold his tears. *Poor Abner.*

Mary returned to her knitting.

Abner's attack raised many things in Ephraim's mind. He wouldn't rush to his father and explain himself. He didn't know what to say. He was complicit, but what had he done wrong? Would the rape not have happened had he acted differently? Could Abner have thwarted the abuser? Is there something in a person's nature that attracts abuse? Ephraim wondered if he had brought his beating on himself—that he was to blame, was cursed. Those feelings stopped when he encountered Jacob Cochrane and joined his society. Jacob Cochrane had taken away his curse. Now it was back, with the same distress and remorse.

Despite Cochrane's great powers, Ephraim knew that his prophet could not understand this inner turmoil. Cochrane would judge him weak or faithless—his deficient righteousness unable to overcome a traumatic past.

Heading toward the kitchen, Ephraim stopped and turned toward Mary. "Is there any coffee? I'd like some, and I'd like to talk to you. I know that I can talk to you and you will listen."

"Yes, there is coffee," Mary looked confounded. "Just a minute. It needs to be warmed." Mary went to the kitchen and Ephraim moved the two empty chairs to the table.

Mary returned with the coffee and two cups. She anxiously sat across from her husband.

"I am terribly sorry about Abner," Ephraim began. "I know that everyone in the family is hurt by what happened, but Abner is the person who deserves an explanation. The violence happened because I took him to the meeting." Ephraim's eyes turned down. "I wasn't thinking about Abner, or Alexander, even their conversions. I took them to please Jacob and bring some new faces to his church. Yes, derelicts and suspicious characters come to Cochrane meetings—his message is for everyone. But I never thought a meeting was dangerous or that the Society sheltered criminals. I have always seen his church as a benevolent place."

"From what I have seen and heard, what you have told me, Cochrane's meetings are not sanctuaries or harmless," Mary said.

"Mary, I want you to listen to me," Ephraim tried to make his point. "I need your advice and help. I can put myself in Abner's shoes. How can I make this up to him?"

Setting her knitting aside, Mary leaned across the table toward her husband. "It's simple. You go to him and you tell him you are sorry."

"It's not simple. After my father beat me I was never sure he felt sorry. I know he was ashamed and could not face his violence directly. Bible stories couched his regrets. But he was not Abraham doing God's will." Ephraim's anger was undisguised.

"It must have made you feel better when your father explained himself," Mary was sympathetic. "That restored some goodness in your eyes, and others in your family."

"I am mixed up about last night and I don't know how to separate my feelings," Ephraim said.

"You have a difficult problem, I know. You struggle with the magnitude of the crime and weight of your shame. But it is not just your shame. It is the shame on your church, the instrument of Abner's tragedy. You can apologize for taking Abner and for leaving him alone," Mary's words stoked Ephraim's agitation.

"Yes, I can. My apology will be earnest and sincere," Ephraim said, his insides stirring.

"I understand your mixed feelings," Mary got to the tough question. "But how do you apologize for your church? You need to justify your church and preserve its reputation. You promote it every day Can you apologize to your brother while protecting your church and its prophet? It is a tangle, a tangle of your own self-respect and the public regard you crave for your Society."

Ephraim left his chair to stare at the sunny yard. "Abner's worse off. I know what he is going through. He's been damaged and tortured. In my heart, I know he will never get over this. He won't feel anger and resentment toward me. They will be directed at the man who ravaged him. I took him there to know the rapture of the Lord, and he ends up cursed." Ephraim cried. He wondered how to mend the damage done, and mask his resentment against the church that allowed his brother's attack?

Ephraim's brooding was interrupted by a knock on the door. Mary got up to answer it and found Jane on the doorstep. "Please come in, Jane," Mary said. "We are glad you are here."

Jane came in the house, and Mary helped her with her coat, the early December chill clung to it. Ephraim said nothing but nodded to his sister while Mary led her into the kitchen for coffee. "You always show up at the right time," Mary said, embracing her sister-in-law.

"How are you feeling? Is the baby restless?" Jane asked. "It won't be long."

"The pain is most troubling, especially when I try lifting and moving things around," Mary said. "The baby doesn't kick or give me problems. This morning I had diarrhea and some stomach cramps." Mary's face brightened. "You think nervous bowels could announce a birth?" The women laughed. "Coffee is ready. Let's join Ephraim."

"The coffee is perfect on a cold morning," Jane said, placing her cup on the table. Ephraim appeared composed as Jane embraced him and whispered, "I am angry. You are connected with some wretched things, brother, and you need your older sister's advice." She took his hand in hers. "Come over to the table so we can all sit together."

Ephraim returned to his chair while Mary refilled his coffee cup.

"Jane, I am glad you have come," Ephraim sounded contrite. "I'd like to hear how Abner is doing."

"I knew you would want to know everything before you went over to Father's house," Jane began. "That's why I've come."

"I am grateful, Jane," Ephraim said. "I am going to see Abner, but all I expect is Father's endless ranting."

Jane turned to face both Ephraim and Mary. "Father and Mother were awakened early this morning by Nathanial Kimball's wagon coming up to their house. Nathanial had both boys covered with a blanket, but all the blood was visible. Abner looked awful, his physical and emotional condition disturbing. Father and Kimball picked Abner up from the wagon, carried him into the house and stretched him out on the table Mother had covered with a blanket. Everyone moved urgently. Father put on water on to boil. Because dried blood behaves like glue, Mother had scissors to cut Abner out of his trousers. His legs and lower body were a horrifying sight. The rest of his garments were removed, and Mother got some sheets to keep Abner warm until the water was hot. She washed off a lot of blood, cleaned many wounds, and bandaged them after applying antiseptic.

"Alexander sat nearby, bewildered and speechless. Father screamed at Kimball, pulling him to his feet. 'Who did this?' he screamed. 'Who did this?'

"Kimball, knowing that Alexander was half paralyzed, answered, 'Some saw a man near Abner, but couldn't recognize him. He had a tattoo on his arm, probably a vagrant.'

"Father was furious and yelled at Kimball, 'People around here don't have tattoos. People in prison have tattoos, and rowdies from bawdy houses.' Father's temper flared. 'Men like that come to your barn? Shameless.' Kimball looked offended."

"I lost track of Abner. But I saw a man last night, a big man with a tattoo on his arm. It was startling—a dagger piercing a heart," the memory alarmed Ephraim. "He pounced on a frenzied boy and pinned him to the ground. That's why I noticed. I didn't do anything because the boy became quiet." Ephraim's look urged Jane to continue.

"Father raged at Kimball, 'You let a criminal into your barn, and lacked the courage to keep that criminal away from my son? Nobody tried to stop him? Nobody is pursuing him—because he has disappeared?'" Jane took time to moderate her voice. "You know that Father never likes losing his temper. He stopped yelling, backed away from Kimball, and fell silent. He stared at everybody in the room." Mary knew all about Isaac's anger, but the blank look on her face suggested her mind was elsewhere.

"Father roared, his voice resolute and strong, like Elijah overcoming his discouragement. 'All of this is that depraved Jacob Cochrane's doing, and the perpetrator is Cochrane's spawn. I know that Ichabod Jordan and Richard Shannon want Cochrane stopped and are filing a legal complaint. They will get Daniel Granger, the Justice of the Peace, to find Abner's attacker. We will see Jacob Cochrane brought to justice.'"

Ephraim toyed with his empty cup, pushing it around the top of the table. "Has Abner talked at all?" he asked.

"Abner's face is so disfigured it is hard for him to speak," Jane said, her gazed fixed.

"Have you been able to speak to Alexander? Has he said anything at all?" Ephraim asked.

"Alexander keeps silent, probably as a way of avoiding a confrontation with Father," Jane said. "He has spoken to me and feels guilty about getting caught up in the Cochrane thrall and abandoning his brother. He's very sorry and said that he had never seen such suffering as Abner's. He is trying to figure out how to explain himself to Father."

"I'm sorry," Mary gasped. "I'm very sorry." Mary scooted her chair back from the table. "Oh no, not now," she said as she stood up, away from her chair. "I can't make it outside." Mary's dress was wet, and it looked like she had peed herself. There was a puddle in the chair. Her face looked startled, but her breath remained even. She didn't appear frightened.

Jane rushed around the table to Mary's side and put her arms around her sister-in-law. "I'm soaked," Mary said calmly, "I must change my dress."

"Are you feeling any contractions? Do you sense labor coming on?" Jane asked.

"No," Mary answered, "I just feel wet. Would you come and help me change?"

"Let's freshen you and get you lying down. Maybe you will want a bath," Jane put her arm around Mary and led her into the bedroom.

Ephraim went to the kitchen, found some coffee left, and took a cup back to the table. He hadn't slept much and felt tired, but he had things he must do. First, Isaac's certain outrage would not keep him from seeing Abner and apologizing for taking him to the Cochrane meeting. He never intended to put his brother in harm's way. It would take some time to figure out how to make things right.

Ephraim also had to come to grips with the new baby. While he bragged about Mary's pregnancy, he knew the baby was not his. The father was Ben Andrews, a brother in the church. Despite Cochrane's teachings, that bothered him. Ephraim was a strong man, but he didn't want more responsibility. A new child? He was not sure he wanted it.

⁓

"It was Ephraim's evil doing," is what Isaac said about Abner's abuse. The words, embedded in Ephraim's mind since Mary quoted them, became an obsession. He needed to get the words out of his head but couldn't do it alone. That's why Ephraim headed to Jacob Cochrane's house on Christmas morning—he wanted a clear conscience when his family gathered later for their holiday dinner.

It was an hour's walk to Jacob Cochrane's modest one-story house on the easterly side of the Buxton–Saco Road, about midway between Samuel Lowell's place and the Cleaves house. Built by Cochrane friends, it was always overflowing with people, his wife and three children, and others staying there.

I must get an explanation from Cochrane of why my brother was raped. Ephraim thought, repeating himself as he walked. *How does God allow this to happen? How can this happen in a place of worship?* Ephraim needed Cochrane's understanding. It was a matter of his own integrity. And, understanding more about the event would help him make amends to his brother. *I never understood my own beating, and my father never told me why it happened.*

There was no activity visible as Ephraim approached Cochrane's house—unusual for Christmas morning. He went to the door, which was not locked, and let himself in. Samuel Lowell was sitting by the fire and he seemed to be consoling Eliza Hill, who was beside him crying.

'We thought you were finally gone," Samuel shouted. As he stood, he recognized Ephraim.

The shouting drew Ben Andrews, only in his drawers, from an adjoining room. Not long after Dorcas Underwood appeared, disheveled, some of her body bare. Deidamia Lane followed, almost fully dressed and appearing more composed.

"What's going on?" Ephraim asked.

"Jacob has been arrested and taken to jail. Abagail took the kids and followed," Ben said. "Our enemies struck out at Jacob, but you know he will be back soon. How can Jacob Cochrane be charged? What can be their case?"

Ephraim did not go into the adjoining room, but thought the arresting officials broke in at an inconvenient time. The room was disordered, male and female clothes scattered about and shoes scattered, kicked off with no thought of their recovery.

"Who arrested Jacob?' Ephraim asked.

"It was Justice Granger. Ichabod Jordan and his brother, Rishworth were with him. Ichabod filed a complaint against Jacob—accusing him of sexual misconduct and adultery," Ben said. "They had papers with them."

"Did Jacob struggle with Granger and the others?" Ephraim asked.

"No, he didn't," Ben said, "It was early morning and a surprise. Jacob wasn't even dressed.'

"Did Jacob leave any instructions?" Ephraim asked.

"Jacob said not to worry and that he would be back as soon as he could," Ben said. "He didn't show much concern. And he could have made it a real spectacle." Ben donned some wool trousers Dorcas handed him and pulled on a shirt which extended to his midthigh. He was now ready for business. "And what brings you here on Christmas morning, Ephraim?"

"I came to talk to Jacob, about a personal matter," Ephraim hesitated. He never had a personal conversation with Ben, but continued, wanting to get the trouble off his chest. "I wanted to talk about my place in Jacob's church."

"If you want to talk," Ben said, "I will listen."

"You are one of Jacob's lieutenants, and I am a major supporter of the Society," Ephraim started. "I professed my rebirth, and with rebirth God is now inside of me. I repented because I owed God my repentance. I was baptized. I have faith in God, and with that faith I can become a more perfect person."

"Yes, Ephraim," Ben's tone sounded indulgent. "That is what is supposed to happen."

"There are people in Buxton who think those who follow Jacob Cochrane are strange, even abnormal," Ephraim said. "That doesn't bother me. I live to honor God and follow His will."

"I know there are those who call us delusional, and use that word in the press," Ben said.

"But I need to know more about what we do, the truth, if I am to obey God, and better serve Him," Ephraim started, knowing that Ben Andrews couldn't answer his questions. "The Bible asks us what good is it to profess our faith without practicing it. How we live, what we do, our good works are most important, not just our appearances, or what we say."

"You practice your faith all of the time," Ben said.

"What if I am practicing my faith and my practice brings harm?" Ephraim asked. "Like my brother's beating and abuse? I took Abner to the meeting. Can people see me as righteous after his suffering? Jacob teaches that God's church is inside each of us. Am I still the same?"

"People see you help Jacob spread his teaching. You raise money for him. Believers see that as righteousness," Ben answered

"Please listen. I take my brother to one of Jacob's service and he is beaten and raped? Does that action undermine Cochrane's call to unbelievers or his ability to reach them?"

"Get this straight, Ephraim. Your brother did not belong at the meeting. Jacob did not want him there. You disobeyed his instructions," Ben said. "And Jacob does his own calling to unbelievers, through God's power of course." Ephraim found it hard to link this authoritative voice with the half-naked man he awoke just a few minutes before. "But you are important, helping people hear his voice. Without your hard work there wouldn't be money for the food Jacob serves at the Lord's Supper. You are a big help and are serving God, Ephraim."

"I obey God and try to please Him. I attend to his church. But the fact that I caused my brother great harm struck my heart. What I did seems far from God intentions," Ephraim said with remorse.

"Have you ever before seen a man as marvelous as Jacob Cochrane? Through him you have felt the love of God in your soul. In your support of Jacob, you have seen how our Lord's love touches many, many others. You please God all of the time," Ben said.

"I need to please God from my heart," Ephraim said.

"Don't you feel Jacob in your heart?" Ben asked boldly.

"I need to talk to Jacob and get all of this clear in my mind," Ephraim stopped. "I must get home for Christmas dinner, and let you get back to your own business."

"Jacob will help you," Ben said. "He knows God's will. Just obey him."

"What is the purpose of obedience if the result is harm," Ephraim said with frustration. His irritation turned to anger. "I know you raped Mary. That happened because Jacob named her as your spiritual wife. I am sure you did not feel you had done harm when you went to Mary, but she feels harmed, deeply. You were cruel, and she will never forget it."

Ephraim, his face bright red, turned and left the house.

⌁

Celebrating the arrival of the New Year was popular in Buxton, some thinking it the best time in the year for merrymaking. The party took place on the evening of December 31 and lasted until the wee hours, but the planning and the work began long before. No different from people in other parts of the country, folks in York County looked forward to better times in the coming year and were eager to get the best possible start for 1819.

The party was Ephraim's idea. Mary, who lost her baby in early December, was despondent and could not imagine receiving guests in her house. Since the end of 1818 was fraught with awful experiences, Ephraim liked the idea of a party where lots of family and friends gathered in an atmosphere of conviviality and warm feeling. New Years was a celebration where no one hid affection, kinship was on full display, and the embracing and kissing of loved ones was common.

A big celebration required a lot of work, most of it done by women in the family. Ephraim assured Mary that he would spend a lot of time on the preparation and enlist the help of his sisters. Mary agreed, despite her exhaustion and poor mood.

Ephraim got to work on the party in mid-December. His neighbors, friends from Coolbroth's Corners, and extended family spread word of the celebration within a couple of days. He enlisted Jane's help in organizing the festivities, and reassured Mary that little would be required of her. People were ready for New Year festivities and many wanted to help.

"We have one day left," Jane said. "Everything will be set for an unforgettable party."

"You are irreplaceable, Jane," Mary said. "I think it's going to work out and be fun too. Making this happen has raised my spirits. Just two weeks ago it all seemed such a burden. I felt so tired. I thought I would be spending the night by myself in the loft."

"You are a strong woman and it's remarkable how you spring

back. I've been happy to help, but you have taken charge," Jane's words weren't hollow. "I am impressed. How you have recovered, gotten some strength back and dealt with your loss. After nine months carrying a baby, I can't imagine how wrenching and distressing it must be to lose it."

Jane and Mary were alone. Ephraim had killed a goose earlier which would be roasted for tomorrow's feast, and Jane was cleaning it. She had a firm hold on its feet and was plucking it with her other hand, gathering a few feathers at the same time and pulling them down in the direction of the growth. The bird was still warm. Mary was making pastry dough for pies and tarts. The familiar routine eased her mind and opened her to talk.

"The death was easier to accept when I knew the baby's lungs didn't work and never fully developed. The loss was a blessing for the child." After mixing the dough, she divided it and shaped it into balls which would be kept cold until the next day. Mary took a deep breath and exhaled slowly, a way of breathing she found calming. She did it again and was careful when she spoke—not wanting to sound uncaring.

"I can say this to you because you know about Ben Andrews. That day, and my rage, I have never forgotten. No matter how sweet and loving the baby may have been, the child would have made it impossible to ever forget the rape." Mary's darkest thoughts were exposed.

There was fumbling at the door and Ephraim appeared, his arms full of greenery. "I know this looks like more work for you, but I saw my sister Elizabeth while I was out. She will be here soon," Ephraim was unusually animated. "The parlor will be decorated with garlands of holly, mountain laurel and pine." The bundle of shrubbery rested on the floor, he rushed to Mary. "I didn't forget a thing," he said as he pulled sprigs of mistletoe from behind his back, stretched a handful above Mary's head and planted a kiss on her cheek.

"Mind yourself," Mary warned with a chuckle, "You'll have flour all over you and you'll have it all over the house."

"This house is going to lift everyone's spirits," Ephraim's enthusiasm brimming. "It's going to smell good. I have some pungent herbs, rosemary and bay, and Eben has some lavender at his store. I'm going to get it now, and the spices and ale for the wassail." Ephraim left, his spirits high.

The goose cleaned, Jane turned to making a special gift. She tied a ribbon around an orange, and stuck cloves in its skin, covering the entire surface. To finish, she dusted the cloves with cinnamon. "There will be gifts for everyone," Jane smiled. "I know my sisters are bringing maple syrup, honey, jam, and Rebecca made an apron. There are toys for the boys, some bags of clay marbles, a hornbook and shuttlecock. We have jump ropes, ribbons, bracelets and some combs for the girls." Jane held up the decorated orange and looked at it with satisfaction, then looked at Mary. "I am not saying who this is for."

Ephraim's sisters and mother were there that afternoon to help with the final preparations. In the morning, Mary made mincemeat pies and apple tarts. Jane arrived not long after to roast the goose and turkey. Women brought beef and a ham, custards, cranberry sauce and brandied peaches which would be set out later. Mary's cousins, Ruth and Mercy, would bring baked acorn squash, candied sweet potatoes and lima beans, and neighbors would bring other vegetables, bread and cheese.

The primary task for Ephraim's mother and sisters was the preparation of the wassail, enough to last well into the night. Ephraim wanted two kinds, one with cider and the other with ale. It would take several hours of simmering, but Mary had everything ready. She had a fire going, and two big pots. There was cider from Ephraim's cousin's mill and ale from Eben Coolbroth's store, along with the necessary sugar, ginger, cinnamon and other spices. Bread was set out to make the toast that would float on top.

Things were just as Ephraim had planned. People started arriving shortly after dark, and children were soon nibbling on cookies. Wassail was ladled from the large bowl on the parlor table. Women exchanged the latest gossip: the departure of the schoolmaster, the virtue and modesty of Sally Fletcher who had sworn she was carrying his child, and whether Sally would hold firm to her accusation. James Thomas had been seen lying in the road drunk. All agreed that special prayers should be offered for his newborn daughter. They talked of weaving and sewing projects for the months ahead.

"Come outside you merry men. We are going to revive a long-revered custom," Ephraim shouted. "Fill your mugs first." He led his friends and celebrants behind the house to his small grove of apple trees. "We are going to have an apple-howling," he laughed, getting the men to form a ring around the trees. All was illuminated by a big fire built nearby. Each man was given a long stick. Ephraim got them hooting and baying, dancing around the grove, rapping the trees with their sticks. Nat Harmon started the singing, and everyone remembered the old verse:

> Stand fast root, bear well top,
> Pray God send us a good howling crop;
> Every twig, apples big;
> Every bough, apples enou;
> Hats full, caps full,
> Full quarter sacks full.

"Hooray," Ephraim led the cheering when the song was finished. "We are bound to have a bountiful crop for next year. Now drink. Let's not allow the wassail to cool."

Ephraim brought out a bowl of the brew and set it on a nearby stump, ensuring there would be no empty mugs. No one was forced to drink.

"I would like to drink to my wife and son. Joanna, may she be bountiful in the coming year and my son Abraham blessed by a little brother," Nat Harmon raised his mug. "And a drink to all my neighbors, who know that I will be diligent in this task. Desire is not a stranger to me."

"My brother Thomas, may he rest in peace. I miss him," John Berry toasted. John did not mention his wife Anna's health which had kept her from the party.

"We all miss Thomas, but we are not missing his cider. Through it he presides over this celebration," Jabez Sawyer bellowed.

"Look, a white owl," Roger Plaisted shouted. "It brings good fortune." Now one else seemed to see it. Roger couldn't have watched it long, his stumbling over himself, falling to the ground. Ephraim didn't toast Mary or her good health, but there was a toast for Ephraim, wishing him another son.

The men drank to more good times, 1818 being a good year for everyone's wealth. Crops had been good, and foreigners wanted American goods. Commerce grew in the years since the war.

"I wish us to keep out spirits high," Paul Dresser said to a few gathered by the bonfire. "But we are headed for hard times. The French and English are closing their markets. It could be hard."

"What's happened to Jacob Cochrane?" John Berry asked. Not part of the Coolbroth's Corners circle, he was behind on local gossip.

"Cochrane was arrested on Christmas Day for taking Eliza Hill and Sally Dennet to bed, they were naked when the sheriff busted into his house," Eben Coolbroth piped in. "It must have been quite a scene breaking in on Jacob Cochrane trying to make another baby Jesus."

"He's already performed a resurrection. The birth had been left undone," Uriah laughed.

"Maybe there will be an ascension in the courthouse," Eben added.

"Yes," Paul Dresser turned to John Berry, "Jacob Cochrane has been charged with adultery and lewd and lascivious conduct. He will be going to court in a few weeks."

"Saco bigwigs, like Ichabod Jordan and his brother Rishworth, have been after Cochrane for a long time," Nat Harmon said. "They actually assisted Justice of the Peace, Daniel Granger, in the arrest."

"Ephraim, you are not saying a word?" Eben teased, "Will this arrest hamper your sex life and the prosperity of Cochrane's Society?"

"I don't know all of the rumors," Ephraim was dismissive. "Cochrane doesn't see himself in real trouble, nor do I. Cochrane is not worried and didn't put up a struggle when Granger came to his house."

"We will see," Paul said. "There is more to this than flesh and carnality. I hear of our Congressman's interest in the case. His daughter was Cochrane's victim for a time and he wants compensation for the injury his family has suffered."

Ephraim had no urge to argue. "I know the power of God and Cochrane will come out of this stronger than ever," Ephraim said forcefully. "Everyone must feel cold out here. Let's go inside."

Those reentering the house found some guests had already gone home. There was still enough food and warm drink to satisfy those who lingered. Ephraim didn't want people to go before they observed another tradition—one involving the Bible. Ephraim cleared a place on the parlor table for a Bible and placed a bright lantern beside it.

"Many of you know this cherished practice. Each of us opens the Bible randomly and randomly points to a verse on one of the open pages. You read the verse aloud, making believe it foreshadows fortunes of the New Year. Eben, will you go first?" Ephraim asked.

"Everyone knows I'm no good at reading the Bible, and have little practice," Eben responded. Shaking his head, he walked to the table, opened the Bible and found a verse with his finger. "It is Isaiah 16:11: 'Wherefore my bowels will sound like a harp from Moab, and my inward parts from Kirharesh.'" Eben paused before a broad smile crossed his face. "Believe me. I have never tried to imitate a harp when farting. And I'm not sure that I could do a trumpet, a far easier instrument. But I will try. All of you must come by the store this coming year to see if I have been given the gift." Everyone laughed as Eben left the table

The Bible-reading tradition interested many in the house, each finding a verse they read aloud. Not everybody made comments on their reading, in some cases the meaning was generally understood. People shook their heads when "faith," "goodness," and "blessings" were mentioned. There was quiet when the verse referenced "sin," "temptation," or "God's wrath." No matter, the readings were engaging, and the tradition proved enjoyable.

"Mary," Jane called out. "It's your turn. Find a verse and read it to us."

Despite her fatigue, Mary smiled and moved to the Bible. "Psalms 127:3" Mary announced, 'Children are a gift from the Lord; they are a reward from Him.'" She said nothing but exchanged smiles with Jane before leaving the table.

"We will not leave the party until Ephraim's found a verse." Nat shouted, "You must find one that promises good luck."

Ephraim took his time, opened the Bible near its end, hoping for a verse by Paul. He looked away as he pointed his finger and then read, "Second Peter 2:19: While they promise them liberty, they themselves are servants of corruption; for of whom a man is overcome, of the same is he brought in bondage." Ephraim was quiet, like everyone.

Reading scripture was not a good thing to do at the party, he thought. *It is not the way to start a new year. Everyone will leave here thinking the Bible is cautioning me against following false prophets.*

SIX

Ephraim had the look of one dealing with a serious problem but the buoyant gait that comes with confidence to solve it. Samuel was playing in the yard when he returned, so they entered the house together. The youngster asked his mother for something to eat. Mary interrupted her mending and went to the kitchen cupboard for some dried apples. With something to nibble, Samuel returned to the yard, stepping carefully over his sister who was playing with a doll on the parlor floor.

After Ephraim removed his winter coat, he went to the kitchen for something hot to drink. "I have some coffee I can warm, or I could heat up some cider," Mary intruded on her husband's prowling.

"I wouldn't mind both," Ephraim said, still looking serious. "It is colder outside than you think." He returned to the parlor, sitting in his usual chair at the table.

"I have a little pudding too, if you'd like some," Mary said. She placed a cup of coffee and a cup of hot cider in front of her husband, along with a spoon and some sugar.

"My stomach feels a little empty," Ephraim said. "Pudding would be good, especially with the rum." His smile was deliberate. "Mary," he raised his voice to be heard in the kitchen, "I have a surprise for you."

"A surprise?" Mary asked as she returned to the parlor.

"Yes," Ephraim waited until Mary was seated. "I've been concerned about you. We had a good New Year's party, although it was more work for you than I intended." Ephraim caught Mary's eyes, and paused. "You don't laugh as much as you did or seem to enjoy life, no talk about the future."

"I have a lot to do," Mary said soberly. She looked down into the cup of tea she had brought into the room. "Neither of the children requires much, but they do need watching. And there are all of the chores."

"You look worried a lot, often sad," Ephraim said. "I know you don't sleep well, and sometimes I hear you crying in the night. It troubles me. I understand some of it. You carried a child for nine months, gave birth and the baby died. And Abner's tragedy has affected you, like everybody else in the family."

"I am all right," Mary responded, slowly turned her head to survey the room, but her eyes not attaching to anything in it. "And Jane comes by to visit."

Ephraim waited, straightened himself, and then leaned across the table, his face closer to Mary's. "After all your suffering, I want to make you feel better, offer you a reward. You are going to have another child," Ephraim assumed the benevolent tone suitable to the awarding of a great prize. "And you are going to have it soon."

"What you are saying, Ephraim? I don't understand," Mary looked bewildered. "I can't imagine conceiving a child right now. There is no tenderness in our lives. And I have no desire."

"Remember the reading you found in the Bible: 'Children are a gift from the Lord; they are a reward from him.' That was a message to you, a message from God," Ephraim said. The expression on Mary's face changed slowly, her left eye began blinking fitfully.

"Please don't joke with me," Mary said. There was a long period of silence before she appeared more collected and less vulnerable. "Does Jacob Cochrane have plans for an immaculate conception?"

"Mary, you can do so much for a child. You find real fulfillment in motherhood, and it makes you happy, "Ephraim said. "You are such a good mother."

"I cannot think of another child right now," Mary dismissed the subject. She picked up her cup and took it into the kitchen. Ephraim followed.

"A baby will be born within a few days. I will bring it here and you will be its mother," Ephraim declared.

A shock jolted Mary's body, and she lost grip of her cup, which slipped from her hand and broke, splattering the floor with tea. "What are you talking about?" Mary barked.

"A baby must have a mother," Ephraim was emphatic. "Nobody can do this as well as you, or make the adjustment faster."

"This is Jacob Cochrane's doing, isn't it?" Mary wanted an answer but continued talking. "It's all to do with spiritual wifery, isn't it? I hear that the faithful equate his wifery with freedom. You Cochranites are told that conventional marriage draws women into unhappy unions arranged by parents and family. Love is of little concern." Ephraim let Mary continue and didn't try to correct her. "Traditional marriage is against God's plan, believers say. It denies a woman the choice of the father of her children."

Mopping up the spilled tea and picking up the pieces of the cup had not affected the pace of Mary's talk. Her anger was not routine, nor was her raised voice. She didn't usually stalk around the house and caught herself when she reached the middle of the parlor. She turned to face Ephraim who had followed her from the kitchen. "Spiritual wifery confers special freedoms on men, they say. And I've heard that in God's plan the father chooses the mother of his children. What I just learned is a new revelation, that the man chooses the woman who will raise them."

Ephraim went up to Mary but didn't try to touch her. "I happen to know of an infant who will need a mother. It is good fortune to know a woman who would be the best possible mother the child could have," Ephraim said resolutely.

"Do I know the real mother?" Mary's voice was icy.

"No, you don't, Mary. The mother is not from here," Ephraim said.

"I suppose that the mother comes from one of Cochrane's strongholds," Mary concluded.

"It shouldn't make much difference. But the mother is from a place where Cochrane's beliefs are respected," Ephraim responded.

"You don't need to know a lot to welcome a baby into your arms."

"The separation of a child from its mother is awful, criminal," Mary said. "I cannot understand how a mother could give up her child."

"There are plenty of things that are difficult to understand if you don't believe that there is a plan," Ephraim said. "What's important is the child have a good and loving mother. And now it does."

Mary settled at the table, where she rested her elbows, burying her face in her hands. She was still for a long time, "I'm not sure that I am physically prepared to do this," she said when she finally raised her head. "There is the matter of the energy and stamina required by an infant. I am not sure that I can nurse or have the milk. Will I be able to sustain the proper health of a baby? I cannot promise that."

"There is no doubt in my mind that you have the strength. Because of your recent pregnancy and the birth, I think you have an advantage. Your breasts are still bigger than normal size, so milk should not be a problem," Ephraim was unconcerned.

"What if I do have a problem? I don't want a wet-nurse around. Getting ready to have a baby in the house requires thinking and preparation, and there is not much time. I don't know how I will get it done," Mary said.

"You will have the help of my sister," Ephraim was quick to answer.

"Jane? Why do you think she would take this on?" Mary asked.

"Because she already knows about this. I just talked to her and she will be at your side," Ephraim responded.

"Jane knows about this? She knew about this before I did? How could you do that?" Mary cried.

"Yes. I didn't want to talk to you before I was sure we had Jane's help. Time is short, and we must make this work," Ephraim halted. "I am not insensitive, Mary. What do you think, that I am a bastard?"

"Yes, Ephraim. You are a bastard," Mary wept.

"This is will be good for you and all of us," Ephraim said. "I am going out." He went to the door, then looked back. "Jane should be along soon."

⌒

Mary had not moved from the table where her head still rested on her arms, when she heard steps in the yard.

"Mary. Mary," Jane called out, entering the house without knocking. "Oh Mary. Let me put my arms around you." She rushed across the parlor to where Mary was still sitting and pulled her up. They embraced.

"I am so glad you are here. I'm desperate and torn," Mary said.

"It is sudden and confusing. How can you not be torn?" Jane said.

"My mind is going in many directions. A baby, but not my baby. Ephraim's infidelities confirmed. Surely, he's the father. My health is not good. Where will I find the stamina? How will I feed and care for an infant, while following Samuel around and attending to Mirinda? And I have to take care of the house and cooking." Mary stopped the unfolding of her fears to hug Jane again. "I am so glad you came."

"I am going to help you, Mary. I was shocked by what Ephraim told me this morning. He is selfish, and his thoughtlessness is unending. He doesn't think of others and how he hurts them," Jane held both of Mary's hands. She calmed, but Jane moved to the tasks ahead. "We both know you will have a new baby within a few days."

"Do you know anything about the baby, the mother, or the birth?" Mary asked.

"I know that the baby will be born soon, and the mother is unable to take care of it. There is a child's life at stake," Jane had sorted the facts on her way to Mary's. "The only thing I know about the mother is that she lives in Old Orchard Beach. The baby will be brought from there."

"Is Ephraim the father? Does that explain why he is doing this?" Mary asked.

"I don't know. He didn't tell me when I asked. That may well be true. He said that he wanted a good future for the baby and wanted you to raise it," Jane said.

"How will he ever change? I want a life where I can trust my husband to put my welfare first, not, without warning, insist that I raise a baby that is not my own," Mary said.

"Mary, my brother has caused you to suffer. I am sorry for that. I am sad for him with his reckless life," Jane said. "But you already have much of what you need to care for the baby, and what you do not have I will bring to you."

"I worry most about the physical demands of the baby," Mary said.

"I can be here as much as you need me," Jane's words were confident. "Samuel and Mirinda can stay some of the time with my parents. Mary, you are much stronger than you think."

Mary resumed her mending. Keeping her hands busy moderated her agitation. She finished patching Samuel's trousers, and went to the room off the kitchen where she kept her spinning wheel, sewing basket, and implements needed for her household chores. The sewing basket hanging from one arm, some recently washed shirts over the other arm and holding a jar of buttons in her hand, Mary returned to the parlor.

"What concerns me most is the milk," Mary said as she placed the items in her arms on the table. "I'm not sure there will be any. The nursing will be a problem."

"I will bring Sarah Brooks, the midwife, and she can offer her good advice," Jane said. "Actually, I talked to her on my way here. She said that the milk and feeding should be simple. You follow the same steps that women have talked about for years. Although you don't have direct experience, it is not folklore." Jane walked around the table to Mary and took the sewing from her hands.

Mary would trust the advice of the midwife. Mary stood, stretched her body to relax herself, and smoothed out her dress.

"And how is Abner?" Mary changed from the subject of Ephraim, wanting to find out about Abner. She had heard nothing of Abner's recovery, since Christmas day at Isaac's house and Ephraim had a bitter exchange with his father, who blamed Ephraim for Abner's rape.

"Nothing has changed. Abner is detached, lurches and bumbles. He doesn't talk much," Jane said. "Something inside of him has stilled."

"He was so spontaneous, such a playful nature," Mary said.

"I would not say he looks blank, but joyless. Father says he can never count on him. Abner takes a rest when he is out working, is refreshed a bit. But there isn't any real change—he really can't work. He is tired the whole day," Jane said. "Father frets about keeping the farm going."

"Maybe he is not getting enough sleep?"

"He's not. Alexander says Abner tosses around a lot at night and sometimes he cries out," Jane shook her head. "Abner is troubled. Alexander takes on much of the blame, which never seems to leave his mind."

"I'm not sure what sticks to Ephraim's mind," Mary mused as she only could with her sister-in-law. "Abner's attack tormented him for a while. He made amends and talked to Abner and I think to Cochrane. With that done, the incident and guilt seemed to vanish from his mind. It's the same way for him as a father. Breeding is a trivial part of fatherhood. The care of the child is the essential element. His job is to find the best person to do the job. That settled, the other requirements are forgotten."

"You will make this child strong and you will make the child feel loved. From you, Mary, the child will also learn how to return love. You know that is so important," Jane said.

"Ephraim sees love as something bestowed, by someone with the power to do that. Like God. My husband sees himself placed to confer love," Mary thought of her one-sided relationship. "But that makes love so small. There is no giving, no union. Loving is also receiving love. He doesn't know how to do that, or maybe he just doesn't want to."

Rumors swirled amid leaked information, and accusations came thick and fast. The York County Court in Alfred called for a hearing to examine the facts and the grounds for the December arrest of Jacob Cochrane. Adversaries characterized Jacob Cochrane as acting in defiance of both civil and ecclesiastical law. Farmers like Sam Swett and Ben Tombs were leaders in the campaign against him. New and sensational stories of Cochrane's abhorrent and depraved behavior were spread. Names of the individuals to testify to specific obscene incidents were whispered in every corner of the county. Clergymen, especially a group of long-standing opponents, made Cochrane the subject of sermons, denouncing him before God and their separate congregations. Some wrote and posted public denunciations of the scoundrel.

Many, though, refused to believe the outrageous stories. There was no change in adherents' evangelism. Cochrane's ministry never slowed, with advocates spreading Cochrane's teaching at meetings in barns, schools, and farmhouses. Followers like Jacob McDaniel and Abner Wood were unwavering in their preaching, despite growing opposition and public attacks.

Cochrane, dismissive of the accusations, distanced himself from the fray. He had no clear strategy for his defense and sought no legal advice. Although Cochrane ignored his summons to the court, Ephraim went to Alfred to observe the Grand Jury and the proceedings. He needed to know what his leader faced.

The courtroom was bright with winter light coming through eight large windows, and full, mostly with Jacob's adversaries. Ephraim recognized Rev. Clement Phinney, who regarded Cochrane as Lucifer, distributing leaflets, as did another guardian of public morals, Rev. Ephraim Stinchfeld. The high-born of Saco, who had expressed great displeasure with Cochrane and funded and organized much of his opposition, took seats on one side of the courtroom, close to the bench. Some seven or eight people in facing chairs appeared to be important functionaries. In front of the bench sat John Mussey, the Clerk of the Court, and Ichabod Jordan, who filed the complaint against Cochrane. Daniel Davis, the Solicitor General, sat in the center with Jeremiah Milliken, the constable from Saco who had arrested Jacob Cochrane, next to him. Rishworth Jordan, who assisted in the arrest, was last in the row with his brother.

The gathering was not unlike a congregation before a Baptist service, convivial and disordered. Voices were loud, and people waved and shouted at friends across the room. Some had food to eat, but the admonition against smoking was observed. A special good humor suggested a few onlookers had visited the local tavern before their arrival, but no one was seen drinking. Nobody seemed to mind the stray dog wandering the room looking for something to eat.

The chamber settled when Justice Granger entered and took his place behind the bench. "This court received a formal complaint," Granger began. "It was made by Ichabod Jordan, on behalf of the Commonwealth of Massachusetts, stating that Jacob Cochrane of Saco, this past July, did unlawfully and lasciviously associate with one Abigail Clark, a married woman." Sniggers and chortles came from all corners of the courtroom. Justice Granger tightly gripped his gavel and pounded the bench before continuing. "Another complaint charges that the same Jacob Cochrane, with force of arms, had criminal conversation and carnal knowledge of one Eliza Hill, a single woman." The jeering and hooting took some time to stop.

Justice Granger asked Ichabod Jordan to present the evidence he had of Cochrane's relationship with Abigail Clark. Ephraim did not see her in the room. The primary witness was Eunice Bond, who was asked to take a chair in the front of the bench. Although Eunice was presented as a former member of Cochrane's society, Ephraim did not know her well. In Ephraim's role in raising money and organizing events, their paths did not cross. *I am introduced to Eunice Bond*, Ephraim thought, *who is as a traitor.* She told the court that she had been at Abigail Clark's house one morning helping her with chores while Mr. Clark left for a day of errands. Jacob Cochrane arrived to tend to Abigail's well-known health concerns and took her upstairs. Two hours later Eunice went upstairs and saw them in bed together, their flesh exposed. Spectators, gasping at the lurid story, wanted to hear more.

Jordan asked Eunice why she had taken more than six months to divulge these scandalous facts. Abigail told the court that members of Cochrane's society were required to keep secrets. She left the society because of the rampant misconduct it fostered in the community and was no longer bound by its rules. Ephraim was disturbed by the testimony and by the fact that nobody in the court, including Justice Granger, challenged Eunice's claims. It got worse.

The appearance and swearing in of Mary King as a witness for the Commonwealth caused a stir and much chatter in the courtroom. Mary was a Saco blueblood, daughter of Cyrus King, a representative of the District of Maine in the U.S. Congress. Her uncle, Rufus King served as United States Minister to England. Mary's involvement with Jacob Cochrane was widely known, as were rumors that she was the fabled "Sister Mercy." Her appearance shook Ephraim—it could not serve Jacob's interests. Ephraim knew her well but hadn't seen her in more than a month. Mary's testimony was shocking and personal.

No one in Cochrane's spiritual realm was given a more elevated position. Mary had no sacred fires to keep burning like the vestal virgins of Roman times. But she was a key feature in the observance and execution of important rituals, like the Adam and Eve ceremony and its representation of God's word. Also her resurrection was claimed a manifestation of God's presence on earth. No follower had a better channel of communication with the spiritual world. Like the vestals she was placed above other women as a symbol of love and chastity. Her primary earthly devotion was to Jacob Cochrane and his service to God. She was beatified by many of Cochrane's followers, and a source of jealousy for those men denied the ardor she showed for Jacob. Sister Mercy was ravishing. Ephraim realized his affection for her and couldn't imagine how Jacob mistreated her.

Beauty alone did not confer Mary exalted status. She was born again, a pivotal event experienced by many believers. And she was blessed with the gift of tongues. Her talking to the Holy Spirit was uncommon among believers and through her celestial visits she described many wonders of the Kingdom of God.

"I was at the Clark house during Cochrane's visit, and remained for the night," Mary said haltingly. "And Abigail made room for me in her bed. I woke up early in the morning to find myself alone. I didn't know the house well but got up and went out of the room to see if something was wrong." Mary looked from Jordan to the rough floor, and with a plea of blamelessness, cried out, "I didn't know what to do. To run into the dark? Away from it all? I found Mrs. Clark and Mr. Cochrane on the floor together, entirely naked except for their linen. I was frozen in place. Mr. Cochrane sat up, raising the palm of his hand in a sign of peace. I was told to pray. The naked man on the floor was telling me to pray," Mary continued.

"How could thoughts of God be in my mind, standing before a naked man mating with my hostess? I told them I could not pray. Could God be anywhere nearby, made to witness to this vile scene? I told them I was hurt and shamed." Her breath shortened, and she crossed her hands just below her neck, as if that might restore the color to her face.

"They just wanted to get me out of that room. I was inconvenient. Interfering. Mr. Cochrane and Mrs. Clark went and laid down on the bed together. As they resumed their business, they told me that we were all bound to keep the secrets of the society. And that I must refrain from watching them."

Ephraim felt a heaviness in his breathing, sensing Mary's rage and suppressing his own. He knew that in a matter of hours the salacious testimony would be spread across the county. But the sensational revelations were not Ephraim's primary concern. *Mary King knows all the secrets of the society,* Ephraim thought. *In her rage and jealousy, she will reveal them to the court and everyone in the District of Maine.*

"They want to convict Jacob and bring down the church," Ephraim told Aaron McKinney the following day in Buxton. "Cochrane's going to be indicted. Abigail Bond told the court she was at Jacob Cochrane's house when he undressed and took Eliza Hill to bed. This was said before a room packed with good citizens of the Commonwealth. The testimony excited onlookers eager to hear the juicy details of Cochrane's sex life. Bond also testified that Cochrane encouraged Ben Andrews to lodge with Eliza and Sally Dennett that afternoon and engage in wanton acts. Worse, it wasn't just the bawdy stories. The court wanted to know about the practices of Cochrane's society. Mary King gave them what they wanted."

"This is worse than what we expected," Aaron McKinney said. "I am grateful, Ephraim, that you went to Alfred and can tell us what we face. When the hearing in Alfred concludes, the enemy plans to lock Jacob up and keep him in jail until the Supreme Court convenes this spring. We can't let that happen."

"Are you certain the verdict will be negative?" Ephraim asked.

"Justice Granger already presumes Jacob guilty and will immediately issue a warrant for his arrest," Aaron said calmly. "Jacob will be brought before the court and told of the charges and trial before the Supreme Court. But Jacob could be released on bail until the spring."

"What do you think the amount of the bail will be?" Ephraim asked.

"Our opponents want Jacob in jail until the trial and will urge the judge to set a large amount. Maybe more than one thousand dollars," Aaron said. "And I don't know where we are going to find that much money."

"That's my job," Ephraim didn't hesitate. "I have raised money before, and Jacob's freedom is at stake. Count on me."

On February 19th, Ephraim saw Aaron's prediction unfold. Granger got right to business. "More witnesses could be called to testify before the court on the five charges, but I would like to move ahead," the Justice said. "The hearing was long, and much evidence presented, sufficient for a careful examination of the facts. I am persuaded to formally charge Jacob Cochrane for his flagrant behavior and abhorrent acts. I order Jacob Cochrane's arrest and summon him to appear before the bench as soon as possible."

Granger motioned Jeremiah Milliken to the bench and handed the constable a rolled-up paper tied with brown cord. "Do this with utmost haste," Granger instructed. Milliken, who left the courtroom with three assistants.

While still in a shock that Jacob Cochrane would be arrested and appear in court that very day, Ephraim was ready to fulfill his promise. He did not know the amount of bond Granger would require, but two men in court with him were ready to post whatever was necessary. Abner Woodsum, who had come from Boston to follow Jacob Cochrane, was both an enthusiast and a wealthy man. Cousin John was enlisted because his wife, Anna, was ill and convinced that she could not survive long without Cochrane's healing powers.

By late afternoon of the following day, a throng gathered to see Jacob Cochrane escorted into the courtroom. He did not look disheveled after his arrest and the journey from Buxton. His bold posture and unruffled appearance disguised all concerns. He displayed no outrage or exhibited an affected air. His black eyes studied the room slowly, hair combed back and complexion robust in the winter light. Ephraim could not tell if Cochrane saw Mary King, but her eyes were riveted on Cochrane. He took no notice of those who had abandoned his society, now sitting before the court. His calm face disguised any contempt or urge for revenge.

Jacob Cochrane stood for several minutes before Justice Granger entered the room and took his chair. Looking directly at Cochrane he began to speak. "Mr. Cochrane, you have been accused of crimes of an atrocious nature. For two days, the court has considered the charges against you, has taken testimony, heard witnesses and examined evidence. It is clear to this court that you have violated the positive laws of this state, subverted wholesome rules of modesty and good manners and failed to give due regard to the good of society. Your actions are detestable." Granger cleared his throat and resumed. "Your guilt, however, is not to be decided by this court. The charges against you are so grave that your fate will be decided by the Supreme Court of the District of Maine, which convenes in this room on the third Tuesday of May 1819."

One clap triggered another; applause filled the courtroom. Justice Granger's gavel restored calm. Cochrane was silent and motionless. "To ensure the defendant's appearance in court, he can be jailed or offer sureties. The sum is eight hundred dollars in one case and one thousand in the other. To ensure their appearance before the Supreme Court in May, four women are ordered to recognize the sum of thirty dollars each." Granger brought the gavel down hard on the bench. "Court is adjourned." The justice left the room.

Ephraim was pleased he had done his job and Jacob would remain free. Abner and John looked especially sober and shaken as they prepared to post enormous sums. Jeremiah Milliken and his three aides stepped up to take the defendant from the court. Cochrane and his ushers moved no more than twenty feet when the prophet broke his silence. "I stand at the door and preach. If any man hear my voice, open the door. Open the door." Cochrane raised his manacled wrists as high as he could. "The Anointed of the Lord will never be allowed to remain in jail." Ephraim watched as Cochrane was taken out the door, the setting sun a halo around the prophet's head.

∽

The pebbled pathway up to the courthouse traversed a bazaar scene. Vendors hawked crosses, religious relics, and objects of Cochrane worship. No virgin Mary was among the obscenely posed clay figures. One hawker displayed small, red cloth bags said to hold the locks of pubic hair of virgins overpowered by Cochrane's unquenchable lust.

Reverend Stinchfield sat in a stall giving out his *Cochranism Delineated,* an influential pamphlet describing Cochrane's "religious hydrophobia" and scandalous frauds. Other York County divines were there also peddling anti-Cochrane tracts. Some operated stalls where prayers were offered to support those with courage to witness against the devil incarnate.

Cochrane had his defenders. A banner stretched between trees identified Jacob McDaniel and Abner Wood as Cochranites, there to spread the teachings of the Society. Posters testifying to Cochrane's rectitude were distributed, and certificates of his good moral character were voluntarily offered and abundant. One given before Cochrane's arrest became part of the public record:

> "I hereby certify to all whom it may concern that I, Mary King, never did see or know Jacob Cochrane to do anything contrary to the character of a Christian, nor any about this house, and I do not believe there is any action by him or any about his house that is indecent or uncharitable.
>
> > "Voluntarily done by me, Mary King
> > "Saco, Dec. 13. 1818.
> > "Attest. Narcussa Robinsin,
> > "A true copy attest.
> > D. Granger, Justice of the Peace."

The notice stuck in Ephraim's craw. Mary King expressed her admiration of Jacob and swore to his good character just a month before she testified against him in Alfred. *Now her testimony before the Supreme Court,* Ephraim thought, *will send Jacob to jail. The bitch!*

Eben Coolbroth set up shop in the middle of grassy patch facing the courthouse. Under a makeshift canvass, he sold rum and cider as well as snacks, sausages, biscuits, and candy which people could eat hastily. The usual gang was there, Uriah Graffam,

Paul Dresser and Jabez Sawyer, enthused and repeating old jokes. Alexander was included in their company.

"Roger," Eben shouted, "I'm not sure I'll allow you any more rum. We'll be calling you Roger Plastered instead of Roger Plaisted."

"Let him alone, Eben," Paul said, "Roger wants to fully enjoy the most important trial ever seen in Maine."

"Important? It's rubbish. Let's be honest," Eben said, "What's going on here is not about justice. It's about quim. We are all drawn here by quim, wanting to hear about women and their sex."

"The preachers and lawyers say it is about public decency, godliness and moral rectitude." Paul said.

"Everybody has come to hear about sex, prostitution and adultery. Women will talk in open court of seductions and depraved experiences. Look at the list, most of the witnesses are women and they will be asked about things that have been hidden," Eben laughed. "Like quim, things kept in the dark too long."

"Maybe I'm sheltered. I don't think we are going to find out anything we don't already know," Jabez said.

"People get things wrong. Look at the fears of the Shakers who think the women were seduced by the devil," Eben said. "Their sex makes them demons of chaos and corruption. That's why they seldom do it."

"Yes. A woman's sex makes a virtuous life impossible for a male," Paul said sarcastically.

"Men's mistrust of women goes deeper than that," Eben continued. "A sailor told me of his travels to Japan where there is great fear of quim, fear that women might be cursed with a toothed quim, which could castrate a man on his wedding night. The sailor told me that one woman cursed with choppers in her quim went to see a blacksmith, who forged her an iron uterus which could break the teeth of her inner demon. She protected the precious member of her future suitor, saved herself from spinsterhood and denied herself no pleasure. In Japan there is a shrine dedicated to that blacksmith. It is so venerated it has been a place of pilgrimage for centuries."

"You are outrageous, Eben," Paul laughed.

"Alexander, you are the youngest man here. I'll bet you have never heard about the toothed quim," Eben laughed. "You have been warned."

"No, I haven't, but I'll take my chances, Eben," Alexander said. "I confess I have begun my search for the elusive snapping quim. I've heard that the toothless sort offers enormous pleasure."

This retort caught Paul just as he snorted another rum and his fierce cough sprayed his friends with liquor. Everybody howled.

"I've heard that the snapping quim also presents some dangers," Jabez smirked. "You don't want to harm yourself in any way, Alexander.'

"There is a problem if you can't find one," Alexander said. "I haven't even found a snapping pussy in training."

"You have rakish tendencies, Alexander," Paul's voice returned. "Like your older brother. Have you ever encountered a merkin? It's a wig, counterfeit hair, to disguise a woman's privy parts should she want of a proper bush. Whores shave to exterminate body lice or evidence of clap. If your quest takes you to Portland, you'll see one."

Ephraim heard the spirited rollicking as he approached Eben's stall. The camaraderie brought back memories of good friendship and fun. With the exceptional responsibilities he assumed, Ephraim was impelled to follow St. Paul's advice. *At a point in your life you must put certain things away,* he thought.

"Given the adventures you've set out for yourself, Alexander, you might follow your brother and be active in Jacob Cochrane's church. Within a harem as large as Cochrane's, chances are good you will find what you seek," Jabez joked.

"My good friends," Ephraim stepped forward, "You are always clever and fun, but I don't like such talk. You must be fair. Jacob Cochrane's trial has not even started. None of the charges against him are proved."

"You have a reputation for honesty, Ephraim Berry, but you have lost it," Eben scolded. "Your friends cannot understand your support, your blind devotion to this faker. But who am I, one rejected by God, to say what's shameful? That is how I think of Cochrane."

"He has never harmed anyone," Ephraim insisted.

"Yes, he has. He harmed our brother," Alexander said angrily. "Both of us were accomplices. Jacob Cochrane's henchmen brought down Abner with a devastating blow, but Cochrane's contagion and dishonesty drew us in. We let it happen. Aren't you ashamed, Ephraim? I am."

Ephraim didn't like what his brother said, especially before his old friends. "Alexander, we have talked of this before. No need to do it again," Ephraim was dismissive. "I've come to take you into the courthouse. There we will see justice done."

"Do that, Ephraim. Go," Eben waved his hand. "You seem prepared for this trial. We have some drinking to do before we can fully appreciate the spectacle." As the brothers left, Eben called out to Alexander, "If you want to join us later, we can take you home in our wagon."

"This is serious business," Ephraim said as he and Alexander walked up the slope toward the courthouse. "I know each of us wants a different outcome from the jury. I see it differently as a believer."

"But look around us. This is comical and freakish. This court deals with the District's most important matters and can send a man to prison. But I sense I am going to a circus," Alexander said.

The brothers didn't talk as they got closer to the courthouse, and it was harder to hear in the growing chaos. Ephraim led his brother up the steps, assuming the role of guide and juridical expert.

"I'm glad we've made it through the mess," Ephraim said as they passed the two constables guarding the door into the large room. "We won't have seats but can stand up front near the bailiff. You will see everything. I may have to move around a bit." They pushed toward the bar dividing the room, the judge's bench on one side and witness stand facing. "Had you been here before, you would see how much has been done to spruce up this old barn. It has been cleared for more space. The bench has been dignified, now polished wood and visible carving. The flag up there is new, too." The Massachusetts naval and maritime banner extended above the bench, a white field charged with a green pine tree and inscribed "An Appeal to Heaven."

Alexander saw the room filling up, but the reserved seats near the bar were still unoccupied. "I can see Mary and Jane are settled into a pew where they won't miss a thing," Alexander said, as he caught the attention of the women and waved.

"Yes. They got here early so I managed some good seats," Ephraim said with satisfaction. The brothers watched Eben's gang find places in a gallery stall. The Coolbroth's Corners bunch were perfectly set to enliven the proceedings.

⌒

A tall man dressed in black stood before the bench and called out, "Ladies and Gentlemen. The Supreme Judicial Court, within and for the County of York, in the Commonwealth of Massachusetts, is now in session." After the room quieted and everyone stood, the bailiff shouted, "The Honorable Judge George Putnam is presiding." The door behind the bench opened, and the judge entered the court. Judge George Putnam was of medium stature, with a handsome, rectangular face. His dark brows and eyes stood out in contrast to his short white wig, with three rows of curls in back.

"We are here on the third Tuesday of May 1819, for the trial of Jacob Cochrane who was arraigned on five indictments for adultery and open and gross lewdness. To each charge he has pleaded not guilty," the judge began.

"Five? Is that all?" Eben's yell was clamorous.

"Order in the court," the Judge was loud and stern. "We will have order in this court. Anyone who disrupts these proceedings will be removed by the bailiff." The room became silent.

"Now I would like to introduce the Counsel of this part of the Commonwealth—the Honorable Daniel Davis, Solicitor General."

Davis rose from a table in front of the bench to the judge's right and turned to the full room. "For the defendant we have two attorneys, Mr. John Holmes and Mr. George W. Wallingford. Please stand." The two lawyers were at a table to Judge Putnam's left.

"Since there are no preliminary matters to address, I ask the Bailiff to bring in the jury," the judge directed.

Mary and Jane watched the twelve men file into the jury box along the wall, not recognizing any among them. Ephraim saw them all and smiled to see David Boyd included in the panel. Cochrane's absence confounded everyone present.

The jury settled. Solicitor General Davis rose for his opening statement. "We are here to address a horrible crime, some of the most disgraceful crimes of the age," Davis began. "The defendant's crimes are particularly atrocious and detestable, because in the guise of a religious teacher he harmed innocent, vulnerable young women, seduced them, and led them down a road of debauchery and depravity. We are concerned with one young lady here, but the harm to her exposes a vast network of wickedness and subversion. Jacob Cochrane has created his own society, drawing in whole families, deluded and fanatic, who become part of his contagion. He corrupts the innocent, our communities, and the rules laid down by the founder of Christianity."

Mary and Jane looked at each other, nodding agreement. Ephraim frowned. Abigail Bond was seated at the witness stand— stiff and upright. For a woman in her early twenties she had a prudish manner, appearing unexposed to matters of sex, much less debauchery.

"Tell us, Miss Bond, about the sixth of December last, when you went to Mr. Cochrane's house in north Saco," Solicitor Davis started the examination.

"I arrived at the house at nine o'clock in the morning," Abigail's words seemed practiced to Ephraim. "Jacob Cochrane came out of a back room and said that Eliza Hill was sick. He wanted all of us, there were probably twenty, to pray for her. He went to Eliza's bed. I could see because the door was left open. Everybody prayed, but I watched, he got into bed with her." Like everyone else, Mary and Jane gasped when they heard Abigail's words.

"Did you see Cochrane undress himself, expose himself? Was his conduct indecent in any way?" Davis asked, coaching the perfect response.

"He had his drawers on. I didn't see them down—everything else was bare. Everyone was told to pray as he got in bed and held her. The embrace, moving around and the mumbling was intended to sooth her. It must have gone on for more than an hour when the murmuring changed. There must have been a convulsion in the bed, with all the tossing and turning. Next was an outburst, and Eliza cried out 'praise the Lord, praise the Lord.' They were breathing hard, she was panting, and shaken when they got out of bed. Still praising the Lord, they came into the room where everyone was praying," Abigail was calm, but her words aroused the room.

"Were you treated to any of this, Ephraim?" Alexander turned, whispering to his brother. Ephraim did not share Alexander's chuckle.

"What can you tell us about Eliza Hill's appearance, aside from her immodesty? Did she look well?" Davis asked.

"She looked flushed, but Cochrane said she had taken cold. It was because she slept alone. He said one of the brethren must go in and lodge with her. Ben Andrews volunteered, took her into the other room and laid with her. When they returned to the room Andrews proclaimed the dead had been raised," Abigail finished.

"I'm sure that wasn't the first time," Alexander joked.

Ephraim focused on the jury, catching Boyd's eyes, wondering if they found the testimony credible.

Nothing new emerged from Defense Counsel Wallingford's questioning of Abigail. She did tell the court that "Eliza looked as well as ever" when Cochrane took her to bed for two hours, and that, "Sally Dennett went with them."

"Jacob Cochrane had a goddam convent," Eben roared from the gallery. The counsel for the defendant returned to his place amid the clamor.

The Solicitor General's last two questions related to Cochrane's society. First, Davis asked, "Miss Bond, were you threatened in any way if you revealed what happened that morning?"

"No," Abigail said, "But Mr. Cochrane said we were not to talk about what takes place in the society. If we did talk about that our names would be blotted out of the Lamb's Book of Life."

"Did you belong to the society and were you forced to leave because you told tales of what happened there?" the Solicitor asked.

"I did belong to Mr. Cochrane's society, but I left because I saw too much improper conduct," Abigail said.

"Your Honor, we conclude the Commonwealth's case of lewd and lascivious behavior against the prisoner," the Solicitor General said as he walked to his chair.

"Abigail Bond does not appear to be a false witness," Alexander jabbed his brother. "She's not foolish either. She showed great restraint, not telling any of your society's dark secrets."

"Her version of the story is warped," Ephraim said. "Once Jacob's defense is presented, God will guide the jury to the truth."

Judge Putnam called Mr. Wallingford to present his case for the defense.

"My call to appear before this court as counsel to the defendant was unexpected, just a short time ago. The window for assembling facts and preparing for this trial was small. This is unfortunate for the defendant, especially because of the grave nature of the charges against him. The morals of society are at issue as well as the prisoner's future, his hopes and prospects in life. The defendant must be tried upon the evidence presented, not on popular stories, gossip or vague reports.

"The counsel for the defense expects to show, through testimony by fair and unimpeachable witnesses, that the story of Abigail Bond is not credible. There was no lewd conduct at Jacob Cochrane's house. Eliza was in feeble health, her parents placed her under the care of Mr. Cochrane, a physician. She slept in a truckle bed at the foot of the bed where the defendant slept with his wife. Miss Hill took ill in the night and was discovered in the morning, her head covered with blood. She was moved into the bed with Mrs. Cochrane. Jacob treated her with urgency and great humanity.

"The jury may not fully share or understand the tenants of Mr. Cochrane's religion. In this country people are free to believe what they wish, insofar as the practices do not intrude on the beliefs of others or subvert the morals of society," Mr. Wallingford concluded.

Deidamia Lane was called and sworn as the first witness for the defense. Miss Lane was at the Cochrane house on the sixth of December. She testified that Eliza Hill had been staying with the Cochranes for a month because of illness. The night before Abigail Bond's arrival, Eliza got worse, started bleeding and then was put in Mr. Cochrane's bed with his wife.

"Did Mr. Cochrane get into bed with Eliza or touch her in any offending way?" the defense counsel asked.

"No. He leaned over the bed trying to soothe her—maybe for ten minutes. I was there the whole time," Deidamia said.

Why doesn't anyone mention Jacob's special healing powers? Ephraim wondered.

"Who else was present during this crisis?" Wallingford asked.

"Ben Andrews was there and some others," the witness said.

"Is Eliza Hill in Saco these days, and can you speak to her health?"

"Yes. Eliza is fine and in good health," Miss Lane said.

"Did Jacob Cochrane get into bed with Eliza Hill when Abigail Bond was present?" Wallingford asked.

"Mr. Cochrane did not get into bed with Eliza. I would have seen it. I was in the house the whole time she was there." The defense had no more questions.

The Solicitor General asked Deidamia about lewd conduct, Cochrane's state of dress and whether he got in bed with Eliza Hill. When he asked about Cochrane's church, the young woman looked directly at Mr. Davis, saying she belonged to Cochrane's society, and that she was not involved in secret meetings. She knew of no secret oaths and had not seen any paper by which members of the society were bound. Deidamia was excused and stepped down from the witness stand. Ephraim thought the testimony proper, the witness forthright, modest and sincere.

Dorcas Underwood was not as young or as fair as Deidamia. She was bigger, and all the brown hair piled on top of her head and flowing down the sides of her round, tawny face suggested she spent little time grooming herself for court or pursuing men. The glow of her cheeks, red lips and dark, flashing eyes did give Dorcas a strange charm.

She was sworn and testified that she was regularly at Cochrane's house which welcomed many visitors and was present December sixth. Dorcas told the counsel for the defense she was at the house the night Eliza bled at the nose and mouth. Her facts were consistent with Deidamia's testimony. The Solicitor General repeated the questions about Cochrane's society and got the same answers.

With the next question, Ephraim noticed the jury's serious and attentive disposition change. "Miss," Davis started, then cleared his throat. "I'm sorry, Mrs. Underwood. I hear you are frequently a companion of Mr. Cochrane. Have you been around the country with him?"

"Yes, all around the country," Dorcas said, her red lips spreading into a wide, lush smile. She raised her head to catch the stares of everyone she could. The catcalls and whistles were immediate. Judge Putnam pounded his gavel but found it hard to stop the raucous cries. Dorcas's saucy manner kept the crowd's attention as she sashayed her way from the witness stand to her chair.

"That's a spiritual wife," Mary said to Jane.

The testimony of Ben Andrews was critical to the defense's hopes of discrediting Abigail Bond's story. His solid, upright manner and resonant voice lent his words gravity, but his answers added nothing to what the court already knew. "Did you go to bed with Eliza Hill?" was the counsel's last question.

"No," Andrews said.

"Do you belong to Cochrane's society and his secret meetings?" the Solicitor General asked.

"I belong to the society that some people say has secret meetings," Andrews said. "We have meetings for church order, public or secret, you may call them what you please."

"That's all for now," the Solicitor General said. "I'd like to call Miss Abigail Bond back to the stand." As soon as Abigail was seated Mr. Davis returned to the subject of lewdness. "Are you positive, Miss Bond, that you saw Jacob Cochrane in bed with Eliza Hill and Sally Dennet?"

"Yes, I'm certain, "Abigail said. "I was there when Sally got up. She asked me to help pin her clothes. I did."

"Since you were a member of the society, Miss Bond, could you tell us if its leaders require an oath from those who become members?" the Solicitor continued.

"Yes, they call it an oath," Abigail replied. "Mr. Cochrane holds a Bible, has you put your hand on it, and makes you repeat after him. When that is finished, Mr. Andrews writes your name on a piece of paper."

"Can you tell us about their creed, any part of it?" Davis asked.

"I cannot tell you entirely. The part I remember best is that anyone who leaves the church, or reveals its secrets, would find his name blotted out of the Lamb's Book of Life," Abigail said.

When Ben Andrews was called back to the stand to take more questions from the Solicitor General, Ephraim knew that testimony was moving against Jacob. Abigail's story was consistent and her character was supported by credible witnesses.

"Mr. Andrews," Davis asked, "Did you write down the names of society members, as the last witness told us, and are you bound to keep the list a secret?"

"I wrote down the articles of faith as instructed by Mr. Cochrane, which were for church governance. When someone joined and agreed to them, I recorded their name," Andrews said.

"Your side is losing," Alexander whispered to his brother. "Your friend can't stick to his story."

"Could you tell the court, Mr. Andrews, about those who choose to leave the society? Are they punished in any way? Is there any coercion?" Mr. Davis asked.

"The names that we write down are of those who are in fellowship, members of our society. Nothing is declared against anyone who chooses not to be in communion with us. It is understood that all who once belonged, who then step out into the world and behave badly, their names would be blotted out of the Lamb's Book of Life," Andrews finished. The court had heard before that the society was held together by informal ties. Now everyone in the room knew that secret bonds existed and were treated as solemn articles of faith. Ephraim hung his head.

"Heretics," "Oh Blood of Jesus," "Rot in Hell, Jacob Cochrane," rang from the gallery. Outcries from every part of the court swelled, mixed with shouts of "Praise the Lord" and "Glory be." Judge Putnam slammed his gavel. The bailiff and two constables rushed to remove the agitators from the room.

"It sounds like you found room in the court for some of Cochrane's defenders, Ephraim," Alexander observed.

"Many people love Jacob. We are all bound together and stand behind him and his truth," Ephraim said.

"Except for those who have been beaten and raped by enthusiasts. Is that part of Jacob Cochrane's truth?" Alexander snarled.

That Jacob's church was responsible for acts of individual abuse was a message Ephraim found hard to ignore, but he didn't respond to his brother. And he reflected that Alexander also dismissed the important fact that through Jacob many people encountered God.

"Would the Solicitor General call the next witness," Judge Putnam commanded. The room calmed. Aaron Libby took the stand and was sworn.

Aaron Libby grinned a lot, which had a peculiar effect on his smooth face. Clear deep creases highlighted his slanted eyes and as his smile broadened, his lips almost disappeared, further exposing his prominent teeth. The small chin was cradled by another crease, crescent shaped and extending his jowl from one cheekbone to the other. Flaring from the sides of his head were large ears and his high forehead was crowned with a mop of thin, brown hair. He looked void of intelligence as he picked his nose.

"Did you belong to Cochrane's society?" the Solicitor asked.

"Y-y-yes, I did," Aaron stuttered.

"Could you tell the court the methods the society used to ensure members kept the promises made when they joined?" the Solicitor asked.

Ephraim could not think why this witness would be called and how he strengthened Cochrane's case. He knew nothing of Aaron's experience in the society. He never had heard of him as an apostate or suffering because of his disaffection.

"I expect," Mr. Davis took a deep breath, expanding his chest to its fullest. "I expect to prove that this society of Jacob Cochrane's was grounded on principles of debauchery. Because of that stark reality, members suffered, members left and continue to leave his church." He turned so all could see his smug expression.

"I object your Honor," John Holmes, the co-counsel for the defense stood. "I do not see that the charges made by the Solicitor General have any bearing on the case before the court. Mr. Cochrane was not indicted for such a crime."

"Objection sustained," Judge Putnam declared.

The Solicitor General's arrogance was undiminished. "Mr. Libby, did Cochrane tell you that the society intended to embrace debauchery and lewdness?"

"Yes," Aaron said.

"Did you hear Cochrane condemn marriage and say that it was useless?" the Solicitor asked.

"I have heard him say that people who were married could stay that way. Those who were not should stay unmarried. He says scripture forbids marriage." Cochrane's views of marriage were not unknown in York County. But Ephraim observed the truly negative reaction of the crowd, the muttering and the shaking of heads throughout the room. Opposition to Cochrane's views was strong.

"Mr. Libby," Defense Counsel Holmes assumed the floor, "Did Mr. Cochrane forbid your marrying?"

"He told me I ought not to think of such a thing. He told me I ought to leave the girl I was keeping company with," Aaron said.

"Did you dissolve your courtship?" Holmes asked.

"Yes," Aaron answered.

"Was this girl of a bad character?" Holmes continued.

"I don't know," Aaron looked puzzled.

"Did Mr. Cochrane tell you much about his society—the one to establish debauchery?" Holmes asked.

"Yes," Aaron responded.

"Where did he say it was?" Holmes asked.

"In the United States," Aaron's quick answer prompted laughter.

"Did he say that the one he belonged to was of that description?" Holmes asked.

"I do not remember that he did," Libby finished.

Ephraim noticed that Aaron didn't say he was pressured by Jacob Cochrane. None of the witnesses before the court, either for the prosecution or the defense, former society members or not, mentioned being harmed or molested, or openly threatened, by Cochrane's church. None of the twenty who took the stand, not Robert Cleaves, Elisha Hill, Polly Moulton, Abrathar Woodsum, false witness or truth teller, mentioned any direct experience with Cochrane that promoted abuse. Only Eliza Hill and Sally Dennet were linked in testimony to sexual predation, and they were never seen in court.

"Jacob Cochrane will be brought down, even though no one speaks in court of the worst injuries, and the violence he spawned," Alexander stared at his brother.

"Eliza Hill and Sally Dennet, two of Cochrane's alleged victims do not want to talk of their personal relations or spiritual life," Ephraim bristled. "If you wanted to see Jacob crucified, and that's important to you, why didn't you bring our brother, Abner, to testify?

"You are detestable, Ephraim," Alexander's eyes flashed. "What in your nature makes you so mean? In your heart you could never want to see Abner on the stand and have him relive his abuse in public. He could not endure another torture."

"We could see if the jury, unanimously, would blame Cochrane for Abner's troubles," Ephraim responded.

"How can you think like this? Even if Abner were strong and able to defend himself, he would never want his attack known, to be regarded as unmanly or at fault. And what about our family? They would be humiliated and ashamed," Alexander was dumbfounded.

"I just want you to understand how complicated this case is. There are so many elements to consider and things not public which must be protected," Ephraim said with condescension.

"And what about you? You would have no stature in Buxton if Cochrane goes to jail. You have been treated as an honest broker by this court, and that is how you got me in here. Are you an honest broker, Ephraim?" Alexander said. "I am not sure that you are aware of how much you have to lose."

The Solicitor General called two more witnesses, Eliza Barker and Eunice Bond. Their testimonies repeated that given by previous witnesses for the Commonwealth concerning secret meetings, the society's covenant, the Lamb's Book of Life, treatment of apostates and Cochrane's fierce opposition to marriage.

When Mary King was called to the stand, Ephraim prepared for his worst fears to be realized. He saw no anger on her face as she sat before the court. But he knew from her testimony before the grand jury in February that she was angry, her words infected with betrayal and degradation. He remembered her talking about that night in July when she discovered Jacob and Abigail Clark together, naked on the floor. Cochrane had no time for her. *"I was expelled from Cochrane's paradise—driven away and then told to say nothing of what I had learned, nothing about the mysteries,"* Ephraim remembered Mary's words.

Mary wasn't present on that May afternoon to talk about adultery. That was business for the following day. Her face was expressionless and without color, disclosing nothing of the betrayal that brought her to the witness stand. Ephraim thought her still beautiful but no longer luminous. The Solicitor General wanted to hear about the precepts of Cochrane's church. "What can you tell the court about the secret meetings of Jacob Cochrane's society?"

"I can remember on a certain Sabbath, Mr. Cochrane told those present that some members of the society had got into the habit of tattling and that he wanted it stopped." Mary's mien was serious, but her tone gave no hint of jealousy or retribution. "He thought brethren and sisters should be bound to keep each other's secrets. At a meeting the next Thursday evening the same subject was again raised. There was agreement. A paper was drawn up and many signed it and swore to keep all things secret," Mary said.

"What was the substance of this writing?" the Solicitor asked.

"Those who signed it became bound to Jacob Cochrane, Aaron McKinney, and Joseph Bryant to keep all things secret," Mary said.

"Can you repeat any of it?" the Solicitor asked.

"Yes," Mary's voice was clear, but unanimated. "It was like this: 'The Society of Free Brethren and Sisters, knowing it is a duty to keep the secrets of the Lord, for the secrets of the Lord are with them that love the Lord. Therefore, I do voluntarily covenant with Jacob Cochrane, Aaron McKinney, and Joseph Bryant, to keep the secrets of the society, and if I disclose any of the secrets of the society, or of the members thereof, that my name may be blotted out of the Lamb's Book of Life.'"

Ephraim watched Mary and wondered if she was getting even with Cochrane for her expulsion from paradise. Jacob offered special gifts and through a new world of physical pleasure Mary's sins were forgiven—and she found ecstasy. Her prophet's special gifts were shared by other women. Did she become jealous? Did Cochrane's intimacy with the others make her feel less beautiful? Discarded?

Isaac had made him feel worthless his whole life. The little Toad had always wanted to feel big and special. Cochrane brought him that, stature and pride. Now Jacob was in great peril and beautiful Mary was responsible.

⌒

Judge Putnam adjourned the court for one hour. The jury retired from the courtroom, and from the presence of the judge and lawyers, to consider the evidence and discuss the final verdict. With the time expired, the judge returned to his bench and the jury filed into the jury box.

"Mr. Prescot," Judge Putnam addressed the foreman of the jury, "Has the jury agreed and is it ready to report?"

"No. The jury has not agreed," Stephen Prescot replied. The foreman was glum.

"What is the difficulty?" the judge asked.

"One of the jurors, Mr. Boyd, says he cannot in good conscience convict a man on the strength of the testimony of one witness." Prescot said. "He has been insistent."

"That's foolishness," the judged sounded irked. "When people lie they can be tried for perjury. There are rules. And one witness, if believed, is sufficient to decide a case."

"As a member of the jury I have the responsibility to weigh the evidence," David Boyd bolted up. 'I cannot agree that the testimony of one witness should send a man to jail, especially when the witness appears doubtful." The juror's interruption was stunning. Some in the room cried out for justice. A few cheered.

Nobody noticed the faint smile that crossed Ephraim's face. He felt a rush of satisfaction at having done his job. But there was more to it. *"The Anointed of the Lord will never be allowed to remain in jail,"* he remembered.

The judge sent the jury from the room, but they were gone no more than five minutes. There was consultation between the judge and the foreman, and exchanges by the lawyers, but no agreement was reached. It was deadlock.

The gavel came down hard and the room was quiet. "I would like to take a moment to tell everyone in the room about our courts and the rule of law in America," Judge Putnam said with great solemnity "The laws of our country are the result of centuries of thoughtful court decisions, aimed at justice for all. The law incorporates the accumulated wisdom of the legislative process and the conclusions of serious ethical debates. Our laws are not primitive—but highly developed. The courts' obligation is to see that our corpus of law is sustained and revered. Your duty my fellow citizens, I suggest, is to take off your shoes. For the ground on which you stand is sacred."

It appeared that many in the court didn't know what the judge was talking about, but they did know they were chastised.

"In a criminal case there can be no verdict without unanimous agreement among the jury," Judge Putnam said. "Order in the court. I will have order. We have a mistrial. We also have four other indictments to consider against the defendant. That will happen tomorrow morning. I order a second jury to be impaneled—a jury which I trust will adhere to the long-established customs of our system. The court is adjourned."

SEVEN

The news spread fast. The Supreme Court jury failed to find Jacob Cochrane guilty of lewd and lascivious behavior. And his followers were enthusiastic when Cochrane immediately called for a celebration. A barn was found near Alfred. Arrangements for the banquet followed a well-established pattern set down by the Prophet. Cochrane called the feast a Passover, where all partake at one table the roasted Paschal Lamb with bitter herbs, large quantities of mutton, bread and wine. Ephraim knew the feast marked the Israelites reaching their promised land.

There was no empty place at the large table set up in the shape of a hollow square, the configuration of King Solomon's Temple. The center, called the Sanctum Sanctorum, is where the lamb was slaughtered, and its blood collected.

A dozen celebrants were accommodated on each of the table's four sides, where they could gaze at the Holy of Holies, contemplate their deliverance from evil, and offer their devotion to the ever-living God. It was a scene of peace and place where followers found refreshment from their labors. A sanctuary to focus love and offer devotion to the eternal God, was also a place to imbibe that evening. It was Ephraim's job to keep the wine flowing.

The drinking and merrymaking was well underway when Cochrane stood silent and imperious before his place at the table, until he had everyone's attention. "'I put on righteousness and it clothed me: my judgement was a robe and a diadem,' just as Job has directed. And we know from the New Testament—from Revelations—that the diadem is a badge of royalty," the prophet thundered. Cochrane's hair was parted in the middle, pulled back and crowned with a wreath of laurel painted gold. He wore a scarlet tunic, a blue toga wrapped his left shoulder and draped from his right, out-stretched arm.

"We are in a consecrated place, a representation of King Solomon's Temple," the prophet lowered his head. "It was in the courtyard of the Temple of Jerusalem where the sacrifice of the lamb took place and its blood was collected in sacred cups. This blood, sprinkled on the door-posts of God's people, protected them, and empowered the exodus to the promise land. In this hour you will be protected and your path to heaven cleared."

At Cochrane's signal a man from each side of the table stood, passed into the Sanctum Sanctorum, and was anointed as a shepherd. Stalwarts Aaron McKinney, John Bryant, Ben Andrews, and Aaron Boynton held cups filled with blood. They dipped into the cups and marked the foreheads of everyone on their side of the table with a spot of blood. "It will come to pass that you will see the land which the Lord has promised," Cochrane's voice rang out. "Raise yourselves. Raise yourselves up. You have been delivered."

Two men entered the courtyard carrying a long wooden tray on which was stretched the roasted lamb, four feet in length, its flesh seared reddish brown with patches of blackened crust. It was placed before the prophet. "My Brethren and Sisters, rejoice and Praise the Lord. Feast and indulge for the Lord's gifts are bounteous." Congregants cheered and clapped, some splashed by wine thrown up from the pounded tables. "You will remember this night—this wonderful supper. It crowns a day when piety, virtue and truth were exalted." Cochrane glowed before the exuberance and acclamation, while waiting for quiet in the barn.

"Think of this night as a time of renewal, an occasion for a new commitment to our church—and to me. This night brings revival, and a new covenant. God has lifted us and embraces us in our sharing of this food and wine. This is the feast of the Lord." Cochrane saluted with his cup.

People were still feasting when Aaron McKinney gave a signal and five basins appeared. Several men formed a chain and passed buckets of water and several pitchers. Extra full pails were placed on the barn floor.

"Jesus taught his disciples servanthood and humility," Cochrane said as he got up from the table and began removing his garments. He methodically folded his robe and tunic in sacramental fashion, placing them on the table. He solemnly moved to the center of the hollow square and the awaiting basins where the bright lantern light reflected off his smooth and well-defined body, covered only by a white loin cloth. "Christ asks in Luke 22, 'For who is greater, the one who is at the table or the one who serves? Is it not the one who is at the table? But I am among you as one who serves.'" Cochrane pivoted slowly to face each side of the table. "We are servants for Jesus, which is how we must think of ourselves and how we must act," Cochrane bowed.

Five people filed into the center of the feasting crowd, Dorcas Underwood, Robert Cleaves, Deidamia Lane, Samuel Lowell, all trial witnesses for Cochrane's defense, and the holdout juror, David Boyd. Dorcas Underwood was the first Cochrane knelt before.

"Are you going to wash my feet?" Dorcas asked as Cochrane lifted her right knee, one hand behind her ankle.

"As Jesus said, 'If I was with thee not, thou hast no part with me,'" Cochrane said.

"Well, I wouldn't want that," Dorcas looked up at Cochrane's face. She giggled as she stretched her foot, trying to touch Cochrane's loin cloth with her toe. Cochrane frowned, then took a small pitcher, filled it with water from the pail, and slowly poured the water over Dorcas's foot. He took the towel tucked under the knot of his loin cloth and patted her dry. He repeated these actions with the next three in line. Ephraim attended his prophet, refilling the pail of water and passing the ladle.

The smooth cadence of the ritual halted upon reaching David Boyd. Cochrane jerked, repelled by Boyd's rotting feet. The odor was cadaverous. Black, swollen flesh with scales and dark red sores were exposed when Boyd removed his socks. Those nearby recoiled from the stench, yet Cochrane motioned Boyd to extend his foot, and poured water over the corrupted tissue turning purple-black as it streamed into the basin. Cochrane's patience showed no limits. He smiled, gave Ephraim the towel to wipe Boyd's foot and returned to his place at the banquet table. The inadvertent whisk of his loin cloth suggested Cochrane was not certain of his immunity to contamination.

Boyd's feet must be miraculous, Ephraim mused. *Those stinky hooves brought Cochrane his freedom. Other jurors had to be tortured by Boyd's stinking feet, all fearing infection through extended exposure in the small room where they deliberated. The resentment must have been extraordinary and palpable, knowing the loner would never agree with them on a verdict.*

Carefully unfolding his garb and robing himself in his ceremonial vestments, Cochrane addressed his followers. "Jesus asked, 'Do you understand what I just did for you?'" the prophet's voice resonated. "'I wash your feet—like a servant. Your servant. You should wash each other's feet. I am an example for you. It is a blessing'"

Cochrane dramatically extended his arms, drooping his head to the side in emulation of the crucified Christ. He raised his head, slowly opening his eyes before he spoke.

"You know that my trial is not over. With the rise of the morning sun I could be betrayed by someone in our fellowship. Someone joined with us in the Lamb's Book of Life could play Judas, might divulge our divinely bestowed truths and rupture the flesh of our communal body," Cochrane paused to hear the collective sighing, a fundamental life-sustaining reflex. His eyes explored the crowd, before he hung his head again. Widespread whispering became a hum, then a cloud of lament drifting to the rafters of the barn.

"Praise Jesus," Cochrane broke the silence. "This is the feast of the Lord, the celebration of our renewal. Start the music and dance."

Everyone stood but Abrathar Woodsom who fell back on his chair, crashing on the floor and pulling Abigail Bond with him. Her raucous laugh broke Cochrane's trance. The tables were removed for dancing. A man on a bench fiddled, a boy drummer stood nearby, inviting another fiddler to join in. With two horns, the ensemble was complete and the music, as well as the marching, began. Revelers young and old joined the party, to cavort and rollick into the night.

⌐

The festivities in full swing, Cochrane left the barn unnoticed, trailed by his wise men, Aaron McKinney, John Bryant and Ben Andrews. Ephraim followed. The prophet stopped by an out-building to let his cohorts catch up and explain his abrupt departure.

"The jig's up," Cochrane's voice was hard. "I am getting out of this nonsense and doing it now. I need you to make it happen, and you can't fail me."

McKinney, Bryant, and Ephraim stood dumfounded, their faces blank in astonishment. Ben Andrews appeared less surprised by Cochrane's declaration.

"There are still charges against you, Jacob. Court isn't over, there is another day," Ephraim said. "You won't suffer defeat. Just use your powers."

"Ephraim, you have kept me well-informed of the proceedings. You have done a good job, particularly managing to get a believer on the jury." Cochrane's words did not hide his condescension.

"Boyd stood up for you. He believes in you and would never let you go to jail," Ephraim said.

"With those hideous feet I am surprised he stands at all," Cochran snapped. "Ephraim, you hold a simple view. The trial is rigged to pull me down. Aaron McKinney told you that. You saw Ben questioned by the Solicitor General, who is after our church. Understand the sinister work that is being carried out. I will not subject myself to more abuse. And I don't want the future of our faith defended by the actions of a putrid leper. Let's go into the house and get some rum."

The men were given beverages and left alone in the parlor. "Where are you going? Aaron asked.

"I am going into hiding. I cannot leave my flock," Cochrane was quick to answer. "You must help me stay here, help me tend the needs of my followers. I cannot be arrested. I must disappear tonight, while it is still dark."

"I must be in court tomorrow morning, first thing," Ben Andrews said. "There will be no immediate suspicion and you will have more time to get away from Alfred. Ephraim can stay with you. He won't be missed in court." Andrews and Joseph Bryant left.

"I don't understand what is going on. Jacob, why go into hiding?" Ephraim asked. "How can you be so detached? You ignored the Grand Jury in February. I never understood why you didn't hire an attorney or find someone with legal knowledge. Now it has come to this," Ephraim couldn't hide his exasperation.

"Can you imagine, Ephraim, and this is not a matter of your capacity, finding anyone in York or Cumberland County who has the required achievements or stature? I know of no one who has sufficient intellect to speak for me," Cochrane said.

"You will forfeit an eighteen-hundred-dollar bond," Ephraim snapped. "You have bragged how you raise great sums of money instantly. But I have done that for you. It's not easy, and you never show your appreciation."

"My risk involves more than cash. Besides Ephraim, you found the bondholders, got their money. You proved you can deal with them. It is a trivial matter," Cochrane said.

You never know what Jacob finds trivial or what sparks his anger, Ephraim thought. Everyone remembered the triumphal procession into Porter which turned disastrous, because Ephraim had picked the wrong white donkey. *It was my fault Jacob ended up in shit.*

"I know that you never needed help responding to the government's charges. You could do it alone. But it has come to this—a situation where it will be more difficult to spread God's Word," Ephraim said. "What has kept you, Jacob, from performing a miracle?" Ephraim's question was audacious but sincere. "You could show everyone again that you have been anointed and under the protection of the Lord. So many have seen your miracles—with their very eyes—and believe in your powers."

"Yes, Ephraim. You have known from the beginning that I have great powers. You were at the funeral of little Catherine when people heard me talk to God. You understand a great deal about me," Jacob responded. "Early on you saw me admonished by Reverend Phinney for trying to cast the Devil out of a man. He was angry that I failed. I reminded Clement that Christ empowered his disciples to cast out demons and perform miracles. The Bible tells us that these delegated powers do not always work." Ephraim had never forgotten Jacob's encounter in the Scarborough churchyard.

"You have worked with me on occasion to make sure that miracles do happen, and the belief of my followers is strengthened," Jacob said. "And maybe your assistance wasn't always sufficient in meeting my modest expectations. I think the unfortunate incident at Lake Sebago could have been avoided had you and Ben Andrews been more diligent."

Ephraim's mind snapped back a year. *Yes*, Ephraim thought. *I remember the contempt your body exuded as you walked from the lake—passing me by without a nod.*

"That calamity is something I have never forgotten, Jacob," Ephraim said. "Others share the blame, but I am sorry for my failings."

"The Supreme Court is not a good stage for me—things cannot be easily arranged there," Jacob continued, oblivious to Ephraim's criticism and apology. "It is alien territory. I will not take the chance of a failed miracle in a mobbed courtroom. I would be doomed, and convicted, if it appeared I had lost my power."

"But your powers are so great, Jacob," Ephraim insisted. "You can save yourself. Isn't that what the disciples wanted when they saw Jesus suffering in the garden, weeping, his eyes streaming blood—that Christ not allow himself to be crucified? Surely you understand that you don't have to make that sacrifice."

Jacob looked at Ephraim with an indulgent smile. "They pleaded, not knowing God's will. At tonight's supper believers would have acted like the disciples had they known what lies before me. We must not forget God's lesson. Jesus wanted to emphasize to his followers that it was God's will that mattered, not his own. We must leave this in God's hands." Jacob was silent for some time, posing as if he had just pronounced a benediction. "Don't just stand there with your mouth agape. I am sure Ben can find you of some help. Every vessel is to be filled according to its measure. Put your mind to it and get out of here."

⌒

"What's happening?" Jane exclaimed.

A sharp jolt was followed by several strong shakes. The courtroom shuddered, timbers creaked, separating molding from walls. An hourglass crashed to the floor when the table before the judge's bench jumped. Papers lifted from hardwood counters scattered across the front of the chamber. Most alarming were the squawking birds, wasting themselves on the crowd as they were tossed from their nests in the swinging chandeliers.

"An earthquake," Mary declared. "I have never felt an earthquake since I married and moved from Scarborough."

"It is God. He is here," a voice from the gallery screamed. "Save us Jesus."

"They never happen here," Jane said, "I have lived in Buxton all of my life. It is disturbing."

"The ones in Portland and Scarborough are usually small, but always reported in the newspaper. They last only a few seconds. You feel the shock most when you are still and sitting down," Mary said.

"The quaking is scary because it is unexpected," Jane said.

"I got used to them growing up, and I read about them," Mary said. "Some experts see them as a warning. The birds here must be lazy, because birds, and barnyard animals also, are supposed to sound the alarm. I never heard those bird sounds. And frogs cease to croak before a quake. But we had no frogs near our house."

"I'm sure that people are afraid of the big quakes," Jane said, "They could have some supernatural origin."

"Yes. One superstition is that they are brought by the gods, who get angry when people give up their belief. Quakes happen when man pays no attention to God," Mary said.

"It doesn't look like they got the attention of anyone in this court," Jane said. She looked around and saw Mary's wide grin. "Jacob Cochrane couldn't have been responsible for this. He would have instructed the gods to wait until the room was full."

"I'm not superstitious, but I think it is a bad omen," Mary grimaced. "I am surprised Ephraim is not in his usual spot. He missed the quake, and the chance to tell us our destiny. I suppose he has more important things to do. Only God knows what."

"It has been four months since he foisted a baby upon you. How are you managing?" Jane asked.

"Isaiah gets sweeter by the day. He has a very easy nature and gives me no problems," Mary said. "I am grateful in many ways, but that surprise is still hard. I love the baby, but I cannot really forgive Ephraim. Yet the baby is so real and uncomplicated. He is more affectionate than either Samuel or Mirinda."

"How do you deal with Ephraim and your resentment?" Jane asked.

"I can hide it most of the time, in a drawer that I seldom have to open. Like Ephraim, it's in the dark, kept out of sight. He is never home, and even when he is, I don't have to be close to him."

"But you don't have a separate bed," Jane said.

"We are in the same bed. At night the drawer opens, but I keep away. I don't want to see inside or think about its contents." Sitting beside Mary, Jane could feel her sister-in-law shudder.

"I can feel you trembling, Mary. I imagine you are thinking about that open drawer," Jane said. "Ephraim has no sense of your discontent?"

"No. And I fear that is part of the problem. It's not in his nature," Mary's sighed. "It will always be like this. I'd like to imagine him out of his own mental drawer, but it is unlikely I will ever see that." Mary threw her head back. The large brass chandelier above was still, its flameless candles in place; there were more than fifty with no way to light them. She could see no pulley to lower the four-foot span, no scaffold nearby. No twenty-five-foot-long candle lighter was to be seen. What a dazzling blaze it might have cast. "There was so much light when I fell in love with Ephraim. Now there is shadow and gloom. It only gets worse."

"I cannot understand the change in my brother," Jane whispered.

"Little Isaiah is now a part of my life. A new light," Mary said. "But life doesn't get any easier or less complicated. I am pregnant again. Ephraim forced himself on me. It was terrible and disgusting how he pounced. A loveless experience, but the innocent I carry will flourish. I know the baby will be loving and kind." Mary started sobbing. "My mind is riddled with dark memories, but the baby will brighten the house. Ephraim, I suffer, but a beautiful child will make me happy."

Mary didn't notice the filled courtroom until the proceedings started. Once she had recomposed herself, she noticed that Ephraim was nowhere around. She saw Alexander with Eben and his unruly friends in the gallery.

The second jury was called and the second bill of indictment against Jacob Cochrane was read: for lying in bed with Abigail Clark, a married woman, and committing adultery and lewdness. The Solicitor General told the jury that Cochrane should be found guilty. "Cochrane is a pest of society," he said, "and he should be removed to a place where no one will be endangered."

Witnesses Eunice Bond and Mary King were again called, Eunice again relived her shock of finding Cochrane and Abogail twice in bed "in the most immodest and detestable posture."

Mary King repeated her testimony of "finding Cochrane and Mrs. Clark in the middle of the night lying on the floor, only linen covering their nakedness." When Cochrane had noticed her, he instructed her to pray, she told the court

After Abigail denied these charges in her testimony, she was asked by the defense why she needed a physician. Her answer was shockingly candid.

"I had two pregnancies. I delivered a dead daughter three years ago. The infant's limbs were deformed and much dislocated," Abigail choked. "A year later I delivered a son. It appeared to have been dead for some time, the skin almost all came off. I have a disorder of a very distressing nature. One doctor said I had a blockage. He tried poking this way and that, every way. I bled badly, but he didn't know what to do. His treatment ended my life as a woman." The witness sobbed.

"Did Mr. Cochrane solve your problem?" the defense counsel asked.

"Mr. Cochrane administered to my sickness with as much, or more, care and modesty, than any physician I have ever seen," Abigail said.

The next three hours became a contest, the prosecution and the defense each trying to show the jury that the other side's case was built on lies. A new witness, Jonathan Newbegin, was introduced by the defense to gain the upper hand. Newbegin, a Cochranite, claimed Mary King's testimony was an act of vengeance.

"I am indebted to Cochrane for saving my soul," Newbegin testified. "Mary King was raised up by him as well, and now abandons him. She has no honor or integrity."

The prosecutor proved ready, asserting that Jonathan Newbegin visited Mary and offered her money if she withdrew her claim and did not testify against Cochrane. Mary told Newbegin that she would tell the court the truth, whether it hurt his prophet or not. Eliza Barker, in an adjoining room, heard the whole exchange and testified to the falsity of Newbegin's testimony. His story was exposed as a complete fabrication.

In his closing argument for the defense, John Holmes focused on the principal witnesses and who the jury should believe. He said the prosecution wanted the jury to discount the testimony of the witnesses for the defense, because they were members of Cochrane's society and of a different religious profession. "Be cautious in declaring the prisoner guilty," he said, "the law in this case requires punishment that is vindictive and severe."

The Solicitor General closed his case, decrying the outrageous nature of Cochrane's crimes and commending the truthfulness of Eunice Bond and Mary King, also noting their unimpeachable characters. Davis said that Abigail Clark's condition was doubtless distressing, but, he asked, should not a woman in a critical or life-threatening state seek someone who is a physician by practice? The witness Dorcas Underwood, a traveling companion of the defendant, could not be considered a substantial witness. And the same was true for Deidamia Lane, a woman with an obscure background, whose husband left her long ago for unknown reasons.

"But the most notorious scoundrel that has appeared on the stand," Davis finished his list of defense witnesses, "is Newbegin, a Cochran associate, who made a base attempt to destroy the testimony of Mary King. I apologize for this warmth of language, but when we see such a scoundrel employed to beguile and disarm the innocent, it is sufficient to raise our indignation."

It was late morning when the presentations concluded, and Judge Putnam addressed the jury. He told the twelve that it was their job to weigh the matter of Jacob Cochrane's guilt according to the evidence. He said they must use their best judgment, so that neither the rights of the prisoner be impaired, nor the dignity of the Commonwealth be abated. The jury was directed to retire until the afternoon, at which time he would enquire as to the verdict. The jury filed out of the room, the gavel came down forcefully and the court was adjourned for two hours.

Eben and his friends sat under a large tree, shaded from the midday sun. He brought beverages out and passed around, along with sausages and bread. All tried to relax, but they were gripped by the court session.

"Alexander," Eben began, "did you recognize Abigail Clark? You have told us how she took you by surprise in the darkness of the barn. Did she surprise you again?" Everybody laughed as Alexander was put on the spot.

"It was a different experience today," Alexander cleared his throat, "not having to attend to her needs."

"I remember your telling us she attended to your needs," Paul said. "From what she told the jury, her needs are exceptional."

"If she and Cochrane fornicated morning, noon and night," Jabez said, "how can she not be extraordinary? And she has a husband."

"Did the tireless voluptuary catch your eye this morning, Alexander?" Paul asked.

"There were many eyes in the room for her to catch," Uriah quipped. "If she spent her time exchanging glances with all of her former admirers, she'd have no time to testify."

"Yes, she would be touching herself," Jabez joked.

Coolbroth's gang was enlivened by the vulgarity, but Alexander felt he had to set the record straight. "One evening at the store I confessed my shameful encounter in the barn. In truth, I cannot say that the seductress was Abigail Clark, it was too dark."

"You are a disappointment, Alexander, we expect full disclosure," Eben teased.

"She may have not been the temptress in the court today, but I can attest to her lust," Alexander smirked. "Even if she's the one who got me started, she is not a contender in my quest for the perfect quim."

"What about that witness, Newbegin, who angered Judge Putnam?" Jabez asked. "Does anyone know him?"

"He appears to be a worthless rascal," Paul said.

"Is he the bugger from up in Porter? A woman in a store there claimed to have seen him act with filthiness, shitting by the fireside. Another said that he showed her his member. He told the court that his belly was 'broke' requiring him to wear especially loose trousers," Uriah finished.

"I heard about that scoundrel. He has a strange attraction to animals as well," Eben laughed. "He was locked up. That was the man in court. Newbegin, I have never seen before. Never been in my store, but I have heard of him. I think he was a Baptist preacher. He pleaded with his congregation to give him a horse, then sold it at great profit. He exchanged a house infested by rats with one owned by a parishioner. After realizing it was a crooked deal, the parishioner could not get his house back from the preacher. The local Baptist church ran the cheater out of town. I guess he found his way to Cochrane."

"Just a small store in a corner of Buxton, Eben but your knowledge of events in York County can be frightening—especially to Baptists. But we know you are not clever enough to make them up," Paul needled. The others laughed. "Alexander, where is Ephraim today? I didn't see him in court."

"I don't know," Alexander shrugged. "Probably running errands for his prophet."

"He is Cochrane's slave. I suspect he pulled some trick to get David Boyd on the jury," Paul observed. "And Newbegin's appearance as well."

"I cannot explain my brother, or why he does Cochrane's dirty work," Alexander said.

"I wouldn't be surprised if Ephraim is behind the conspiracy Judge Putnam talked about," Paul continued. "It was probably your brother's flawed plan to bring down Mary King, invalidating her testimony. He arranged Newbegin's visit with Mary King and the attempt to extort something from her that favored Cochrane's cause. Who else would do this?"

"I don't know, but Ephraim is not the only one involved in Cochrane's defense," Alexander said. "What do I know at nineteen? You are his old friends. Why does he find Cochrane attractive and none of you do? What is it about my brother?" No one wanted to answer.

"Ephraim came by the store a lot. That stopped after Cochrane came to town. He drew your brother away from us," Eben said. "He is searching for something more than the perfect quim, Alexander. My guess is that Ephraim thinks Cochrane will show him the way. Now his prophet is going to jail, and he is up a creek. I doubt he will look to old friends for help."

Mary did not move from her place in the pew but leaned against Jane for reassurance. Ephraim was nowhere to be seen and he did not come home last night. She was overcome by dread.

Jacob Cochrane has absconded, she thought, *and my husband is at his side. Is he so possessed by his prophet that he doesn't think of his family? He has deserted his children.*

⁓

The courtroom filled, the jury was in place and Judge Putnam took his place behind the bench after a two-hour recess was over.

"I have a question for the foreman," Judge Putnam said full-throated. "Is the jury agreed?"

"Yes, your Honor," the foreman responded after standing.

"Is the prisoner guilty or not guilty," Putnam asked.

"Guilty," the foreman said.

"Bailiff, bring in the prisoner," Judge Putnam commanded.

The crowd anxiously awaited while Cochrane failed to appear. Mary noticed the accelerating motion of fans—women trying to keep the powder on their faces dry, while hiding their growing anxiety. Men with overactive sweat glands stretched their legs, pulled at the cloth around their crotch, refreshed themselves with their flasks. Cochrane's foes fidgeted, erratically scanning the room, looking left and right, frustrated by the delay. Others smoked and chewed, unconscious of their own drooling or those coughing nearby.

"We will have a short recess while the prisoner is found." Judge Putnam finally announced, appearing dumbfounded. He stood and left the room.

"The prisoner has absconded," the judge said when he reappeared and settled at the bench. The room was overwhelmed by confusion and disorder by the declaration. Order was not easily restored despite the pounding of the gavel and frantic efforts of the bailiff and his assistants. "With the flight of the prisoner, the court will be paid the sureties promised. Since the bondsmen have defaulted on their recognizance, they will forfeit the sum of eighteen hundred dollars." Eyes turned to John Berry and Abner Woodsum, their faces red with shock. "The prisoner will be apprehended with utmost dispatch. The court is adjourned."

The gallery emptied quickly, everyone wanting to tell of the astonishing disappearance. Eben and his friends took time to stand, stretch and collect themselves. "My wicked streak has not completely erased my religious education," the storekeeper said. "Today I do remember some scripture, which I think is from Proverbs: 'The wicked flee when no man pursueth: but the righteous are as bold as a lion.' Despite his ostentatious displays and claims of greatness, we see today that Jacob Cochrane is not a lion."

❧

In his disappearing act, Cochrane kindled a new flame of excitement, which swept across the county from Fletcher's Neck to the New Hampshire line. Old men and women would give each other significant looks and say, "Ah, that Cochrane is an arch fellow; they can't hold him." Cochrane seemed more respected as a convict than as a preacher. There were mingled feelings of joy and indignation among people who talked of nothing else. The story was news in Portland and in faraway Boston.

One news article cited the fabled story of the flea and the man. It seems a man was annoyed by a prick on his leg, put his finger on the place and found a flea between his fingers. "Why is a tiny animal sucking my livelihood from my carcass?" the man asked. "It is the livelihood that Nature allotted me, and my stinging brings no mortal danger," the flea replied. "You shall die by my hand, for no evil, large or small, ought to be tolerated," was the response. The flea was there one moment, but in the blink of an eye the flea was gone. Like Cochrane, the evil flea was around one second and gone the next.

The rule of common justice, the reporter said, was live and let live. This respected rule is changed when someone is troublesome on the one hand, no more than that, and on the other hand, there is an obligation to discharge every cause of distress. Is that justice? People asked themselves this and Jacob Cochrane's cause drew sympathy.

The night of the Lord's Supper Ephraim arranged for horses and the flight. In the early morning hours of May 22nd, he and

Cochrane left Alfred. Under the cover of darkness, they rode to Francis Grace's farm near Parsonsville, arriving there by daylight. Devout followers were closely connected, and it was through these connections that Ephraim and his prophet moved through Cornish, Limerick, Limington in York County, Standish and Gorham in Cumberland County, and then across to the New Hampshire line, to Acton and Newfield. Despite Cochrane's boundless need for admiration, Ephraim kept all meetings small, not wanting to attract undue attention. To divert the authorities, he got sympathizers to make false reports of the prophet's whereabouts.

The presiding judge in Alfred issued a warrant for Cochrane's arrest immediately after his escape, but the authorities did not grasp the magnitude of their job in catching the fugitive, or the number of warrants and writs that would follow. A warrant was issued to John Banks in July to surround a house in Parsonsville and arrest the escapee. Six of Cochrane's followers were in the house, but the wizard had already been secreted away.

Cochrane eluded authorities by traveling at night but found the restriction of moving only after dark confining. A disguise for traveling around in daylight was agreed—he would assume the appearance of a woman. Jacob knew of the admonition in Deuteronomy that "a woman shall not wear an article proper to a man, nor shall a man put on a woman's dress: for anyone that does such things is an abomination to the Lord thy God," but he had no problem with this travesty. He did have differences with Ephraim over the exact costume. Cochrane, who liked to stand out, wanted a more elaborate dress than the country outfit Ephraim thought appropriate.

Ephraim was acquainted with Deidamia Lane, Dorcas Underwood, and Abigail Bond because of the preparation for Cochrane's court defense, and arranged for all to meet at Dorcas's house. They knew the plan: to make it easier for Jacob to move around Saco Valley, they could disguise their prophet by dressing him as a woman. All were enthusiastic and couldn't wait to get started.

"It's going to be fun dressing Jacob," Dorcas said, "But as a woman, I'd rather undress him."

"Jacob can undress himself," Ephraim snapped. "Your job is to make him look convincing as a woman."

The talk moved to fashion, which was changing, from full skirts and blouses with long sleeves and high necks to trimness and a slimmer silhouette. Dorcus thought the older style would suit Cochrane's large, muscular frame, and they wouldn't have to shave his arms. Since Cochronite women lived simple lives, the materials they brought, including hair for a wig, suited their purpose.

Cochrane was presented with the ladies' scheme. He favored the current fashion that emphasized physicality, vigor and the attractiveness of youth, but Ephraim convinced him to restrain his desire for attention, keeping in mind his need for disguise.

The ladies persuaded Cochrane to try on the old-fashioned wardrobe they brought, including a voluminous skirt and petticoats. He insisted on having a whalebone corset to show off his narrow waist and provide a platform for resting small pillows to simulate breasts. Understanding the great pride Jacob took in his hair, Deidamia persuaded a young girl to sacrifice her long, dark locks to crown the head of her prophet, the locks sewn into a bonnet. Cochrane seemed pleased with the way it rested on his head and did not cover his own hair above his brow. Ephraim found some shoes to complete the wardrobe.

"I never imagined this," Cochrane said, as he twirled around the room "I could pass as a pretty young girl."

"Sit down, Jacob," Dorcas said, "We must do your makeup. It will make you even prettier. And keep your legs together so I can concentrate on your face. Besides, ladies don't sit with their legs apart."

Cochrane enjoyed the application of the makeup. Dorcas started by coloring his lips with beet juice mixed with lard. "This looks luscious, Jacob," Dorcas said. "You have full lips. Some women bite them several times a day to make them lush, but you don't need to."

"Do you think my lips will look more alluring if you powder my face?" Jacob grinned.

"You are not going to have powder. I preferred blush, though blushing is nothing I do naturally," Dorcas laughed. "Rosie cheeks also lend a touch of innocence." She applied beet juice mixed with talc to Jacob's cheeks. She rubbed the rest of his face with a cream made of bacon grease. "This will make your skin glow and look fresh."

"Fascinating," Jacob said. "Bring me a mirror."

"We just need to do your eyes and we will be finished." Dorcas said. She plucked his full, dark eyebrows, making them thinner, then moistened his eyelashes and cautiously applied some coal tar. "You have to be very careful with this, it could do damage. Now stand up. Let us have a look at you."

"I want to have a look at myself," Cochrane said as he jumped to his feet, mirror in hand. "Well, well. If I weren't a man of God, I'd say there is a hint of decadence lurking in that mirror."

"You must be demure and not try to turn heads, or our purpose will not be served," Ephraim warned.

"It's a tempting picture, that attractive woman," Cochrane couldn't take his eyes from the mirror. "I suppose there is no way I could make love to myself," he said to everyone's astonishment.

"There are other choices," Dorcas said, sidling up to her prophet.

"Are you interested in playing around with girls?" Cochrane winked.

Cochrane needed practice walking, gesturing, and moving decorously. Dorcus and Deidamia guided the first daylight ventures around the Saco Valley, the dolled-up prophet imitating their posture and bearing. He learned fast and went unnoticed. He mastered riding, since he could see more followers traveling on horseback. The sidesaddle was rarely seen in York County where women rode astride. Cochrane had no trouble mounting a horse, but there was more to riding than that. While dismounting his horse in Gorham the sham was nearly exposed. Cochrane's skirt became entangled around the saddle, and despite his fabled agility, he fell to the ground. Any observer around could not mistake the figure with skirt and petticoats flung above the knees for a woman. They could not ignore the sausage.

∽

The disguise made traveling easier, but the novelty wore off. Cochrane realized it was a diversion from his true calling, performing miracles. While hiding out, there was much to do, tending to the sick and those struggling with the devil. But those deeds did not give him prominence. His obscurity and need for adoration seized his mind. Things had to change. He talked to Ephraim incessantly of the need to manifest his greatness, restore the majesty of his life. Ephraim listened, pledged help whatever course his prophet chose to follow, while reminding Cochrane he was a fugitive.

"I was thinking about you and your family," Cochrane said out of the blue. "You don't see enough of your wife and children. Since you miss them a lot, take some time for a visit." They had come to Gorham because of a girl's unending seizures. Cochrane raised the girl's head to rest on a pillow to prevent its involuntary banging on the floor, pulled out her tongue to prevent choking, and calmed the child.

"But Jacob," Ephraim said, "You are being hunted. I must be around to keep you hidden and safe."

"You must spend some time with your family, Ephraim," Cochrane said. "You've been away too long. You must come back, because I count on you."

"Are you sure you want me to do this?" Ephraim asked.

"Yes. But I am counting on you to do something for me while you are home," Cochrane said.

"What do you want me to do?" Ephraim asked.

"You are very good with your hands and working with wood. I want you to make me the Staff of Moses. The staff was wondrous. There was the miracle of the exodus. The staff produced water from a rock. It transformed itself into a snake and then back into a staff. With that rod David slew the giant Goliath. It disappeared long ago, but it will be restored. I possess a relic, wood from a sacred pew which was the only thing found from an English ship lost at sea. The wood is from the cedars of Lebanon, called in ancient times the Cedars of God. It was ascribed great power, and Solomon used the timber to build the Temple of Jerusalem," Cochrane explained. "This relic retains its power. People resting on it have prayed and found their prayers answered. It will make an extraordinary staff."

"I am not sure that I am up to this task," Ephraim said.

"When you finish making it, I will do marvelous things. I'll show you what it should look like," Cochrane ignored Ephraim. The prophet knelt, took a stick and drew a figure on the ground. "The staff should be four inches across at the top, tapering to a smaller girth at the bottom. A serpent will be coiled seven times around most of its length. The staff will be topped by a nob, the shape of a head. You will carve on it the bearded face of Moses, his eyes heaven-ward, beseeching God. Paint the snake green and the rest of the staff gold. You have to make it look old."

The next day Ephraim was at his workbench with his tools and a rough, oak timber that would become the staff. Samuel was with his father, sitting on the ground surrounded with some wooden blocks, and occasionally stood up on a sawhorse to watch the wood carving underway. Ephraim, enrapt in his work, paid little attention to the boy as he moved around the workbench, until he heard his son howl.

"Father. Father," Samuel cried as he raised a bleeding finger. "Oh. Oh, I'm hurt. Look."

"Stand up and show me," Ephraim commanded. Samuel's left index finger was bleeding profusely, and when looking down he saw that his son had been playing with one of his carving knives. The tip of Samuel's finger rested on a block of wood. Ephraim tried to quiet his panicked son, as he tightly wrapped the wounded finger with a handkerchief. He picked up the fingertip and rushed the boy to the house. The screaming brought Mary to the door.

"He has been hurt," Ephraim said, "You know what to do. I'm not sure you can do anything with this." Ephraim handed his wife the fingertip, then turned to return to the barn. Mary's concern as she rushed Samuel into the house, became incredulous when her eyes caught Ephraim bustling toward the barn.

Mary's customary pattern was one of indifference towards Ephraim's presence. She prepared meals, kept order in the house, but did not pay much attention to her husband's comings and goings. Her movements showed increasing urgency as she tended to Samuel's injury, worked to staunch the wound, calm Samuel down and make him comfortable.

Ephraim was drawn in by his task, working skillfully and fast. Mealtime passed, and he never left the barn. All the tools he needed were within reach. It was quiet in the barn, except for the sounds made by the saws and chisels, all the animals out to pasture. Work continued until dark.

"You are shameful, Ephraim Berry. Shameful," Mary entered the barn screaming. "You don't know your own kids. You don't care about them. What kind of father are you? Your prophet must have told you about kindness. Cochrane preaches of Paul, why doesn't he teach what Paul said of kindness and enjoying the fruit of the Spirit? He doesn't preach about love, joy, peace, goodness, or gentleness either."

Ephraim was stunned. He stopped his work but did not turn to face his wife. "I left because I was in the way and had my woodwork to finish. I wanted to get out from underfoot."

"Why does cruelty have to be repeated? I know that you feel marked because your father never knew you or loved you. Do you think that you will ever let Samuel know you and experience your love? Didn't you promise yourself never to be like Isaac?" Mary asked.

"I don't know what you are talking about," Ephraim said. "What has my father got to with anything?"

"Look at what is happening, what just happened with Samuel," Mary was exasperated.

"So, he cut his finger. That happens to kids. He will learn to be less careless," Ephraim said evenly. "Spending too much time alone makes you overly sensitive. You need to get out more."

"You are not here for your son, ever, and you were not here for him when he cut himself. And he will remember this morning his whole life. Every time he looks at his shortened finger, he will remember that you did not embrace him when he needed to be in your arms. Just as you have denied him affection, you diminished him by not taking time with him, rushing him into the house so you could get back to whatever you are doing for your prophet," she spat.

"Mary, stop making things up. Clear your head for God's sake," Ephraim said.

"What you did was abusive and unforgiveable," Mary said. "You isolate yourself from your son. You let him know that your own thoughts and feelings are more important than his. Incredible. Your father didn't teach you those lessons. Now, you are treating Samuel just as Jacob Cochrane treats you. Cochrane abuses you to establish power and control, he cannot do it any other way. You shouldn't need to do that with your son."

"Mary, you are crazy. I'm glad there is no one around to hear your words," Ephraim said.

As she tried to quiet her anger, Mary's voice turned cold. "It is not just about Samuel. You don't understand anything going on around you. What you are doing stifles your awareness, disregards decency and your obligations to your family. At your age you ought to be able to move on from the traumas of your youth and recognize the false promises of your prophet. You are swallowed up in darkness, blind to all the goodness in front of you. Maybe they don't strike you as miracles, but you have great blessings before your very eyes that you cannot see."

Ten days at home was good for Ephraim, his life adjusting to a normal pace. He finished the staff except for the paint he could find at Coolbroth's Corners. Ephraim spent time each day with Samuel and Mirinda, and regularly held Isaac in the rocking chair. A visitor would see little good will between Ephraim and Mary. They barely spoke. Their estrangement was fixed.

Pounding on the door woke Mary first. "Ephraim," she nudged, "you must get the door. I can't imagine who would wake us this time of morning." Ephraim got out of bed, went to the door in his nightshirt. It was his cousin, John Berry.

"Thank God you are here, Ephraim," John said, breathless. "Anna is deathly ill. I must find Cochrane and take him to her immediately." John was sweating in the chill air.

"Come in, John," Ephraim said. "I'll get my clothes on and we will go as soon as possible.

"Here is some water," Mary passed a cup. "You will find it refreshing. I am so sorry to hear about Anna.

"Time is short, Mary," John said. "Anna is feverish and it's hard for her to breath. I have never seen her so bad."

⤳

"You know that I am not a believer, Ephraim," John said as they left the house. "But Anna has great faith in Cochrane. She thinks he is the only one who can restore her health. We must get him right away."

"I know where he is. We will take him to Anna," Ephraim said. They headed west from the farm. Ephraim carried the new staff, which his cousin didn't mention.

Cochrane frequently visited John Berry's farm to help Anna with her ailments. It was risky, being a Cochrane haunt, and the place was frequently watched. He took the chance because John was a reliable source of money.

Ephraim found Cochrane in a shed on the farm of Phineas Towle. He was bundled under a blanket with Dorcas Underwood. John kneeled next to Cochrane in desperation. "I fear for Anna's life if we waste any time," John pleaded.

"Of course, I will go. God is calling," Cochrane stood and put on his clothes.

"I am coming too," Ephraim said. "And you will find this useful." He took great pride in handing over the staff.

"Oh. You found it where I was told it would be," Cochrane grasped the staff with his powerful right hand and raised it toward heaven. "It has an immortal beauty. Who would guess it to be thousands of years old? Let's get to Anna."

The three men went by Duck Pond, along a creek to Long Plains Road and arrived at John's house. The place was dark except for the light coming from the bedroom. Mehitable, Anna's older sister, stood stroking the sick woman's hand. Cochrane prayed. Anna seemed unaware that her prophet had entered the room.

"We must prepare for the reception of the Lord," Cochrane commanded. He directed the placement of aromatic candles and their lighting. Camphor oil was poured into small dishes and set aflame, its distinguished smell permeating the room. "From ancient times this oil is known as the balsam of disease. I call it the balm of Gilead. It will carry away Anna's pain. Ephraim, stoke the fires. We must remove the chill from this room."

Cochrane sat by Anna's bedside and held her hand. John guided Anna's wrist to the prophet's fingers, because Cochrane would not loosen his grip on the ancient staff. Anna's pulse was erratic. It would surge and then vanish.

"The demons of disease are in our presence," Cochrane thundered. "Each of us knows the Kingdom of Heaven resides within. It is present in us, and He is anchored within Anna." He gently laid his left hand on Anna's chest and raised the staff of Moses with the other. He pressed Anna's chest harder, rhythmically, more forcefully with each thrust. Anna looked pained—Ephraim found it distressing to watch.

"Anna, come forth like Lazarus," Cochrane cried out. "Holy Father, make Anna strong. In her cause, come down, bring the healing power of the Blood of Jesus, and infuse her body. Rebuke the evil punishing Anna's flesh. Rebuke the evil—drive it out now." He stood and raised the staff of Moses. Cochrane genuflected, then reached out to touch Anna's heart.

"It is struggling," Cochrane whispered. "The rhythms of her heart are intense, chaotic." Anna's breathing was desperate, her open eyes strained and became transfixed. Cochrane exhorted, prayed, and called again upon the Lord to cast out the demons taking control of Anna's body.

Anna's breathing stopped, her eyes closed. There was no pulse. Cochrane's prayers became more fervent as he pressed hard against her chest, released and pressed hard again, calling out to God. John looked frightened before tears rolled down his taut face. The room was silent, without any signs or sounds of breathing. Cochrane remained motionless, not taking his hand off Anna. John hung his head. Ephraim prayed God would reach out to Anna as he had to Catherine years before.

"I feel a faint heartbeat," Cochrane whispered. Moments later, "And there is another." Cochrane's sigh was deep and unbidden. "Her heart is coming back. Anna has not passed from this world."

John stayed with Anna as dawn broke, while Cochrane and Ephraim left the room to rest.

Late in the morning Anna regained consciousness. "I passed. But they sent me back." Anna muttered. "Yes. They sent me back to love. I saw the Kingdom of God before me. And found a reflection of something already inside myself but never saw before." John raised Anna's head to sip some water. "I guess it was clouded by selfishness and worthless distractions." Her voice became more fluent. "I praise God I passed. My heart stopped, my blood slowed, and I wandered from the body on the bed. Pain was gone, and I felt peace. Light transformed my tranquility into elation, magnificent and irresistible light.

"Heaven was before me and I was asked by attending angels if I was ready to enter the Kingdom. I said that I did not know what to do in heaven. I knew there was so much more for me here, more loving to do. I understood that God is love, that I have the power to love, and that I have so much to give my devoted husband and my children. Love will replenish my family, and my family will enrich me."

Ephraim could not recall such vitality in Anna. Something ineffable powered her revival.

"The angels told me to go back home, enjoy the blessed love I have there, and let everyone know that they can experience God on earth." Anna's body settled back on the bed and she closed her eyes.

Ephraim was stricken by Anna's revelation. *Anna met God,* he thought. *It's true, just as it happened to me. But people won't believe her and how it will change her life.*

It bothered Ephraim that Mary never understood his belief, and this diminished his faith. He wanted her affirmation, but understood the belief was not shared. *If I experience God one way, Mary can experience God differently. Why can't she understand that my beliefs and experience are as true as hers? She rarely worships and doesn't seek an encounter with God. She cannot comprehend God's power and glory. We will never bridge the spiritual gap separating us.*

Ephraim knew that Anna's revival was a miracle. There was no delusion. Anna's revelation reaffirmed the powerful gifts of Jacob Cochrane, gifts not exercised since his arrest.

As Ephraim awoke from his rest, he thought how his encounter with God differed from Anna's. The old traveler told Ephraim that he loved him, and he was embraced. Anna experienced more, was given instruction. Anna was told to share her love of God, that she had the power to love, and love would enrich her life and her family's. She should fill those around her with love.

I wasn't given power and I have not found it through my devotion to Jacob. Ephraim thought. *Love is not part of what I have been taught. I thought that holiness flowed from unbending service to my prophet. Anna's revelation is different because one's bliss is seen in their love—its expansiveness and potency. Jacob never told me how to use the love God bestowed on me, and I never asked.* Ephraim never related love for family to his redemption. He understood its source in his devotion to Cochrane.

Ephraim remembered Sister Mercy's resurrection in the same way. There were no divine lessons learned as part of her celestial voyage. She didn't talk about love, generosity or selflessness. The experience itself was paramount, and for Cochrane's congregation the important thing was that he made it happen.

Cochrane did not teach me to live as a man of God, Ephraim thought. *He taught me to live as his servant.*

༄

Rishworth Jordan and John Banks tracked Jacob Cochrane the length and width of the Saco Valley for nearly five months. Numerous writs for Cochrane's arrest were issued by the Solicitor General in Alfred, but no arrest followed. They were paid by the county for their time, assistants and horses, but catching the elusive criminal became an obsession. More than just a job, Cochrane's arrest was a moral duty.

On October 8th, the two were detailed to the house of John Berry in Buxton, where reportedly Cochrane could be found. They had a plan, which they reviewed before they rode north from Alfred. When they reached John Berry's house they scouted the surroundings, making sure they were familiar with the terrain and the location of windows, doors and cellars of the house.

Jordan and Banks went to the front door, knocked and waited. When the door was opened, a cloud of fumes engulfed them, the scent of camphor and myrtle, exotic herbs. There was the smell of body odor and sickness. John Berry appeared haggard in the evening darkness and he sounded short of breath.

"What may I do for you, gentlemen?" John said in a weak voice.

"We are looking for the whereabouts of Jacob Cochrane," Jordan replied.

"I hope you understand, but my wife is very sick, and I must be with her. Anna needs calm and sleep. She is suffering. You must excuse me," Berry said.

"Jacob Cochrane with his storied healing skills is not attending to her?" Jordan asked

"Look elsewhere for Cochrane. He is not here. We face a grave situation, so please do not trouble me further," John said as he closed the door.

"Did you hear him bolt the door?" Jordan asked Banks. "Does he need to do that?

"I'm sorry to see a man in his early thirties in such grief," Banks said. "If Mrs. Berry is severely ill, Cochrane must be nearby. Let's stay and see what happens."

Everyone in York County predicted Cochrane would be hard to catch, and that proved true. Cochrane's extraordinary strength and fleetness were part of local lore. People knew he jumped a four-foot fence like a deer and believed he could resist the draft of two horses. The plan for Cochrane's capture also considered that the fugitive faced imprisonment, making him especially dangerous and difficult to control. At least six men would be needed to hold him.

Boys in York County attended school until age twenty-one. Many, being energetic and having nothing to do, would be anxious for action and willing to join the force of justice. Four such boys came and were hidden nearby.

After checking their backup, the two officers concealed themselves in foliage near the house and waited. The officers had heard rumors that Cochrane frequently disguised himself as a woman. But it was a trouser leg that first emerged from a side window, followed by another and the appearance of a staff. Before long Cochrane thrust his entire body out of the window, planted himself on the ground and raced to the woods. Jordan and Banks pursued him.

Cochrane had a large staff and when the officers reached him, he turned and struck Banks down with it. He gripped the staff like a spear, aiming it at Jordan. It must have dismayed Cochrane that his target was not impaled. But in successfully dodging the staff, Jordan ended up on the ground. When Cochrane ran, again dashing toward a fence, the boys gave chase. Cochrane did not leap the fence like a deer. With his front foot caught on the top rail, he ended up astride it. Two boys grabbed a leg to pull him off the fence and the other boys got hold of an arm. Cochrane's fabled power to resist the draft of two horses was never seen, and in no time the prophet was on the ground, subdued by the heft of the four young brawlers.

Cochrane looked stunned as he was pulled to his feet, allowing Jordan and Banks to bind his wrists together and hobble his feet. The prophet summoned all his oratorical powers and called out, "The Lord will never allow His Anointed to be jailed." There was nothing to do but exhort. He had no other assistance.

Ephraim observed the ambush from a distance, making no move to help his prophet. He wasn't sure his intervention would matter against the force of six. And he didn't want to fight with his brother, Alexander, one of the young men who had sprung from the bushes.

When Ephraim appeared, Cochrane's confusion vanished, and anger took possession. "Ephraim, you bastard. You imbecile. This is your blunder," the prophet raged. "I knew all along I could not count on you, that you would betray me. Judas. You led me into this trap and didn't come to my rescue."

Jordan and Banks worked methodically on Cochrane's restraints. By no sort of legerdemain could the captive muster to be free of his bonds.

"Can one of you boys go to the house and get some lanterns?" Jordan asked. "We want to see what we are doing." Cochrane was searched and disarmed, but his involuntary muscle contractions and fitfulness made the officers edgy.

"You are disloyal, irresponsible and unreliable. I should not have trusted you to make Moses' staff. It's ugly, uninspired and worthless, devoid of power." Jordan and Banks did not react to Cochrane's acknowledgement of defeat.

"I did as you directed," Ephraim said, while trying to grasp the fact of Cochrane's capture and helplessness. "I followed your instructions."

John arrived with two lanterns. After asking about their placement, he set them down so all of Cochrane's body was illuminated.

"You are a thankless wretch, Ephraim, after all I have done for you," Cochrane bellowed. "I showed you the way, brought you before God. My love was wasted on you."

"Yes, Jacob, you revealed to me that the Kingdom of God is in myself," Ephraim ordered his thoughts. "I was at the bottom of the river, called out for God and was delivered. I thank you for that."

"So many times, I placed my hopes on you, Ephraim. I taught you many things. Many times you disappointed me," Cochrane said. "I had much faith in you. You had the chance to realize God's magnificent plan for you, manifest His glory."

Cochrane was now secured by so much rope he could not move. Jordan, sure the captive would remain secure until behind the bars of the Alfred jail, called for the horse.

"Jacob, you are wrong. You were never interested in my glory," Ephraim choked. "You have never been my teacher or given me lessons. Much of what you said to me these years was in derision, never to advance my spiritual growth or welfare."

Banks led a large brown gelding next to Cochrane. Ephraim didn't understand the plan to get the captive on the large horse. "Ephraim, you never got anything right," Cochrane said, "You're hopeless."

The boys were helpful in lifting Cochrane's body, slinging him across the back of the horse like a sack of grain. Alexander looked like he enjoyed the task. Ephraim flinched at the indignity shown his spiritual leader, but his concern passed.

"I am not stupid, Jacob, and I now see that your advice was self-serving. You never told me how I should live, every day, as a man of God—how I should give love to others, my family, those who do not follow you. I know God's glory rests in love, but that was never one of your lessons."

"You are lost, Ephraim," Cochrane hissed as he twisted his face to look at the former acolyte. "You are condemned to hell."

"I was so fixed on the future, travelling the path to heaven and sitting at the right hand of the Father, I never understood that my life in the present is incomplete. Anna's miraculous experience links the future with the present. Mine does not," Ephraim lamented.

The official party assembled together with the boys to begin the journey to Alfred.

"You gave me a place in the world," Ephraim wailed as his prophet was taken away, "but not as a man of God. You elevated me in your band of followers, but I was no more than a servant." Ephraim was on his knees, in the darkness. No one saw his tears or heard his anguished sobs. He felt empty as Cochrane faded into the night

Cousin John carried the lanterns away, returning to the house and his ailing wife.

"Help me find my way, God," Ephraim mumbled, unsure his plea would be heard. Cochrane had been his guide. His teacher's fellowship offered solace, but without a prophet there were no ecstatic congregants to lift him up or mask his desolation. Mary could never be of help. She was unable to grasp the depth of his loss. Ephraim was alone.

EIGHT

"Damn it," Ephraim yelled. He flung the warped scythe blade across the barn. "Goddamn it." He ripped off his gloves and threw them after the blade.

"Those don't sound like the words of a righteous man." An unfamiliar voice drifted through the open barn door.

"I seldom say such things," Ephraim said warily. "Almost never. I was hammering the blade of my scythe to make it even and thinner. I thought the anvil was properly secured to that heavy stump, but it wasn't. I ruined the blade the way I hit it. I doubt it can be fixed. We have a field to harvest."

"Sorry. I did not mean to embarrass you. And I don't want to get on your wrong side before an introduction," the stranger said. "I occasionally have those moments myself."

"What brings you and your friend to my farm?" Ephraim nodded to the man who stood next to the stranger. "Do you have something to sell?"

"No. We have nothing to sell. We are missionaries of the Mormon Church from Ohio. My name is Orson Hyde, and this is Brother Samuel Smith," Hyde said.

Hyde was an imposing man and vigorous seeming despite receding brown hair with determined, dark eyes and a resolute mouth, broad with pursed lips. He struck Ephraim as the type of man who would accomplish whatever he set out to do. Smith had a bland, not quite likeable appearance.

"Good to meet you," Ephraim said as he moved to shake their hands. "But I have had my fill of religion and no longer spend much time at church. You are wasting your time with me."

"We came to Buxton upon the recommendation of Jacob Cochrane," Hyde said. "He is a friend of our prophet, Joseph Smith, the founder of our church. Cochrane told Joseph of his devoted followers. He singled you out as a stalwart and told us our first stop should be here, to meet you at your farm."

"I have not seen Jacob Cochrane for a long time. His flock has scattered. He is not welcome in the Saco Valley. He was not treated fairly. But I am no longer drawn to his beliefs." Ephraim, trying to sound indifferent, had to repress his excitement. Some bad memories did not restrain a smile.

"Well, you have not been forgotten by Cochrane. He still reveres you and considers you one of his most trusted followers," Hyde said. "He said that you are generous and kind and would make yourself helpful to us."

"My wife won't like it that you are here," Ephraim said emphatically.

"We don't want anything of you. We are not after your soul, your conversion, or baptism," Hyde grinned. "We would be here only a couple of days. We will get our bearings and move on to see more of southern Maine and meet as many people as we can."

"People here don't easily take to outsiders. They particularly dislike those peddling religion. Folks have their own way of looking at things," Ephraim said.

"I cannot deny that we have a mission and are spurred on by heavenly revelation and a compelling belief. We know that new ideas are not always welcome in this part of the world," Hyde did not sound pessimistic. "There was a decent reception in Boston, although we were disturbed by false spirits, a man and a woman who muttered, grumbled and shook. They believed in Cochrane's teachings. There were those who listened. Three confessed their faith in our gospel and were baptized."

"In this household we try to stay away from anything controversial."

"Controversy is inevitable, but we are not agitators. It does not advance our cause," Hyde said. "We were just in Rhode

Island where we baptized two converts. That led to threats of violence. We left the state after only twelve days."

"You won't be threatened here," Ephraim said. "Although you may feel unwelcome."

"You don't make us feel unwelcomed," Hyde looked at his companion who nodded in agreement. "We wouldn't be an imposition. We try to be helpful. It looks like you have a lot of work, getting ready to harvest that field of wheat. You have a good crop."

"I have five sons to help me. But thank you for the offer." Despite himself, Ephraim was pleased by their persistence. "This is a full house."

"Harvesting that crop could take more than a week," Hyde continued. "You cannot refuse the aid of four experienced hands when the weather could suddenly turn."

Ephraim walked across the barn, fetched the scythe from the floor. He picked up the tool and inspected it with displeasure.

"Samuel and I know about the harvest," Hyde continued. "And the Bible. In Matthew, we find Jesus's parable of the wheat and the tares. With experience, the two can be distinguished. We are reapers, skilled with the scythe, but gatherers too. Following the Lord's instructions, we can distinguish between the good and the bad. We know how to bind the tares and cast them into the fire. We know how to gather the good wheat into sheaves, dry them and get them safely into the barn. We know how to bring in the sheaves and are here to do that."

Ephraim was impressed by Hyde's reference to scripture. The comments about the wheat made him think back to Cochrane services, the dancing, and exercises of "reaping and winnowing."

"Is dance a part of Mormon religious practice?" Ephraim asked. "Cochrane's followers, men and women, had a lively dance which portrayed the separation of the grain from the chaff. But in the dance, women were not separated from the men, making it quite enjoyable for everyone. The dance was popular and became a common feature of Cochrane ritual." A smile crossed Ephraim's face.

"I should say nothing untoward to my prospective host while asking for a place to rest," Hyde paused. "What you speak of does not sound like the activity of a righteous man or a righteous church. Dancing is not part of Mormon worship."

"I know how worship and dance come together and have taken pleasure in the liveliness of it all. If you are here for a while, I can tell you more about it," Ephraim brightened, his thoughts lingering on Cochrane's services. "As I recall, the gospel says, 'the harvest is plentiful, but the laborers are few.' We can always use help with the harvest. You can stay here in the barn for a while but leave my soul alone. I'll tell my wife, Mary, you are here and to set two more places for dinner."

⤸

Everything was ready, and the entire family was gathered. With Mirinda's help, Mary made room for ten around the table. Two visitors sparked excitement, particularly since the guests traveled hundreds of miles from a place not easily found on a map.

Ephraim's interest in the visitors had grown since the afternoon, particularly with the mention of Jacob Cochrane. Mary made sure there was plenty to eat and that the guests felt welcome. She routinely complied with Ephraim's commands when guests were invited unexpectedly. Ephraim mentioned that the two young men were missionaries but explained that no evangelizing would occur during dinner.

Ephraim responded to the knock on the door, and invited Hyde and Smith into the parlor.

"Welcome to our home," he said as he shook their hands. "Let me introduce you to my wife, Mary, daughter Mirinda and my sons Samuel, Isaiah, Josiah, and the two youngest, Jonathan and William."

"We are pleased to meet you and honored to be in your home," Hyde said, as he bowed. Smith did the same. "My first name is Orson, and I would feel comfortable if you called me that."

"I am Samuel Smith. Call me Samuel," Smith said.

"Let's eat," Ephraim said as he moved to the head of the table. "Orson please sit at my right and Samuel take your place here on my left." The boys sat down. Mary and Mirinda brought roast pork, potatoes, carrots and spinach from the kitchen. Freshly baked bread was on the table.

Ephraim loudly cleared his throat to get everyone's attention. "Let's bow our heads and thank God for this food. Bless us, Oh Lord and these thy gifts which we are about to receive through your bounty, through Christ, Our Lord. Amen." The host raised his head and looked at everyone at the table before lifting his knife and fork. He noticed Orson looking across at Mirinda, who caught the glance and blushed.

Ephraim's lead was followed with haste as family and guests clanked utensils on plates.

"Orson, could you please tell us about your travels?" Ephraim began. "I've never been west. Ohio seems so far away."

"Thank you again, Mr. Berry, for your hospitality," Orson said. "Samuel and I come from Kirtland, Ohio, which is south of Lake Erie. We set out eight months ago, traveling through New York and all of New England, before reaching Maine."

"That's quite a journey and a long time on the road," Ephraim said.

"Yes, it is. But we are on a mission and carry good news. We were assigned to take our gospel here," Orson said as he stood and reached under his coat. He handed Ephraim a plain brown leather book with a black label on its spine. "This is a gift from us. I wanted to wait until after dinner, but my enthusiasm wouldn't allow it. We are here at the direction of our prophet, Joseph Smith, to present you with the *Book of Mormon*. It is wondrous, a volume of Holy Scripture, a new Bible. It explains the ancient roots of Christianity in the Americas, draws upon the doctrines of the Old and New Testaments, and includes the prophecy and revelation of many ancient prophets. With Christ's imminent return to earth, it discloses His plan of salvation, tells us how to prepare for the coming tumult and eternal life." Orson exhaled and sat down.

The silence at the table was awkward. No one was prepared for Orson's remarks. The intrusion reminded Ephraim of Cochrane's audacity and selfishness.

"Had I known in advance the importance of our guests' good news, I would have arranged a more sumptuous repast," Mary's sharp voice reminded Ephraim to demonstrate his authority.

"The platter is empty, Mary," Ephraim said, "Would you please bring some more food? And, Mirinda, there is more cider. Please fill the pitcher." As the women left the table, Ephraim didn't miss Mirinda's fleeting look at Orson.

"You have never read anything like the *Book of Mormon*, Ephraim," Orson was exuberant. "It was written in times we know nothing about, inscribed on gold plates and hid by an angel, Moroni, in a hill in remote New York. The Angel Moroni appeared to our Prophet Joseph Smith, led him to the buried records, and showed him how to read the ancient text. That was nine years ago. Guided by the power of God, Joseph Smith published his Bible and made it available to all of the world."

Having replenished the food and drink, Mary and Mirinda took their places among the men who were stunned by Orson's account.

"That is quite a story, young man. I have never heard anything like it," Ephraim said. "Gold tablets."

"It is the word of God, and like the Bible, recounts the religious histories and struggles of ancient civilizations on this continent, including the Nephites and the Lamanites, ancestors of the American Indians," Orson paused. "I realize that this is not a usual dinner conversation, and I have gone on too long. Please excuse me."

"Moses found tablets, but they weren't gold. No one has ever talked about finding sacred tablets in this country," Sam said. "What do they look like? Where can you see them?"

"You cannot see them," Smith answered. "When my brother finished translating the plates, he gave them back to the Angel Moroni, who keeps them in his charge. Some say they are in a cave, deep in the Hill of Cumorah where they were found. But I have no idea where they are."

"Joseph Smith is your brother!" Sam exclaimed. "Then you can tell us about the treasure?"

"Yes, I can tell you. I have seen the plates. I have handled them, touched them with my hands and fingered the engraving, which looks like Egyptian characters," Smith said. "Turn to the back of the *Book of Mormon*. There is the *Testimony of Eight Witnesses* who swear to the authenticity of the plates. I am one of the eight."

Ephraim opened his gift to the back-cover page and saw Samuel Smith's name among the "Witnesses." He nodded his head and passed the volume to his eldest son.

"What did the plates look like? Were they bound together like a book? If someone wished to steal them, are they too heavy to pick up and run?" Sam's curiosity was aroused.

"The plates were whitish yellow in color and they were held together by three rings. My brother, William, lifted the plates and thought they weighed about sixty pounds. No one could ever steal them because they are protected by the Angel Moroni," Smith answered.

"They can't be stolen because no one can get their hands on them," Mary interjected. "Eight people have seen this astonishing relic, but their existence depends on the testimony of those eight witnesses."

"No. There are eleven. Along with my brother, the first to see the plates were Martin Harris, Oliver Cowdery, and David Whitmer. They assisted in the translation," Smith said.

"Your tale of the plates is fantastic," Mary said. "How is a person to believe this? They cannot be seen. Their existence is established only by the statements of eleven witnesses. I am dumbfounded," Mary blurted. "Your story is not compelling."

"You know the tablets are real when you read the *Book of Mormon*, observe its precepts, and accept the commandments," Orson said authoritatively. He stood and motioned Smith to do the same. "We traveled a long way today and are tired. Thank you for the sumptuous dinner and good company. There is a lot more to talk about, particularly after you start reading the new Holy Scripture."

"I think my boys will like reading about the fighting between the Nephites and the Lamanites," Ephraim said as he led his guests to the door.

"You will read about the legendary sword of the wicked Laman, which his brother, Nephi, used to kill him. The sword is now hidden in the same place as the plates," Smith added.

"I am sure the story is engrossing. Goodnight," Ephraim said as the missionaries left the house.

Ephraim sent the boys to bed and Mirinda helped her mother clear the table and put things away. Ephraim sat down in his rocker and filled his pipe for the final smoke of the day. The tranquility of the moment was interrupted by the clanking and banging of pots in the kitchen. Mary was annoyed.

"Why are these strange men here? Why have you taken them in?" Mary asked.

"They are hands who will help with the harvest. The men are experienced and need a temporary place to stay," Ephraim puffed.

"I do not understand how you and such odd creatures are drawn together," Mary said. "Where do people with these outlandish stories come from?"

"Ohio," Ephraim answered. "Kirtland, Ohio."

"It is bizarre, this talk of ancient scripture and golden tablets. And a new Moses, from Ohio. Where else?" Mary tried to temper her agitation.

"Most talk around here is about cows who stray, as well as the occasional roving wife," Ephraim yawned. "Tonight's conversation was not boring."

"You mean the talk of Laman and Nephi?" Mary said. "How could they have forgotten to mention Pocahontas?"

"I cannot understand, Mary, why you are so overwrought," Ephraim said. "I think you need some rest."

"There is something portentous in the arrival of these men that worries me. Goodnight," Mary left Ephraim to himself.

I'll never understand how Mary can become so excitable, Ephraim thought. *Of course, she would have been even more agitated to know that Orson mentioned the name of Jacob Cochrane.*

⤿

The prospect from the ridge where the house and barn sat allowed a panoramic view of the work done. The mowing was finished, but the rakes and tools had not been put away. Sheaves were collected in stooks to dry, each twelve bundles leaning upright with their heads together. They would retain their golden-brown hue, more vibrant than the mown field, looking parched although dappled with patches of bright green. Heavily leafed trees marked the stream at the far edge of the field, separating Ephraim's land from the Dresser place spread along the horizon.

"Your father must be pleased, as is mine, Sam," Smith said. "Seeds of faith yield sheaves of joy. You know Psalm 126. 'They shall come back rejoicing, carrying their sheaves.'"

"We've done a lot of work." Sam wanted to ask how Smith learned so much scripture but didn't. "And work goes on." He looked at his mother setting the table where the field hands would eat. Mirinda emerged from the house carrying dishes and cloths to cover the rough planked top. "There is still work to do. The threshing will take a lot of time."

"Your sister is quite pretty," Smith said. "Does she have a suitor?"

"Mirinda stays at home most of the time, and is shy with boys," Sam was short. "Did Orson ask you to find out? I see him eyeing her. Please. She doesn't need a match-maker or a playmate."

"Her blush is a display of modesty. I was making a complement," Smith said. "Orson has a sweetie in Ohio he pines for."

"Orson left Ohio ten months ago," Sam said. "If he is lustful, he should look among the Cochrane followers, and leave my sister alone."

"A warning isn't necessary, Sam," Smith said. "Orson is virtuous and is driven to do God's work."

"People say that Orson performs miracles," Sam said.

"The power to perform miracles is a gift conferred by the Holy Spirit. All of our Elders possess the gift," Smith said. "Orson is not yet an Elder."

"What about the exorcism in Kennebunkport?" Sam asked.

"My brother performed the first miracle in the Mormon Church. Jewel Knight was possessed by the Devil, and Joseph purged the man," Smith said. "But he avoids doing exorcisms and sternly discourages the practice."

"Orson and you work hard every day," Sam said. "Nearly every night you hold a meeting, attracting enthusiasts, young men and women. God blessed you with a lot of energy."

"They are coming here tonight. You will see them after dinner," Smith said with exuberance.

"My mother is not going to like that, particularly if my father is involved," Sam said.

"Your father gave permission," Smith said.

～

The small crowd of field hands and neighbors finished eating before the rambunctious train of young men appeared, following Orson up the road toward the house. Orson's deeply resonant voice was heard above all those shouting "Halleluiah" and "Praise Jesus." Stopping near the tables which Mary and Mirinda had almost cleared, Orson lifted his arms exhorting, "Raise yourselves up. Ready yourselves for redemption. Prepare for the Gates of Zion."

Mary, returning for the last table items and soiled cloths, ran to Ephraim, who was observing the scene. "Stop this," she said to her husband, "Send them away. Tell Mr. Hyde to take his yelling someplace else."

"He's doing no harm, Mary," Ephraim said. "He is teaching these young men, waking them up to something important."

The young men had clustered together. Some were beseeching and exhorting, others' mouths were agape and mute. Eyes heavenward, closed and sharing some vision while fervently embraced by fellow novices. All were in a separate world.

"How did this get started? You let this happen," Mary accused. "You know how I feel about this."

"If this is distressing you, Mary, go back to the house," Ephraim said. "You don't belong here."

"This is my place. A sane, peaceful and serene refuge for my family." Mary's objection was futile. She turned from the chaotic ritual to return to the house, not seeing Brother Smith lead Sam to the edge of the swaying pack.

"We are here to receive the wisdom of our Prophet. His instructions from Almighty God and the gift of the Holy Spirit are true," said Orson, standing on a wooden box, where he could be seen by all. "We keep His commandments and await His promised blessings." Orson spread his upper limbs and, lowering his arms, motioned the novitiates down. Everyone was on his knees.

"Each of has cried out to the Lord, and promised to build His kingdom on earth," Orson began to preach. "Through the power of the Holy Spirit, your blood has been cleansed and you are empowered to fight off Satan's temptations. The Holy Spirit has opened your souls."

"God is real" was whispered within the group. "Honor me, Jesus," was faintly cried. "Enter my spirit," quickly followed. "Ahkanda, ee ki kirreh," "Ok kah rah, zfende." Strange chanting in tongues broke out.

"You receive God's message. Whisper in His spirit," Orson rumbled. "Blessings greater than Jupiter await. Stand and shine like the sun. Fill yourself with the Spirit and follow it."

Stricken men fell to the ground. One assumed an apish posture, a ridiculous grimace, arms swung sideways as he roamed aimlessly. On hands and knees one crept, head raised and howling. A reenactment of Indian warfare began with the encirclement of the howling man, those in the circle chanting, and side-stepping around the prone figure. One "brave" left the circle, grabbed the hair of the howling figure, pretended to take his scalp, shook his upraised fist in the air, then rejoined the chanting ring. Another from the circle stomped toward the bleating man and flipped him on his back. He feigned a brutal attack, ripping open the victim's stomach and tearing out his bowels. The distribution of the disgorged parts to his unmerciful cohorts followed. Pleasure possessed the crazed faces as they pretended to eat the cursed vittles.

"See the wrath of God," Orson bellowed. "'Vengeance is mine,' sayeth the Lord. Witness the impending calamity, when doom will consume all."

From the edge of the aboriginal scene, Sam appeared fascinated and fearful. He looked at his father who appeared enrapt, drawn to the frenzy. His mother was nowhere in sight, despite noise so loud it traveled fields away.

"Can you see the fate of sinners, Sam?" Brother Smith asked. "Can you see what awaits those who have no faith, who do not repent? Those not baptized for the remission of their sins?"

"I fear for Mother and Mirinda," Sam panted after a long silence. "They will never understand this, what is taking place by their house. It must be alarming for them. Father's fascination with the extraordinary clouds everything, even concern for his family. My mother feels safe around familiar things. She is strong but needs support when startled by something weird." Sam looked toward the lamp-lit house. He moved in that direction.

"Don't go until you hear about God's gifts. Orson tells how God the Almighty bestows powers on the righteous," Smith grabbed Sam's arm and pulled the young man back next to him. "It's through the Holy Spirit and the laying on of hands that you can become one with God."

"When mother is upset, I must help her," Sam resisted.

"You must listen," Smith refused to release the young man. "It's important for your soul. With the new Bible there are new miracles."

"Behold the heavens. Witness God's firmament," Orson intoned as he pointed toward the sky. "See God's house spread across the heavens. It is the dome of righteousness. There is no moon. The brilliance of a thousand stars is undiminished."

Worshipers emerging from one trance were invited into another rapture. Heads raised in awe, others pressed the earth with their skulls like petitioners, mouths opened wide in expectation. One man bit his lip so hard it bled.

"Behold. Heavenly light sweeps out the darkness of your soul," Orson exclaimed. "Look up, open your eyes and see God's authority, the path of your sacred journey."

Then a meteor shot through the sky accompanied by blinding flashes of light., as if by the missionary's command. All were shocked, especially Orson whose surprise registered in a flat smile. Had it been announced by a clamor, he might have jumped in surprise and been unable to lay claim to the meteor shower that followed.

"Look. A cannonball of light. A ball of fire manifests God's power," Orson roared in a revived voice. "He shows that he wants us closer, wants to take us in his arms. He wants us to be one with Him."

A miracle began, the marvelous, fantastically radiant shower of meteors, one brighter than the other. Some stars had tails extending their brightness. The persistent trains of others radiated sheets of light. Dazzling surges and spectacular outbursts bleached out the movements of other racing matter.

"Run from the waking dragon. It spews the fire of hell," a worshipper screamed as he tried to dig himself a hole. One beholder desperately gripped the ground to keep from being swept away by the streams of light. Those needing to fasten themselves clung to trees.

"Embrace your God!" Orson stood tall like Moses parting the sea. "Do not hide from Him. Pursue His glory."

Orson's words were a call to action. Young men started running across the field, chasing the shooting stars, racing after the balls of fire, dodging stooks, vaulting tree stumps, while calling out to God.

The spectacle of leaping, bounding and jumping began, and soon became a contest among believers to reveal who was closest to God. A man with a long plank and a barrel tried to catapult his friend into sainthood. As time passed, no jumper was signified, spirited away with a gale of stars or rendered to his knees by a beam of heavenly light.

"Be of faith," Orson spirited them on. "Persevere. Keep going. The Holy Spirit is here, present in this wondrous night. Don't give up. Gifts are not granted to the faint of heart."

Sam remained on the sidelines of the inexplicable event. His concern for his mother increased with each shower of light. The childhood memory of his helpless mother returned along with guilt of not trying to stop the attack on her. Sam was awestricken and confused. He was overwhelmed by the unending celestial display but immobilized, unable to move toward the house. Smith remained quietly at his side, occasionally gripping his upper arm in assurance that all was part of God's plan.

"Jumping has its rewards," Smith spoke over the surrounding tumult. "Gifts come from the sky. God transmits his authority materially, signaling His approval to preach and spread His gospel. In Kirtland they are known as *Arial Commissions*. Each commission is written on parchment and signed and sealed by Christ. After the gift is read and copied, He takes the commission back for safe keeping. It is stored on high as a perpetual record."

Sam looked around for his father but could not see him among the disordered throng. He was unconcerned; his father would be at home among the chaos. Sam did not feel grounded, nothing appeared clear and defined. He saw the trees and fences transformed into a luminous swirl of starry light. The contours of the field seemed pliant, the large trees yielding, yet deeply rooted in the earth. Movements in the sky were dynamic and charged, but things, even the house in the distance, wavered like a heat mirage.

Brother Samuel held Sam tightly, keeping him upright as the dawn approached, but Sam could not wait to see the morning light. Much had happened, too much to understand. Exhausted, he let himself fall to sleep in the missionary's arms, thinking of the day to come and its promise of a return to normal life.

⁓

"These Mormons appear to be as wanton as rabbits," Eben chuckled, "they come here and cannot stay away from our women. Their Apostles are the worst. Since they arrived in Saco, all eligible women pursue them. My cousin, Agnes, does. Who is given the name Don Carlos? It sounds dark skinned, but he is her interest. Maybe because he's the brother of their prophet, Joseph."

"Remember Mary Baily. She went back to Ohio with Samuel Smith last year. It seems the Mormons have come to prize the women of Maine," Nate Harmon said.

"Our men are prized too. People around here have the reputation of being properly endowed," Paul Dresser quipped. "Samuel's younger sister, Lucy, came here and snagged Arthur Milliken. She took him west."

"It is the lasting infection of Jacob Cochrane's promiscuity," Paul Dresser said. "He is again in the newspapers. They report that he showed up in Massachusetts as 'Jacob the Prophet.' When found out he fled to New Hampshire with a bevy of women. Couldn't take everyone, so he sneaks back, in the guise of a woman, to hold secret meetings." Everybody laughed.

"He never gives up, seeking a revival of his golden days here. They say he started a community in New York, but people complained life was too hard. Cochrane never spent much time there, to get them enthralled. He left a Mormon in charge who didn't have the prophets's charm."

"Important business must have kept Cochrane away, or his tumescent member," Eben quipped.

The banter, joking, and the mugs of cider, enlivened the gathering. The two brothers at the door went unnoticed.

"If you want to talk about Jacob Cochrane, we will come back later," Alexander Berry spoke. "There is nothing about him we find funny."

"Don't go, you are welcome here," Eben stood up. "There is plenty to gossip about, especially the Mormons and their trip to Zion. Alexander and Abner, join us, have a drink. How is your father?"

"He has no relief from the rheumatism," Alexander said. "His joints are too stiff to move much, or he would have come with us."

"Nate had to bring me in a buggy," Nathaniel Harmon said. "I have a year on old Isaac."

"And how is your sister, Aphia?" Eben asked.

"Much the same. She would do better with a woman around the house," Alexander said. "But both Elizabeth and Anna come by now and then. They are kind and understand her needs. That is a help." Alexander held his brother's moist hand.

"Both of you can sit on this bench," Eben got up from the plank suspended between two boxes. "Do you want some cider?"

"Sure. I'd like some," Alexander took his brother to the sagging timber. "Abner doesn't drink."

"We were talking about the Mormons. They are disrupting everything. Some hereabouts have joined that deranged church. They are selling their land, disposing possessions, and preparing to go west. They come in here for provisions," Eben said.

"Yes. I hear they are breaking free of Babylon and going to Zion," Paul cracked. "We could be missing out on something, wasting time here gabbing."

"Alexander, what about your brother, Ephraim? He keeps to himself. Does he talk of Babylon or Zion?" Nate Harmon joked. "I was there the first time Ephraim had sex in church."

"We don't see much of him," Alexander said. "He keeps so busy, he has no time to come by the house." Abner's face was expressionless, but his breath was audible and short.

"I hear he is kept busy down in Saco," Nate smirked, looking around at the regulars in the room. "I know the Mormons had a conference there, and nine of their twelve Apostles showed up. The bigwigs from Ohio are not the only attraction."

"I don't know what he does. I don't look to my brother's example," Alexander said.

"The Mormon exodus offers some a new opportunity. If you want to buy more land, Alexander," Eben said, "There is a lot for sale. I know Phineas Butler and Benjamin McKinney are getting rid of their farms."

"We just sold some land to our brother-in-law, Jabez," Alexander said. "Our farm suits the four of us. We have what we need to get by. Abner and I can handle the work."

"I understand that your brother, Ephraim, is dabbling in land," Paul said. "He has done business with Joseph Moulton. They were drinking at Wentworth Tavern and had papers with them."

"We don't know what he is doing," Alexander barked. "Ephraim doesn't come by. Damn Ephraim."

The room fell silent.

"Ephraim. Ephraim. Help me," Abner cried out. "Help me, pleeese. Pleeese." Abner's mouth didn't close, his eyes froze. He trembled, jolted and frantically clenched his chest with both arms. His fingers scratched at his shirt. The rigid body constricted, gulping for breath in short, guttural snorts. Sweat ran down Abner's face, and his head shook with fierce jerks.

Alexander latched on to his brother, pulling him close, grabbing Abner's convulsing head with both hands to still it. "Calm. Calm," he pleaded. "You are safe, Abner. Look in my eyes. It is me, Alexander, your brother. You are safe. I will take care of you." He clutched his brother's head.

Abner stilled, but the shaking continued. His clothes clung in sweat.

"Here is a blanket," Eben handed a heavy spread to his nephew.

"Put the blanket on the floor," Alexander commanded. "Get another."

Alexander got behind his brother. Wrapping his arms around Abner's torso, he eased the rigid body back. Alexander rested his brother's frame on the blanket Eben stretched out on the rough planking. Extending the arms along Abner's sides to improve circulation, Alexander noticed the piss-soaked trousers. Alexander lay down next to his brother, pulled himself close, bolting Abner in his arms.

~

"Where's the laughter and the jokes?" Ephraim burst into the store. "It's time to celebrate, loosen up. Pour the cider." Ephraim stopped short.

Every man in the store huddled around the two figures on the floor. No one turned to welcome the ebullient newcomer.

"We have something serious here," Eben looked up. "Abner has had a fit. He is resting now. Nate has gone for his buggy to take Abner home."

"My sisters tell me that Abner is sometimes overcome," Ephraim said. "These episodes are part of his nature."

"What do you know about Abner's troubles? He never had attacks before you took us to that Cochrane meeting." Alexander's red face turned toward Ephraim.

"You were at the meeting too, Alexander," Ephraim's voice turned gritty. "How was it that he got out of your sight? The flesh is weak."

"What do you know about us? Nothing," Alexander stepped toward Ephraim. "We never see you. You never come by. You have money, but no sympathy. Do you ever think of your ailing father, or your sister, who cannot take care of herself? Look at your brother." Alexander pointed to the motionless figure on the floor. "He can do no work, know happiness or feel joy. There is no healing, no cure."

"The buggy is ready," Nate stepped into the store.

Eben pulled Abner upright, tucking the spread around him before Alexander maneuvered his brother toward the door.

"Be kind, Alexander." Ephraim said. "Show some understanding. I have a farm and a family to care for. I have responsibilities in the community."

"Show. What do you show? You are a phantom, hiding your land schemes and financial deceit. You think your cheating and romping in Saco are secret. People know the disgusting things you do, things which discredit our name." Alexander spat toward his brother. "God bless you," he said, and took Abner from the store.

Ephraim was abashed. Some time passed before he seemed conscious of the spittle on his shoe. Eben, Nathaniel, and Paul stared at the churlish man before them in disbelief. Eben, Jr. couldn't look his childhood friend in the eye, and turned away.

"We are all set. I'll be back once Abner is settled, Father," Nate stuck his head in the door.

"A drink is called for," Ephraim broke the silence and moved toward the store's counter. "I'll help myself." He filled a large cup with the liquor. Casually, he walked back to face his former friends.

"Alexander knows nothing of God," Ephraim said with authority. His thin face was transformed with a smile of unexpected warmth. "Please don't expect me to drink alone." He raised the cup.

"You said you came here to celebrate," Paul grabbed the decanter and poured cups so everyone had a dram of liquor.

"I came here to celebrate," Ephraim said, raising his arm again. "And to spend time with old friends. Let's drink."

"I can't imagine what you are celebrating, since you keep everything a secret," Eben said.

"I sold some land," Ephraim said, "And got a good price."

"Like Phineas Butler and Benjamin McKinney? Are you going away, with the Mormons?" Eben asked, shaking his head in disbelief.

"Yes. I am going to join their wagon train. I am heading west." Ephraim took a swig of whiskey.

"You are leaving everything behind," Eben said.

"I am taking my family, my children," Ephraim responded.

"You are leaving Buxton, your farm. My sister passed, but you are leaving your father and Jane, Rebecca, Elizabeth, Aphia, Anna and two brothers," Eben listed the names in solemn cadence. "How can you part from your family?"

"My father never liked me. No one will forget Toad, and I will be mocked by that name until my death. Everybody knows how he worked me. He never respected me or listened to a word I said. My father is never satisfied. He is a hard man, without affection. I owe him nothing," Ephraim's words poured out. "I will not be stuck in this hole. The land is difficult to farm and there is not enough to divide up among my boys."

"Are you caught up in that Mormon hocus pocus? Do you know verses from Nephi and the revelations of the New Bible? Will you become a saint?" Eben found his caustic voice.

"You men do not understand, because you have never experienced God," Ephraim said. "It is a gift from beyond, to be one with Him."

Itinerant preachers stopped at Coolbroth's Corners. Mendicant, dervishes, fakirs and monks had drifted through. But Ephraim's testament was stupefying to the store regulars.

"You are a changed man, Ephraim," Eben announced after some brief deliberation. "And a changed man understandably changes his domicile. But I don't see the nascent saint in you. The Ephraim I remember over the years was kind and accommodating, preferred conciliation to conflict, extended emotional support and empathy to others. What I see in you now is just the opposite. You are not delusional, just callous and self-seeking."

"I expected scorn," Ephraim said. "That doesn't make it easy to suffer."

"The qualities Eben mentioned are said to make men sexually attractive to women," Nathaniel cracked. "Does Mary know how irresistible you have made yourself to that woman in Saco?"

"You pride yourself with your fatherhood, but your children suffer most from your deplorable judgment," Paul said. "At least they have a caring mother."

"Say whatever you want. Spread every vicious rumor you can make up. I won't take any more abuse. I'm leaving for good. Rot here in hell." Ephraim dashed from the store.

Mary heard the front door slam loudly. *Who could that be in the middle of the day?* She thought. *The boys are out working and Mirinda has gone to her grandfathers to visit with Aphia.* Ephraim didn't say a word as he tore through the kitchen and went into the storage room.

"Where is my rifle?" Ephraim yelled, "Who has been playing around with my rifle? It isn't here. Mary, are you listening to me?"

Mary put the bowl of flour on the counter, wiped her hands on a towel, and walked to the storeroom door. "I haven't seen your rifle, but I have no reason to look for it," Mary said.

"You have so much junk in this room. I can't find anything," Ephraim clamored.

"Why do you want your rifle?" Mary asked.

"There could be trouble," Ephraim looked at Mary for the first time. "I got into a fight at the store."

"A fight? At your uncle's?" Mary walked into the small room, where Ephraim raged among the disorder, dust swelling up in the dim light.

"It wasn't a fight where we came to blows," Ephraim said. "There were sharp words. It was bitter, and I never want to see them again. But they could come after me, to even things out. I let them have it."

Mary returned to the work counter and making bread. Ephraim came out of the storeroom, stroking the barrel of the rifle. He had a faint smile.

"They are cowards and won't come," Ephraim sounded confident. "I won't have to defend myself. But I cannot leave on the trip without the rifle."

"Leave? Trip? What are you talking about?" Mary turned to face her husband.

"I have converted and become a Mormon. Hyrum Smith, an Apostle of the Church and brother of the prophet, Joseph, baptized me. I am joining the wagon train to Zion," Ephraim said.

"Mormon. Zion. Where in hell is Zion?" Mary paced the kitchen floor trying to make sense of what she heard. "I have heard insane stories, of people selling their land, everything, and moving west. That's not what you are doing?"

"Yes. That is what I am doing. Taking the family on a marvelous journey to a new life," Ephraim looked around the room which had not changed in twenty years. The wooden beams overhead sagged, discolored by smoke, their corners laced with spider webs. The old glass in the windows distorted the outside view and shaded the incoming light.

"You want to leave all of this? A place that through work, sacrifice is a part of you. Separating from this land is like rending your flesh and tearing out your heart."

"It is a break with the past. You have to leave the awful scars and brutal memories to become new again and fresh," Ephraim said.

"Fresh and new. Like that woman you have been seeing?" Mary's tone was flat. "It hasn't been that long since you stalked her at Nate Harmon's social. In two years, the bonds with her cannot be feeble. Gossips say you spend a lot of time with her. How are you going to give her up?"

"I am not going to give her up. She has been baptized and is now a Mormon. She will come along." Ephraim didn't hesitate.

"What about me?" Mary gasped.

"You are not coming," Ephraim said firmly.

"You bastard," Mary screamed. "You shameless bastard." She rushed at her husband in rage, swung at him and swung again.

Ephraim parried the blows. She grabbed for his face; he grabbed her arm. She twisted until she freed herself, falling to the floor. He reached down, grabbing each side of her head and pulled her up. The large tortoise shell comb in her hair caught in his cuff, and Mary's thick locks fell loose.

"You lout. You dissolute rake," she screamed.

He gripped her thin shoulders with calloused hands and shook her violently. Mary's loosened hair tangled, and her head rolled around, puppet-like. Her wailing turned to choking.

Ephraim threw her on the floor. In falling, her hand caught the bowl of flour, tipping it over, covering her face and hair in white. She stayed on the floor, sprawled, catching her breath. She shook the flour from her hair as she got up and dashed toward the stove and the frying pan. Mary took it in both hands, lunged toward her husband, swinging the pan toward his face. Her rage erupted into a surge of energy.

Ephraim was surprised "*Where did this all come? What has broken loose?* He asked himself. As he ducked, he went for her waist, and brought her crashing to the floor with his heavy weight.

They hadn't been this close in years. As he pressed into her body, he looked down at her battered face dappled with flour, at her tangled hair streaked with grey. Some of it, wet with perspiration was matted to her scalp, but the awful, dark red scar Ephraim hadn't seen since his wedding night was fully exposed.

Choking for air, her transfixed eyes leaked tears into the white powder on her face. Ephraim's finger traced the ugly wound as if it were newly discovered. The alien weighing heavily across her trembling chest offered no comfort, his look that of an explorer eyeing an exotic curiosity. He caught no sense of her horror and ignored the bloody drool escaping her mouth.

Ephraim pulled off and sat in a footstool beside Mary. "Yes. I am starting a new life, and I am taking the children," Ephraim said, as if the struggle with his wife had been only a minor intrusion. "They too will have a new life. They will be a big help in settling our promised land."

"How can you take the children?" Mary boosted herself up. "You don't even care about them.'

"I am their father and know what is best for them," Ephraim said.

"You have given Samuel some of your time, teaching him to run a farm," Mary avoided her husband's face.

"He is a good worker, listens to what I say and knows what to do," Ephraim said.

"You give some attention to Mirinda, your only daughter, but have no idea how she sees herself. She could have greater confidence and self-regard," Mary struggled to speak. "You don't want her to have an education and show no interest in her future."

"I am very fond of my daughter," Ephraim said as he brushed flour off his trousers.

"Aside from what you demand in the field," Mary said, "the others are largely ignored.

"I was ordered to mother Isaiah and I love him dearly. But you don't see how hard he tries to please you, and his hurt from your inattention." Mary sat straight up, pulling her skirt over bruising legs. "You wanted the adoption of William, but you have no interest in his grades at school, or his impulse to help others. When Josiah fractured his shoulder, you wouldn't pay to have it reset by a proper doctor. He lacks strength in his left arm. Everyone can hear the pop when he stretches it, but you take no notice."

"I spend more time with the boys than you, Mary," Ephraim said. "You can't tell me anything I don't know."

"You think only of yourself, Ephraim," Mary wasn't finished. "You never liked your father calling you "toad", but you belittle Jonathan by calling him 'puff guts.'"

"It fits him," Ephraim retorted.

"You have been shaped by your father's abuse, and pass it on," Mary said. "You do strike the boys and don't hide your brooding anger—it terrifies them. Your rage is not balanced by expressions of love. You don't know how to love. Your indifference and neglect are forms of abuse."

"Mary, you have a small life. Nothing changes for you, except the children get older. You no longer talk about the color of their shit or worry about getting them dressed. Kids learn fast how to take care of themselves. You may prepare new food, but the bread is always the same. Our bickering is no different than it was five years ago," Ephraim said.

"We don't bicker, because we don't talk," Mary said. "Change is not always good, and you are the best example of that.'

"My children have the chance to experience something new and marvelous. They will see things they never imagined," Ephraim stood. "I cannot deny them revelation, and revelation is attainable."

Ephraim is delusional and caught up in craziness. Mary thought. *I am sure he sees himself radiating the light of God.*

"That is what you want, Ephraim?" Mary was livid. "You did not deny Abner your prophet's revelation. I want my children protected from that risk."

"You have nothing to say about this," Ephraim said. "It is done." Ephraim turned to leave the house. "You are welcome to help them get ready for our departure. It will be a long journey." Ephraim was out the door.

Mary hated Monday but started her washday early. The open fire was burning well, with the water boiling in the big pot sitting over it. Everything was assembled. Dirty linen and clothes were strewn on the ground beside the half barrel used as a soaking tub. She would submerge the laundry in the soapy water long enough to loosen the dirt, then lift the clothes on to the washing bench placed beside the tub. The batting block, a rectangular plank on legs, was sturdy enough to withstand the blows from the laundry bat Mary used to beat the grit from the soaked items.

"What are you doing?" Jane's voice was a surprise.

"What I do at the beginning of every week," Mary straightened up. She put lye and ashes into the hot water. "Why aren't you washing clothes? Ignoring laundry just makes it worse."

"I had to see you," Jane hurried to embrace Mary. She started to cry. "How horrible. Anna told me that Ephraim is leaving you, leaving Buxton and taking the kids."

"This water won't stay hot forever," Mary's voice broke. She picked up the dirty clothes.

"Mary. Oh, Mary," Jane reached around Mary's shoulders hugging her sister-in-law again. "Don't move away from me. I'm here to help you. I can."

"With the washing?" Mary turned around, clutched Jane, tears breaking loose. "It's awful. I don't know what to do, Jane. Nothing is clear to me."

"Don't think about anything now," Jane said. "Let yourself cry. He hurt you. He is going and cannot hurt you anymore. You will be rid of him. His harping, complaints, beating, all of that will be over. Your pain and heartache will be over."

"It is not his leaving that hurts," Mary wailed. "I'm not sorry he is going. But I am losing the children. The bastard is taking them away. I can't stop him." Mary cried.

"Mother. Mother," Mirinda called as she walked from the house. "I have the rest of it, every dirty rag."

"Thank you, dear," Mary called back. She pulled away from Jane. "Put them on the ground with the others." Her broken words could not hide the hurt etched on her pale, contorted face.

"Mother," Mirinda cried. She dropped the clothes and ran to hold her mother. Jane reached out to both.

The women were alone. No one was around to see the grieving cluster or hear the helpless sobbing. When they pulled apart, they kissed and exchanged small, reassuring smiles. The fire under the water pot faded and the laundry was abandoned.

"You go back in the house, Mirinda," Mary said. "I'll finish later. There is not much more to be done." Jane stayed to help.

Mary left the tub to cool and would later ask the boys to dump out the water and move it and the soaking barrel into the barn. She and Jane took the undone laundry, the batting block, the laundry bat and the black soap into the house. Mirinda disappeared, Mary guessing that she had retreated to the loft.

"Please sit down, Jane. I will stoke the fire and make us some tea," Mary said.

"I'd like that, but don't go to any work," Jane said as she took her place at the table.

"It is no work. I would like some myself, and it keeps me busy," Mary said as she tended the coals and filled the kettle.

"Ephraim and I never planned the births of our children, but I have never thought any an accident. They are blessings and something about each of them is spiritually profound. Love for them leads me to life's mysteries, it takes me to God. I cannot imagine losing them." Mary faced Jane and started to cry. "Unlike Ephraim, I do not have to go west to feel God's presence. I feel it when I play with my children, when I am with them. Each one is different. I am losing so much."

"Husbands never ask their wives about their children's spiritual welfare. At least, my James doesn't," Jane said. "But, James doesn't talk about religion. I cannot imagine him mentioning revelation."

"Ephraim doesn't talk to me much, on any subject," Mary brought the teapot and the cups to the table and poured the tea. "Revelation came up when he said he was leaving and taking the children. He can rant on about the Bible."

"Everybody has heard him talk about fatherhood," Jane said. "His authority on the subject is scripture."

"I know," Mary halted and wiped her eyes. "But he doesn't know how to be a father."

"Women need their own Bible, a book which acknowledges our nature and how we live," Jane said. "What we have is a man's book, written by men, and concerning the interests of men. Caring for children is given few words."

"Ephraim recites Bible verses and talks of rules to live by," Mary opined. "The rules do not countenance women. Though ignored and discounted by the Good Book, what would men do without us? Men find no rules for raising children. Children suffer from that contradiction. The Book says that children shouldn't suffer."

"Women suffer too," Jane said with a deep sigh. "How different it would be for us, and our husbands, had the Bible included accounts written by women. A book by Mary, or Elizabeth, the mother of John the Baptist, would offer women satisfaction. Their experiences should have been recorded. If not by them, written down by other women. There is no wisdom on motherhood. In the Bible motherhood is vulgar, while fatherhood is something for my brother to preach about."

"We complain about this with each other, Jane, but it makes no difference," Mary said. "My children are leaving. Understand? And grumbling does not stop my heartbreak." Mary reached across the table, and caressed Jane's wrist, having nothing else to say.

"You are a strong and capable woman, Mary," Jane said tenderly. "Do not concern yourself with men's scripture. You must take your soul into your own keeping."

BOOK TWO

The New Testament

NINE

"Never took you as a man who sits around looking at sunsets," Orson interrupted Ephraim's solitude. "I see you as a man of action."

"You've got it right, Orson. I like to keep busy," Ephraim said. "But this is a nice spot and it is quiet here."

The wagons below were scattered among the trees at the edge of the meadow, a dull brown in the fading light. The sun settled behind the far mountains, but its glow on the water highlighted the figures of the children at the river's edge.

"I'm glad to have you among this flock of pilgrims, Ephraim. You pitch in. You are always ready to help anyone fixing a wagon or having trouble with their animals," Orson said.

"I do know how to fix things. My boys can take care of our wagon. I have time to lend others a hand," Ephraim said.

"Your boys are helpful. My herdsman, Elder Butterworth, tells me they know how to work cattle. We only have thirty head in the train, but that is a lot for one man to handle," Orson said.

"I know cattle will go in the direction they are headed, but also that if they want to go to that patch of woods, that is where they will go," Ephraim agreed. "You can't count on them to follow."

"Your boys saved us when we forded the Deerfield. The cattle started to move when they smelled water. With the boys on their flanks, the cattle were herded to the best spot, and we crossed the river without losing one," Orson said. "We traveled more than one hundred and fifty miles in our first ten days, and I think that water crossing could have made for the worst day of all."

"We have a long way to go," Ephraim stood and pointed at the dimming horizon. "I'm glad you know this trail, and how to get where we are going."

"I was not surprised by your decision to come," Orson said. "You always had a faraway look in your eye. But I was curious when I saw your new companion and realized that Mary stayed behind."

"Yep. Mary stayed behind," Ephraim paused before elaborating. "She has her own way of seeing things and doesn't have a spiritual nature. She didn't want to convert. Hannah did and was baptized. Hannah has some child-bearing years ahead, along with a lusty nature. And she brought a cow along. How could I refuse livestock when I am starting a new farm?" Ephraim laughed.

"So, despite your spiritual inclinations, you never take your mind off the practical," Orson said. "That is a combination I revere. Men like you are especially useful to our church and its future. I understand that you contributed a lot to Jacob Cochrane's successes, and that you were devoted and loyal to him."

"Jacob Cochrane has not been part of my life for many years. I haven't kept up with him. He could be dead," Ephraim said.

"The Mormon Church offers many opportunities to a man with your abilities," Orson said.

"An important part of my life was spent at Jacob Cochrane's side, advancing his vision and tending to all of the mundane thankless work. That experience needs no repeating," Ephraim said. "I don't have to relearn those lessons."

"That stewardship was important for you. I think you know about true belief and what it takes to make man's belief stronger. You were part of some storied events and must have learned much about the spiritual nature of men. From those varied tasks you know your own nature better. Now, with God's new revelation, and Joseph's new Bible, you have renewed your belief," Orson said. "You can be a big help in the restoration of God's Kingdom."

"Thank you, Orson. With compliments, I easily become a half-wit," Ephraim chuckled. "I will be pleased to help out as I can, but I want to be just like every other pilgrim—no special position. I need to work more on my own salvation than on the souls of others. I will be of more help in spreading God's New Word."

"Ephraim. You must serve God's Church," Orson said.

"This trip is a big change for me. I am on a new path, making a new life. I have thought about that life a long time. At twenty-four I wanted to leave and join the war. Didn't happen. Now, everything is left behind, Buxton, its old stories and tired ways. Connections to the land I spent years cultivating are severed. I am no longer bound by my family's parochial ways, no longer bound by my father's commands and whimsies. There is much to do before I will be adept at discharging any new responsibilities," Ephraim said. "I am grateful that your Church has given me the path."

"I'll let you be, Ephraim, for now," Orson said. "But you haven't left everything behind. That is why I know you can be of help to me and to my Church."

◠

The Berry boys were fascinated by American Indian lore, the Oneida, Cayuga, Tuscarora nations and the native landmarks along the Mohawk Trail. They knew the Seneca still lived near their destination in Western New York; the settled farmland they traversed was the historic homeland of a great Indian nation. Early on, they passed through what was once Mohawk land, and villages with names like Canajoharie and Schenectady. Chittenango had been home to the Oneida tribe, another part of the ancient confederacy. Onondaga County was named after yet another people of the Indian nation, the "Keepers of the Fire," hundreds of years before the "Great Peacemaker" had appeared in this place. It was at the time of a solar eclipse, and the sky turned pitch black at midday. When sunlight was restored, all the tribes from miles around joined to form the great and powerful nation of the Iroquois.

Camillus, New York, where the Mormon party stopped for provisions, had no Indian history. It was named after the Revolutionary War, when the New York Legislature divided up two million acres of land for settlement by veterans of the war. From the encampment in a grove above Lake Onondaga, the rich history of the region could be imagined.

Levi Sloper usually left the cooking to his wife, Emma, but she was attending to the accumulated laundry. Slope, as he was called from childhood, was impatient and hungry. He got the fire going and put the slabs of bacon he had bought the day before into the large, hot pan.

"Be careful with your cooking, Levi," Emma cautioned.

"Stop telling me what to do. I'm not an idiot, Emma," Levi carped. "Just pay attention to those dirty clothes. I got the water for you, and all you need."

"I need some peace, Levi, and to be left alone for a bit," Emma sighed.

"Alone. You wouldn't be anywhere without me," Levi retorted.

Levi was exasperated but was calmed by the late afternoon sun reflected on the lake. Everything seemed peaceful.

"Look! Turn around!" Emma yelled. "The pan's on fire."

It was indeed. The swell of flames from the pan of bacon surprised Levi. He looked back at Emma and her bucket of water and frantically ran to get it. Pouring water on the fire only made it worse. It was a tiny explosion, an eruption of grease that splattered oil in all directions.

"You know not to do that," Emma's voice was harsh and pleading. "Never."

"Goddammit! I will take care of this," Levi cursed, grabbing a cloth from Emma's pile of laundry. He swatted the fire with the cloth. Fanning the flame spewed more sparks. They landed everywhere, including the laundry pile which started to fume. Little flames littered the surrounding area. The fire brightened and grew hotter. Levi lashed again for the fire's source.

"Stop. Leave the pan alone." Emma's urgent voice was unheeded.

Levi lifted the pan, searing his hands. Reflexively, he flung the pan and it skidded to rest in the wagon bed.

"Help! Help! Please help!" Emma screamed. At the same time the wagon caught fire, the pile of laundry burst into flame. The Slopers were helpless. Emma was sobbing, while Levi blacked out.

Those nearby immediately pitched in to stop the fire. The camp alarmed, men formed a perimeter around the Sloper campsite moving wagons, any material that might catch fire. Shovels cleared brush. Hurriedly a trench was dug to confine the fire, the dirt flung on the surrounding flames to smother them.

Men and women with buckets formed two long chains from the lake to the burning wagon and surrounding trees. With clock-like precision, large quantities of water passed efficiently through the stifling smoke and were hurled at the leaping flames. Older children kept the younger ones out of the way. With every able body at work, the fire was finally extinguished.

As the smoke receded, Emma was seen lying on a blanket attended by several women with clothes, balms and various home remedies. Orson Hyde, who had supervised all the emergency measures, was there with horses to take Levi into town for medical attention. Benjamin McKinney boosted Levi on his horse and got behind him, so he wouldn't fall on the way to the doctor. Many of the waggoneers had gone back to their own business, but a small, silent crowd watched as Orson, Levi and Benjamin set out to find the closest doctor.

The Berry boys followed the whole scene from a distance.

"It's sad to see that Levi will never shake off his name," Samuel broke the silence.

"What's that, Samuel?" Jonathan asked his oldest brother. "Slope?"

"Yep. You are too young to know, but it was about his prick," Samuel said.

"His prick?" Jonathan's broad smile held back a giggle.

"When he was young, his friends joked that his dick sloped. Because of that, they were sure he would never get it to stand up," Samuel laughed.

The boys broke out in laughter and found it hard to stop.

"Well, each of us has his blessings, and that includes Levi," William smirked.

"So, how was Levi blessed?" Josiah asked.

"He was blessed to have been born in Buxton and not here," William continued.

"I never considered being born in Buxton a blessing," Josiah said.

"Levi was lucky he wasn't born in Onondaga. He would have been an outcast." William said. "He could never have been a "Keeper of the Fire.""

～

Despite its steep banks, the Chenango River was shallow at its ford. The spot was called Swift Run because of the fast water, but the rocky bottom would support heavy wagons during the crossing, if everyone took their time. Orson had two men posted on horses down river to catch anything that got caught in the rapid current.

Because the scent of water had its expected effect as they neared the river, the cattle crossed first. Samuel stayed with the wagon on the bank, but the other Berry boys herded the livestock to the ford, where the animals wouldn't get mired in sand. In the deepest part of the stream the water came up to a cow's withers, but all had their noses up and heads well above the river's surface. The herdsmen kept the cattle together until the other side was reached. Not all the herd wanted to leave the water, and it took time to round up the strays.

In the late afternoon each wagon took its turn crossing the Chenango. Small children stayed in the wagons, but those big enough crossed the wide stream on foot. Children were carried on shoulders. Some pilgrims stayed upstream from their wagons, giving them something to grab if the stream became overwhelming. Not all the wagons were reliably stable, and the Bentley rig rolled on its side. Righting a swamped rig was rarely successful, but those nearby scrambled to the task. Spilled contents, such as a toolbox, sank to the river bottom. People shouted over other articles carried downstream, alerting men in their path to retrieve fleeing possessions. A young boy snatched up a yapping dog that stood precariously on a floating wooden trunk. People cheered the rescue.

Mirinda, holding her boots waist high, trudged across the river with bare feet, halting at sharp rocks and avoiding the holes others fell into. Having hitched up her skirt to keep some of it dry, she found her balance difficult. In the middle of the crossing, she slipped on a slick rock and plunged into the stream.

"Help," she cried, arms flailing. "Help." Her head went under and she came up coughing and spurting water.

Orson Hyde was supervising the crossing from the far shore. He jumped off his mount, waded to the screaming woman and grabbed Mirinda before she was pulled into the strong rushing current. After grabbing her hand, he wrapped his arm around her waist, lifted her into his arms and headed to shallow water. Tight already as they headed to shore, Orson's hold on Mirinda went beyond that needed for safety. As they sloshed out of the river the savior's hand moved up the wet bodice of her print dress, swaddling her breast. The caress, given the urgent nature of Mirinda's situation and general chaos among those in the water, went unnoticed. But the bold embrace was a new experience for the young woman.

When the packed sand at the river's edge stabilized the young woman's feet and her balance was restored, she wrested herself free of Orson's arms. Pulling back the hair pasted to her forehead and cheeks, Mirinda's flushed face became completely visible.

"Thanks, so much for your help, Mr. Hyde," Mirinda said. She smiled, then rushed away to find the McKinney wagon.

Mirinda was confused by the encounter in the river, and by the revived memories of Orson's flirtations months before. His glances that night in Buxton were the first to make her feel attractive and aware of her womanhood. She had been aroused. Now, she couldn't settle down and could not go back to the McKinney's wagon. She wandered around the encampment, among exhausted pilgrims who drank and smoked. Fires were set to cook or dry out garments still wet from the crossing. Desperate to compose herself, she decided to seek the advice of her father.

Ephraim was not with his wagon, but Hannah was, surrounded by company. Her father's mistress ignored Mirinda as she approached the gathering of women. Mirinda knew all of them except the dark figure who sat in the center.

"That's Nittawosew," Sarah Bentley whispered to Mirinda as the newcomer eased herself into the group. "She is a midwife who knows Indian magic. They call her Blossom because she knows how to help women get pregnant."

Pregnancy was the last thing on Mirinda's mind. She wanted to ignore her sexual urges, not aggravate them. "Everyone here wants to get pregnant?" she whispered to Sarah as she looked around at her father's girlfriend, Sara Butler, Martha Junkins, Susan Guptail, and Hannah Libby.

"Yes. Some are only curious," Sarah amended. "Blossom has wisdom from the ancients about women, their womb, the courses, and conception. She has potions and medicines."

"I'm no longer a slip of a girl," Sara Butler stood, and laughed as she rubbed her generous belly. "Though I'm getting older, I'm still built for pleasure. I've been married twice, am older than my husband, but would like another baby. Can you help me, Blossom? My husband would find me more endearing."

Blossom's lustrous complexion, her lineless and unblemished fawn skin, and full mouth contrasted with her dark, immutable eyes, making her age difficult to peg. Her gaze was fixed and serious but her small gold earrings, a wide choker of small white shells, and the bright ribbons tied at the end of her dark braids made her less forbidding. Blossom sat rigid, but her hands, palms up, reached out from her lap in an offering. "Yes, I can help you. But your mind must be as willing and committed as your body," Blossom replied in an even tone. "And your mind must be respectful of the child you will beget."

"Respectful?" Sara asked.

"You must care about the child from the very beginning. Your husband must want an offspring," Blossom said. "Take care that your actions foster the gentle growth of your egg and know that everything you eat is its food. Don't eat things that would be harmful to the baby. Eating raccoon or pheasant will make the baby sick or die. Speckled trout can cause birthmarks and eating black walnuts could give the baby a big nose."

"I want another child. That's why I came. I am not here to hold on to a husband, and don't like raccoon, or black walnuts. God's command to replenish the earth means nothing to me," Sarah Bentley blurted. Sarah was twenty-two, unmarried, independent and seeking a new life with her daughter, Lucy. "It's easy to find a man to screw, but you can't always count on a baby after. I am here, Blossom, to buy your potion. How much does it cost?"

"A husband is important. We are given husbands by God to multiply believers. That is what the Prophet says. Childbearing is doing God's work," Hannah said. "A child binds a woman to her husband and draws attention away from his other children." Hannah turned toward Mirinda, finally acknowledging her presence.

Mirinda despaired as she looked at the women around her. There was no one to give her the advice she needed. All the women gathered around Blossom wanted to get pregnant. She was not ready to lose her virtue and saw no reason to do so.

Everyone knew Martha Junkins liked sex, she couldn't keep it a secret. Her husband, Joe Gilpatrick, had a similar constitution, and, under the sway of Jacob Cochrane, had left his wife and family to live with Martha. They had a two-year-old daughter, Elizabeth, but wanted another.

Susan Guptail also married an older man and former Cochrane leader. William, the "Swamp Fox," was known for his randiness and had introduced the popular "lights off" novelty to Cochrane's services. Susan's fruitfulness was not in question, with daughters Elizabeth and Matilda always by her side, but she wanted to honor her husband with a son.

Mirinda laughed to herself about the three Hannahs present. Hannah Ridley and Hannah Redlon, like her father's mistress Hannah Grace, were childless and complained about it incessantly. They would buy anything the Indian woman had to sell.

The ladies chattered. They talked candidly of needing a good tumble in the hay, stimulants for boosting husbands' carnal drives, and personal ways of managing sexual frustration. There was little talk of glorifying God by producing more offspring.

Blossom spread a blanket on the ground where she set out her special wares. She pointed to a bunch of leafless stalks, variegated in color—brown, red and shades of tan. "You call this yarrow. In our tradition it is life medicine, because it is so useful. Pour a mixture into your ear and it stops aching. Inhale its steam for headaches. It kills pain." She paused, leering, "Chew the root and place the saliva on any appendage as a stimulant. Any one of them is vitalized."

"That is for me," Martha's brash words broke the solemn tone Blossom had set for her sales pitch.

"All women suffer stomach cramps and bleeding inside. The extract from the seeds in these fan-shaped pouches will help," Blossom said. "Just put a few drops under your tongue."

Blossom reached into a small mound of pebble-like chunks of wood that she called wild cherry bark. It made a strong tea, which sped a delivery. Mirinda thought the women looked bored.

"This is what you come for." Blossom's hands cradled a small earthen vessel with a leather plug. She raised the vessel slowly as if it were a sacred object. "This potion is older than our memory and served generations of women. The oil comes from the seed of a beautiful yellow flower, which you call a Primrose." Blossom rubbed the vessel between her hands as if to warm its contents, removed the plug to give the women a whiff of the potion's light, sweet aroma. "It is medicine of the Gods."

Martha and Susan reached for the vessel, but Blossom drew it back to rest in her full bosom. The women were excited. Their heavy breathing stirred the evening air.

"You must be careful with such a powerful potion. This smooth liquid warms the womb. You rub it in and purge all innocence. Men are drawn to you, finding you irresistible. They cannot hold back," Blossom said.

"Show me how to use it," Martha commanded. "I want some now. In my womb? On its lips and helmet?" The excited woman leaned back on her elbows, pushing her pelvis toward the Indian healer while pulling up her skirt, grunting.

"Me first," Hannah bleated, knocking Martha off balance.

"What is going on here?" Ephraim bellowed. He appeared from behind the wagon.

Mirinda was jolted by her father's voice, and embarrassed being part of the wickedness.

"I'm ready for my dinner," Ephraim said, indifferent to the various exposed pudenda.

The women scattered, reminded of their own hungry husbands. Hannah hurried to restore the fire and tend to the food. Mirinda stepped toward her father, hoping for a few words.

"How are you, my lovely daughter?" Ephraim bowed for a peck. "I see you have dried out. The water seems to have refreshed you."

"I am fine, Father," Mirinda said. "I came here to talk to you."

"Father. Father," Josiah called out. "We have trouble with one of the horses. She may be lame." Mirinda's brother appeared with an urgent look on his face. Josiah caught his sister's eye and smiled. "Hello, Mirinda."

"We can talk later, my dear," Ephraim said as he left with Josiah.

Mirinda looked blank, realizing she lost the sense of urgency that brought her to her father's wagon. She didn't know what she would say had she the chance to talk.

Mirinda knew that her father was a philanderer. Her cousin, Mary Ann, repeated her mother's stories. She knew her father played a snake in a church enactment of the story of Adam and Eve, and that he had been the only clothed participant. Like other men on the train, her father had been a deputy of Jacob Cochrane and hip deep in his sordid tales. Ephraim was at Cochrane's right hand during his famous trial for debauchery. He helped Cochrane escape from the county marshal and kept him hidden for months. Mirinda knew of the decadent religious services, one where her Uncle Abner was attacked. Her father had taken Abner to that meeting.

People waved at Mirinda as she walked back to the McKinney wagon through the gentle smoke of campfires and snatches of night music. Everyone seemed kind.

Mirinda had heard that her father consorted with women in Cochrane's fellowship and may have fathered children outside her family. The boys kidded about having different mothers. Isaiah was teased most because of his dimples, the only family member with them. Mary Ann told Mirinda of her mother's rape. Her mother went undefended, according to accounts. Ephraim took no action. The tragic event was never mentioned in the immediate family, except that Samuel was said to have been a witness of the violence. Mirinda didn't have the nerve to ask her brother if it was true.

I have always loved my father, but how do I fit in his world? What would he say if I asked him? Is his world any different than Orson Hyde's? Is he different from Benjamin McKinney, who makes advances on me in the presence of his wife? Mirinda saw no solution to her problem. *The Mormons are no different. There is no condemnation of adultery. My father and Hannah were baptized with no questions asked of their union. No concerns were raised about my Mother and her abandonment.*

It was not hard to find her way to the McKinney wagon, despite the darkness and the silence. Next to the wagon a small fire was burning, and Benjamin had his back against a wheel. He was cushioned by a heavy blanket. His legs were extended so the insides of his trouser legs were warmed by the embers. He sipped from a tin cup.

"Where is Mary Ann?" Mirinda asked.

"She's gone to bed. Headache," Benjamin said. "Sit down. There is nothing left to eat, but I'll pour something that will warm you up. Cider?"

"No, thank you," Mirinda said. She sat down facing her host, curling her legs and tucking the full skirt under them. "I don't care for any drink and I'm not hungry."

"I know that you would have preferred to travel with your family," Benjamin said. "I know that Mary Ann and I cannot replace the excitement of your brood, but we are glad to have you with us."

In the firelight, Benjamin did not look much different from her father. They were nearly the same age, both physically trim under loose-fitting clothes. Neither had a naturally welcoming nature, but they could assume an easy manner when necessary. Mirinda thought her father's face kinder, though, reading something aggressive into Benjamin's smiles.

"Hannah has to be jealous when you are around. She's something you no longer have to suffer as long as you are with us," Benjamin said.

"I will learn to get along. I have to," Mirinda said.

"Everyone knows that you are your father's favorite. You are older than all of them but Samuel. You know everyone's needs," Benjamin continued.

"My father has his own needs. That is why Hannah is there," Mirinda was irritated by Benjamin's conversation. She had no idea how long Hannah had been seeing her father. Since leaving Buxton she grappled with Hannah's presence and the position this woman had in the family.

"I am sorry if this is a sore subject," Benjamin sounded apologetic. "You are a generous and caring person, Mirinda. That is all I have to say."

"Thank you, Mr. McKinney," Mirinda lowered her head.

"It is remarkable. You played with Isaiah, Josiah, William and Jonathan as babies. You must know almost as much about them as their mother. You have an important place in their lives," Benjamin said.

"Please, Mr. McKinney," Mirinda implored.

Benjamin drew up his legs, idly adjusted the crotch of his trousers and moved around the fire. He put his arm around Mirinda's shoulder. "You will never be treated with indifference around here, never ignored, Mirinda. I promise." Benjamin's embrace became a hug. It didn't end soon enough but he finally pulled away. He didn't take his eyes off her.

"Your beautiful hair shines in the firelight," Benjamin said. "I have noticed all of the care and attention you give it. That is telling and shows that you don't let the grit and dust get the best of you. It is a kind of self-respect. I see no vanity because you are blind to your beauty."

Mirinda was impressed by the tenderness behind Mr. McKinney's tough exterior. There was more to this man than she had seen before. He noticed so many things. His words were soft and smooth. But she did not feel calm or composed.

"You must be a little hungry, Mirinda," Benjamin said. "I have something in here especially for you." He reached in his pocket but locked his eyes on the young woman, smiling. Mirinda looked down, wondering what all the fumbling in his pants was about.

"Rock candy. You must like rock candy. It is sweet and hard," Benjamin said. He held a small white crystal between his fingers. He teased Mirinda, moving his fingers toward her mouth, then pulling them back. "Stick out your tongue." When Mirinda did, he put the candy in her mouth. "Nice and sweet. Huh?"

The sugar tasted good. She smiled before she looked down. His stare wore her out. *No.* She thought. *No. This can't happen.* Benjamin's pants were open, and she could see his flesh.

"You must be cold. We better cover your legs. That skirt is not enough to warm them, even though it keeps them hidden. I've got a blanket here." Benjamin reached for the bedroll he had been resting on. "I noticed how you managed to get yourself out of that rushing water. Those legs are strong." While he covered her lower body with the wool spread, he stretched out her legs and massaged them. "You are a hearty girl. Your body feels ready for any challenge."

Before she had her bearings, Benjamin pushed her torso to the ground. Mirinda struggled, but his strength and body weight were overwhelming. He pulled up her camisole and blouse to expose her breasts.

"I saw you in the water," Benjamin panted. "I could tell Orson Hyde liked these teats, the way he played with them. Did your nipples get hard?"

"No. Don't do that. Please. Stop, please." Mirinda cried, as her head rolled back and forth on the hard dirt. Her strength quickly failed her, as did her voice, muted, but for desperate gasps.

He got lighter. But a moment later he had torn off her underwear and was between her legs. "Argh! Argh!" Mirinda wailed. "Help."

"Shut up," Benjamin barked. He clamped her mouth shut with his hand. "I don't want to hurt you. You don't want to spoil your journey."

Benjamin's hand did not stop the tears and his weight could not subdue the involuntary thrashing of Mirinda's body. The oppressive heap moved in a ferocious rhythm, stopping only after a beastly shudder. His short-lived thrill was concluded by a hideous belch.

The assailant took no heed of the sobbing girl as he sat up, stretched his neck and took several deep breaths. He climbed into the wagon, and shortly reappeared with a bedroll that he tossed to the motionless figure on the ground. "We have a long day ahead. You should probably stay where you are. This will keep you warm enough."

A long time passed before Mirinda raised herself and got the bundle of bed linen. It was hard to move, and it was cold. She wrapped herself in the covers and lay back down not knowing what else to do. So sore, feeling like she had been torn open, she touched the residue on the inside of her thighs and cried. She wiped her brow. Near her face, she could see the sticky blood on her fingers. *Where is my mother? Who will take care me? How can I find my way? This cannot by my life.* There seemed no end to her sobs.

"You are going to be all right." The words woke Mirinda. It was less dark, and she could make out the face of Mary Ann. "This will make you feel better." Mary Ann wiped the drowsy young woman's forehead with a warm cloth, then her mouth.

She tried to sit up by herself but couldn't. "Could you please help me?" Mirinda whimpered.

"That is why I am here, dear, to help" Mary Ann spoke softly. "Benjamin means no harm. I had a peek under your covers and saw the blood. I will get another cloth and more warm water. You will be fine."

⌒

"What a blessed night we had," Elder Dunham exclaimed as he approached the McKinney wagon. "The Holy Spirit watches over this camp, Benjamin."

Mirinda was wakened by the voice of Orson's acting engineer. During the night, her move under the wagon provided shelter. Now, she curled up behind a wheel to hide her sorry state.

"What's that you said?" Benjamin emerged from the back of the wagon, hitching up and buckling his trousers. "The Holy Spirit?" He jumped to the ground.

"The camp was glorified last night," Jonathan said. "Did you see it? There wasn't a lot of swooshing, but the light was seen everywhere about. It is a reminder that God is always with us."

Benjamin stepped toward Jonathan and shook his hand. "It is a good morning, too." Benjamin's eyes searched for Mirinda, and briefly locked on those staring from behind the wagon wheel. His face did not register her terror. "It was a good night, but I saw no light."

"It was a luminous orb, which moved through the encampment close to the ground. It was not part of a shower, or random in its movements, but deliberated, purposeful as it traveled through the camp, assuring every one of their comfort and well-being. It also warded off evil spirits at the same time. After the visitation, the globe whirled around some forty or fifty times, zigzagged overhead and raced straight for the hills over there and disappeared," Jonathan's voice broke with excitement. "Amazing. Didn't you feel some special comfort last night, Benjamin?"

"I did," Benjamin smiled. "But I saw no ball of fire. I know what they look like, because I saw them on Ephraim's farm once. Orson was there."

"You were blessed," Jonathan nodded his head, having heard the story.

"You better get up girl, and do your part around here," Benjamin turned and looked down at Mirinda. *"The idler shall not eat the bread of the laborer.* Isn't that what you say, Jonathan, when you withhold a person's rations?"

"Yes, I do, Benjamin," the acting engineer said. "But I came for your help. We must fix that wagon and get rolling. Come on."

Mirinda crawled from under the wagon and grabbed the top of the wheel as she stood. Her legs were stiff, and her knees cracked as she straightened herself. Seeing no one around, she lifted her messy skirt to check the bruises and sores on her thighs and see if she needed to go and wash herself. She had heard of contagion, infection. Mary Ann had cleaned her up well.

"Here. You can wash your face, Dearie," her hostess magically appeared with a pail of water and a washcloth. "I have a brush for your hair, and some ribbons. You will look just fine."

Mirinda could not understand the attention she was getting. She was pleased by Mary Ann's presence, but her deepest urge was to disappear. She couldn't—there was no place to go.

"Are we staying in this place awhile?" Mirinda slowly scanned her surroundings.

"Yes. There are lots of things to be done before we move on," Mary Ann said. "There's that broken wagon from yesterday, and Jonathan said that many others need attention. They are going to be setting wagon tires, repairing hardware, and shoeing horses. The horses will be checked too, for worms and ticks." Mary Ann continued to brush Mirinda's hair. "We can find you a fresh skirt and wash this one."

The brush through her hair was comforting, but its sudden encounter with an unyielding tangle revived memory from the night before.

"Get away from me," Mirinda shook her hair loose from the comb and sprang to her feet in a rush of anger. "You heard the whole thing. You knew what was happening to me, and you didn't try to stop him." Mirinda's increased blood flow became visible, her whole body pulsing. The fury that abandoned her the night before was taking over. "How could you sit by and not try to stop him? You didn't make a sound?" The pulsing made her hands shake and her cheeks flush before her face turned a bright red. "Did you watch?" Her voice got louder; the words came faster. "Was he doing it for you?" Miranda's facial muscles tweaked her expressions into an ominous look, with lowered eyebrows, open mouth and strained lips framing wet, clenched teeth. Her ferocious appearance warned Mary Ann to flee. When the strain made Mirinda's appear ready to explode, she collapsed. Her core gave way to sobbing.

"Women face tough things," Mary Ann's voice stayed calm, like the morning air.

"I cannot stop him."

Mirinda pushed herself up and looked at Mary Ann with disbelief. "But you are his wife."

"What difference does that make?" Mary Ann retorted.

"You are supposed to give him what he needs. Don't you show him that you care?" Mirinda bawled. "You must not give him enough love."

"That's what preachers say, Dearie." The older woman reached to Mirinda, helped her sit straight, then looked her in the eyes. "You will understand as you get older. No matter what I tried, it didn't work. We have been together many years, and I still cannot explain what drives him."

"He doesn't want you?" Mirinda asked. "Because you haven't given him a baby?"

"Those are different things," Mary Ann said. "We have been intimate, but I never had a child. I never got pregnant, don't know what it is like to have a miscarriage."

"I am sorry," Mirinda inched closer. "Does he blame you?"

"He never said that," Mary Ann said.

"Did you give him pleasure?" Mirinda asked.

"At one time I am sure, but I don't know anymore. He wants me, sometimes," Mary Ann took her time. "I know there is resentment. I gave him no sons to help with the work."

"Did that give him doubts—about himself?" Mirinda continued. "Is that why he goes after other women, to prove his manhood?"

"I don't know. I am acquainted with some of the women he has been with, but I don't think he fathered any children," Mary Ann said.

"Have you ever desired him?" Mirinda asked.

"Yes, but I can't change anything. Stop his interest in other women? I gave up on that long ago," Mary Ann said. "But not the resentment."

"I don't understand any of this. Why did he choose to attack me?" Mirinda paused. "He didn't care who I was."

MaryAnn had a look of resignation, her expression saying, "That is the way it is."

"Men have such license, seeking out other women and ignoring their own wives. Where do they get such a sense of privilege? We are in a community that tolerates such oppression. Is that why we are going with the Mormons?" Mirinda sobbed.

"You are so young, Dearie," Mary Ann said. "But you know what happened in Buxton. You have seen what happened in your own family."

"What do I know?" Mirinda asked.

"Maybe the Mormons came for more than our souls. They may want to live the kind of life Buxton became famous for," Mary Ann said. "Maybe Benjamin, and your father are on this trip because they don't want to change. Mormons will let them live a life they prefer. Men have no reason to stick with just one woman. That's what this is all about."

"You mentioned my family. What about it?" Mirinda asked.

"Families never like to talk about their secrets, but those outside cannot shut up about them," Mary Ann said. "And they don't forget."

"My mother prides herself on her family," Mirinda admitted.

"But she doesn't pride herself on her marriage. Have you ever talked to your mother about her life?" Mary Ann asked. "Has she ever mentioned her own submission? Her rape? I'll bet not."

"My mother never talked about brutality and violence," Mirinda said.

"But you do know what she endured. You know about your father's indifference. And his unfaithfulness," Mary Ann said flatly.

"My mother doesn't speak badly of my father," Mirinda said. "She is never disrespectful."

"And Mary never said anything unkind to you about Hannah, I suppose." Mary Ann shook her head sadly. "Even in her abandonment, your mother has not railed against the bitch your father left her for?"

"No. Aunt Jane got very angry, but Mother never showed her feelings," Mirinda said.

Mary Ann moved closer to Mirinda, tightening her embrace. "You get it, don't you, Mirinda?" Mary Ann squeezed the woman beside her. "The code. You've learned the code and your eyes are open."

A butterfly fluttered before the silent women. With its unfurling the tiny creature became more luminous in the morning light and was utterly dazzling in its ascent. Too soon its figure was lost in the brightness of the sun.

⌒

"Look at what we have here," Orson said. A storm had washed away a whole section of the trail, and no bridge or roundabout had been constructed. "There is no upkeep on this road. Most people use the canal, so this damage remains. God knows when it happened or when it will be repaired."

"You deal with this kind of problem all of the time, Orson," Elder Dunham said. "We will find another way."

Orson and Dunham spent several hours scouting the surrounding terrain before deciding how to move forward. Orson led the wagons up a long, steep slope, part of a range of hills bordering the regular path. Moving up was an hour's long slog, lengthy and slow, but not an impossible climb. At the top of a ridge they found the road which would take them down to the village of Mt. Morris. Camp was set up for the night.

After sunrise Orson gathered the men to survey what lay ahead. The road was poor, but the drop down was the biggest challenge, along with managing the safe descent of everyone in the party. Most would walk the distance but keeping the animals together for that trip would not be easy.

"The road is badly rutted by use and rain, but the surface is hard and dry," Elder Dunham observed. "It looks to me like all of the wagons should make it."

"I'll have a problem," Rufus Warren said. "There will be an accident if I don't have a man to handle the brake on my wagon. It has been giving me trouble and my wife is not strong enough to manage the brake arm in an emergency."

"I'll handle that," Ephraim volunteered. "My son Samuel can drive our wagon and I can ride with you, Rufus. I would hate to see you lose all your belongings on the way down to that village. You wouldn't enjoy yourself when we get there."

Rufus's wagon was a little different than the others. It was bigger, and the bed was curved, not flat. Like most wagons, the front wheels were small, to make turning easier, wooden and rimmed with a steel ring to enhance durability. The rear wheels were larger, and the brake was on the left. A wooden block brought the wagon to a stop when pressed against the tire. Several mechanisms were involved, but Ephraim would man the critical one—the brake arm. When moved forward, the lever activated the braking system. The brakeman rode either standing or seated on a pull-out board. Ephraim stood to stay apprised of any danger ahead.

Rufus kept his team at a steady gait, a good distance behind the rig ahead. Nell, Rufus's wife, walked alongside the wagon while his son, Johnny, sat next to his father on the driver's bench.

The boy held to the backrest, happily singing "Turkey in the Straw." Ephraim paid strict attention to the road, which became more arduous by the minute.

The forward wagon pulled over and stopped. As they passed Moses Hanson, Rufus and Ephraim saw Moses adjusting the harness, collars and bridles of his team. Johnny waved, but his father and Ephraim could not afford distraction. They kept their eyes on the road as the village and the Genesee River came into view below.

Halfway down the slope the left rear wheel got caught in a long, downhill rut and Rufus couldn't get out of the trough before reaching a large boulder lodged in it. The wheel withstood the impact of hitting the obstacle, but the wagon pitched on to the two opposite wheels, tossing the riders in the air. Johnny bounced from his perch but held tight to the backrest as the wagon was righted. Rufus grabbed for Johnny, but momentarily lost his grip on the reins. After he regained his hold and pulled hard, it was too late. The horses picked up speed.

"Brake. Brake," Rufus yelled. Ephraim's hands turned scarlet from the stress, squeezing the brake arm, but the pressure on his left leg and ankle was just as great. Ephraim extended his leg back against a strut on the side of the wagon bed to gain leverage. He pushed the oak shaft forward with all the strength he could muster.

"Brake harder, goddammit. Push. Harder," Rufus yelled. "Hang on, Johnny. Hang on."

The smell of smoke reached Ephraim's nose despite the stifling dust. "The brake shoe is catching fire," he shouted. "We've got trouble." The wagon pitched and lurched as the wheels skidded on rocks and slammed across ditches in the road. Running faster with the weight of the wagon behind them and their harness breeching loose, the horses were free and headed straight toward the river.

The cattle leading the convoy panicked from the noise behind them and raced in all directions. Ephraim's sons jumped out of the wagon's path. Storefronts appeared on the right, Rufus yanked the reins to force the horses left, away from the river. The quick turn of the front wheels checked the wagon's momentum so abruptly the wheels broke away from the front axle. The horses broke free as they turned, the wagon careened and flipped, landing on its side and sliding to the roadside. Ephraim was hurled toward the buildings, but his fall was cushioned by the canvas bowed across the top of the wagon. Rufus was face down in the intersection of the street. Johnny was nowhere in sight.

Ephraim pulled himself off the wagon canvas and on to the wooden sidewalk where the wagon's top was perched. He faced a storefront, a smashed window and shards of glass covering the walkway.

"Help. He needs help. Get a doctor," a woman screamed as she ran from the dry goods store, turning up the street bordering the riverbank.

Off the tarpaulin and on his feet, Ephraim staggered through the broken glass and to the store's entrance. Gaining balance, he wobbled in the front door. After a few paces, he stopped beside a table stacked with bolts of cloth, embroidery hoops, yarn and knitting needles. Adjusting to the interior light, Ephraim's restored vision fixed on Johnny. The boy lay face down on the plank floor, hair soaked with blood which flowed into a pool around his body. It was a gruesome sight. Horrified, Ephraim started to cry as he bent over the small, unconscious body. He didn't know the child. Although they had never spoken, he felt a profound loss. A memory long buried inside, cracked open. *No one is here for the boy. No one to help him—to restore him.* Ephraim thought, paralyzed by a growing sense of helplessness. *What can I do?* Those around him were numb and motionless, adding to his own awful sense of emptiness. He had no power, no skill, nothing to give. He had no prayer and felt that there was no one to hear it.

Ephraim stood up and raised his head, remembering Catherine from long ago, and Jacob Cochrane talking to her lifeless body. She was assured that the Kingdom of God was inside of her, there from birth, and present at her passing into heaven. Cochrane told everyone standing by the grave that they too were filled with God's grace. Ephraim had thought he witnessed a miracle and would be forever changed by it. The strength of that belief diminished, just as the limits of his physical power had been exposed when he lost control of the wagon.

Ephraim carefully turned the boy on his back, felt his heart and pressed his ear to the bony chest. "It is still beating. The heart has not stopped." Ephraim's voice rose as he wiped his face. "We need a doctor. Get a doctor."

Ephraim had no jacket to cover the child. "Get some covers," he ordered. The clerk who brought a blanket hesitated when she saw the blood-soaked figure.

"Damn," Ephraim growled. "I'll pay for that." With a recklessness triggered by despair, he yanked the unblemished cover from the clerk and wrapped it around the boy.

"Let me see what is going on here." Dr. Douglas Bennet was loud, but in no other way imposing. Ephraim scooted sideways, allowing the healer room to examine Johnny. Bennet pushed Ephraim further away as he placed his satchel beside him. He opened the bag, removed a thermometer and stuck it between the boy's tight lips.

"His fingers tracked the paths of blood flowing from the boy's cracked head, then moved his hand to the chest and limbs. There were no other fractures. Bennet's nose wheezed as he sucked in a deep breath and leaned back.

"What can you do for him?" Ephraim asked. "There must be something you can do." Ephraim knew that frontier doctors were minimally trained. Bleeding and purging therapies were popular no matter a patient's problems or condition.

Bennet reached down, retrieved his thermometer and put it back in his bag, next to some knives, jars and dressings. The way he closed his satchel it appeared he thought his job was done.

"What can you pay?" Bennet looked Ephraim in the eye, showing no sense of urgency.

"The boy is dying. Do something to keep him alive," Ephraim implored. The murmurs from the crowd, mostly women, supported his plea.

"You are not from around here," Bennet's voice was flat.

"What difference should that make?" Ephraim barked.

"Mormons are not welcome here. We know about your kind," Bennet stood.

"You are the only one who can help—make Johnny better," Ephraim shouted.

"You people don't care about us. Over in Rochester, your prophet Joe ordered a couple of his stupid and wicked followers to murder non-believers. They didn't succeed, thank God. The last thing we need around here is another Mormon," Bennet picked up his satchel.

"Please. The boy needs you or he will die," Ephraim cried in desperation.

"He has a prophet," Dr. Bennet said as he backed away from Johnny. "An amazing healer who performs miracles, they say. Take him to your prophet. Or, call one of Joe's angels."

"No. No," the hideous cry came from the small woman charging in the entrance of the store. "You can't leave. You can't leave my dying boy." She leapt up on to Bennet's back and viciously wrapped her arms around his neck. She was wild, whirling with his spastic motions to free himself, her skinny legs kicking and flailing.

"Get off. Get off me," Bennet yelled while trying to shake the woman from his back. He pounded the clinging figure with his bag. "Let go, you shrew."

"Doctors make promises. Every doctor," the woman screamed. "You made a promise to heal."

"Get her off of me," Bennet yelled. "Get this nag off."

Despite the wildly thrashing legs a bystander grabbed the skirt of the raging attacker. Another got a good hold on the hem. Together, they pulled to dislodge the furious woman.

"You will never forget this. You will remember my son. You bastard," she yelled into the doctor's ear. She clamped her teeth on Bennet's earlobe. More women tugged at her skirt and her legs, while the kicking gradually abated. Her arms slackened. But the teeth were unrelenting, and her mouth was the last part of the body to lose touch with the doctor.

Nell flopped on the floor. She moaned and choked as she turned her head to the side, coughed up blood and discharged the doctor's earlobe.

"Arghhh," Bennet staggered away. "You heathen bitch. You barbarian whore."

Subdued by her own fury, Nell did not resist as she crouched behind a worktable, trailed by bloody drool. Dr. Bennet bent down to retrieve his earlobe, gave it a cursory look and shoved it in his vest pocket. He grabbed his open satchel, stuffed its scattered contents inside, and left the store without a word.

Everyone but Ephraim seemed to have forgotten Johnny, whose ashen figure rested apart from the bedlam. The boy was lifeless. He stooped beside the boy, looked at the innocent face, and began again to cry.

"I am sorry, Johnny, so sorry that I am of no help," Ephraim whispered. "By the grace of God, you have been lifted up, and are now resting with Catherine in the Kingdom of God. God's grace may no longer fill your wasted body, but I will take care of it. The only thing I have to give you is my tears."

Ephraim bent down. He kissed the boy on his cold mouth before reaching under the body with both arms and scooping up his pallid frame. "I will take care of you, Johnny," Ephraim whispered as he got to his feet. He settled the boy in his arms and walked out into the afternoon light, tears streaming down his face.

TEN

"I like the Seneca better than the other nations," William said, "But they could be really cruel. They would burn an enemy captive alive. Nastier still, they tied an enemy to the back of an untamed colt, with his face towards its tail and turned the colt loose to run wild."

"Why face toward its tail? So, he would have to see the colt shit?" Jonathan cracked.

"No," William said. "To make the endless ride more terrifying."

"Where do you come up with such twaddle? Is it just your twisted thinking?" Isaiah asked.

"I got a book from a Seneca. I lifted one of Orson's special Bibles and we made a trade," William confessed. "There is so much to explore in this ancient forest and Seneca hunting ground."

"Orson stopped here to baptize locals," Isaiah said. "He said that he heard God's call to stop. After that doctor's misconduct, people around here must be led away from the darkness of their heathen ways."

"While we are stopped maybe we can find the Seneca's ancient city, Genundewah," William exclaimed.

"Or the bones of a man tied to a horse's skeleton?" Jonathan jested.

"Genundewah was the center of Seneca civilization, where important councils met and prayed to the Great Spirit," William kept talking while the boys struggled up a steep, densely wooded bank.

"You know so much about the Seneca, William," Jonathan asked. "They drink?"

"No. Drinking is a white man's corruption. Most stay away from spirits," William took the lead.

It was a beautiful landscape. The slopes were completely forested with white and Norway pine, interrupted with steep rocky outcroppings breaking through the dense green. The boys slid down deep ravines covered with long brown needles and scurried through tall heather shrubs and troublesome expanses of berry brambles.

"At one time their sacred village, Genundewah, was taken over and surrounded by a monstrous serpent, whose head and tail came together at the gate. Many Seneca were trapped inside, and no outsider came near the entrance for fear of the beast's foul and deadly breath," William had the full attention of his brothers.

"After a long imprisonment the villagers resolved to escape. Armed with furniture, barrels, staves, whatever they could find, they charged the gate, but ended up marching down the serpent's throat. All were swallowed up."

"Ugh," Jonathan roared. "Fighting the foul and deadly breath the whole way."

"Shush." William continued his tale. "There were two orphan boys who never got into the compound. They were outcasts without family but decided to save their tribe. They found an old, decrepit shaman deep in these woods. He told them to subdue the snake with a willow bow and a small poisoned arrow. They had to get close, sneaking up under the cover of darkness, and wait until light before shooting. When the arrow pierced the flesh under the small scales of the serpent's neck it jerked upright on one side. It stood, a large, towering hoop. Balance was difficult for the snake, and it started to roll down the mountainside.

"It was an abominable sight as the snake picked up speed. Trees fell in its path, blight clouds of dust and debris were left in its wake. The snake bounced and bounced, striking rock outcroppings, crashing through gullies. The relentless descent caused uncontrollable discharges as the snake spun down the mountainside, coating the forest with dung and a noxious fog. The heads of the Seneca were spewed out its mouth, also rolling and crashing downward, into a long, narrow lake."

"William, your mind is warped and disgusting," Jonathan guffawed. "You've been drinking firewater."

"Quiet," Isaiah snapped, "I want to hear the story."

"It is sad," William said. "Over time, the carcass of the serpent dissolved in the corrupted water, but the Indian heads still lie at the bottom of the lake, petrified and hard with the appearance of stone. The lake is sacred for the Seneca people, who go there to visit their ancestors."

"I see no ruined city, or lake, William," Jonathan said. "There is nothing here."

"Could we find the falls in the canyon?" Josiah was eager to continue. "I've heard that they are marvelous, it is believed that the sun halts its passage every midday to behold their beauty."

"We have been gone for quite some time. Remember, Orson wants us present for the baptism." Isaiah had grown tired of the pointless exploration. "He said that the Lord will be displeased if we are absent."

"It is not about the Lord," William said. "He just wants a crowd to make the dunking more impressive. No need of a crowd. Just one person would do—a simpleminded convert."

"Be respectful of our leader," Isaiah said. "Father believes he will get us to Allegany County."

"If we found the Big Tree and climbed it we could probably see to Allegany County." William's enthusiasm did not ease. "I am sure we can find the tree."

"How are we going to find one tree in this thick forest?" Isaiah grumbled.

"The tree is huge and venerated by the Seneca. It is east of here, over by Keshequa Creek," William said. "Let's go." William seemed to know where to go.

The watershed they crossed was a primeval forest of massive trees, with immense trunks and swooping limbs. They crossed a few open spaces, clearings made by natural causes, fires, slides or wind and ice. Finally, an opening of light appeared. In a plot of rough grass stood a giant tree. The leaves of the lower limbs rested on the ground, and branches spread as much as a quarter acre. The top of the towering monolith could not be seen.

"Let's climb it," William ran to a sturdy branch close to the ground, wrapped his arms and legs around it and started climbing. He reached an elbow where the limb turned and attached to the trunk. William stood triumphantly on the branch, one of his shoulders resting against the soaring trunk.

"Come on," William yelled. "Get up here."

His brothers followed.

"I see something up there," William exclaimed from twenty feet above. "There is something stuck in the tree."

The brothers scrambled higher, anxious to see William's discovery.

"Jonathan," Josiah called to his brother. "Will you give me a hand? I can't pull myself up with this weak arm." Jonathan reached down and pulled his brother next to him, where they saw William and Isaiah just above. Both caught their breath, taking the time to survey miles and miles of treetops. Somewhere to the southwest was Allegany County.

"It is a tomahawk buried in the tree trunk," William said with excitement. "There are initials carved into the tree, a circle and an X. The X, is crossed bones."

"People's initials?" Josiah asked.

"There are three sets. JJ, TJ and JJ. Incredible," William said.

"What? Do Indians use initials?" Josiah questioned.

"They are brothers. All murdered by this tomahawk," William said. "I am sure."

"How would you know?" Jonathan scoffed. "Besides, it is morbid."

"John Jemison, Thomas Jemison and Jesse Jemison, sons of Mary Jemison. She is legendary," William said. "Mary was a white woman kidnapped by an Indian raiding party at age twelve. All her family were killed, and she was carried away and adopted. She married a Delaware and had a son, Thomas. They travelled here, seven hundred miles, but on the way the husband died. Mary married a Seneca and had six more children. John and Jesse were two of them."

Everyone heard the loud flapping of wings, and a bird call, a loud, sharp, krak. A sooty black raven, with expansive, four-foot wings lifted itself from a nest above them. More flapping and deep rasping calls followed, the sounds deep and musical. Soon three large singing birds were in the sky, circling the treetop with easy flaps.

"I think we are being watched," Jonathan said. "Don't do anything foolish, William."

"John became a doctor," William continued. "But many in the tribe tagged him a witch. His mother wrote of his great vices, noting the child's evil disposition and suspicious ways."

"An Indian woman knew how to write?" Isaiah asked.

"Before she died, Mary wrote a book about her life. That is what I traded for the Bible. I read some of it." Although the birds still soared overhead, William regained his brothers' attention. "John was jealous of his half-brother Thomas, resented him deeply. Thomas constantly reprimanded John for having two wives. He told John that it was indecent to live that way. The unrelenting taunts ended one night, when John grabbed Thomas by the hair and split his head open with this tomahawk."

"And he went after another brother?" Jonathan whispered.

"Two years later. Jesse was younger than John and afraid of his brother because Thomas's blood was on John's hands. Two years after the murder of Thomas, John picked a fight with Jesse, stabbed him repeatedly and finished him off with the same hatchet. Of all her children, Mary had loved Jesse most."

"John's initials are there too. Who killed John?" Jonathan asked.

"Many Seneca wanted to. Finally, John quarreled with two drunken Squawky Hill Indians. When John started home, the drunken Indians grabbed John, dragged him from his horse and struck him on the head with a big rock. They took John's tomahawk and smacked him so hard that his brains leaked out."

"The tomahawk was placed where it would no longer be used for evil," Isaiah concluded.

"Indians have a custom of burying the hatchet. A friend of Mary's probably hid the tomahawk here, high in the great tree so it would cause no more harm," William said. "Burying it in the ground would draw attention. You could dig it up and use it again."

"Take it," Josiah declared.

"Leave it here." Isaiah was the oldest present. "There was purpose in planting it in this tree, marked with the dead brothers' initials. God have mercy."

"Josiah is right. It has great power. But I will use it for good," William insisted.

"You are a good brother, William," Jonathan said, "but keep that weapon away from me."

"Don't come near any of us," Isaiah commanded. The brothers laughed.

"I know that one day you will be glad I have it." William stood tall, anchored his feet, and pulled the ax from the tree. His face beamed with pride.

⌒

The Livingston County Sheriff took out a warrant against the Mormons for assault on Dr. Douglas Bennet. Jonathan Dunham and two others passing the courthouse were arrested and jailed. Mormons, camped at the edge of town, received threats and warnings not to pass through Mt. Morris. The train's passage through town was unavoidable, with no alternate route. No violence occurred as the convoy moved through the village, but the city fathers had arranged for repeated blasts from a small battery of cannons, to frighten horses and scare women and children. Those trailing the cortege of pilgrims received a salute of rotten eggs from a house they passed.

The court was in the final days of its fall session and convened at eight the next morning to hear the case of the imprisoned Mormons. With the sheriff not present, the court could not find sufficient cause to hold the defendants. Charges were dismissed, and Dunham and his cohorts returned to the camp in time to perform the baptisms Orson had announced.

Local farmers congregated for the ceremony, but Indians appeared in greater numbers. Mormons called them Lamanites and considered them to be descendants of Laman, son of a Jewish prophet. They were lured by promises: a gift, the "Stick of Joseph," their name for the Mormon Bible, a revelation, the appearance of an angel and a celestial blessing. The lure attracted a sizeable gathering.

"Have you ever seen Elder Dunham in a wet robe before?" Jonathan asked. The Berry boys squatted on a bank above the stream. "He is so scrawny he'll be turned away at the Pearly Gates."

A dozen converts entered the water in a line and waded toward the waiting Elder. Children, local, Indian and Mormon, ignored the solemn rite and played in the sand at the water's edge. Orson was nowhere to be seen.

"Do you think Dunham is strong enough to support that fat woman after he pushes her underwater?" Jonathan was watching every move, and the heavyset female was next in line.

"Are you boys alright?" Their father's voice and sudden presence startled them. "I didn't see you all morning."

"Hello, Father." Isaiah turned around. "We did not expect you. I thought Orson would be keeping you busy." He stood up and the other boys followed. William kept the tomahawk hidden behind his back.

"Orson did ask me to help him out, but there were things I had to get done," Ephraim said.

"There is nothing he cannot handle by himself," Isaiah said.

"Look. Look." Shouts came from the crowd. "There is the angel. The angel came, it is here."

In the dense woods across the stream, a blob of white briefly appeared accompanied by flashes of light. The crowd roared. After the sound peaked the mysterious form disappeared, only to bubble up again nearby. The insubstantial figure rose from one thick clump of shrubbery and then another. With a flash of light, it was gone again.

"Praise, Jesus. Glory Be." The crowd summoned the ghost's reappearance.

When the incorporeal blur emerged for a fourth time, shrill, blood curdling shouts rang out, and a group of young men sprung from a hidden lair. Armed with sticks and clubs, the intruders jumped through the underbrush, charging toward the blotch of white. Trapped by a hedge, the ghost bolted upright, and became a human figure, swaddled in a white sheet. With a desperate dive, the man, naked, swam downstream with all his strength, sped by the rapid current running along the far riverbank. Four assailants plunged in the water in enthusiastic pursuit of the Mormon angel. Clothes hampered the young men's advance, as did their apparent drunkenness. The fugitive was soon out of sight. Everything happened so fast no one was sure of the imposter's identity. The ragtag men laughed as they staggered from the river.

Elder Dunham now stood alone in the water, while the confused converts slowly headed to the shore.

"The Spirit is still with us," Dunham called out frantically. "The angel has departed, but the Spirit is still with us. Come back, wash away your sins so you may enter the Kingdom of Heaven."

Nobody rushed away. Congregants had planned an afternoon of celebration, and had food, chairs, blankets to pack and campfires to put out. Some Mormons withdrew to their wagons, and others observed the disbanding of the assembly from the sidelines in silence.

"I am grateful you are here with us, Father," Isaiah turned to Ephraim. "It is unclear what help you could offer Orson today. People here will have to struggle with the disappointment on their own."

"I could be of no help to Orson. At least no one has been harmed," Ephraim said. "I am glad to be with you, my sons. Let's get the wagon loaded, I am sure we will be moving on as soon as possible."

The children playing on the riverbank were oblivious to the surrounding disorder.

"Stay away from me, Lamanite," a child yelled as he pushed a Seneca boy. "You Redskins make me itch."

"You make me itch, paleface," the Indian grabbed a handful of wet sand and threw it at the troublemaker. "Look at yourself. You have red spots all over your sorry body."

Another Indian boy ran up behind the instigator and jumped on his back, bringing him to the ground. A second white boy ran to pull the Indian off but was tackled by the Indian who was pushed. Before long, there were a dozen boys in a pile, whacking, hitting, and pummeling each other. All were too busy to scratch. Peace was haphazardly restored by parents, already exasperated by the day's events, who tugged the wrangling children apart and dragging them away. The fighting made it even plainer that it was time to go.

The Mormons left Mt. Morris before dawn. No baptisms, no new believers, no endowments left behind. But their children's presence would be remembered. Locals had immunity to chicken pox, and bouts the young suffered were easily endured. It was different for the Indians who had no immunity to European diseases and no healers or shamans with medicines to treat them. The Indian youngsters were helpless. Their parents had come to see the angel and receive a celestial blessing, the children went home with a plague.

⌒

The end of the journey was arduous. Two days before, Orson split off from the train to head west to Kirtland, Ohio, the Mormon seat. Goodbyes were not warm. Ephraim found the leader's farewell dismissive and final, sensing that Orson blamed him for the failed baptism and his public embarrassment at Mt. Morris. Ephraim would have preferred a more cordial parting but turned his mind to the road ahead.

After the village of Nunda, the road became a trail. They passed through rugged terrain, and a pile of rocks marking the

Allegany County line. The band of pilgrims finally reached their destination, Granger Township. Each family had property documents and deeds from the Holland Land Company with instructions for reaching their individual properties. The party split up before noon, abruptly, each family anxious to find their own land. Ephraim moved on in such haste, he failed to say goodbye to Mirinda, who headed with the McKinney wagon in another direction.

Ephraim moved through the woods with his compass, counting his paces. Samuel, an extra pair of eyes, looked for landmarks his father cited from the property documents. Upon discovering his plot, Ephraim scouted out the best way forward. With Samuel's help, a path was cleared along Rush Creek to ease their passage.

They finally stopped where Ephraim surveyed his new domain with great satisfaction. The unspoiled vista overwhelmed all thoughts of hardship and the trials of his journey. Yes, he thought. *This is where I belong, a place to settle, to farm and live out my days.*

He saw the makings of a fine farm once the land was cleared. Situated in a small valley, a stream bordered one side and the land gently sloped up to a ridge on the other. The higher ground offered protection from high winds, and the downward gradient eased any worry of standing water or flooding. He heard songbirds and saw evidence of wildlife. Nature was in harmony in this Promised Land.

"Are you sure you did the right thing? We struggled through so much and there is nothing here. It is godforsaken. Even the Indians are gone," Hannah complained at Ephraim's appearance. "Is this the world I'll give my baby?"

"Yes, it is," Ephraim said. "Now, clean up and make yourself useful. There is a lot of work to do."

Before dark, the boys set up camp in the meadow. The horses were hobbled close by to keep them from straying. Ephraim had an unobstructed view of the unspoiled land around him, so anything that approached was visible. Bedrolls were set out on a canvas tarp, a fire built and dinner prepared. Isaiah sat on a water barrel cleaning the two possums his brothers killed for dinner. Hannah shucked corn to boil in the water that William fetched from the stream.

They had not traveled far that day, but everyone was exhausted. After eating, all were ready for bed. Ephraim and Hannah slept in the wagon. The boys clustered together on the ground, bracing for another cold night.

"Aaa…Rrooo. Aaa…Rrooo. Aaa…Rrooo."

"That's a wolf. That's a wolf." Samuel exclaimed as he sat up. "Did you hear the howls? Get up and into the wagon." He quickly herded his brothers to the wagon, climbing in after them.

"Now keep quiet and stay still," Ephraim whispered.

"Stop pushing me. I don't like it," Hannah protested.

"Hush, or you'll be wolf food," Ephraim snapped.

It was crowded and black inside, but Ephraim fumbled around the floor and found the two rifles, loaded them and passed one to Samuel. Father and son moved to the side of the wagon closest to the source of the howling. Everyone was still.

Howling was replaced by snarls and sharp grunts from the trees bordering the meadow. Ephraim pulled back a flap of the wagon cover. No prowling wolves could be seen. With no moonlight or fire, there was only darkness. From the silence came short whines and the rustling of the horses.

"Quiet," Ephraim whispered. "They are close."

His sight became keener in the darkness and Ephraim saw a large wolf emerge from the trees, moving stealthily toward the horses. He waited before raising his rifle. Samuel did the same. Ephraim's breathing was even and audible. The wagon was jarred suddenly as William sprang from his hiding place and ran straight toward the wolf, tomahawk in hand.

"Yurrrhree! Yurrhree," William screamed at the top of his lungs, unwavering in his assault. The wolf was not frightened but poised to pounce on the unexpected prey as it neared. Alerted by the boy's cries, more beasts emerged from the darkness, moving behind their leader to join the attack.

"Come back, William. Come back," Ephraim yelled. "We will shoot them."

"Yurrhree! Yurrhree," William wailed again.

Ephraim raised his rifle and aimed at the nearest wolf but couldn't get a good bead on his target from the rocking vehicle. Samuel jumped from the wagon and raced to catch his brother. Ephraim leapt to the ground, and lifted his weapon, only to see William in his line of sight. Samuel dove at his brother, bringing William to the ground. He shielded his brother's body with his own and pulled a Bowie knife from his waist band. Ephraim finally had the closest wolf square in his sight. With a startling flash, the growling head was blown apart and its splayed body was thrown back into the darkness. There was no sound but the loud report of the rifle. Samuel stood and watched the rest of the wolf pack turn and flee soundlessly into the trees.

Isaiah and Josiah ran to William to help him up. He looked unscathed, the hard tackle leaving him with dirty clothes, a few abrasions and a big smile. He never let loose of his tomahawk.

Samuel went to inspect the remains of the dead predator. The wolf head was too damaged for anyone's trophy, but the remains would certainly be worth a five-dollar bounty.

ELEVEN

"BANG." A single report from the rifle broke the silence of the bleak morning and started the pig's fitful thrashing.

"Stay back. Those hooves are sharp. They can hurt you bad," Marmaduke Aldridge commanded. "Keep that rope taut, Ephraim. Pull back yours, Samuel. Benjamin, bring me that pan." The rifle bullet was perfectly placed, and the pig quickly stilled. Marmaduke slit the throat of the inert sow with his large sheath knife, reached for the pan Benjamin had passed, and began to bleed the animal. Skill ensured that the jugular vein was severed so the blood flowed freely, and no damage was done to the prized shoulder meat.

Marmaduke Aldrich knew all about pigs and sold Ephraim the sow sprawled on the cold ground. As part of the sale, Marmaduke agreed to bring the sow to the Berry farm, along with the equipment needed for the slaughter, and to oversee the day-long enterprise. His daughter, Mary Polly, came to help the women.

"Let's get this hog to that trough," Marmaduke said as he handed Benjamin the pan of blood. "Boys, bring that big skid." The wide plank was laid next to the animal's side, and Ephraim stretched two large ropes across it. It took all eight men to lift the skid and carry the pig carcass to sawhorses next to the large, wooden trough.

"Bring the water," Marmaduke ordered.

After their brief greetings, the busy women barely exchanged a word all morning. Fires were set and tended. Gallons of water boiled, and preparations made for processing pig parts. Hannah's complaints were constant. The women were called to bring pails of boiling water to fill the hog cleaning trough.

"Follow me," Mary Polly said, filling a pail from the large tub and rushing to pour it over the dirty and hairy carcass. Hannah, Mary Ann, and Mirinda tried to avoid spilling water on themselves as they scrambled between the tub and trough. With scalding water, the men scrubbed the hog with brushes before taking up their tools, wooden pegs with shanks on each end, to scrape the coarse hair that covered most of the pig's body. The large ropes under the beast were occasionally pulled to rotate the body so that no part of its flesh was unattended. The head was brushed and scraped too, before it was laboriously severed from the body and set aside.

Marmaduke had brought his dog, Duke, who constantly barked and jumped, trying to get any scrap to eat. In his affection, he jumped on Mary Polly as she poured a bucket of scalding water into the trough. Most of the water splashed over the exposed milky-white flesh of the bloodless hulk, but she slipped and fell on the wet ground.

Samuel dropped his scraper to help the young woman up.

"You are too pretty to be in that cold mud." He smiled. "And Mary Polly is too long of a name for you."

"My mother's name is Polly," the girl responded.

"My mother is Mary," Samuel grinned. "Can I call you Polly? You will be the only Polly I know."

"That's nice. Call me Polly." She smiled, picked up her pail and scurried back to the tubs of boiling water and the women.

"Let's get this old sow back on that plank," Marmaduke said. "Then I can show you how to get the goodies we will eat this winter. And help me keep that dog out of our business."

The ropes steadied the slippery carcass as they raised the pig from the trough to the wooden bench and turned it on its back.

"Hold your noses," Marmaduke said as he made a slit the length of the animal's belly. "Get some more water." Samuel followed his instructions.

Marmaduke pulled the entrails—lungs, heart, stomach, liver, intestines, kidneys, bladder—from the carcass, identifying each organ and handing the parts to Samuel to dunk in the water and put in a wooden box.

"Samuel, take these innards to Polly. She knows what to do with them," Marmaduke instructed. "Take the head, too."

Ephraim, Marmaduke and Benjamin did most of the butchering, dividing the meat according to which would be cured, hanged, or stored. The boys watched and learned. Isaiah collected the scraps left from the cutting and took them to the women who chopped the chunks before tossing them into the stewing pudding used in making sausage.

"Thank God we will have food this winter. We will be fit to clear more land," Ephraim said.

"And we will have a ham at Christmas," Isaiah smiled.

"This winter we will bring more wolves, and I will have some cash from bounties," Samuel boasted.

"We may get a mountain lion," William joined in enthusiastically.

"You better hope they stay away. All are trouble," Marmaduke said. "You should get a dog." Duke happily nipped scraps at his master's feet.

"You are lucky having all of these boys, Ephraim, getting the skills they need. And they have stamina." Benjamin said.

"It may take you a little longer getting settled, Benjamin, but you will be eating some nice vittles," Ephraim said. "And Mirinda is around to lend a hand. I am sure she is helpful to Mary Ann. Mirinda can learn a lot from your wife."

"Yes. It is good having her around. Mirinda offers much more than a helping hand," Benjamin smiled.

"Mirinda knows how to cook, sew and is good with children. She is kind." Samuel glared at Benjamin. "She will make a deserving man a good wife."

Ephraim appeared indifferent to the exchange.

"I think I will take these scraps down to the ladies and keep them busy," Samuel said, as he left to join the women. The women were not far away, but the loud, high-pitched voices set a boundary, marking off a domain of complaint and bickering.

"I don't like this work. It is hard, it is dirty and it stinks," Hannah said as Samuel approached.

"This is your first slaughter, Hannah. You will get used to it. We only do it once a year," Polly said. "And cooking the fat for the lard isn't a smelly task, particularly if you don't stand in the path of the smoke." Polly's remarks made Mary Ann and Mirinda snicker.

"I will never get used to this," Hannah said. "And I won't do any of this while pregnant and nursing."

"That can't be anything to worry about right now," Mary Ann quipped. "At least from what I can see."

"What do you know?" Hannah asked as she raised her apron and rubbed her belly. "There is magic going on in there. Understanding the divine aspects of an ancient balm is beyond your grasp. And what could you know about conception or having babies?"

"I know how to hump, sweetheart. And I'll keep at it until it works," Mary Ann said sharply.

"Sure. But you are getting less practice. What are your chances of conception with another woman in your house? When you have to share Benjamin's juice?" Hannah sneered.

"What man can get aroused by a shrew who bitches constantly? A harpy. A scold," Mary Ann retorted.

"You old battle-ax. Why would Benjamin want your dry, old quim when he can get a young, tight one?" Hannah asked, looking at Mirinda.

"Jacob Cochrane knocked on your uninviting door twenty years ago, Hannah," Mary Ann shot back. "Men have been walking through it ever since. You might give yourself a thrill in applying your pagan unguents, but they won't make that well-traveled passageway more alluring."

"Stop. Stop. I don't want to hear such talk," Polly interrupted. "There is so much to do before we finish. Let's get back to work." Mirinda's crimson face teared as she stared at the pile of entrails before her.

"What is all of the cackling about?" Samuel asked as he stepped among the tubs and pots of boiling water.

"We are just fussing over who gets to take the garbage you keep bringing us," Polly said. "You can put those scraps here by Mirinda and me. We are the custodians."

"What do you mean by that?" Samuel kept his eyes on his sister.

"We decide what goes to Mary Ann for the sausage or to Hannah for the lard," Polly said. Mirinda was trembling and seemed unable to speak. "William came asking for the bladder and we decided that he could have it. He carried that smelly bit of pig remains off with him. He said that he was planning a surprise."

"That sounds like William," Samuel got his mind off his sister's distress. "He always has a surprise."

"You are welcome here, Samuel, even if is it only to bring garbage," Polly said. "But we have work to do. Don't use us as an excuse for laziness."

"Yes. I want to show my industry." Samuel winked at Polly and left to help with the endless butchering.

The women got back to their business. Hannah cut the pig fat into chunks and tended to the pans where other fat was cooking. Pudding was stirred, and more scraps were cut up and added to the sausage cauldron. Polly moved her stool closer to Mirinda, placing her arm around the young woman who could not stop shaking.

"It takes two of us to clean the intestines, Mirinda," Polly said in an even tone. "I cannot do this alone." Polly carefully removed the intestines from the tub and started to meticulously separate the maze of tubes from the mesh tissue holding them together. As they loosened, the jiggling flesh began to look like a rope.

"I cannot do this," Mirinda seemed to search for each word before saying it. "I can never do this." She muttered and turned her head to look away.

"Yes, you can, Mirinda," Polly leaned toward her helper, looking her in the face. "This is just a task. It is not what you think."

"It is slimy and awful to touch. Repulsive," Mirinda managed to whisper. "Playing in garbage and filth. The stink on my fingers will never go away. I will become more disgusting."

"None of that is true. We are doing a job. I do the same as you. We keep our minds on the task before us. That is what we do," Polly was encouraging. "The slick tissue is easy to hold. It keeps you from puncturing or tearing the casing."

"The smell. I'll never be rid of the smell," Mirinda's voice waivered.

"We'll get rid of the smell. That is part of the job," Polly continued. "The pig wasn't fed yesterday. Most food is out of its system, so it is not bad to begin with. We get rid of it all by washing with cold water, rubbing with salt, and lots of chopped onions."

"Polly, I can never do this," Mirinda said.

"It is a job you must do. And you do it for others," Polly affirmed.

Polly reached down and cut a length of gut, just long enough not to touch the ground after standing. Polly poured clean water into the top end, worked the water through with a squeeze of her hand, rinsing out the inside of the gut. Repeated a few times, the water eventually came out clean.

"You see it isn't that bad," Polly said, placing her fingers next to Mirinda's nose. "Now we turn it inside out and do it again. This time you pour the water and I will do the squeezing."

It was a laborious job and would take all day. Some of the larger pieces of gut, having more loops and bulges, were harder to get clean

"Run and catch it." William's voice was not far away.

The yell attracted the women's attention. They heard the pounding of feet, saw Jonathan running toward them and an object in the air above his head. It was odd, spherical, the size of a large melon and wobbled in its irregular trajectory. Jonathan jumped to catch it, but it slipped from his hands, landing on the ground with a thud and negligible bounce. Jonathan picked up the egg-shaped ball and wiped it on his trousers.

William got the pig bladder from Polly and his sister, and the idea from a peddler on the road to Granger of making a ball from the bladder.

"Your turn, William," Jonathan shouted. "See if you can catch it." The ball disappeared.

"I've got it. Good throw," William's voice got closer. As he appeared, heading in the direction of the women, Isaiah and Josiah came into view. The boys' laughing brightened the grey afternoon.

"Let's see who can catch this," William cried out. Holding it with both hands, he stepped forward and kicked the ball high in the air. It soared, crested, and after a brief halt, set its own course. In its descent it swooped, suddenly changed direction, even accelerating as it whirled and danced. The amazing spectacle had everyone agog and laughing, until the ball froze in the air and plummeted to earth.

"Eek! Eek!" Hannah screamed. She was resting in an old wooden chair when the deflated bladder plopped in her lap. "Heavens. Help." Outraged but unhurt, she bolted to her feet, the bladder slid down her skirt leaving a track of stinky goo.

"Ephraim. Come, see what your boys did," Hannah cried out. "They hate me. Their tricks and rowdiness are ceaseless. What kind of world will my child face with a mother always under attack?"

Ephraim had dropped his butcher knife and rushed to Hannah's side. After appraising the scene, he shook his head and exhaled with a long grunt.

"Ease your mind, woman. You must conceive first. Keep those worries to yourself until then," Ephraim scowled. "I have work to do, Hannah, as do you. Get to it."

"I deserve better than this," Hannah shuddered, sitting down in the chair while wiping the ooze off her skirt.

"I think you are going to need some extra unguent tonight," Mary Ann teased.

⌒

"Father. Do you ever miss my mother?" Josiah's words came out of the blue. Ephraim and his son were on the road to Hume. They left home in the afternoon on an overnight trip to pick up timber for a new barn. Ephraim liked to take his sons on trips for company, and possible help. Samuel had accompanied him to Angelica to conduct business at the county courthouse. Nunda, the place for buying farm tools, had been Isaiah's turn. Now he'd asked Josiah to go with him to Hume, the place for buying timber.

"What's that, Josiah?" Ephraim felt confident guiding the team and wagon over the rugged road through Granger, but the gullies, fallen limbs and erosion of the road required all of his attention.

"My mother. Do you ever miss her?" Josiah repeated.

"Do you miss her, Josiah?" Ephraim asked.

"Yes. Sometimes. My brothers, too. I don't know about Samuel, since he has been courting Polly."

"And Mirinda? Ephraim asked,

"We hardly see Mirinda. Nobody brings up Mother's name," Josiah said. "We miss her, but don't talk about her."

"Do you miss her because you don't like Hannah?" Ephraim asked.

"No one likes Hannah," Josiah said, "But that doesn't have anything to do with Mother."

"What is it you miss," Ephraim asked. "Her cooking?

"I am not joking, Father," Josiah said. He was comfortable sitting by his father, despite the unusual talk. "She cared for me and made me feel loved."

"Fathers provide for their children," Ephraim said. "That is the job. I'm good at that."

"Yes, Father. You are." Josiah said.

"How did she make you feel loved?" Ephraim asked. "She didn't yell and scream at you, like Hannah."

"Never." Josiah said. "I haven't thought exactly about what she did, but she was always present."

"I taught you how to farm, Josiah," Ephraim said. "We spent hours in the fields. I showed you how to fix things."

"Yes. You did, Father," Josiah said. "I will be a good farmer because of that."

"And do I make you feel loved?" Ephraim asked.

Josiah rocked back on the seat, looking up for the first time. With no trees around the sky was wide and clear, but for three ravens circling high above. He couldn't take his eyes off the soaring birds.

"Look. Look in the sky," Josiah said pointing. "The ravens. Do you think they are listening to our conversation? The Seneca say they do that. The birds want to remind us to seek knowledge of ourselves."

"No," Ephraim scoffed, looking up at the circle of black fowl moving forward with his wagon. "Such nonsense. You are too old to be superstitious, to believe in omens."

"Do you think the people by that river would have believed they saw the Holy Ghost, had it not been for those ruffians?" Josiah asked. "Isn't it the same?"

Ephraim paid attention to the road. Not a washout, but a deep rut required careful negotiating. He bypassed a couple of stumps before getting back on the tracks down a long decline.

"I heard the county wants to put a bounty on ravens, saying they damage crops," Josiah said. "They don't know how important they are, and sacred."

"Josiah, I asked you about love," Ephraim persisted. "If I were apart from you, would you miss me in the same way you miss your mother?"

"No," Josiah said after a long pause. He avoided looking in his father's face. "It is different with her, always asking me how I am. She did nice things for me, unexpectedly. I was surprised how often she listened to my dumbest remarks."

"Fathers don't do those things," Ephraim snapped.

Jason became quiet and looked ahead at the Genesee River flatland. It was scattered with bogs and pools of standing water, begetting blankets of morning fog.

"She took time," Josiah said. "You were often away. When you were home, your mind was somewhere else."

"By example, fathers try to be an inspiration to their sons. Devotion, hard work, and steadfastness speak for themselves,"

Ephraim said. "Fathers are revered for what they do in the world, the lessons they teach, like the courage to lead a family to a new life."

"To kill a wolf," Josiah added. "Father, you are an inspiration. But I feel I must earn your admiration. Your respect isn't free."

"Yes, Josiah. I expect a lot from you and your brothers," Ephraim said. "Anyone who comes to our farm knows I did not clear the land by myself. Or plant the fields, dig the well and build fences. My sons have earned the admiration and respect of my neighbors. I am proud of all of you."

"You tell your neighbors you are proud of your sons," Josiah said. "But you never tell us."

"I don't need to," Ephraim said. "That goes unsaid."

"It's not hard to figure out when we fall short," Josiah said. "That is clear."

"I suppose. That is part of teaching my sons how to make their way," Ephraim said. "You will see one day that I have done a good job."

"I would be nice if you expressed affection," Josiah said.

Ephraim and Josiah reached their destination. Blakely and Drake's sawmill was in the hilly terrain on the western side of the river. A dam spanned a narrow gap on Cold Creek, a few rods from the Genesee, and a sawmill had been built. Its primitive construction was no ordinary achievement. The castings and stone had been brought all the way from Albany. The gearing, cogwheels, and moving parts were made of wood by special craftsmen. A frame millhouse was made from local timber. A bridge crossed the rushing creek. Ruby's blacksmith shop sat on the north end and Ingham's tavern on the south.

"The wagon on the bridge, Father," Josiah pointed ahead. "That Indian is going to fall into the water." A toddling figure on the side of the buckboard tumbled into the creek. "That is sad."

"It happens all of the time," Ephraim said. "With the success of the sawmill, Blakely and Drake built a grist mill, bringing people from miles to grind their corn. Indians gave up the mortar and pestle and came too. With all the corn, stills were built and whisky sold. That is money and Indians have a special attraction to booze."

Ephraim planned to spend the night in Cold Creek, load the cargo in the morning and return to the farm later that day. He found a place near the mill, sheltered by a rocky escarpment, where Josiah helped park the wagon, tie up their team and set up for the night. They were hungry when they finished.

"What can I serve you two," the tavern keeper asked. Ephraim and Josiah seated themselves at the end of a communal table.

"Yes. Something to eat," Ephraim responded. "I'll start with a whiskey. Do you want one, Josiah?"

"That is too strong," Josiah said, "Not whiskey after seeing that poor drunk Indian. I will have an ale." Josiah settled on his stool, looked up and saw an old Indian with a smooth, expressionless face, staring at him from the other end of the table. "I am sorry. I meant no offense."

"I am not drunk," the dark man chuckled. "I was resting. My name is Little Beard. I did not mean to be rude."

"Little Beard?" Josiah asked. "That is funny when you don't have one. How did you get that name?"

"My Father," Little Beard laughed. "As always, he did it without my consent." The man smiled.

"That is the way to show your father you didn't like his decision," Josiah laughed. "You shaved it off." Everybody laughed. "Funny. Why do you look so serious?"

"There is going to be a terrible storm," Little Beard said.

"A storm is coming?" Josiah asked.

"A shaman told me a terrible storm is on its way," Little Beard said. "I am sober and worried, not drunk."

"Did you say storm?" Ephraim heard the prediction.

"Yes," Little Beard said. "Seneca know about storms. We have always lived here. Settlers pushed us out, but we know the weather."

"I'm Ephraim Berry. My son, Josiah," Ephraim said. "We are from Granger. We have been in Allegany County two years. Move closer and tell us about the weather."

"Thanks," Little Beard said, changing stools. "Never know around here what will happen with the weather. It is always changing. Three years ago was the Great Flood. Yep, 1835. I don't know about Granger, it is higher up and not along the river. All the bridges on the Genesee were wiped out by that storm, from Pennsylvania to Rochester. Awful, hard rain lasted two days. Everyone's corn was destroyed. Fences, houses, barns, mills and dams, all were taken away. Never seen anything like it."

The tavern keeper brought the drinks to Ephraim and Josiah. "We've got some deer ham and corn. Would you like some? Little Beard want another whiskey?"

Ephraim ordered food. The Indian nodded his desire for another drink and pulled his stool closer.

"Brother, there was a crowd in here when that storm came on. People got really scared and left," Little Beard said. "Some didn't make it home. It took a long time before the bridges were back. People managed, because the river could be forded in some spots. One of them is right nearby."

Ephraim and Josiah did not stay late at the tavern. They were tired and aware of the work facing them. The next morning, they were not the first to load their lumber and had to wait for those first on the docket.

Loading finished in early afternoon, just before the weather changed. The wind picked up and got increasingly fierce.

Ephraim and Josiah found shelter against a stone retaining wall built to ensure that the slope behind the mill did not slide against it. The wall protected the Cold Creek mill and sheltered the men as the brutal north wind whipped through Hume.

The howling storm seemed interminable and damaged everything. Houses were leveled. Scarcely a tree was left standing. All kinds of rubble, parts of wagons, timbers from barns, pieces of roofing were strewn across the ground. A horse carried by the twister lay sprawled on the road leading to the river. There was no water in the river, it had been scooped up. The maelstrom pushed it upstream, leaving the river channel as mud.

"Now is our chance." Ephraim grabbed Josiah as he ran to their wagon. "There is not much time. God has given us a shot to make it home." They rushed to untie the team, jumped onto the loaded wagon and headed down the embankment to the empty riverbed. Ephraim couldn't make the wheels move fast enough across the muddy bottom, although he drove the horses as hard as he could.

"Are you sure?" Josiah asked, worriedly searching the black sky. "The storm doesn't look like it's over."

Ephraim's mind flashed to the Bible and the fleeing Israelites confronted by the sea. "God parted the waters for Moses and He'll part them for us as true servants."

The horses bolted before the men heard the crash of water and turned to see the dark, plumed wall, studded with logs, a tree trunk, a screaming cow, and a wooden gate surging toward them.

"My God," Ephraim screamed. "Hold on, Josiah."

The awful power of the water and its cargo of wreckage struck the wagon, tossing it into the air. Everything in Ephraim's immediate world was split, timbers scattered against the dark sky, terrified horses discharged from a wagon rent of its wheels and moving parts. Desperate Ephraim and Josiah were hinged to a raft, engulfed and swept up in the vicious current.

Ephraim held fast to the capsized wagon and tightly gripped Josiah's arm. The debris in the convulsing water knocked against their bodies, the remnant of a buggy hit hard. Josiah's ceaseless screams for help were interrupted, choked off by the turbulent water. Ephraim's strength diminished, and it became harder to hold on to both the wagon bed and to his son. He prayed to God, but his muscles felt no resurgence of vitality.

Holding on to each other became more difficult. Ooze made Josiah's cramped hands slippery. Ephraim felt the limits of his stamina before the real calamity. Pulled by the fury of the water, Josiah's shoulder popped. Ephraim heard it, and the muscles in Josiah's hand slackened. Ephraim tried to tighten his grip but could not compensate for his son's worsened state. Josiah's eyes widened in surprise as he lost touch with his father, who fixed Josiah's gaze as he washed away and disappeared in the torrent.

Ephraim blacked out.

He opened his eyes to a new landscape of destruction, leveled by some awesome power, everything brown and covered in mud and slime, much obscured by a vaporous fog. The surging in his stomach told him he was not paralyzed, a notion he did not test by raising his head. That happened involuntarily. His head jerked up to expel the garbage in his stomach. The vomit running down his bruised chest merged with blood, bits of sod, some nuts and lifeless tadpoles. There was no serpent rising from his gut or splendorous bird to brighten the nonexistent sky. Heaven was absent from this world.

His head flopped down on the wooden bed; he was overcome by the stress of briefly lifting it. *What can I do? What brought me such misfortune? Why this punishment?*

Ephraim knew that God was present to open the path across the river, just as he was there to part the sea for the Israelites. Jews were saved from the threatening waters, but his son, Josiah, was carried away by them. God's power was seen in the dead bodies and wrecked chariots lying on the shore of the Red Sea. He was alive, wrecked atop a muddy wooden bed on a riverbank. His son had been taken from him. *Why? My selfishness? Because I did not tell him I loved him?*

Joseph Smith preached that the devout man, fully exercising his faith is privileged to see the Lord face to face. With full exercise of his faith, he beholds God in all his glory. *I did not see His face. God did not appear today in all his glory. To me, He unmasked his abominable wrath and took my son. Because I did not practice my belief in Him? Because I did not show my love for Him?*

Ephraim felt wretched and unredeemable. He was powerless and could not move. It was night when Ephraim mustered his strength to call out again: "God have mercy on my son. Have mercy on Josiah. Loving God, please find a place for my Josiah in heaven."

"Nobody will say how nice I got this room looking," Hannah said as she finished dusting the wooden table. "All the work I have done for this visit and nobody will notice."

"This parlor has never looked better," Ephraim said. "I meant to tell you that."

After Josiah's death, Ephraim lived in a fog, remorse clouding important family events. Soon after Josiah's burial, the family celebrated the long-anticipated marriage of Samuel to Polly Aldrich. His mood was unchanged by that milestone and the birth of his son, Eli, which followed. Ephraim seemed unaffected by the news of his father's death in 1840, or by the financial panic that gripped the nation and threatened the family's fortune. His confusion finally lifted but it was a long passage.

"It is not easy to get things done while keeping track of a two-year-old," Hannah carped. "My Eli is into everything and always in my way."

"But you are happy to finally have a son," Ephraim smiled at the blond-haired boy playing on the floor. "He is strong and fine looking."

"I worked hard for him," Hannah retorted as she set out cups, saucers and napkins on a low table in front of the settee. "You can thank God for him, Ephraim, and yourself. But I climbed that mountain every night for years."

"I never thought you took it as a chore," Ephraim chuckled. He stooped down and picked up Eli, who was heavier than he thought. "He is a cute fella."

"You don't give him much attention, or me," Hannah said. "You spend all of your time on your boys, when you are not brooding or drinking."

"Their futures are important to me. Samuel understood that when he married, I would set him up with his own farm. That's done. Still three more to provide for and worry about. And I must plan how to take care of this place as my sons move on,"

"At fifty-two you don't hide the years," Hannah jibed. "You know, Ephraim, you are no longer a promising young man. You have obligations to me and Eli, too."

"I remember when all of the boys fit in a single room," Ephraim said, surveying the expansiveness of the almost-finished house.

Jonathan's knock on the door was a courtesy, giving his father a few seconds to prepare himself and a warning he was not alone.

"Please come in Jonathan," Ephraim said as he opened the door, standing back to let pass his son and the companion holding his arm.

"Father, I would like you to meet Harriet," Jonathan said. "Harriet, this is my father, Ephraim." Harriet smiled and nodded her head. "And this is Hannah."

"I am pleased to meet both of you," Harriet said. "These are for you, Hannah." Harriet smiled again as she handed Hannah a bouquet of wildflowers.

"Very thoughtful," Hannah said, taking the flowers. "Excuse me while I get a pitcher for them."

"Please sit down," Ephraim said, extending his arm toward the settee. "Make yourself comfortable." Jonathan sat next to Harriet.

"I made tea," Hannah said as she entered the parlor. "I hope it suits everyone."

"It is nice to have you here, Harriet," Ephraim's interest was genuine. "Have you spent time in Granger? Jonathan tells me that you are from Amity. It is a lovely place with beautiful views of the countryside."

Ephraim aged rapidly after Josiah's death. Patches of dark brown remained in his receding hair, but the center of his full beard was grey, untrimmed and bushing down from his skewed mouth. The dark eyes were remote, burdened by the deep lines etched across his wide forehead. He reached back to the armrests of the chair, steadying himself as he sat.

"Yes," Harriet replied. "I live in Amity with my mother. It is a hilly place, From our house the views are ordinary. We like it there."

"Tell me Harriet. Are you related to David How?" Hannah's question was unusually pointed for a first meeting. "I have spent some time over the past week and a half to ask people about you, what they knew about Harriet How from Amity."

"Yes. He was my father," Harriet seemed surprised. "I am complemented by your effort." Ephraim noticed the girl was caught off guard.

"Tell me more about yourself, Harriet. You appear lively and discerning. How did you ever get interested in my son, this rascal, Jonathan?" Ephraim grinned.

"It is hard to turn away one so persistent, always at my doorstep. He doesn't give up, or lose his smile," Harriet said.

"The tragedy was long before we arrived," Hannah interrupted. "Everyone still talks about poor Othello Church."

"We invited Harriet here to get to know her. I wanted to see if you were as pretty as Jonathan described. Do you have a big family?" Ephraim gave Hannah a harsh look.

"I have a sister at home, Mr. Berry," Harriet said. "I have five half-brothers and sisters, but they are not in Amity."

"Othello Church was the first man murdered in Allegany County," Hannah said, as she poured Harriet a cup of tea. "But that was long ago."

"It was seventeen years ago when my father was hanged," Harriet stood, still but for her blinking eyes. She ignored Hannah's offer of tea. "I was four years old. I still remember the day he said goodbye. He kissed me."

"You were there when your father went to the gallows?" Hannah asked.

"Hannah," Ephraim barked. "Stop. There is no excuse for cruel behavior."

"It is important to know about persons who may become members of the family," Hannah rested the tea pot and cup and moved behind Ephraim's chair. "You must know their roots, what kind of blood courses through their veins."

"Hannah," Jonathan sprang to his feet and put his arm around

Harriet. "Stupid slut. How could you bear such scrutiny? Harriet, I am sorry. I will take you home." Jonathan clasped Harriet's hand, pulling her to the door.

"No, please. I beg you to stay," Ephraim stood, giving the young woman a kind look. "Please sit down."

Harriet, taken by Ephraim's sympathetic tone, moved back to the settee. Jonathan sat beside her.

"I know who you are, Harriet. I know about your father, David How," Ephraim said. "And I have some idea of what you have gone through all of these years."

"Harriet's past makes no difference to me," Jonathan glared at Hannah.

"It makes a big difference. David How was a cold-blooded killer," Hannah said, brandishing a pamphlet she pulled from a chest. "It is all here. It is his confession."

"Where did you get that?" Harriet gasped.

"A fruit of my labor," Hannah gloated. "Someone I asked about you was around for the famous trial and got a copy of this record."

"Get that away," Jonathan rose to grab the booklet from Hannah, who jumped behind Ephraim's chair.

"Jonathan," Harriet's voice was sure. "I want you to know everything I have lived through and lost."

Harriet stood and picked up the pamphlet resting on a side table. She thumbed through a few pages before she began.

"My father gives account of all the business he did, his handling of property and his hardships over eight years. There were many projects." She thumbed the pages of the short document. "He planned a turnpike road from Friendship to Hamilton and lost two thousand dollars. He turned to farming. In one harvest he raised two thousand bushels of corn, but his creditors fell upon it and left him nothing. He had highs and lows but descended to a desperate position."

Harriet sounded detached as she began her tale, as though she had done it before, and looked at no one. Ephraim did not take it as routine discourse. It was tragic.

"He traveled to Connecticut and borrowed thirty-five hundred dollars from friends. After his return he paid off his creditors, but they took undue advantage of him. They wanted everything and took it." Harriet's breath quickened. "Within a few weeks all his crops, horses, cattle, even his farming utensils were taken from him. Othello was the greediest among them."

"We didn't come here for this," Jonathan was impatient. "This was planned as a social visit. I didn't bring Harriet to expose herself."

"Let me finish, Jonathan," Harriet said, touching Jonathan's shoulder. "My father asked the scoundrels to leave enough grain to supply our family during the winter, but they refused, and tore up the vegetables in his garden. Othello Church, when asked to leave some onions, refused and spat in my father's face."

"Othello had bad reputation," Ephraim said. "He took advantage of those with little power and no money. He was vulturous."

"David How was a cold-blooded killer. He woke Othello Church in the middle of the night, shot him in the heart, and left him bleeding to death in his doorway," Hannah snarled. "It is all here in his own words." Hannah grabbed the pamphlet from Harriet's hands.

"Deep wrongs were inflicted on David How, or he never would have been a murderer," Ephraim countered. "Othello Church was evil, conniving and heartless. He and 'the seven devils' were relentless in taking advantage of How's destitution and drove him to complete ruin. They destroyed a whole family."

"Listen to me," Hannah shouted. "Justice was done. Think of Othello's poor wife and his family."

"You never fail to show your callousness, Hannah," Ephraim said. "You don't know the full story. Public sympathy for David How was overwhelming. Without the confession, he would have escaped the gallows. People for miles around saw him as a victim of great wickedness. Ten thousand people came on the day of his execution from Cayuga, Steuben, Livingston, Wyoming, Cattaraugus, Potter and other counties. Along with scores of Indians."

"So?" Hannah screamed.

"You'll be fortunate to have ten people at your funeral," Ephraim shot back.

"They came because they wanted to see him hanged," Hannah was unrelenting.

"Hannah, have some compassion," Ephraim said, "Guards were placed around the jailhouse. With all the sympathy How garnered, the Sheriff and the Court worried about a jail-break."

"I'm taking Harriet home," Jonathan said. "I am fed up. This has nothing to do with Harriet and me."

"It is important to all of us," Ephraim said. "Please, stay a little longer."

Jonathan moved closer to Harriet who looked for his approval.

"I have read this tract," Ephraim said. "Half of it is a record of How's trial and the other, as you know, Harriett, is your father's confession."

Hannah appeared furious at being ignored. Anger left her face when she heard a clatter from the corner where Eli was playing.

"Your father, Harriet, writes about love and salvation. During the forty-two days from the jury's verdict to his last hours, he learned about man's salvation, which is unconnected to how he appears in the world." Ephraim raised the pamphlet to read. "'I have labored for uncertain riches, and treasures that vanish away. Now I see the vanity of all earthly pursuits.'"

Harriet listened attentively. Hannah snorted in exasperation, picked up Eli and left the parlor.

"The confession makes it clear that David How reflected on material pursuits, and found them a distraction," Ephraim said. "Listen. 'I see how I was led from my home and failed to care for my precious family. Most simply, I never let them know how much I love them.' How realized that it was easy to be ensnared by greed and covetousness." Ephraim paused and closed his eyes.

A bird that had been resting in the rafters smacked against the window to get outside. It broke the silence. Jonathan opened the bay, picked up the rattled creature and watched it fly away. Harriet's eyes were on Ephraim.

"In this confession your father's mind and his heart are transformed. You see God working, taking a man who performed ungodly acts and making him righteous. Salvation does not come from Holy Declaration, but through a divine act of grace." As Ephraim described a profound process, his strong feelings were manifest in heavy breathing and sighs of intense sorrow.

Harriet lowered her head, her sniffles a mystical sharing of Ephraim's breath.

"I can feel your father's deep remorse," Ephraim choked. "It is here in his words. 'We seldom appreciate the worth of our family while we enjoy them. We glide through life surrounded by blessings and mercies, but we live ungrateful. When family is taken from us, we realize that life is precious, and loving is urgent.'" Ephraim stopped and sobbed.

Jonathan's move toward his trembling sweetheart was cautious, suggesting he did not know how to calm or console her.

"Daniel How felt the magnitude of his loss in body and soul," Ephraim declared as he pictured Josiah's hand pulled from his grasp by the raging water. Involuntarily he stretched out his rigid arm. He wiped his eyes. "'And my blessed children, from whom my sins, my dreadful sins, are forever separated from their father.' It was awful for your father, Harriet."

Ephraim moved closer to Harriet, as if his emotions would be less exposed by the diminished distance. He rested his hands on each of her shoulders and remained still until she raised her head and looked at his eyes.

"David How was won back to God through selflessness, all-embracing love," Ephraim said. "Dear Harriet, God saw in your father's love for you, and in his open heart, true atonement. Full forgiveness followed."

Harriet's eyes widened, tears gushed, sobs overwhelming. Ephraim put his arms around her to contain the profound grief.

Jonathan appeared stricken by discomfort as he watched his father embrace Harriet and saw a passion in her response, a passion he had never seen.

"Salvation is a healing of the heart. You captured your father's heart, Harriet," Ephraim choked. "And his love for you made it full. That flourishing heart empowered his salvation." Ephraim and Harriet clung together, bound by irretrievable loss.

⤳

Ephraim was on his knees, elbows resting on the wooden chair and eyes closed when Hannah returned to the empty parlor. She picked up the cold teapot, scattered cups and saucers, unconcerned about the noise she made.

"Well, that's the end of that," Hannah said. "Jonathan won't be bringing her back."

"Clean up later, Hannah," Ephraim raised his head and blinked his eyes, adjusting to the late afternoon light. "I don't need that clatter right now."

"You need to get out of my way," Hannah swung her leg against Ephraim's thigh, trying to roust him. "Jonathan called me a slut," Hannah nudged him again. "In front of the daughter of a hanged criminal."

Slowly Ephraim got up, straining against the chair's arms to stand while looking around the empty room.

"Jonathan gets it all from you, Ephraim," Hannah said. "No respect. And you making her the center of attention."

"Harriet was our guest. Guests deserve attention and respect," Ephraim said. "It's called good manners."

"Is it good manners to have your arms all over her, embracing her when she hasn't been here for half an hour? I saw it from the kitchen," Hannah said.

"Be quiet, Hannah," Ephraim said. "Get me a cup of coffee."

Ephraim couldn't easily calm himself. As he cleared his mind, the wildflowers in the pitcher caught his gaze. He didn't know how to make sense of the afternoon's events. His son brings home a young woman unknown to him, fresh like the flowers. Hannah dislikes the girl and wants her out of the house because of her father. But the girl is not cowed and hides nothing of her past. No turbulent storm or raging water attended the grim unfolding of Harriet's story. The tumult of the afternoon occurred outside the human realm. The Holy Spirit was there. He and Harriet shared the overwhelming embrace of God, carried away by Him in wonderment. Would Ephraim ever be the same?

"Don't go back to sleep on me," Hannah yelled from the kitchen. "I am not finished with that mess they left."

The afternoon's experience was illuminating, but not forgiving. Ephraim's selfishness was made blatantly clear, and his solitary life lived in disregarded of others. He was baptized and soldiered for his religion, but unaware of the need to sacrifice and the presence of love. There was much to be forgiven and those most dear to him deserved amends. David How's love for his daughter, Harriet, showed Ephraim a path forward, a course toward forgiveness and new way of living in the world.

"You need to treat me better, Ephraim," Hannah said as she reentered the parlor. "You show me scorn in front of others. I deserve better."

"Yes. That is true," Ephraim said, as if in a trance.

"You don't treat me as a person. You order me around like a slave," Hannah talked as if no one listened.

"I can be better to you," Ephraim said. "You deserve more attention and consideration."

"You treat me like a slut," Hannah continued. "That is why Jonathan feels free to humiliate me."

"Stop. Listen for a moment, Hannah." Ephraim said. "I haven't shown my appreciation. You deserve more from me. That is going to change."

"You sorry bastard, Ephraim," Hannah sat on the settee, wiping her brow. "What more do you want from me? Maybe you don't want me and want that young bitch who doesn't know her way around a mattress. What is your trick?"

"I will try to treat you better," Ephraim cleared his throat. "I am not kicking you out. I will try not to demean you and will make you feel more appreciated and secure and provided for."

"That's new, something I have not heard before, Ephraim," Hannah said. "You gave a farm to Samuel and Polly when they married. You go to the county courthouse to provide for the other boys. You give them land and plan to support their families."

"You deserve proper treatment," Ephraim said. "You are the mother of my son, Eli. His well-being is important to me."

"You won't marry me?" Hannah asked. "That would be a sure guarantee of Eli's welfare."

"No. Marriage has never been a consideration," Ephraim said. "I know you will take care of him. As he gets older, he will take care of you."

"You are a bastard, Ephraim," Hannah said.

"I've told you what I will do, what I can do," Ephraim said. "There are things you never learned, and I have not bothered to change your thinking. It is too late to start now. You are unlikely to change. I know that my failure to pay attention to you has fostered your selfishness. The same is true for your lack of empathy and pettiness. I accept blame for that."

Ephraim thought he had built a solid house as he looked around at the ample space, the light from the windows welcoming. In some way it was unfamiliar, despite the time spent building it. Unlike his home in Buxton, it was never a haven offering contentment. The creaking from the roof hinted at careless construction.

"I am not going to kick you out. I will try not to demean you. But many things will never be improved. It is not the time for marriage, and I don't have the inclination," Ephraim broke the silence.

"Ungrateful son-of-a-bitch," Hannah yelled. "You made me what I am, your nastiness and conceit. Why stop now?"

"I cannot tell you how to be nice to other people, Hannah, or be empathic. People's nature doesn't change. I don't know how people are moved to feel anything beyond themselves. Harriet's suffering stirred no interest in you. I have never seen you express concern for any of my sons, or empathy. You don't want them around. You have always been hostile toward Mirinda," Ephraim said.

"I don't remember that you ever showed her any deep attachment, not in my presence," Hannah sneered.

"You will have to learn about forgiveness on your own, Hannah," Ephraim continued. "Although David How was executed, you know he was offered forgiveness. And mercy is every bit as important as justice. Salvation is from sin, not the penalty of sin. I cannot explain that to you."

Ephraim thought he heard a snatch of laughter.

"Is sin next, Ephraim? I do not want to hear any of your dreary lessons on sin," Hannah yawned. "I think sins are best dealt with by thinking of them as little as possible." She stretched back on the settee and closed her eyes.

"I'll let you be, Hannah," Ephraim knew he could not change her deportment or thinking. "I stand by my commitment to Eli and providing for his future."

A welcome quiet descended. Silence was not part of Ephraim's sacred tradition, which prized noise and disorder. He heard of Quaker practice, where sustained silence in a meeting brought members together and made them receptive to higher truths. They said the Holy Spirit was the companion of silence.

"Ping." A sharp, high-pitched sound rang out. Ephraim jerked up his head, unable to place the noise in his mind. Looking around the room gave him no clue to its source.

"What's that?" Hannah barked when the strange sound was repeated. As she rested on the settee, there was another "ping."

"I need peace and quiet," Hannah's yelled aimlessly. "This is my house."

Ephraim was puzzled and focused on the source of the unknown noise. "Ping." The sound was just in front of him, but he saw nothing.

"Ephraim. Do something about that noise," Hannah yelled again. "You are worthless."

Hannah sat up, her head moved fitfully, while the searching eyes appeared lost.

"Ping. Ping." The interval between the sounds shortened and Ephraim got a better fix on the source of the disturbing beats. He looked at the low table in front of the settee. It was bare after Hannah's cleaning, except for the bowl at its center. The dish was small, round with sides curved upward to a fluted lip, handles fastened on each side. Made of polished tin and copper, it gleamed and was a wedding present from Marmaduke Aldrich to his daughter Polly and Samuel. They forgot to take it with them when they moved to their own place. As Ephraim leaned forward, he heard another "ping" and saw a metal bead bounce from the bottom of the bowl, roll around and settle with several others. He looked up. Directly above the dish was a hole in the roof and a clinched hand sticking through it.

"Haw! Haw!" Ephraim's laugh was loud, and taken as encouragement, a request for the stream to continue.

The "Pings" increased, more beads falling from the ceiling, as Hannah's screams became a series of undulating howls, reverberating through the whole parlor and rattling every moveable object. Each bead appeared the same, but behaved differently, some bouncing more than others, others raced in unexpected trajectories.

"It got me in the eye, Goddamit!" Hannah wailed. "Ephraim stop this downpour. Stop this devilry."

Hannah stood up swatting the air, then whirled around as if swarmed by a hoard of mosquitoes. "Goddammit! Goddammit! Ephraim, you worthless piece of shit. Stop this."

"Close your mouth Hannah, before you swallow something," Ephraim laughed.

"It's an avalanche. We will be buried if it doesn't stop." Hannah's eyes fixed on the overflowing bowl of beads and grabbed it. "Out you devils." She wheeled around, sending the pellets to every nook and corner of the room. "Out."

The torrent suddenly stopped, Hannah's undefended head and shoulder, free from assault. Seeing nothing in the air, she looked up defiantly and screamed, "That's that, Fart-Catcher! It's over." Hannah raised the bowl militantly, saluting the ceiling in victory.

Her moment of triumph was short. With the first shift of weight, her foot slipped on the bead-littered floor, arms scrambling for balance. The other foot slipped sideways as she bore down on it, and the spinning started. She would not let go of the bowl, convinced of its shamanic power, adding to the disarray and un-likelihood of her regaining balance.

Strange forces were at work. The potent air in the room, moving restlessly in whirls and flows like the weather, added to Ephraim's sense of helplessness. He could be no more than an observer.

Hannah bolted when the light flashed from the suddenly open door. The room was brilliant. Spasmodic reflexes flung back her upper body, thrust her legs forward and up, locking them straight at the knees. She levitated briefly before she plunged, pounding the floor with a loud thud. The bowl which was flung into the air, rested on her head like a crown. She was not bleeding or scared by the vessel's impact, since the fall threw up her flounced skirt to cover her entire face. Her naked legs had the look of wood.

"Are you all right?" Ephraim reached down to Hannah, who had not budged since her fall. "Hannah?"

"That's that," William laughed from the open doorway. Isaiah, stood behind, rolling in laughter. They were doubled up by the chaos before them.

"She has stopped complaining for once," William cracked.

"And making cruel and foul remarks," Jonathan's words were harsh.

"Get up," Ephraim said as Hannah stirred. "Take my hand. You need to head into the other room and rest." He did not look at his sons, still hooting in the doorway.

TWELVE

"Where is she? Where is Mirinda?" Samuel asked as soon as Many Ann opened the door. "Can we see her.?" Samuel's wife, Polly, entered the house first.

"She is in her room." Mary Ann answered. "I don't know if she is awake right now. I have tried to let her rest."

The McKinneys' white frame house was small and unwelcoming with its rough, unsheltered front door and small porch. The two small windows that flanked the entrance did not lend much light to the room Samuel and Polly entered, and the recent addition to which they were led was no brighter.

"You will have to excuse the mess," Mary Ann said. "Mirinda usually takes better care of this place. She has been distracted. That table was overturned in Big Bear's haste to get her to bed."

"What happened to my sister, Mary Ann?" Samuel asked. "We were told Mirinda was hurt and to come as quickly as possible."

"We couldn't get here any faster," Polly said.

"I don't know. I paid no attention when Mirinda went outside," Mary Ann. "I did look out and saw her walking towards the woods. I didn't think anything about it until she was gone a long time. I went outside and called for her but got no answer."

They stopped at the door of the room where Mirinda was resting. Mary Ann put her finger to her lips. "Shhh. She is sleeping." Samuel and Polly looked in and saw Mirinda, her eyes closed, lying on a spread dappled with blood.

"She looks awful," Samuel said as he eased the door shut. "What do you know?"

"Not much. I went looking for her, calling her name all the while. I got no response. Mirinda never went into the woods without me when she could help it. But she thought she knew her way around enough not to get lost. I got close to the creek, and above the sound of the water I could hear some low moans," Mary Ann said.

Mary Ann never paid much attention to her appearance but must have taken some time with herself since the incident. Her dress was not mussed up: no burrs, twigs, or signs of having trudged through the woods in search of Mirinda. She seemed unaware of the nervous fidgeting of her hands.

"Mirinda was lying in a patch of grass. She was covered in blood. Her skirt was up and dark red streaks ran down her legs. She wore no shoes. I found them later at the base of a tree. I couldn't tell if the patches of blue on her flesh were bruises or from exposure. There was some blood in a pool at the edge of the creek; maybe she was trying to wash herself or drink." Mary Ann leaned back against the wall, the recounting of her tale a source of exhaustion. "She needed help. I tried to lift her and get her back here, to the house. She was too heavy, and I had no strength to help."

"How did you get her back here," Samuel asked.

"Benjamin went to Short Tract on business this morning. Today, Big Bear was here to dig a new well. He is strong and good at that kind of work. I found him, took him to Mirinda. He carried her back to this house and left her on the bed."

"Have you called a doctor?" Samuel asked.

"She did not ask for help, but she doesn't like doctors. She's made that clear," Mary Ann paused. "You know, she doesn't talk much. But she did say your name, Samuel. You are the one she called for," Mary Ann said.

"Let's go in and let her know we are here," Polly said.

Samuel and Polly sat by the bed where Mirinda lay motionless, no sound except for the shallow breathing. Her pale lips were parted but expressionless, disguising any pain or anguish.

"Mary Ann, could you bring some water and a cloth?" Polly asked. She stretched Mirinda's arms along her sides and gently unlocked her clenched hands, finding no secrets among the stains of blood.

Mary Ann brought a stool with the small basin of water and cotton cloth and set them next to Polly. After dampening the washcloth, Polly softly wiped Mirinda's forehead before moving to her bruised cheeks. The inert young woman stirred and slowly opened her eyes. Samuel stood to look at her face and smiled.

"Mirinda, Polly and I are here," Samuel whispered.

Resting back on a pillow, Mirinda's head was tilted up. She faced her surroundings, but she did not turn or look at her brother. Her position appeared unchanged since she had been set down by Big Bear, her tangled hair the same as when she was found in the woods.

"We came to help you, Mirinda," Samuel leaned down. "What can we do for you? Would you like some water?"

Mirinda did not respond. Polly clasped Mirinda's hand, and gently stroked the top of it. There was no reaction, no squeeze of recognition.

"You have nothing to fear, Mirinda," Samuel said. "I am here with you. I will stay with you."

Polly took the cloth and again wiped Mirinda's motionless face, no blinking of her eyes. After setting down the cloth, she began to comb out the snarls in Mirinda's hair, hair being more venerated than hands for making an intimate connection with its possessor, a gesture of affection and trust.

"We love you, Sister. We want you to feel cared for and safe." There was no response to Samuel's words.

The frustrated brother stood and straightened his back, assuming the appearance of confidence. His deep breaths, his arms folded across his chest, did not disguise his frustration. His patience disappeared.

"Mirinda, who did this to you? Who did this?" Samuel's voice shook the room. He seemed to regain control as he bent over his sister and looked into her eyes. They were unblinking. The black centers were dilated, as expected in the dim light of the room. As he got closer and looked directly into them, their centers did not change. They were not aroused, got no wider, appearing insensate, dull. Samuel seemed embarrassed by the outburst and his face looked sad as he gradually pulled away.

"'The eye is the lamp of the body,' Luke tells us," Samuel choked. "I don't see the lamp." Samuel took a deep breath before he called out. "Mirinda. Come back to us." He looked at his sister again. Nothing changed but for the tears streaming down her cheeks.

⮑

"Everybody wait here," Samuel said, dismounting his horse. "I want to take a look."

He walked to the top of the bald ridge trusting Swift Hill would offer a good view of the settlement below. Samuel paused briefly for a general look before homing in on Higgins Mill, tilted into a depleted stream. Too dilapidated to serve as a meeting house, Samuel figured that gatherings took place in the large clearing beside the building. The plot's red clay surface was fully visible through the wooded slope that descended before him. A large pole stood in the middle of the open space and two men stacked wood nearby. No one else appeared through his vigil.

"What did you see?" Jonathan asked as Samuel returned to the members of his party.

"Just two men carrying firewood," Samuel said. "There's an abandoned mill, a clearing they probably use for services, and some dozen log cabins scattered through the surrounding woods. Smoke is coming out of all of them, so dinner must be under way. The cabins don't look well-constructed. I guess there are twenty men down there, at most."

"What do you want us to do, Samuel?" Jonathan asked.

"Station yourself on the ridge and keep watch on what is brewing down there, Jonathan. Stay out of sight," Samuel said. "The rest of us can relax for now and stay quiet."

Samuel watched his friends tie their horses to trees and settle on the ground. Brothers Isaiah and William were in the rescue party, along with Jonathan, as well as Mark Guptail, Joe Horton, Hiram Williams, Nate Ridlon and Ezra Gibson, friends he knew and could count on. Despite his age and objections to the enterprise, his father had come along.

Ephraim hadn't understood Samuel's need to defend his religion. The conversation of several days before would not leave his mind.

"Libby's atrocious deeds are not what my Church is about," Samuel told his father. "No wonder people call Mormons crazy."

"I am not going to go with you, Samuel. It a job for a level-headed man, not one who makes rush decisions," Ephraim said.

"There are prophets, men like Joseph Smith, who talk to God and have marvelous revelations," Samuel said. "But quack holy men show up all of the time. None of those has blessed us with the Book of Mormon."

"I have come across a few imposters over the years. I have also known Joseph Libby for a long time. He is no prophet." Ephraim frowned and shook his head sideways in disgust. "Back in Maine, we were both followers of Jacob Cochrane, both overwhelmed by his moving sermons and glorious feats. Libby was a young man and as a Cochranite he learned to talk to God."

"You heard him talk to God?" Samuel was amazed.

"That is when he started talking in tongues. I heard him babble," Ephraim said. "Cochrane called it a gift of God, but I never understood a word. Like Cochrane, Joseph Smith places great emphasis on prophesy and revelation. Since Libby's conversion to Mormonism, he has fully developed his gift," Ephraim continued.

"He claims to be the 'mouthpiece of God,'" Samuel said.

"Since he settled here. Experiencing God and his talking in tongues is unrelenting," Ephraim said. "Those who have known him over the years doubt his gift. He moved away, to Centerville, because of the rumors. He has followers there, call themselves 'Libbyites.' They are a noisy and unruly lot."

"All over the county, they are thought of as Mormons. They make us look bad," Samuel said. "Libby makes it harder for us to live here."

"Lots of people don't like Mormons and the newspapers don't make it any easier. Now, everyone is talking about Joseph Smith's many wives," Ephraim chuckled. "Are there really thirty-three?"

"Joseph Smith wants a multitude of believers. With more wives, there are more offspring and more followers to spread his beliefs," Samuel said. "Polly and I have two children. That suits us, but we may have more."

"I am proud that you have resisted the self-indulgence of your prophet," Ephraim joked. "And your character has proved stronger than your father's."

"I have watched you, Father, put your scruples first. That is not Libby, who says he lives by God's commandments. He has etched his revelations on a hunting knife and brandishes it all the time. Followers come to his meetings because they are promised heavenly visitors," Samuel couldn't take his mind off Libby.

"I've heard that," Ephraim said. "But unlike Mormons, Libbyites are not evangelical and don't seek converts. They want to be left alone."

"They can't be left alone. Not any longer. That is why we are going to their meeting at Higgins Mill tonight," Samuel turned to leave. "We can't tolerate injustice or turn our backs on murder."

After dark, Samuel's party silently crept through the woods toward the clearing. A group of about twenty, mostly men, gathered before a fire that brightened the pitch-black night. "Cast him out," they chanted. "Cast him out."

Joseph Libby, the self-proclaimed prophet, head lowered, solemnly appeared in a long dark robe, cinched around his middle with a wide belt. Tucked into it was his famous knife. He carried a rope in his left hand that served as a leash and pulled behind him a child with slim limbs and long, matted hair. She moved on all fours, head up, sniffing the air like a dog. She growled from a misshapen mouth with long canine teeth and seemed unable to speak. Easing back on her haunches, she finally rested in front of the gathering, her wet tongue hanging from a panting mouth.

"This creature, this hideous creature, has invaded our community," Libby shouted while searching the crowd to see if any intruders had joined his clan. "In a vision, God, our Almighty God, sent me a message. He revealed to me that this foul creature before you has been sent among us by the Devil, to corrupt us and debase our families. You can see in her disfigured form and abhorrent manner that she is satanic."

The girl was agitated, alert to the hostile environment, fearful yet keenly vigilant. Her nervous black eyes flashed as they stalked the surrounding darkness and her cowered head twitched toward every sound.

"God has ordered this ugliness be cleansed by fire. Like witches before her, she will be burned at the stake." Both of Libby's arms shot up, calling for a sign or heavenly command to affirm the murder he was about to commit. "Keep chanting, brothers and sisters. Summon the Holy Spirit. Bring down His fury."

Behind the fire, stood the tall, charred post Samuel had seen from the ridge. As Libby pulled the girl around the fire toward it, she violently resisted and began to bark. The bark became the long howl of a wolf, a cry for help. It grew louder as she was dragged across the cleared ground, her hands and feet finding nothing to grip. She howled again.

Two followers raised the struggling child upright and bound her roughly to the post. In a desperate spasm the howling stopped. Her grotesque mouth hung wide open, frozen silent in place. The child's eyes were filled with terror, but there was no gasp or whimper. Her hands were tied behind her and the hairless, unbathed body was striped by rope. In firelight, the subdued frame showed an abundance of scars, bruises, and calluses on the palms, elbows and knees. Her sex was covered by a dirty rag.

On Libby's orders, his helpers stacked firewood on the ground around the girl and placed dried brush on top for kindling. A sharp howl of a wolf broke the tense air.

Libby ignored the ominous sound and moved toward the campfire with a homemade torch. He lit the torch in the campfire, then waved it in the air as he strode toward the traumatized girl. "Strike down this wretch, Lord. Show your wrath, your powers of destruction. Stamp out this evil. Banish her from this earth."

A loud splintering of underbrush alarmed Samuel, who saw the large, furry-coated beast charge past his hiding place in the direction of the helpless child.

"Arghhh. Arghhh." The furious growl frightened everyone. The group fractured, astonished at the fury of the wolf as it leapt toward their prophet. The beast's jaws aimed for Libby's throat, but he dodged, swinging around the torch to parry the attack. In the fierce rush, the torch fell from the prophet's grasp. He grabbed his knife from the sheath tucked in his belt. The polished blade flashed.

"Save the child." Samuel yelled, rousing his eight companions to take advantage of the moment. "Get the girl." As the rescue party raced for the child, her voice was set free. She began to howl. The torch had fallen on the brush around the pyre and the kindling flared into tall flames.

Several of the Libbyites belatedly rushed to save their prophet, one fired a rifle at the raging beast. Many remained paralyzed in the face of the assault.

The blaze did not stop Samuel or his brother Isaiah from working to free the child. The rest of Samuel's band kept the Libbyites at bay while the brothers freed the child. There was no intention to harm them, so they kept their weapons in reserve. And the hand-to-hand tussling made shooting rifles difficult. One Libbyite tried to club Jonathan with the stock of his weapon, but Jonathan ducked and Joe Horton downed the assailant with his knife. Hiram Williams and Nat Ridlon pulled burning brush and wood away from the girl and her rescuers.

Libby struggled for his life. The fabled knife, adorned with accounts of God's commands, penetrated the wolf's thick coat, and blood gushed from the deep wound. But the beast's jaws remained locked on the prophet's shoulders until another shot rang out. Wounded a second time, the wolf released Libby and fled, the shining knife still lodged in her loin.

"Get the knife. Get that bloody knife," Libby screamed, devastated by the thought of losing this important connection to his Almighty God.

Samuel's trousers caught fire and Isaiah coughed for breath when they pulled the child away from the post and into clear air.

Libby remained on the ground, disabled by the struggle. Two more rifle shots aimlessly blasted into the darkness of the forest. Most of the Libbyites fled to the shelter of their cabins.

Samuel and his deputies faced no further resistance as they wrapped the unconscious child in a blanket. Samuel mounted his horse, and Isaiah and Jonathan lifted the girl so their older brother could cradle her in his arms for the journey back to Granger. There was no hurry to return. They were slowed by the shock of what had transpired, but as they rode on, comforted by the just outcome of their mission. The child was safe, and they were unharmed.

〜

"Let's get a table and sit down." Ephraim tried to get his sons inside the lobby, but found it was hard to get their attention. "I see a place on the other side of the room. Let's head over there." Samuel and his brothers lingered by the door, relishing their newly found celebrity. The compliments seemed never-ending.

Folks in Granger were proud of their young men who secretly traveled to Higgins Mill and saved a child from being burnt to death. For the past several months, family and friends celebrated their courage and bravery. The story of the daring rescue spread throughout Allegany County, but few outside of Granger had the opportunity to meet the plucky heroes. The appearance of the Berry boys in Angelica caused a stir and when they were noticed at the Exchange Hotel that afternoon people would not let them alone. Ephraim was proud of his sons but wanted to finish the day and return home.

"Thanks for all your kind words," Ephraim finally shouted so all could hear. "My sons are worthy of your respect, but we still have business to finish this afternoon. Please excuse us."

Samuel and Isaiah immediately followed their father's lead through the crowded room. Jonathan had difficulty leaving his admirers, and eyes remained on William as he slowly swaggered to the table where the family settled.

"Anyway, I'm glad that business is settled. Let's have some refreshment before heading back to Granger," Ephraim said.

The Exchange was the most popular hotel in Allegany County, situated across West Street from the county clerk's office and around the corner from the courthouse and county prison. Numerous law offices were nearby, and it appeared that most of the lawyers in town had come to the lobby to finish business or to enjoy a late afternoon beverage. Ephraim liked being there with his sons after a day of meetings with the county clerk. They would never have found themselves in a place like this in Buxton.

"The land has been transferred as promised," Ephraim said. "I'll keep these papers." A barmaid brought the beers they had ordered and set them on the round table. "Cheers," Ephraim led a toast. "Nobody owes me any money. But I want you boys to make your own way, be independent and be good providers for you families."

"Thank you, Father," the three sons said in unison.

"Of course, it is wise to be married before you start a family," Ephraim laughed. "William has got a start on that. Isaiah, you are planning a wedding. I know, Jonathan, one day you will tire of sowing your wild oats." Ephraim took a drink from his tankard and nodded at his son.

"You envy my freedom, Father," Jonathan joked. "And you know how hard it is to pick the right woman and settle down with some peace of mind." Ephraim didn't lose his smile at the reference to Hannah.

"Family is important to a man, Jonathan, and how he regards himself," Ephraim said. "You will watch your brothers change and be jealous of the pride they take in their children."

None of the boys had a full picture of their father's business dealings or the extent of his holdings. They heard talk of properties beyond Granger, in Allen, in Birdsall and as far away as Scio, but Ephraim kept these affairs secret. Samuel had traveled to Angelica with his father several times, but this was the first trip for the other three.

"Father, I want to ask you something," Isaiah said. "Would you mind if mother came here for my wedding? I have thought about how special that would be for her."

"I would like to see her too, wedding or no wedding," Jonathan said. "It has been more than eight years since we said goodbye."

"All of us boys would like Mother to come," Isaiah said. "I have talked to Samuel too. We would share the expense of bringing her to Granger. We even plan for her to stay."

"I haven't given any thought to Mary being in Allegany County," Ephraim was surprised by the conversation. "I don't know what that would be like."

"You do not have to see her, Father, except at the wedding," Isaiah said. "She would be living in another part of Granger. Gideon Aldrich lives next to my new farm. He has a big house and lots of room. He told me that Mother can live with his family. I think that would be fine with her."

"It seems like you boys have done a lot of talking and planning," Ephraim said. "And I'm the last to hear of this scheme."

"You talk a lot about family, Father," William said. "Mother is part of our family, even though she was left in Buxton."

"Why did you leave Mother? And take us with you?" Jonathan asked, emboldened by William's remark.

"She didn't like the idea of coming. She didn't think at all about the grim future in Buxton. I saw it. There wasn't going to be enough land for you boys to farm, where you could sustain yourselves and your own families," Ephraim said. "We had barely enough money to support ourselves in good years. Bad weather meant disaster."

"Mother would have been a lot of help here, and worked hard," Jonathan said.

"Your mother could not comprehend my dream," Ephraim said.

"Hannah came. I can't imagine the kind of dream she had." William joked.

"I did not dream small, William," Ephraim said. "I wanted a new start and saw the chance to get it. Buxton will always be small. Minds there are small too."

"Mother didn't want the family broken up," Isaiah said. "She's said that in letters."

"I had to make a change," Ephraim said. "I had to get out of that house."

"I don't remember well, Father, but you were often not there," Isaiah said.

"Even before I married, I wanted to get away from Buxton. I wanted to go fight in the war," Ephraim said.

"You wanted out of Buxton when you were young, before you married?" Isaiah asked.

"I felt unsettled, even before your mother came along. And she wasn't from Buxton," Ephraim reflected. "She didn't change my feeling about not belonging there. That never changed. The hard work on the farm, my endless efforts to make the house a place to be after a long day in the fields, didn't make me feel more rooted."

The noise in the lobby grew as more alcohol was consumed. The drinking, Ephraim mused, was driven by the surprise of someone exposing a hidden life. *Spirits never did that for* me, *like those who spent their time in Coolbroth's. They knew only what I wanted them to hear.* Ephraim thought.

"Go on, Father," Isaiah said. "Tell us more."

"Your mother tried to make things more stable. Having children did ground me somewhat. With the births of Samuel and Mirinda I became more attached to my home," Ephraim said.

"You shouldn't have stopped before having me," Isaiah injected. "You took a long break."

"Mary miscarried," Ephraim hesitated. "After that a big change came over Buxton. My restlessness abated with the arrival of Jacob

Cochrane. His astonishing presence focused my restlessness, settled me down and quelled my deep longing. But my spirits soared with his orations, and his divine pageants carried me away. It didn't matter where I slept, so I was away from home a lot."

"Some of my friends in Buxton talked about Cochrane's orgies," William smirked.

"He was exposed as a fraud and was sent to prison for lewd and lascivious behavior," Ephraim said frankly. "As for me, I could not shake off his wondrous vision, and I didn't lose all of my Cochrane habits. I did stop going to church. My attachment to Cochrane's ways brought on fights with your mother," Ephraim said. "The quarreling made me want to stay away."

"There were the other women too, who kept you away," William teased. "You were infamous in Buxton for getting around."

"I was adrift and taken over by emptiness," Ephraim said. "For me, the flirtation was a way of stepping out of my dreary surroundings, and entering, temporarily, a different world."

If Ephraim were caught up in some reverie, it ended with the woman at the next table falling into his arms. She got up to leave while managing several bags and packages. Her parcels were difficult to balance, stacked one atop the other, and she slipped with her first step. She was unexpectedly pitched across Ephraim, but the woman didn't seem to mind the hand across her breast. Ephraim laughed but didn't want others to see how much he enjoyed the incident. Before he extracted himself and got to his feet, Isaiah came to the rescue. He helped the woman up and, along with her possessions, got her to the door. The sons howled with laughter at the helpless and embarrassed look on their father.

"Excuse me, Father, but I was asking about Mother coming to the wedding," Isaiah said.

"You can see that still I do not always behave well," Ephraim smiled as he straightened himself in his chair. "Your mother is a good woman. I could have treated her better, but I am best with only one task at a time," Ephraim stated. "Getting out of Buxton was foremost on my mind."

"Why did you take us with you and not leave us in Buxton?" Jonathan asked.

"I am your father," Ephraim asserted. "It my job to show you how the world works and how you make your way."

"That may be true. But you knew nothing of us when we left Buxton. Samuel was different than the rest of us, because he is the oldest. You knew nothing of our needs or the way we thought. You were never curious and didn't ask. You told us to be quiet and listen. Mother wanted to understand us," Jonathan said. "Taking us from her was a wrenching loss."

Ephraim never wanted this encounter, although the subject was on his mind since the loss of Josiah. He wasn't sure how to explain himself.

"It has taken some time, but I have started to understand loss," Ephraim said. "I knew you had bonds with your mother, but I didn't realize how strong they were, or how enduring. Getting close is hard. It takes time and is not natural to me." Ephraim's eyes looked sad and far away. "In fact, it's not what I was taught and goes against my instincts."

"Father, it isn't anything you do alone," Isaiah said.

"A man doesn't learn how to let down his defenses. Exposing any part of himself, much less reaching out to others, shows weakness. A son expects his father to know the truth, and that truth must be absolute. Otherwise, a father's authority is degraded," Ephraim said.

"But Father, we can learn from each other. Don't you think that is possible?" Isaiah said. "You know that I am different from my brothers, and Jonathan and William have their own talents."

"Yes. That is true. You are not as good with an axe as either of your brothers," Ephraim smiled. "It takes you longer to fell a tree."

"And I am the best with a tomahawk," William bragged.

"We think differently, from each other and from you," Isaiah said. "We don't act the same. William is the most stubborn. And Josiah's positive disposition brightened up a room. He never had a bad word for anybody."

"Yes," Ephraim said, sadly. "He is an inspiration. There is a lot I can learn from my sons. I will try my best to make our affection mutual."

Ephraim pushed his chair back and stood, his eyes looking straight ahead.

"And I will pay for your mother's transport. My sons will not foot the bill for my sins. Now, it is time we started home. I will meet you outside."

THIRTEEN

"Mary. Mary, wake up. Please wake up." Jane nudged her semi-conscious sister-in-law. "Talk to me. Please."

"Ummgrh," Mary grunted. Another shaking prompted a snort.

"Mary, listen," Jane pleaded, placing her hands on each side of Mary's face to raise her head. "Please. You can hear me. Open your eyes and look at me. I want you back."

Mary had stopped eating days before. As she retreated from life, letting go, Mary drifted in and out of consciousness. Her color paled, and expression dulled.

The sad figure on the bed had given up. There was no cure for her loneliness and the crippling isolation. Mary suffered almost a decade of painful emotions. Each thought of her children's departure was a blow to her heart, and eight years of blows left it in fragments. It was impossible to restore, and she had no urge to try.

Jane's affectionate pleas drifted through Mary's consciousness. Memories of friends and neighbors, their kindness and endless compassion salved her diminished spirit, and the whiff of imagined primrose soothed her pain. But Mary's mind was unable to connect the descent into profound sadness with her ultimate extinction.

My ties to Buxton are abiding and substantial, Mary's thought surfaced, *but they prolong this life made unnatural by the absence of my children.*

"Mary. Mary, you must pay attention. Listen to me," Jane pleaded.

I wonder if my children will understand. I am unresisting to this consuming sadness, not wanting to make them suffer. Mary thought. But I never want to foist upon them the awful burden of loss.

"Mary, look. This came in the mail," Jane shook some papers in Mary's face. The rustle of the discolored sheets checked her squirming and irregular movements. "Look. Your children are calling for you. They want you to come. They have sent tickets."

Days of semi-consciousness and lassitude hampered Mary's ability to focus. Physical surrender and inactivity made movement difficult. A shift in Mary's body prompted Jane to grab the floppy shoulders and pull her up.

"Careful, Mary. Raise your head, slowly," Jane directed. "Breathe deeply and compose yourself. Rest your weight on your hips."

Mary sat upright, unsteady and speechless. Her face seemed frozen until her eyes widened, their sockets had turned red. Tears came when she read the letter. Mary covered her eyes with both hands before breaking into sobs and fitful shaking.

"Jane," Mary's voice broke out as if she had never stopped speaking. "My children. I am going to see my children. God is returning them to me. He is healing my heart."

"Your children want you back. They sent for you," Jane said. "Mary, you will rejoin your loving family."

Mary's sense of hopelessness had grown over eight long years of separation, and the fear that her children were gone forever deepened. She did not turn to God or call out for His help. But she increasingly thought about Him. She longed for Him and remembered His promise of hope. While yearning for love, mercy and forgiveness, she had surrendered, stopped eating. The void left by her children was filled by the deity who took them away.

༅

The long trip west was like a pilgrimage. Each day of the journey Mary fought to restore her body's weakness, endured unexpected physical demands and prayed for divine assistance. Every hardship was eclipsed by the longing to embrace her children again.

Crossing New York was easier for Mary than the journey described in Isaiah's letters. The Erie Canal reduced the number of days it took to traverse the state, but early winter ice slowed Mary's boat and froze shut the doors of some canal locks. Traveling on land was much less comfortable, but Mary did not have to trudge through mud and ice until the stagecoach from Mt. Morris to Nunda skidded off the road. Passengers had to get out and freight had to be unloaded before the coach was righted and the journey resumed. Nunda had a decent hotel where Mary bathed and rested well. The final leg of the trip was easy.

"Hello, Mother," Samuel said as Mary stepped out of the stagecoach from Nunda. "Don't you recognize me?"

"Oh Samuel. Of course, I recognize you," Mary said, collecting herself. "My eyes were adjusting to the light. Come here and hug your mother."

Samuel steadied his trembling mother with a strong embrace. Mary overcame her tremors but could not stop the tears.

"Mother, don't forget me," Isaiah said. "I'm here too, no longer just a memory."

Mary welled up again as she recalled the last words to her son when they parted years before. She was swept up in Isaiah's arms.

"Mother, you can tell by these sturdy arms around you that you didn't lose me." Isaiah cried. "I have missed you."

Samuel got his mother's things from the coachman and placed them in the wagon.

"We have a two-hour ride ahead, Mother," Samuel said. "Would you like to refresh yourself in the hotel first? I have a jug of water in the wagon if you are thirsty."

"I'll be fine, Samuel," Mary said. "I am anxious to see the others." Mary took a handkerchief from her sleeve and wiped her eyes.

"Isaiah and I will help you into the wagon, Mother. Let's move over to that front wheel." Mary followed Samuel's instructions. "Now, put your foot on this hub," Isaiah "I will lift, and you grab hold of the side of the seat."

The sons stood on each side of their mother. Samuel helped her position her foot, then lifted Mary and got her into the front of the wagon.

"Mother, you will sit beside me on the seat and Isaiah will ride in the back," Samuel said. "Make yourself comfortable. I have a blanket for you in case you get cold."

Mary watched Isaiah scramble into the back of the wagon. Samuel got himself on the front seat, took the reins in hand, and headed out of Angelica. The sun was bright, but the chill in the air prompted Mary to unfold the blanket and wrap it around her. It was quiet but for the horses and wagon creaks, when Mary settled herself against the back of the seat.

I cannot believe this is happening, that I'm back with my children, Mary thought. Isaiah was a good correspondent and had kept Mary aware of goings-on with him and his siblings. She knew about her children's chores on the farm and some Granger gossip. *I never thought I would see them again.*

Mary knew that she could have come to Granger before, that money could have been scraped together for transport. *But I could not have come without an invitation*, she thought. *I had to know I was wanted.*

Early after her abandonment, Mary thought she could never forgive Ephraim. He had gouged out her heart, but she survived. Healing came, and the hurt subsided along with thoughts of Ephraim and retribution.

The road from Angelica to Granger was all up hill, stretching over brown fields splotched by patches of snow, and through evergreen woodlands.

"We are almost there, Mother. You will get your first glimpse of Gideon's house after we round that far bend. It is not much more than a mile," Samuel said

"Stop, Samuel. I must get out." Mary knew the last of her pilgrimage must be completed on foot, a demonstration of her humility and submission to God's will. There was no other way to demonstrate her gratitude for the unfolding miracle. The wheels beside her clanged on rocks, the wagon groaned as it bounced across the ruts in a stream bed, but the winter brought no washouts or difficult crossings. Feet numbed by the frozen earth and the regular incline kept Mary's pace slow and shortened her breath. The terrain wasn't hard or overly demanding. No obstacles required her to crawl on her knees or lift herself. Twice her skirt caught in briars. Mary was tired from the day's journey, but her mission asked nothing but patience.

It isn't just the invitation telling me I am wanted that brings me here. Mary thought. *God is restoring to me a lost treasure. I am granted His forgiveness.*

"Would you like to stop for a moment, Mother? It is not far, and you may want to catch your breath." Samuel paid close attention to his mother's considered steps and careful pace.

"Yes. I would like that," Mary said.

Samuel pulled his team to a halt, the wagon resting in the shade of an evergreen.

"Isaiah, could you hand me that brown leather satchel behind the wagon seat?" Mary took time to catch her breath and compose herself. Isaiah handed his mother her satchel which she rested on the wagon wheel.

Mary removed a small mirror from the bag and set it on top. She carefully removed her bonnet, picked up the mirror and inspected her tousled hair. She combed up the strands that had fallen loose, pinned them back and replaced her hat. The scar on her head still caused her shame, and she wouldn't risk it being seen.

"That will do. I don't want people to think my travels were a hardship or unpleasant," she said as she took a handkerchief, patting her face to remove barely noticeable grit. She replaced the mirror in her bag, then passed it back to Isaiah. "Please help me back up."

The silver-grey hair confirmed Mary's fifty-plus years. Her eyes were still bright. The deep lines around her mouth and chin, which make older women appear grim or scornful, did not detract from a pleasant countenance.

"I'm fine. Let's go ahead," Mary smiled at the boys. She would look her best when presented to the rest of her family. The faint worry that she might not recognize her other children after eight years did not go away.

Mary had expected Gideon Aldrich's residence to be large, since ten people lived in it. And the sprawling, white frame house was unmistakable in the distance. She could not distinguish one figure from another, but many people gathered for her arrival.

"Mother. Mother," Mary heard as they halted. Two men came forward to help her from the wagon. Behind the manly faces of Jonathan and William, Mary could see the youthful outlines she remembered from long ago. Strong arms helped her down.

"I have to do this one at a time," Mary said as tears appeared. "I can't hug you both at once. Jonathan, I am so happy to see you again," Mary embraced her son. "And hear you speak. The last time we were together the cat got your tongue."

"My dearest Mother. Welcome home to Granger," Jonathan said.

"And William," Mary turned to embrace her other son. "I am glad to see you have your feet on the ground, and you do not have to be summoned from a tree. I am too old to crawl up after you."

"I missed you, Mother, and didn't want to make myself hard to find," William smiled.

The endearments and embraces continued. Mary turned to find Samuel off the wagon with a young woman and two boys at his side.

"Mother, this is my wife Polly, and our boys Amasa and Pembroke," Samuel said.

"I have heard so much about you, Polly," Mary said as she embraced her daughter-in-law. "And about these dear children. I notice there is another on the way." Mary stepped back for a full view of her daughter-in-law's expanded profile.

"Yes. In less than a month," Polly said, and motioned to the man a few steps away. "This is my brother, Gideon, he is your host and will make your move to Granger as pleasant as he can."

"Welcome to my home, Mrs. Berry. I hope it becomes a pleasant one for you," Gideon smiled, extending his left arm. "This is my wife Rachel, my grown sons James and Allen, and the youngsters, Nathaniel, Polly and Edwin. Frank and Ester Faller, over there, also live in the house."

"I deeply appreciate your hospitality, Gideon. I hope not to forget anyone's name. This is quite a reception," Mary was taken by the flurry around her, children throwing gumballs at each other in the brief pause.

"The introductions aren't over, Mother," Isaiah said as he walked forward with two women. "This is my bride, Saphira Eli, and her mother Sallie White."

What a pretty girl, Mary thought, *Isaiah has an eye for women*. Saphira's dark hair was parted in the middle and pulled back, highlighting her beautiful, brown eyes and prominent cheekbones. She could have appeared haughty, but for the wide, smiling mouth below the graceful nose. The high-neck red wool dress was buttoned up the front, surprisingly stylish for western New York.

"You are a charming young woman, Saphira," Mary smiled as she reached out. "I have heard so much about you. I am hoping you will tell me the things my son won't, and we can be even better friends. Many blessings on your marriage to Isaiah."

Mary stopped abruptly before greeting Saphira's mother, carefully scanning the crowd around her.

"Where is Mirinda?" Mary asked aloud. She looked about again.

"Where is my beautiful daughter?" Mary asked loudly. "Samuel. Samuel, where have you hidden Mirinda?' Mary sensed something was wrong.

"Mother, Mirinda is not here." Samuel appeared immediately and put his arm around Mary's shoulder. "Mirinda didn't come."

"She didn't come?" Mary was stunned. "What kept her away?"

"Mother, let's talk over here," Samuel said. He put his palm behind her back and led her away from the others.

"What is going on?" Mary asked firmly. "Is this some secret others can't hear?"

"It is hard to talk about, but Mirinda didn't want to come," Samuel kept his voice low.

"Did she tell you that, Samuel? That she doesn't want to see her mother?" Mary asked in disbelief.

"She didn't say that, Mother," Samuel said softly. "Mirinda can't talk."

"Can't talk?" Mary asked.

"Mirinda doesn't speak and goes nowhere. She doesn't go out," Samuel said.

"Doesn't go anywhere at all?" Mary asked.

"Mirinda won't leave the house," Samuel said. "She doesn't leave her room."

"You can't get her out of her room? She can't be persuaded?" Mary asked. "Can she hear you? She hasn't become deaf and dumb?"

"She can hear, Mother. But to get her out, she would have to be forced," Samuel said. "We can't do that. It would make matters worse."

"What in God's name has happened? What has happened to my baby girl?" Mary wailed. "I should never have let her go."

"There was a terrible accident. We don't know what happened. She has never said. She doesn't say," Samuel said.

"Where is she? We must go to her at once." Mary said.

"She is at the McKinneys', but there is no reason to rush over," Samuel said with grim resignation. "Her condition doesn't change. She will be the same tomorrow as she is today."

Mary was befuddled. *I thought the crying ended. So many tears. I nearly drowned in sadness when my children were taken. The dark cloud that came with news of Josiah's death closed me off from God. The invitation was a piercing light. On the road up from Angelica today I felt I had traveled my way of sorrows. It is not over.*

"You are tired, Mother. You have had a long day. We will see Mirinda first thing in the morning," Samuel put his arms around his mother.

"No. No." Mary cried, freeing herself from Samuel. "I must go. Get the wagon. I must go to my baby now."

The team was still hitched to Samuel's wagon, but the departure was not immediate. Samuel had to make sure that Polly and his children had a way home, that Mary gathered personal things she might need and that family members knew they were going to see Mirinda. They would not be back before nightfall.

Samuel tried to keep his mother calm as they crossed Rush Creek and took Davis Road south. As they traveled he pointed out Mary's new neighbors, the Weavers, Reynolds and Fullers. Mary's mind remained gripped by thoughts of her daughter.

"Tell me Mother, when Mirinda and I were young, were we very different?" Samuel asked.

"You were young and paid no attention to your sister, Samuel," Mary said. "Unlike you, Mirinda was a quiet child, but surprised me. She started talking when she was ten months old and walking at one year. Picky about food, she liked to eat things that were white."

"And I was slow, loud, naughty and ate everything in sight," Samuel joked.

"Mirinda was content by herself, she preferred being alone. She liked to read, which can set a child apart," Mary continued.

"I was never interested in reading," Samuel said.

"Look. There is a fire over there, Samuel. I can smell the smoke," Mary pointed to the sloping field on the right.

"Everything's fine," Samuel said. "George Voss tends the fire. He is burning crop residue left from the harvest. People do that here before spring planting, something not seen in Buxton."

Samuel slowed the wagon as they approached a junction. Mary remembered a story from school and was filled with dread. In the tale from long ago, the traveler had to choose a path knowing that none would lead to anything good. Mary thought of Mirinda's plight, and that at the end of one road she would find Mirinda was a victim of violence; at the end of another, her daughter would not have suffered had she been kept in Buxton. Mary could also be led to find that Mirinda had brought everything upon herself.

Samuel turned north on the county road to Portage, and Mary did not ask her son to slow or stop. She knew the choice of road made no difference. For some reason God had decided that her daughter should have a tragic life. Like the Old Testament perhaps, God required evidence of Mary's obedience. *Mirinda was the price for God's love and for the return of her children.* Mary shuddered.

"What was the accident?" Mary blurted. "You said there was a terrible accident."

"I don't know what happened. I have only seen Mirinda once. She called for me," Samuel started to tell the story. "Mirinda disappeared and was found in the woods unconscious and disheveled. Her dress was up, she had blood and bruises on her legs. She could not have run from an attacker., with no shoes on. We saw her only after she was carried to her bed. She opened her eyes as Polly washed her face, but she didn't talk, not a word. Every time I went to see her after that, I was turned away," Samuel said.

"Was she attacked?" Mary asked.

"I don't know who would do that," Samuel said. "The only man around was Big Bear, who occasionally works around the farm. He carried her into her room. Benjamin McKinney was away."

"She hasn't recovered, she stays by herself and won't see anybody, even her own brother," Mary said. "You are closer to her than anyone."

"Maybe she cannot talk to a man," Samuel said.

"Samuel, what happened to Mirinda? Do you have any idea what brought her to…," words failed Mary. "Why she stays apart?"

"We don't see much of Mirinda," Samuel paused. "That started on the journey here."

"You didn't see her at all?" Mary asked.

"She traveled here with the McKinneys. She was with them most of the time on the trip. Hannah was jealous from the start and showed her dislike when Mirinda came around. I am sure my sister never felt welcome to visit. I am sorry to say my brothers and I were too busy to seek her out. She and Polly get along, but don't see much of each other." Samuel said.

"Did Mirinda see your father? Did he visit?" Mary asked.

"On the journey here, she came by and asked for him. But Father was always busy," Samuel said.

"Does he see her now, in Granger?" Mary asked.

"I don't think so. He's busy with the farm," Samuel said. "Mirinda shows up for barn raisings, pig slaughters, quilting bees. She comes with the McKinneys. Father sees her then."

"Was it after the accident she stopped talking?" Mary asked.

"It may have started before. Polly told me Mirinda was becoming quieter. I don't know when she stopped altogether. You can ask Mary Ann McKinney," Samuel said.

When they pulled up to the McKinney house it was getting dark. As soon as Mary was out of the wagon, she rushed to the front door and knocked loudly. Benjamin McKinney finally came to the door, looking annoyed.

"I want to see my daughter. Take me to see Mirinda." Mary demanded.

"Wait here. She's always sleeping." Benjamin closed the door in Mary's face.

"I don't care if she is sleeping. I must see my daughter," Mary pounded on the door. "Let me in." Mary waited.

"Hello." The door was opened again by Mary Ann. "Please come in. I am sorry to keep you waiting."

"I would like to see Mirinda. Please." Mary had seen Mary Ann once or twice in Buxton, but they never spoke. "I am her mother, Mary Berry."

"I will take you to her room. She likes her rest," Mary Ann said.

After a few strides through a disheveled parlor, down a step into the new addition and through a short hall, they reached a closed door.

"Let me look in first," Mary Ann said. "Maybe she shouldn't be disturbed."

"No," Mary said. She pushed the woman aside and entered the dusky chamber.

Only the exposed hair suggested a human being huddled, inert and silent, under the dirty bedding. Mary could not tell if her daughter was breathing as she settled on the wood frame of the bed. Mary fingered the faded stars on the old quilt, slowly searching out her lost child.

"Mirinda. Mirinda," Mary intoned softly. "This is your mother. This is your mother, Mary, and I have come for you. I have been away too long, my dearest. I am sorry I let you go. I have missed you, my child. I didn't tell you how much I love you. You couldn't really know if I didn't say it." Mary pressed her hand down until she felt her daughter's body through the covers. Mirinda remained unresponsive.

After Mary spread her hand and lightly stroked the daughter's scalp, Mirinda lifted her head. Her eyes locked on her mother's, a look of disbelief rather than alarm. She turned her head away, took a deep, gasping breath and stared back as the tears began to flow. A flood of emotion followed, the quilt no longer an obstacle to Mirinda's arms which tightly gripped her mother. When Mary returned the embrace, her daughter gagged, her body started shaking.

"I will never let you go, my darling," Mary whispered. "I am here for you. I will stay with you."

Samuel observed the stirring reunion and left the room.

Mary stayed on the bed holding her daughter. She dozed but found no actual sleep. She remained motionless until she felt something digging in her back. She tried to slide away without disturbing her daughter, but the continued scratching tracked her movements.

It is something in Mirinda's hand, she thought. She lifted her daughter's wrist and found it stiff and turned down at a sharp angle. The top of her hand was flat, but at the knuckles her fingers turned up and curved back down, like a claw. *Oh no,* Mary thought. *How awful. What's happened to my daughter?*

Mary rolled Mirinda on her back to check the other hand, which felt deformed in the same way. *My baby. What happened to my child?* Mary stretched out on her back and cried. *I must know what happened, everything that happened.*

"Mirinda. Mirinda, precious one," Mary said moving close to her daughter, snuggling against the still figure. "Come next to me. I love you and want to be close to you." Mary kissed her face and touched her daughter's eyes. "Look at me. Look at your loving mother. I want to take care of you, end your suffering. Please let me help you." Mary brought her daughter's hands to her lips and kissed them. She pressed the gnarled hands against her face. As Mirinda shifted on the bed, Mary heard a deep sigh. A long silence was followed by several quick, short gasps.

"Mother," the voice emerged timidly. "Mother," Mirinda choked. "I need you. Oh, I had given up. My life is horrid."

"Let your tears flow. You don't have to hold them back any longer," Mary pulled herself closer to Mirinda, felt her heart pounding.

"What happened to your hands, my darling?" Mary whispered. She had to ask.

"That comes with the sadness. It happens slowly," Mirinda said. "They don't hurt much, but it is hard to dress."

The room was drafty and getting colder. Mary noticed a blanket at the foot of the bed, which she pulled up and bundled around both. They watched traces of their breath.

"Mirinda, I am going to take care of you, but I have to know what happened," Mary finally mentioned the accident. "Samuel told me that you were hurt. Since that time, you don't want to see anybody, or go out. Were you attacked?"

Mirinda raised herself, drew her knees to her chest and wrapped her arms around her legs.

"Mother, I am sorry. I never wanted to tell anyone, but I got pregnant," Mirinda burst out in sobs. "I couldn't have a baby. I had to stop the pregnancy." She wiped her eyes with her arm. "Women do this, especially Indians. Big Bear's wife brought me herbs and plants, which I chewed and used to make teas. I was desperate." Mirinda lowered her head and rubbed her eyes with the bottoms of her hands.

"One day I tried ergot, and before long I had terrible burning sensations in my arms and legs. Then seizures started, and

I ran into the woods. I don't know how I got there, I kept falling down." Her daughter sniffled. "Violent contractions started. I squatted with my back against a tree like the Indians, my legs apart, so I could push hard," Mirinda pulled her raised knees even closer to contain the heaving torso. Mary hung tight. "I suffered violent pain, it went on and on. I bit my tongue, so no one could hear me. There was blood everywhere, my mouth, my hands and legs." The high pitch of her voice became a muted scream. "I blacked out."

Mary was conscious of her breath, not wanting to exhale, fearing a loss of power, and with it one more betrayal of her precious child.

"Who?" the whisper burned. "Who raped you? What monster?"

"It started a long time ago," Mirinda uttered.

"Started? It happened more than once?" Mary's voice roiled.

"Mr. McKinney sees me as a spiritual wife. I am his property. He claims it his right," Mirinda choked. "You know what a spiritual wife is. What I have become."

"How could this evil happen?" Mary hissed.

"I traveled here in his wagon. There was nothing I could do, no place to go. I carry so much shame," Mirinda whimpered. "Who around me would care?"

"Twit-twooo." The long, loud screech of the owl startled Mary, who jumped from under the covers.

"Did you hear that?" Mary whispered.

For a moment Mary thought she heard her own shudders, but it was the flapping against the window. Before it settled on the outside sill, the bird's wings spanned the width of the window's glass surface. The owl appeared surprisingly small when its wings folded, a large broad head but no more than ten inches in height. When poised, the bird's head moved closer to the glass and it started tapping with the short, curved beak. The beat was regular, too rapid to be code, but Mary thought it ominous, a chilling warning.

Mary quietly got to her feet and moved toward the window. When close, she started flailing her arms to shoo the night creature away. It disappeared.

"She doesn't mean any harm," Mirinda said, her voice above a whisper. "She keeps me company. Owls are helpful spirits. She is telling us we need to leave."

"Well then I agree with her," Mary said with urgency. "Get something warm to cover yourself and I will find Samuel. Hurry."

When Mary returned with Samuel, Mirinda had on a heavy coat, a couple of blankets clamped under her arm, and other belongings bundled in a sheet.

"Can you walk, honey?" Mary asked. "Samuel, get her things."

The threesome rushed through the darkness, but Mirinda stumbled at the raised floor of the main house.

"Eeekk," Mirinda screamed as she looked up and saw Benjamin sitting across the room in the darkness.

"You can't go, Mirinda," Benjamin shouted as he stood. "You belong here with me and Mary Ann. Go back to your room," he threatened, raising a bottle in his hand like a club.

"Mother. Get Mirinda to the wagon," Samuel commanded before turning to his sister's abuser. "My sister is coming with us, Benjamin. You will never harm her again."

As Samuel stepped to block Benjamin's movements, the older man lunged forward, swinging his glass weapon. The violent thrust of Samuel's arm took control of the drunk assailant's body, bringing Benjamin down in a palsied twirl. Samuel stared in amazement at the figure on the floor, sorry that he never got to hit the brute.

It was not a quiet exit but took less time than I expected, Mary thought as Samuel emerged from the house and raced toward her.

Samuel helped his sister and mother into the back of the wagon. They huddled low as Samuel squared himself on the driver's seat.

"You can't leave," Benjamin yelled from the porch but did not try to stop the fleeing party. "I'll get you. I'll get you back, Mirinda."

Samuel whipped the horses and they raced away.

FOURTEEN

Isaiah and Saphira could not have their wedding in the new Methodist Church because it wasn't large enough to accommodate everyone they wanted to invite. It was smaller than Gideon Aldrich's barn and less convenient for the bride's family, who made most of the preparations. Saphira was not a Mormon and Isaiah stopped practicing that faith after most of Joseph Smith's followers moved on to Illinois several years earlier. Everyone who attended the afternoon ceremony thought Enos Baldwin, the new Justice of the Peace and friend of Gideon's father, did a good job tying the marriage knot.

Ephraim served as his son's witness in the ceremony. He spent much of the day attending to Hannah, who hadn't wanted to come at all. Tired of hearing Hannah tell other guests that the bridal couple was mismatched and the wedding was Isaiah's excuse for bringing his mother to Granger, Ephraim finally asked his friend, Phineas Butler, to take the unhappy woman home. It was time that Hannah made dinner for the six-year-old son she left at the farm.

Because the father of the groom was not involved in the wedding's arrangements, Ephraim had no reason to visit Gideon Aldrich's farm after Mary's arrival. His first glimpse of his former wife in a decade was just before the service. Because Mary was not in the wedding party, Ephraim was never close enough to her that he felt obliged to speak to her. Having traveled so far for the wedding, Mary was a center of attention and the whole day was never without company.

Much of the late afternoon was spent playing courting games. Gideon's sons James and Allen erected a maypole from a thirty-foot-tall pine tree with the help of friends. Young men and women grabbed the colored streamers hung from the top and danced and frisked around the pole to music, drumbeats and the occasional gunshot. Others watched and sang. Unlike those who stayed for the evening's dancing, Ephraim went to the house, tired of the clamor and loud music in the barn. The parlor was warm and offered solitude.

"Hello, Ephraim." Mary's unexpected voice was surprisingly familiar. Ephraim turned his head and saw her seated on a large chair in the corner.

"Oh Mary. Hello," Ephraim responded. "You caught me off guard. It is good to see you."

"I am happy to be here and with my children again," Mary said. "It is a delight to have Isaiah married. And I get satisfaction seeing he is choosey in picking a spouse."

"His good judgment is a gift he gets from his mother," Ephraim said.

"Seeing Samuel with Polly and his kids makes me happy too," Mary continued. "He is building a good life for himself. Since my arrival he has showered me with attention, introduced me to people and helped get me settled." Mary smiled and settled back in her chair.

Ephraim marveled at Mary's ease, the natural way she occupied the seat. He recalled his children being snuggled and comforted in that warm lap and held fast by Mary's capable arms. *Mary is a natural mother, a mother of hope and generosity.*

"William has matured the most and left his prankish ways behind. Sarah appears to be very self–assured and her father's gift of a farm encourages his industry. That endowment could turn William into a squire," Mary chuckled. "Which means I will probably never see the fabled tomahawk. He will have to hide it."

"The tomahawk," Ephraim laughed. "Isaiah has kept you well informed,"

"Yes. He has, especially in matters of his siblings," Mary said.

"Yes, Mary," Ephraim murmured. "The only son who hasn't exhibited your gift of discernment is Jonathan. He is not near choosing a spouse. He has inherited his wanderlust from me. I understand why he finds it difficult to settle down."

"Some time ago Isaiah wrote that Jonathan was courting an attractive girl, but she disappeared." Mary said.

"Harriet was an unusual young woman," Ephraim replied. "Jonathan seemed quite fond of her and, as far as I can tell, did nothing to drive her away. He brought her for a visit. She was unprepared for our ill-mannered family."

Mary nodded. "I understand that Hannah played a part in Harriet's disappearance. Isaiah's letters hinted that. Since I have been here, Jonathan has told me about Hannah's rude conduct," she said.

"I wish Harriet hadn't gone away. She faced remarkable struggles in her life, which she overcame," Ephraim paused. "Harriet remained strong and courageous despite her great loss. Her experience taught me a lot about myself."

Ephraim would not have noticed the cat in the room, had it not stopped to lean against his leg. Blackjack didn't usually call attention to himself. Ordinarily, he rambled around a room before returning to the outdoors. Ephraim took the cat's presence as an omen. *Like the cat I come out of the darkness and always go back into it.*

The cat rested at Ephraim's feet, indifferent to his surroundings.

That afternoon when Harriet was here, I felt I could see the way out of the blackness. Now, it is not clear what I learned from her, or how to find my way.

"When I see so much restlessness, people moving around, families breaking up, times like Isaiah's wedding must be cherished," Mary continued.

Birth was my first coming out of darkness. Ephraim thought. *With it came the knowledge that my father didn't like me. The riddle of my being was also born and being here remains a mystery.*

"I am happy to see my children again. Of course, Josiah is gone." Mary teared up, then took a moment to compose herself.

"I did offer my final respects to Josiah. I asked Samuel to take me to the Weaver Cemetery and spent some time at his grave."

"It's foolish to visit his grave," Ephraim snapped. "You can't call him back." The sharp tone registered in Mary's face.

I failed my son. God took Josiah from me and Josiah knew I could not stop it. I saw the disappointment in his eyes as he slipped away. The thought betrayed Ephraim's purported indifference to emotion.

"I know, Ephraim, that you were devastated by his death, just as I was." Mary didn't assign blame. "Isaiah told me about the accident. He sensed the depth of your grief."

"I never had experienced such loss," Ephraim said. "I felt helpless." He gathered strength for his next declaration. "It was my fault."

"I hear remorse in your voice. You never talked like this before, Ephraim," Mary said. "You hide your emotions."

"Yes, many. Some I cannot name and others, like sorrow, are hard to manage," Ephraim said.

Mary grasped the carved arms of the walnut chair, straightened her spine, scooting back into an upright position. The formal posture lent authority; tilting her head forward she appeared resolute.

"You never imagined what I felt when you took my children away," Mary's voice was hard.

"No," Ephraim said. "I knew what I had to do. Emotions were not part of it."

"You were never sensitive," Mary said, "Or sentimental."

"I learned from my father to protect myself," Ephraim said. *Expose yourself and others see weakness, were my father's words.* Seeking attention, the cat pawed his trousers.

"If you never show your feelings to others, you cut yourself off from them," Mary said. "That makes it hard to relate to others and understand them. And you were impulsive, never thinking things through."

Mary planted her crossed arms under her breasts, while her rapid blinking seemed to suppress her breathing.

"I did some things right, instinctively, with no thought of feelings." Ephraim claimed. "Like bringing Isaiah to you as a newborn.

I knew that his chance for a good life was with you as his mother. You would be good for each other."

"Isaiah is a wonderful part of my life. He is why I am in Granger," Mary said.

"I knew that you would love him," Ephraim said. Covering a cough, he stilled his fidgeting hands.

Not a creak in the frame house broke the extended silence. And the quiet from outside did not reduce the tension.

"But you didn't think about love, not when you took all of my children away from me?" Mary, no longer able to control her rage, leapt from her chair. The cat jumped under a side table, but was not driven away by the skirmish.

"Please sit down, Mary. Listen to me. I am sorry for any pain I have caused you. I have thought a lot about the past. Memories of things I did torment me." Ephraim was contrite as he stood and raised his hands, motioning Mary to sit. "I was selfish and uncaring. I am trying to rid myself of my conceit and thoughtlessness."

Mary, her face taut, reluctantly sat. Her squeezed eyelids, straight and tight like her lips, restrained her anger, and her clenched hands, welded to the kneecaps under the rumpled skirt, kept her in place. Long, deep breaths relieved some internal pressure.

"But I was right to bring Isaiah to you. I was right about that," Ephraim persisted.

"Ephraim. Oh, Ephraim," Mary erupted. "Your mind is scrambled. That selfish nature will never change. Is there anybody but you in this world?" Mary bolted up the stairs. Blackjack raised himself from his spot on the floor and disappeared into the night.

Mary's abrupt termination of the conversation stunned Ephraim, as did finding himself alone. He had to finish what he started.

"Please come down, Mary," Ephraim implored. "Please come back down."

With no response to his repeated calls, Ephraim scrambled up the stairs. Only one of the five doors he faced was closed. Behind it, Mary was fixed in a corner.

"We have got to talk, Mary," Ephraim said as he rushed into the room. "I have more to say."

"About yourself?" Mary, voice and posture firm, looked up from a dark nook. "There are things you have to explain to me." Mary moved along the wall to a bedside table and lit a lamp. "Why did you cheat on me? You were not a faithful husband. Or a good father. Can you tell me how I ever fit into your intoxicated world?" Mary asked. Her voice was hollow.

"I know there is a better way I can live," Ephraim insisted.

"The world is not just men, your sons, patriarchy and property. What about the women in your life, Mirinda, who got swallowed up by your spiritual wifery? Have you seen your daughter and what has happened to her?"

"Many things I didn't think about. I treated people with carelessness," Ephraim confessed.

"You had to know that would happen with Jacob Cochrane guiding your way. The trip here with the Mormons was not to find a new life. It was just another adventure driven by lust. You didn't want to change your ways. It was not a divine enterprise for Benjamin McKinney either. You had Mirinda travel with him. Despite Mary Ann, you knew that all the days in Benjamin McKinney's company would lead to her rape. You are alike, you are brothers in filth. You are as responsible as McKinney for Mirinda's degradation and shame."

Ephraim was dumbstruck. He felt like he was waiting for his father.

"I didn't see much of Mirinda on the trip. It was a big wagon train and I had many responsibilities. Orson counted on me," Ephraim stammered, searching for an explanation. "Mirinda could have come to me, asked for my help. She didn't."

"You idiot, Ephraim," Mary wailed. "Do you honestly think Mirinda knew she could count on you, that you would understand the danger she faced and protect her? Did you ever tell her you would shield her from men like yourself?"

"I would never mention Mirinda's personal life," Ephraim winced. "I am her father."

'What does fatherhood mean to her for God's sake?" Mary screamed. "Your misguided piety allows you to ignore your selfishness and your devotion to physical pleasure. She knew what you were like, heard the rumors of your misbehavior. She may have known of Ben Andrews and my rape. Samuel was there and saw it. He could have told her that you didn't defend me."

Mary retreated to the corner of the small chamber, while Ephraim slumped on the bed. No sound came through the open door. Silence ruled the house as the black cat entered, meandered toward Ephraim and pawed his leg. He looked down to see the cat staring back. As Ephraim slowly raised himself he started choking, the tightness of his neck blocked his breath.

"I have seen Mirinda," he stuttered, "and talked to her." Ephraim looked down. "She has suffered greatly, still spiritless despite Samuel and Polly's care. I visited. She didn't talk. Again and again, I said I was sorry. I am trying to make things up to her but am not sure how I can. Can she know I care after years of indifference?" Ephraim started to tear, looked at the bed spread and pulled at a protruding thread. "I am grateful to you for rescuing her and ending her torment. Samuel too."

How do I find myself in this place? Ephraim thought. *I have tried to get past this. Is there a way I can atone for Mirinda's suffering and find her forgiveness?*

"You know, Mary, I have a good son," Ephraim said. "A better man than I. He is a man of courage. Faith is important in how he defines himself. It brings him closer to God."

"You have talked about God with Samuel?" Mary asked with surprise.

"He tells me that Mirinda will get better with the care he and Polly offer. He thinks Mirinda will heal through love and kindness. He has those qualities—because of you. There is a solid sense of right and wrong, a sense of justice. He acts on it," Ephraim said.

Tired, Mary moved from the corner and leaned against the bedpost. Dampness on Ephraim's face reflected the lamplight from the table.

"You have heard about the rescue of the girl from the fire? It happened before you arrived," Ephraim turned to Mary.

"Yes. I'm told our boys are heroes," Mary said.

"Why would God give instructions to burn a child at the stake? Joseph Libby, you remember from Buxton, claimed he was commanded to do just that. And some around Joseph were willing to help," Ephraim recounted. "Samuel was outraged by the news and told me that he was going to stop it. Sadly, I gave him no encouragement.

"But I did go along. It was night. From the bushes I watched as the bedraggled child was brought out. She was tied to a post, wood stacked around her and the fire set. There was a throng gathered, but no one called out or objected to the murder. Not a man in the crowd tried to stop it. Samuel sprung from the woods, rescued the girl and is now taking care of her." Ephraim trembled at the thought of it. "Since that night, I cannot take my mind off Mirinda, realizing it was far worse for her. There was no one to stop the perpetual violence. She had no way of escape, was helpless."

Mary nodded, and she looked at the brooding man beside her on the bed. She had no words of consolation for Ephraim and made no gesture of encouragement. Mary bit down on her curled lower lip before moving to stare out of the window.

"It looks like nobody is leaving. The party may last until dawn," Mary said.

"I am not what my father wanted." Ephraim struggled for words before he stood and yelled. "It made him angry. I didn't look strong and robust, no more remarkable than a toad he said. I tried everything to be what he wanted. My life was spent trying to please him, showing the manly attributes that inspire respect. To be valued." He clomped across the plank floor toward the open door.

"I am not what I wanted." Ephraim yelled again. "Bringing harm on my own daughter. For God's sake. No compassion for anyone, and I didn't listen."

Ephraim paused to catch his breath, but his expression remained grim.

"It is years now." Ephraim halted. "On the trip here, there was a runaway wagon. The race down the mountain was frightening for the family hanging on to it. I was there too, but not scared. I faced the danger. The child thrown from the wagon was injured and lay dying. I was at his side but did not know what to do, how to save him or persuade a doctor to help. My father's lessons were useless. I felt sapped, couldn't think of what to do."

Mary went to the window and stared outside. "I too was depleted and helpless. I had to seek," she murmured. "You need to look beyond yourself."

"I am trying to be less selfish, open up my heart. Selflessness is frightening to think about, even if it promises love. Maybe I deserve no love. Opening my heart will bring trouble, cause me more pain," Ephraim paused. "But you are right, Mary. I must find out my purpose on this earth."

"God says that if we do not seek the truth, we will not find it," Mary's voice was clear.

"My children can choose whomever they want. Would they choose me? No one is drawn to selfishness. Do I still command their attention?" Ephraim questioned. "What can I do to win back their love and make up for the harm I caused?"

"If we do not find the truth, we will not know it," Mary said.

"What person, even most dear to me, would seek my advice if I could not fully give myself, remain imprisoned by my own wants?" Ephraim stepped toward Mary. "No one is willing to open themselves, to love those who do not know sacrifice, whose own personal world is placed above all things."

"You must show that you care," Mary's words were deliberate. "We have to act. We cannot be indifferent to others and love them at the same time. That is impossible. I had to come here to know my children."

"We talked about Harriet How, the young woman Jonathan brought home," Ephraim said. "I have not seen her since, but she was a gift to me."

"It is easy to forget the things our children do for us," Mary said.

"With Harriet I realized people escape damnation. She knew the way out of the dark because of the journey with her father. He was a murderer, the first man hanged in Allegany County. While in jail he understood the price for his sin was the irretrievable loss of his children."

"Yes." Mary shuddered. "That can be the price." The winter chill settling in the room prompted Mary to retrieve the shawl from the top of her trunk. She trembled as she covered her shoulders. She rolled up her fingers and pulled at her sleeves.

"The days before hanging were misery for David How. Harriet spent that time comforting her father. A pastor came every day to pray with the condemned man, but it was Harriet who fueled her father's passionate search for a way to keep his precious children. His faith grew, and he was transformed by God's grace. David How found atonement, forgiveness—and matchless love," Ephraim said. "I will never forget that afternoon I held Harriet. In her eyes, I saw that her father's love rested in her heart. And she would never be without him."

"Is there anyone you carry in your heart, Ephraim?" Mary's voice was stinging.

"There is a path for me, Mary," Ephraim continued as he sat down, "I can be selfless and embrace my children. We will be connected by love, a chain of enduring love. There is a lifetime of amends to make, but I will start and do what I can."

Mary's irritation, registered in her frown, seemed to go unnoticed by Ephraim.

"I will be less concerned about my life and more concerned with the lives of others. How I live and what I do will connect me to my children and their future." Ephraim raised his voice. "They may have some good memories of my life which, as they grow older, will influence the way they live. They may do laudable things in the future because of the advice I offer," Ephraim said.

Ephraim's sigh of satisfaction sent Blackjack leaping up onto the bed. He huddled against the man's trousers and lightly poked his thigh.

"Unfortunately, we leave this life incomplete, and pass on to our children burdens left undisposed. Every child must bear their parents' unfinished business. God bless them with the courage to take on mine." Ephraim ended his lament.

Mary could not bear Ephraim's satisfied look from across the room or control her building rage.

SMACK. A stinging silence followed Mary's hard slap against her husband's face. The sudden charge and loud blow came spontaneously, Mary's smoldering anger released. She started beating his chest with her fists.

"Stop," Mary screamed. "You want me to relive all of my horrors? You think I could forget your cruelty? You crave to torture me more. Is that it?"

"No," Ephraim cried. "Don't hit me. Don't." He leaned back, raising his arms to shield his face. There was nothing else to do. He couldn't get away. Blackjack's shriek ended with a hiss and he darted from the room.

"Still. You cannot not fathom my loss. That seems to have never crossed your mind. Ever," Mary raged. "You want my forgiveness? Is that it?"

Ephraim said nothing, passive to Mary's violence.

"Was all of the talk your way of seeking my forgiveness?" Mary snarled. "I do not have the power to absolve you of your pitiful wrongs. You are wasting your time with words. No one gets absolution through words. That only worked for your fake prophets."

"You say there is a path for you," Mary screamed. "Shouldn't you try to find it? You followed the path blazed by Jacob Cochrane, which landed him in jail. Joseph Smith went through forty wives and was murdered by a mob. That is not what you longed for, is it? You must find your own path.

"I have been through trials you could never imagine." Ephraim gulped.

"Can't you stop that whining? Muster courage to think of what you must do, forgetting how much you must make up for." Mary was unrelenting

"I have poured it all out. Exposed my weakness and shame." Ephraim was sobbing now.

"You ended your story with a plea to God, but not for yourself. You asked that your children be given the courage to assume your unfinished business," Mary roared. "Why not shoulder those burdens yourself? You are just fifty-seven and able. What keeps you from doing that?"

"I have experienced helplessness and know abandonment. Action can be difficult," Ephraim said.

"You are not condemned like David How. There is much that you can do. Show that you truly care about those you love. Build that chain which will bind you to your children and shape their future. You can restore their trust, but you must fully reimagine the hurt you caused. Have you asked Mirinda for her forgiveness, or tried to make amends?" Mary asked.

"You cannot imagine how my past has tormented me," Ephraim groaned.

"You must seek. Do more than talk. Get started on your journey for forgiveness and atonement. No one else can do that. Your mistakes make that clear," Mary said.

Ephraim did not move, frozen in place and speechless. Not getting his attention, she kicked his leg

"Get out of here. Get up and out of my sight. I do not want to see you again," Mary commanded. She yanked his arm, compelling him to stand.

Trance-like, Ehraim rose, crossed toward the door and stopped. His shoulders swelled as he took a deep breath, coughed and left the room. Ephraim's slow descent down the stairs was marked by regular, resonating steps.

Mary was alone, undisturbed by the sound of wedding revelers or night creatures.

He is gone. Mary thought. *It is finally over.*

She let go of years of suffering. Some pain was Ephraim's doing, some self-imposed. She started to tremble. Violent shaking of her hands followed. Spasms transformed into heaving, then endless weeping. Her whole body cried. This shrine of tears faded as Mary's normal breathing was restored.

Mary pulled the shawl tight around her shoulders and moved to the window. No one was on the road; no figure moved across the empty field or disturbed the gentle dawn.

∽

"Ephraim Berry was buried in Buxton, Maine on September 30, 1852," John Meserve wrote in the Buxton Town Record. The recorder noted, "We do not think he died here."

ACKNOWLEDEGMENTS

I am grateful to Ben Farmer, who taught me how to write fiction and Guy Biederman and Rachel Schwerin who help me improve my craft. Those to whom I am indebted for reading and offering advice on the novel during its period of gestation include: Alice Berry, Harry Blair, Robert Hardgrove, Charles Ludolph, Christine Ryland, Lucie Vallee and James Wilson.

ABOUT THE AUTHOR

Chasing Gods is Willard Berry's first work of fiction. After graduating from Pomona College, he entered a PhD program at Duke University, where his master's thesis was published. After earning his doctorate, he taught for ten years at Georgia State University.

He moved to Washington, DC to work on public policy. Demonstrating expertise in international trade and business issues, Berry spent the next 33 years as the chief executive of several trade associations. He wrote several studies, policy papers and op-eds which received wide attention in the US and Europe.

Before retirement, Berry began to look at his long family history. An elderly aunt had told him to look for Ephraim Berry, but had difficulty finding him. In his search, several astonishing facts came together: Ephraim "went with the Mormons," abandoning his wife and taking her children; Ephraim had been a devotee of primitive evangelist, Jacob Cochrane, who brought polygamy, and lascivious practices of worship to Buxton, Maine; and, Jacob Cochrane and Joseph Smith knew each other.

A novel about Ephraim Berry's life was irresistible. Five years later *Chasing Gods* was finished. Berry's dream to become a writer came true.

Made in the USA
Middletown, DE
17 January 2020